Better Angels

Better Angels

The Cobb Variations

David Floody

Implosion Press
Fiction with Attitude

Design: Felicity Perryman

ISBN 978-0-9919004-8-0 Soft cover
ISBN 978-0-9919004-7-3 eBook

www.davidfloody.com
Published by Implosion Press
P.O. Box 653, Tofino, British Columbia
Canada V0R 2Z0

email: defloody@telus.net

Be under the perpetual guidance of the better angel of your nature. Starve and drive out the demon that lurks in all human blood and ready and anxious and restless to arise and reign.

— from a letter by
William Hershel Cobb
to his son Ty

Contents

PART 3. COBB'S CARD

PART 4. COBB'S CRISIS

PART 5. COBB'S LEGACY

prologue

Windsor, Ontario – 1969

Now that Frank thought about it, everybody has at least one big hero in his life. Not just guys like him, but men, women, and girls too. And some, probably only a few, get to meet that hero face to face. The year before, when Frank was twelve, he became one of those few. But he had to take the worst beating of his life to do it.

His friends are still envious of that meeting, and Frank's tired of telling the story. Now he doesn't even mention the sucker punch and the brutal kicks, his head hitting the cement, the blood, and the blacking out. He just says a fight, and guys think they know what he means because they've all had them. Dr. Elmore, a friend of the family, told Frank later that you could never remember pain. A doctor should know. But when he looks in his mirror and feels the white new scar tissue on his forehead, and it all comes flooding back, Frank wants to tell the doc he's wrong.

Frank thought it began when his grandfather, David Charles Phelan surprised them all by winning those impossible-to-get tickets to game five of the 1968 World Series in Detroit, and he met Ellie Fitzgerald for the first time. Her parents named her after the Black jazz and blues singer, and Ellie has a voice that's bigger than any other girl he knows, even his sister Fancy's, and that's saying something. Frank didn't know any Blacks, and watching Detroit burn in the 1967 Detroit Race Riots the summer before had made him apprehensive about the whole Black-White thing. But it was Ellie's guts that day in the stands that stopped the beating and probably saved Frank from becoming a human vegetable. She took a lot of pain and bruises too, and almost got the life choked right out of her.

Then last week, his grandfather, David Charles Phelan, took Frank duck hunting to his special place that's not marked on any maps. He had found it by accident one fall and named it "Lost Man Lake." David would go by himself, just once in a season, with only his talented duck dog and black Labrador retriever, Cobb. It was like a holy pilgrimage. The same kind of journey his grandfather had made with his own father, before Wallace Charles Phelan disappeared on Lake Erie in 1938, the same year their team, the Detroit Tigers, lost the World Series to the St. Louis Cardinals, and pitchers Dizzy and Daffy Dean.

Frank was only the second person David ever took with him to reveal Lost Man Lake's secret location.

The other one was a duck hunter named Big Al Greathwite, a wealthy Chrysler car dealer from New York State. But more importantly, a talented duck hunter, a rare sports card card collector, and an avid baseball fan who was as dedicated to his New York Yankees as Phelan males are to the Detroit Tigers, going all the way back to Frank's great-grandfather, Wally, at the turn of the century. Frank never met Big Al, but from what his grandfather David told him, after their shared dedication to the duck hunt, the two men were as different as two people can be, and their meeting was just as unlikely.

Frank still didn't know the whole story.

Frank used to think heroes were the famous people you looked up to from a distance and shared with thousands of other people. That's still true. But now, he counts Ellie, his grandfather, and even David's black Labrador retriever Cobb, as heroes—not famous, but special in their own ways to him. His grandfather still can't believe what Cobb did that day on Lost Man Lake, or forgive himself that he let it happen. It changed him, and it changed the big duck hunter from New York too.

So, Frank thought it all began with he himself, in a way, even though he wasn't there. And with Yankee Al, because he had that very rare and special 1954 Topps #201 Al Kaline rookie card, more special than Frank ever imagined.

But grandfather David had laughed and said no. In the longer historical view, it really began with the Irish, and with Frank's great-grandmother, Lulu Pearl Phelan.

"You think you're the first one in this family to get an almighty crack on the head with a baseball bat, Frank? It's time you heard the whole story. But at least my father, your great-grandfather Wallace Charles Phelan, deserved it.

"The irony is, that crack came from a rare, chestnut-oak baseball bat, hand-carved by the great Tyrus Raymond Cobb himself, in Royston Georgia, from the rare chestnut-oak trees that grew there. Wallace Charles recovered the bat from a garbage bin while working as a carpenter on building the new Navin Field stadium in Detroit in 1912. The bat had developed a serious crack and was no longer usable by Cobb in his Detroit Tigers American League games, so he threw it out.

"Ty Cobb's old chestnut-oak bat became Wallace Charles Phelan's most valuable and treasured baseball souvenir and possession, and he built a very special glass-fronted case to hold it.

"But my mother, your great-grandmother, Lulu Pearl Phelan, was the one who came to wield that heavy wood. And what a memorable blow she struck! And after that, it was 'Lulu's Bat' and no one else's.

"Now my mother, your great-grandmother, Lulu Pearl Phelan, was *not* a violent person—but she surely was a *proud* one."

Part One

Cobb's Journey

Windsor, Ontario —1918

1   A Rare Picture

The sound of shattering glass pulled David Charles Phelan out of a fevered sleep into the thick heat of his bedroom. He sat up gasping and crying out. *Sma-a-sh!* The sound came once more by the open door of his room, and he shivered and cried out again. "Mama?"

"Get up and get dressed, Davy. We're going out." It was not a dream, but he wished it were. By the yellow light of the street lamp beyond his bedroom window screen, David saw his mother standing in front of the hand-carved case mounted on the facing wall. Lulu Pearl Phelan ran the black poker around and around the inside of it to scythe away the remaining shards and reached in to remove the bat. David flinched and stared at the ruins of his father's special case and could not believe his eyes. The special bat had a crack and been discarded. But it had been hand-carved by Ty Cobb from the wood of the rare chestnut-oaks that grew in his hometown of Royston Georgia. His father Wallace Charles treasured it.

"But Papa will..." What? He sensed his father's absence from their well-kept house on Gladstone Avenue, just west of the Hiram Walker Distillery and the Ford City auto plant, where Wallace Charles Phelan worked as an interior carpenter. "Why, Mama?" David couldn't imagine the shape of his father's anger.

"Quickly now, Davy." Lulu stepped carefully over the glass into the dim light by his front bedroom window, the bat in one hand, the poker in the other. "It's himself I'm going to deal with." No hint of the Spanish in his mother's Irish cream skin and the red hair, piled

3

neatly atop her head, with a single strand escaped from the hold of the pins and tortoiseshell combs from her exertions. The unprecedented sight of that escaped hair scared David more than anything else.

The bat looked too large for his mother's slim stature, but her anger had given her strength, and the force of her will was irresistible, even to his father. David thought of the sharp spike on the wicked looking axe head so prominent at the entrance to his King Edward Elementary School: USE ONLY IN CASE OF FIRE. The head and handle were painted blood red. Now his mother seemed to burn in the half-dark, red rising until her cheeks glowed with colour. "Get a move on, Davy." She gestured with the bat.

David got his shorts and clean shirt from the top of the dresser, where Lulu had laid them out herself, put them on over his under shorts, then sat back on the bed to pull on his socks and the boots he kept neatly together under the single bed. His fingers were sweaty, and David had a hard time with the shirt buttons and shoelaces, but finally stood up in his mother's shadow.

"What time is it?" The steel alarm clock on the side table faced away, but its ticking was loud in the room, the mechanical chewing of an animal.

"It's just gone half ten. Mind the glass."

"Where's Father?"

"Well now, that's the question, isn't it?" His mother's tone upset him further. It had the same quality as the clock.

Wallace Phelan was a skilled carpenter and wood carver, his talents in demand on both sides of the Detroit River, especially in the throes of the Great War, when both Detroit and Windsor had worked continuous shifts to supply its monstrous appetite for men and material.

Those four years had been a dark time for young David, and even now he had not fully taken it in. There had been an edge of desperation in his parents' hugging and expressions of reassurance, even before he was old enough to understand all the words. The effect was the opposite, leaving David more fearful, with a childish anger that was all the more disturbing because it was so diffuse, so lacking in focus. When the war broke out, David's single bed had been moved back into his parents' room just before he turned three. It remained there until he began half-day school at four, when embarrassment over the situation in the presence of his new schoolmates trumped his fears. "I think I want my room back, Father." David had announced it after grace at their big meal on a Sunday afternoon.

"There's our little man!" His father had praised him. "We'll take the bed apart and move it over after supper. Your mother and I could do with a wee more privacy." He winked at David.

"Wallace! Not in front of the boy." His father had laughed and squeezed his shoulder, and his mother blushed, but was drawn into the laughter, in spite of herself. His father had that gift. David warmed to feel the love between his parents, and the old anxieties continued to recede.

Yet his mother's sudden embarrassment intrigued him—until he remembered those sounds coming from his parents' bed some mornings, before he was all the way awake. The moving shapes like sawing wood. Lulu softly crying out. At first it was just an annoyance he tried to ignore that drove him more deeply into his bedclothes. Awake, some instinct told David not to raise the subject, especially with his mother.

Then there were the older boys at his King Edward Elementary School, on Ottawa Street. After school was out, David often saw them at the school gate, talking in lowered voices behind their hands and watching the girls go by in laughing groups—but with quick glances back too, as if they knew the boys talked about them, and didn't mind it, and exchanged whispers of their own. "Toddle your arse home, Phelan. Come back when you have some hair on your pecker," Brian Broder had mocked, aiming a kick at him.

It was another mystery to David and his friends, one of many, quickly forgotten when the bat and ball came out and the raucous choosing of the sides for scrub baseball on the cinder playground began. Still, he thought his father might be more approachable when it came to the subject of girls.

David had been born in 1912, considered a banner year by Wallace Charles Phelan. His wife, Lulu Pearl Phelan, had given birth to a fine son and, almost as important, the old Bennett Field had given birth to Navin Field, which became the new home of his favourite Detroit Tigers baseball team and its genius of the bat, Tyrus Raymond Cobb, the 'Georgia Peach'. "Tyrus, the man's father named him, after the ancient city of Tyre on the Mediterranean Sea. Supposed to have admired the way the people there didn't give in to a siege by a powerful army led by a general called Alexander the Great."

"Sounds like Mama," David said.

"Indeed, it does. So, a professor the man was and knew such things. Wanted his son to be a doctor or a grand lawyer. Too much hard drinking, cursing and tobacco-chewing in the sport for his tastes."

"Mama doesn't like those things either."

"And aren't I just the walking illustration?" Wallace struck a dignified pose.

"Sometimes you are."

"You have the Phelan wit and tongue, and I hope the sense to know when to hold them both."

"It would be hard to talk with a cherry all-day in my mouth." His father laughed and took him by the shoulders.

"You drive a hard bargain, my son." But they walked west, all the way up Sandwich Street, and he bought David the special hard sweet on a stick from N. M. Meisner's Confectionery—and then one for himself, to David's surprise and amusement. "I believe you're right, Davy."

"Ah, Davy! You and the stadium, the luck of the Emerald Isle and the luck of the faithful gamesman, coming together in one glorious concert," his father would declare more than once.

6

David's parents had met while riding one of the Detroit Belle Isle and Windsor passenger ferries between the two cities, on a Sunday afternoon in the summer of 1909. Lulu, with her cousin and friends from the Central Methodist Church, was on her way to a combined Methodist Church picnic that had been jointly organized by the Detroit and Windsor congregations, this one near Detroit's Corktown village. The village was the place where many Irish immigrants had settled, resisting a farther move southwards to the larger Hibernian enclaves in Boston and New York, but working as cheap labourers in the expanding city, now with its thriving auto and manufacturing industries on both sides of the Detroit River.

But sectarian divisions remained strict between the British-leaning Protestants and the generally poorer, but numerous Catholics, mostly descendants of the so-called "Famine Irish," living, worshipping, and breeding under the paternal eye of Rome in a new country where it was easier to be a good Irishman, a good Catholic and a good American, than in the monarchist-loving Dominion of Canada to the north.

Lulu was often angry at the situation. "Don't the parish priests know the poor families can barely feed the children they have? The little ones starving and the poor mothers worn out with childbearing and bearing still." But she felt sad too, David knew.

In Canada, where British citizenship remained the key to success, the Catholic priests and bishops damned from the pulpit all support for Irish nationalism, on the altar of recognition and social acceptance for their Republican-leaning parishes. Thus, the rebellious sentiments of the Fenian Brotherhood, and even the later, less extreme Ancient Order of Hibernians, remained anathema to the Irish Catholic Church in Canada, and were considered evil sedition by Irish Protestants like the Phelans. "We stood ready at the Boyne, and the Orange stand ready still," Wallace would pronounce—but only out of his mother's hearing.

Lulu Pearl was passionate on this matter too. "Did the Irish famines and the Great War teach us nothing? Leave the Troubles in Ireland where they belong. Canada is our hearth and home. I'll not have you filling our son's head with that old hate, Wallace. We have a new century and a new cause and trouble enough here. Devote your energies to the breaking of the Devil's cup!"

Now it was his father's prize bat case that was broken, and David walking out into the humid night. His right hand was in his mother's left and her right hand was holding Cobb's bat. David had the sick feeling his father had indeed gone to the Devil, and his mother was about to drag him back. Or worse.

It was July 12, 1919—celebrated, not quite accurately, as the 229th anniversary of the Protestant Orange victory of good King Billy over the Catholic hordes of the deposed James II, in his unholy alliance with French forces, at the river Boyne. That was the old cause. David knew his mother's love for his father, and his father's love for her in return. But Temperance was the new cause, her cause, and Lulu Pearl Phelan was as dedicated and fierce in its defence as any Fenian.

"Stay close now, Davy. And do exactly what I say." Standing on their front porch, David held Cobb's bat while his mother fastened her blue cloth purse at her waist, tucked the stray hair under her narrow straw hat and took his hand. They turned north on Gladstone Avenue, headed toward the Detroit River. "Exactly what I say. You hear me?"

"Yes, Mama."

But David began to cry. And when his mother, Lulu Pearl, looked down at him, he saw the tears in her eyes too.

2   The Claddagh

David loved the tale of how his father Wallace and mother Lulu Pearl first met. It was his family's favourite, and oft repeated at his request. David remembered it now as they marched along Gladstone Avenue in search of his father—

That July afternoon on the Windsor and Detroit ferry back in 1909, Wallace Charles Phelan and his friends, young Orangemen all, were attracted to Lulu Pearl and her ladies' group, and bold enough to invite them, instead of the church picnic, to join the Orangemen to watch a Detroit Tigers baseball game at Bennett Field, in the same Irish Corktown area. The young men's trip was organized under the auspices of the Royal Black Preceptory, Loyal Orange Lodge No. 539, but it was decided not to wear any regalia to avoid confrontations with the Catholics. They would save their boisterous aggression for the opposing team and any of its fans brave enough to confront them. His father had recounted this story many times to David.

"Your future mother sitting there in the middle of those lovely girls, with her straw basket in her lap and her nose in the air, proud and distant as an English lady. And Jesus wept, Davy, that beautiful Irish red hair to her shoulders, just catching the river breezes. The blessed tongues of St. Patrick and All Angels could not have moved her." Wallace Phelan always dropped his eyes at this point. "It was our whisky flasks, you see. And the game, of course, even then."

Lulu Pearl Phelan was already a formidable force in Windsor's Methodist Community, and one of the youngest leaders of the Women's Christian Temperance Union. "Success Needs Self-discipline" was its motto. Alcohol was an obstacle to that self-discipline, and so alcohol was an obstacle to success—and a man-made, self-inflicted abomination in the eyes of the movement. Abstinence was promoted, but prohibition was the goal. Lulu Pearl had high hopes of success before the war and spoke out passionately on the issue. "Poverty will decline. Crime will be brought to its knees. Faith and God's grace will spread among our sodden, our downtrodden masses."

David would soon accompany his mother to the local meetings of the Women's Christian Temperance Union, where Lulu would speak of this God-granted choice as a rare gift. "Because it means perfection on this Earth is possible. The conquest of sin is possible—a lofty, but attainable human goal. Discipline and self-control, Ladies, that is the Method at the heart of Methodism." Lulu almost never failed to receive a round of applause from the assembled women.

That is how David would remember Lulu best, marching against Windsor's most notorious *shebeens*, its waterfront beer and liquor establishments, Bible raised high and him at her side with the other children, handing out Temperance tracts of Lulu's own composition to sheepish men, some with their wives, some fewer with companions whose virtues were less certain. But all of them more disposed to accept the "Truth of Temperance" from the hand of a child.

But that Sunday afternoon Wally and Lulu met, the sight of that smooth silver whisky flask, a gift of his father, made him suspect. The further admission that he, though undeniably a fine figure of Protestant Irish manhood, regularly attended these low sporting contests, where the consumption of cheap wine, beer, and the more powerful, spirituous liquors by opposing baseball fans spawned dozens of violent brawls, was reason enough for Lulu Pearl to refuse the invitation to accompany him. She encouraged her companions to do the same and directed her tart reply at his future father.

"Have you not heard the saying, 'Good as drink is, it ends in thirst'?"

"And have *you* not heard, 'The light heart lives long'?"

"Then would you be floating off now to your home in the clouds and not putting us cold in your shadow here?"

"I will ... if you would consent to telling the name of the person that has so cruelly shown me my place on this Earth—or above it." Lulu had said nothing. But her cousin, Siobhan, had her own cheek.

"It's Lulu Pearl Connor, and her heart is not yet given. Though you're not the first to discover it and be the worse for the knowing."

"Siobhan!" But it was too late. The young man swept off his cap and bowed low.

"Wallace Charles Phelan, God's gift to the fine working of wood, and his heart held the same—if you wish to curse me by name." And in making his obeisance, Wallace caught sight of the ring on her right hand before Lulu could hide it under her left.

"Ah, Miss Connor, I see you're wearing the 'Claddagh' ring, and I'm guessing by the age of it, it was your mother's before you." Siobhan gasped at the quickness and accuracy of the young man's insight.

"And no business of yours if it is."

The village of Claddagh is thought by some to be the oldest fishing village in Ireland, the home of legendary 17th century goldsmith Richard Joyce, who was taken by pirates the week before his marriage and sold as a slave to the Moorish goldsmith who taught him his trade. The hapless young lover crafted a beautiful ring for the woman at home he could not forget. Set free years later, Richard returned to Claddagh to find the woman still waiting and offered her the ring, with its two hands gently holding a crowned heart. Such rings were taken ever after in Ireland to mean that love and friendship will reign supreme in the wearer: the hands to symbolize friendship, the heart love, and the crown loyalty.

"Maybe not," Wally had replied, "but just to note the wearing on that lovely white hand—and with the heart turned out."

"You are mistaken, Sir, in your words and your attentions."

But Wally was not. It meant Lulu Pearl Connor was truly not spoken for by any man. Wallace Charles Phelan vowed he would see that ring on her left hand, the heart turned in, and she his wife in lasting love and friendship, his loyalty hers forever.

"Then I take my leave." David's future father did—but not before entertaining all present, so that Lulu Pearl Connor was the only one to look pointedly away, fixing her gaze on the banks of white clouds above Detroit.

> *"May neighbours respect you,*
> *Trouble neglect you,*
> *The angels protect you,*
> *And Heaven accept you."*

Siobhan laughed the longest, hand over her mouth, aware she had, herself, caught the shy looks of Wally's best friend, Garrett Bryant.

3 The Oath

Now, as Lulu Pearl Phelan, bat in hand in her determined march toward the Windsor waterfront and the tall silhouettes and varied lights of the Detroit skyline spread out beyond it, her fears of where and what she might discover of Wallace's activities grew. She glanced down at her son David, saw the tears slowly tracking down his cheeks and the haunted look in his eyes, and regretted bringing him along. But what alternative did she have? There was no-one at home to mind him in her absence, and the impact of that absence might be even worse.

Lulu Pearl smelled the rich urban aromas of smoking chimneys, sour river water, vehicle exhausts, rotting alleyway garbage, unwashed bodies, restaurant kitchens, and occasionally, just a hint of perfumes she rarely wore herself.

"Mama, where are we going?" his white face looking up at her.

"I'm sorry, Davy. I'm not sure yet."

"I'm worried about Papa."

"So am I, my love. And that's why it's up to us to find him."

"Yes, I know, Mama."

Lulu paused a moment, reached down, and hugged her only son close, looking even now, so much like his father. "I know you do. Remember that fine Irish wish and wisdom: 'If God sends you down hard roads, may he give you strong shoes.' Strong shoes, Davy. Strong shoes!"

David sought refuge in his favourite family story of how his father had first met his mother, Siobhan and their friends on that Windsor and Detroit River ferry so long ago, and learned her name. And his father's pleasure and laughter in the telling of it, with his mother blushing and snorting in embarrassment, but ending in laughter and tears.

"And didn't that set the fox among those pretty chickens, Davy? 'A pearl indeed,' I said to myself. And swore to win that hard heart. And thus began..."

"...the Siege of Castle Connor!" David would finish, gleefully.

"Ah, you've heard of that grand battle, Davy?"

"Haven't we both, one too many times? Enough of your nonsense, Wallace. That story is tired from the telling."

"Yet the sweeter each time. And you with it."

"Enough! Or this sweater will have three arms on it."

"All the better to hold you with, my peerless Pearl." It was his mother's look then that drew a booming laugh from his father, and ended the recounting. But David knew the rest of their story, almost by rote, from Wallace Phelan's repeated telling.

A previously indifferent Wallace Charles Phelan had joined the Central Methodist Church and did not feel too uncomfortable in its largely Irish congregation. He attended regularly, added his fine Irish tenor to the choir, and kept his whisky flask, his Irish Protestant, Loyal Orange Lodge regalia, and his baseball sportsmanship out of sight. Wallace Charles was there every Sunday morning before Lulu Pearl Connor arrived with Siobhan and her friends.

"A fine, bright morning to you, Miss Connor!" And waiting for her when she left. "A sermon to make all angels weep, Miss Connor." But it wasn't enough. Wally needed something more, something special to incline that distant heart he sought favourably toward him.

"The walls of Castle Connor stood high and hard, Davy, resisting..."

"...all Love's sweet assaults!" David would crow.

"Exactly, my son. It needed a rare plan of attack to reach its hidden heart. And on that blessed day, December 19, 1909, the last Sunday before Christmas, I found it."

Again, it was his mother's cousin, Siobhan, who had made it clear to all within hearing that fateful morning in church—

"It's yours, Pearl! Yours! Sure, and it must be!"

"Ah, my son, our Lulu Pearl Connor, at worship on that most memorable and glorious Christmas week, the day of my demonstration of my love and devotion for her, was the soul of piety, Davy."

How, at the end of that Central Methodist Church Christmas service, as he did every year, the Reverend Ballymoney would confirm by a nod that Mrs. Ballymoney should ready a select group of the congregation's children in the hallway at the entrance of the church. Then a second nod, and all adults and parents stood up in their polished oak pews and turned to see and smile warmly, when more than a dozen of the youngest members of the Central Methodist Church, each meticulously scrubbed, combed, and polished by proud parents, and well-rehearsed by Mrs. Ballymoney, trooped up to stand in front the pulpit of the church in mixed pairs.

The Reverend Ballymoney stepped down from his high pulpit and directed them into a line facing the congregation, with each child carefully holding his or her painted, plaster piece of the Nativity: the shining Baby Jesus; the empty Manger; the haloed parents Mary and Joseph; the three well-travelled Wise Men; the small offerings of gold, frankincense and myrrh; two Shepherds with Crooks, one kneeling, one standing; assorted stable animals and farming implements. "Let us rejoice once again in the miracle of Christmas and fill our human spirits with the sure and certain coming of the Resurrection and the Life."

Touching four-year-old Sarah Feeney on the right shoulder, the Reverend Ballymoney deftly removed the sparkling white linen sheet that covered the large, wooden-model stable while the girl stepped forward, held up her offering, and delivered her line in a pure child's voice: "The Holy Baby Jesus!"

But the warm murmurs of appreciation and the ceremonial placement that was to follow, slowed to a quiet halt. The Reverend Ballymoney, the congregation, Sarah Feeney, and the other children, stared at the stable—at what *was* and *was not* the Stable of the Nativity.

It was of the same dimensions, had the same shed roof, the same raised centre for the manger, the same stick-built stalls, the same ancient-looking small lamps, the same bedding of fresh straw—yet it was as different from its aging predecessor as glowing white wood, softly highlighted in decorative shades of muted colour, could be from dusty, painted brown.

Following a period of gasps and exclamations from the congregation, and ooohs and aaahs from the children, all eyes returned to Reverend Ballymoney for some explanation.

"It appears ... appears we have had a ... a Visitation."

"It's beautiful!" Sarah Feeney clapped her hands and spoke with a child's wonder for the whole Central Methodist Church assembly. "A miracle!" Then, remembering her role and training, Sarah stepped forward along with the manger-carrying boy beside her, and laid her infant charge in His traditional place. "The Holy Baby Jesus lying in a manger." Then pausing for a closer look, she asked the question the whole congregation was thinking—

"Who's the Angel?"

And that's when Lulu Pearl Connor's sharp-eyed cousin, Siobhan, delivered her considered opinion. "It's yours Lulu Pearl! Sure, and it must be." She meant the delicate, carven face of the newly added White Angel.

"If it hadn't been the Christmas Day celebration, I would never have forgiven Siobhan!" Lulu Pearl always made clear to her husband and son. But she no longer denied the conclusion, as they always smiled at the oft-repeated declaration.

The fourteen inch tall White Angel, carved from the same pure white wood hovered ceremoniously over the Holy Baby Jesus with its beatific smile, and proffered its own gift. There was no paint or colour of any kind adorning the image, but the artistic carver had textured the spreading wings so the feathers appeared an even purer white, the robes white also, but a different shade from the wings, and different again from the skin of the hands and feet and face, which seemed to glow with a mortal blush of life. The long hair, blown by invisible winds, was the most intricate feature of the carver's art, with an impression of individual hairs, and one curling strand caught naturally under the tiny pointed chin.

But it was none of these artistic features that lead Siobhan to her verdict and caused her cousin, Lulu Pearl Connor, to stiffen beside her in the polished oak pew.

The White Angel's billowing, sumptuous heavenly robes were held at the waist by a wide, carven belt in the form of two delicate hands, the hands holding a heart, and the heart crowned. But the gift the Angel's hands held was less certain—rounded and burnished, so it caught the light of the large candelabra in their pewter sconces at either end of the altar table, so the eyes of the viewer would rest on it last—as did Siobhan's.

Siobhan was about to speak aloud her guess at it, when her cousin pinched her arm to silence her.

Lulu Pearl Connor didn't have to look closer to know that the burnished white offering was a pearl, and the heart of the Claddagh was turned upward, in love and loyalty.

"The very thought of it, now, still turns me red with embarrassment. I should have stood up and walked out of our Central Methodist Church right then. But I wouldn't give the man that satisfaction." She meant, Wallace Charles Phelan, before he became David's father.

"That's my precious Lulu Pearl!" And Wallace Phelan would try to give her a kiss, but Lulu would drive him off with a knitting needle. "And Castle Connor still can stand, Davy!"

A day later, Reverend Ballymoney passed by the Nativity Table on his way to join the weekly meeting of the Christian Temperance Union in the front pews, where Miss Lulu Pearl Connor would finalize the Christmas week Temperance Campaign plans. These Protestant Christian women judged the temptation to sup of the Devil's cup was keenest at this holiday time, and the New Year's to follow, when epic drunkenness was a certain expectation among the weak-willed and fallen. But the Temperance women were equally certain that the Promise of Redemption, and the decent Godly life they so fervently spread to the wider community, were equal to the challenge.

The Reverend was just rehearsing his own words of inspiration to them, when something made him suddenly pause and turn back to the Nativity Table crèche. The carved White Angel was gone!

And a further mystery, even possibly a Holy Mystery, was born. And would remain.

But suspicion and then near-certainty in the Central Methodist Church congregation abounded, as Siobhan's comment regarding Lulu Pearl's as the delicate carven face of the White Angel was repeated in the days and weeks following. Although neither of the parties in question, Lulu Pearl Connor and Wallace Charles Phelan, would admit to private knowledge, nor speculate on the significance of these events.

But all knew there was only one individual well-versed in the carver's art who might have wrought such a miracle and later removed it: Wallace Charles Phelan.

"Keep up, Davy. Keep up!" his mother admonished him at her side.

Further strands of auburn hair were escaping Lulu Pearl's straw hat when the Detroit River waterfront breezes grew more vigorous, as mother and son approached the bustling Windsor Ontario business district along its shores, with the noisy swell of men's shouts and raucous peals of laughter from the crowded saloons and restaurants. Lulu Pearl Phelan tightened her grip on David's right hand, almost to the point of pain, but the son bore it in silence. He sought refuge in the past.

David remembered well that, as the early months of his parents' relationship had slowly progressed and evolved after their momentous meeting on the Detroit Ferry, Lulu Pearl Connor and Wallace Charles Phelan used to walk north through the Windsor summer crowds, toward the mile-wide Detroit River and its busy ferry terminal. They sought a refined evening meal at the luxurious British American Hotel at the Sandwich Street corner. Lulu Pearl would only come in through its west side entrance, to avoid the wide front lounge with its hanging smoke and heavy scents of beer and alcohol, and sit in the smaller restaurant area with patrons who only smoked tobacco.

Lulu had her Women's Temperance Union principles, but could not resist partaking of the better class and luxury of the lavish hotel—and increasingly, the ready wit and warm compliments of her handsome Irish beau—finally allowing herself to use the term. Lulu consoled herself with the thought that its better class of civilized company would be mixed and genteel, with an acceptable level discipline and restraint. Still, she did somewhat punish Wally by insisting he *not* use his tobacco during the meal, claiming it would pollute the savour and quality of the sumptuous dishes they ordered, shared, and consumed with great pleasure and relish.

"Wonderful, wonderful times they were, Davy!" his father would say. "Your mother in a white voile and lace blouse, and a lovely Irish-green dress skirt, showing just a wee bit of shapely ankle, with her red hair down under that neat straw hat, finally wearing the fine pearl earrings I'd given her and drawing every man's eye in the place. But you know, my son..."

"...it was *Terpsichore* that took the Castle Connor Keep!" David would exclaim, on cue.

"Yes, indeed, boyo! A lively German polka followed by a Boston or Viennese Waltz."

"Please dance, Mama! Please." And in the best times, Wallace Charles would bow to Lulu Pearl who would make a great show of reluctance, and of finally giving in, put aside her intricate needlework and waltz around their small parlour." Then, a short while on, his father would direct a sly wink at David.

"May I cut in?"

"Sure, and your father's not the only man in the world." Then David would dance badly with his mother while his father noisily hummed the tune, until the whole of the small Phelan family was stumbling together, hugging in raucous fits of joyous laughter.

"Not a word to the Good Reverend Ballymoney, now!" his mother would warn her Phelan men, wagging her finger and with her own sly look.

"Our lips are sealed, Mrs. Phelan," Wally promised. And David and his father would ostentatiously button their mouths. The Good Reverend had always disapproved of such dancing, and the further, more intimate liberties it might lead to, from his high pulpit.

Lulu Pearl Connor had fallen completely in love with waltzing, despite the Reverend Ballymoney and her own higher principles— and also with the skilled Irish worker of wood who held her so naturally, so warmly in his arms, showed her the steps and swung and dipped her until she was giddy.

The first week in August, David's father took Lulu Pearl to the motion pictures at the New Empire Theatre for a showing of Edwin S. Porter's 1903 film *The Great Train Robbery*, brought over from Detroit. Caught up in the novel excitement of shootings and wild horseback pursuits across the rugged landscape, Lulu Pearl Connor let Wallace Charles Phelan kiss her more than once, and didn't resist at the end when Wally deftly removed her mother's Claddagh ring and turned the heart around. That traditional Irish act sealed their engagement, their future as loving husband and wife, and their child to come.

David's father was Best Man and his mother Maid of Honour at Lulu Pearl's cousin Siobhan Connor's wedding to Wally's best friend, Garrett Bryant, that fall. Again, no other extended family made an appearance at Siobhan's wedding. And again, Lulu Pearl warned Siobhan with a sharp look when her cousin seemed about to respond to Wally's polite inquiry as to her "growing condition."

The newlywed Garrett Bryants moved into their own small apartment further up Sandwich Street. But, despite the Claddagh heart's turning and their "understanding," Lulu Pearl Connor refused to be alone with Wallace Charles in their old apartment, now hers alone. When her handsome fiancé protested his respectful and loving intentions toward her, she finally revealed to him the reason, realizing the Good Reverend Ballymoney and the rest of the congregation would guess soon enough.

"Siobhan is already carrying their first child, Wallace, and all three will reap the unfortunate consequences of their act. Sure, and certain it is, that Mrs. Ballymoney and Mrs. Talliberry can count to nine." Wally was genuinely taken aback—Garrett had not told him! But after much pleading and entreaty, Lulu Pearl *did* allow him, earning a good wage in the carpentry shop at the Ford Auto Plant, to help her with her apartment rent on the strict understanding that it conferred no entitlements.

When he was old enough to understand, David had been told by his father Wally the importance and significance of the Claddagh in their Irish culture and traditions.

Wallace Charles Phelan had turned Lulu Pearl Connor's heart and her Claddagh ring around. Their own marriage banns were announced for consecutive Sundays, and the following spring they married. Wallace Charles' wedding ring to her was a sparkling white pearl costing three months' wages, mounted in a wide, engraved gold band. And, despite cousin Siobhan's swollen belly, Lulu Pearl insisted Siobhan and Garrett stand with them at the marriage altar, and with a single, intense warning look, dared the Good Reverend Ballymoney, Mrs. Ballymoney, Mrs. Talliberry, and the entire Lincoln Road Methodist congregation to raise the issue to her face.

None of them did.

The two Phelans, mother and son, continued pushing through the raucous and growing riverfront crowds in front of Windsor's *shebeens* and dance halls.

But as his mother had been careful to remind an older David, their marriage came only *after* Wallace Charles Phelan, in genuine sacrifice and with all the sincerity in him, had sworn the Temperance Oath of Sobriety, administered by his intended, to the energetic applause of Reverend Ballymoney, Mrs. Ballymoney and the Christian Women's Temperance Union in those same front church pews. This was followed by Lulu Pearl's inspired vision of a bright, prosperous, and righteous future for them all, and for Canada, their chosen country, now that her fiancé had been redeemed and saved from the ravages of beer, spirituous liquors and other potent *poteen* concoctions.

"I expect nothing less than a new Canadian standard of dignity and morality. One which will inspire and encourage others like ourselves, still arriving on Canada's shores from all parts of Europe and America, seeking, as we have so recently ourselves, a life of hope and fulfillment that will replenish the mind, body, and spirit. Can we, in good Christian conscience and charity, offer them any less?"

Lulu Pearl had not allowed David's father to mount his fine White Angel anywhere in the respectable Clifford apartment they had rented on Ouellette Avenue, south of Wyandotte Street, a few steps away from their church and Dumfries Fine Ladies Wear, where Lulu Pearl continued to work in the lingerie department.

Both newlyweds had worked hard, and Lulu Pearl managed their savings minutely, so they soon had enough funds for a down payment on their Gladstone Avenue home when David was born. But there, his mother kept the fateful White Angel, wearing her very own carven face, wrapped in fine Irish lace on top of her wedding dress in her Hope Chest. The Connor family's vintage Claddagh ring remained on her hand with the gold and pearl wedding ring, and out of sentiment for things handed down, Lulu did allow Wally to keep his father's silver whisky flask in the bottom drawer of their dresser, that locked with a single key under Lulu's control.

Lulu Pearl would explain about her own parents' uncomfortable marriage history to her new husband in time, but the memory was still painful, and she did not want to risk clouding the special joys of marriage and motherhood with the brooding it would bring. Wallace Charles Phelan was content, and Lulu Pearl loved him much the more for his patience and sympathy.

But David Charles Phelan would learn of it all years later and, in the painful circumstances surrounding that difficult revelation, struggle mightily to understand and accept it. So that very first year, as loving husband and wife, his mother put the sad story away as carefully as the White Angel wrapped in its fine white linen.

But now, here David was, along the extensive Windsor waterfront, struggling and out of breath, keeping up with the determined Lulu Pearl Phelan, the mother he so adored. And David couldn't help but wonder, if that love for her and the love his mother bore for his father Wally, might all be at grave risk. More family memories crowded his boy's imagination as his mother pulled him along.

And David suddenly felt he might be on the longest journey of his young life.

4

Battle of the Boyne

As David Charles Phelan was maturing in the arms and hearts of his loving family, Wallace Charles Phelan had taken great pains to pass on to his eager young son the richest, most significant baseball lore and history. David was as hungry for this knowledge as he was for his mother Lulu Pearl's roasted wild duck, or the sweetness of N. M. Meisner's cherry all-day suckers. And so, the most significant, engaging and noteworthy Major League Baseball legends unfolded for him, year after year, with his father Wally the masterful tutor.

And Wallace Charles Phelan, Canadian, proud Irishman, Protestant, Methodist and now former member of Windsor's Loyal Orange Lodge No. 539, expected his maturing young son to master the most significant events in their proud Irish and Canadian history. Lulu Pearl Phelan was no less insistent, as long as matters like Ireland's "Troubles" were not glorified and putting their son at risk of prejudice and hate. Lulu, especially, unfolded for David the troubles and trials of their adopted Dominion of Canada nation. David was less enthusiastic about these subjects than baseball, but well knew it was important to his mother, so did his boy's best to be attentive. And after a while, began to enjoy it.

The Great War to End All Wars, the First World War, had been over for one year when "Shoeless" Joe Jackson and seven other members of the Chicago White Sox, one of the greatest teams the game of baseball would ever know, were accused of accepting bribes to throw the 1919 World Series. "Say it ain't so," a young baseball fan had supposedly begged his hero. But the scandal caused the eight White Sox players accused to be popularly dubbed, the 'Black Sox,' as the scandal took deep root in baseball fandom. By September of 1920, all eight so-called 'Black Sox' players had been indicted by a grand jury headed by Kenesaw Mountain Landis. By 1921, Charles A. Comiskey, a player, and later, founder and owner of the Chicago club that was known as the White Sox, formerly the 'White Stockings' of 1894, *suspended* the eight so-called 'Black Sox' players for the season.

Yet later in August, a jury pronounced the eight accused *not* guilty!

But Kenesaw Mountain Landis was now Major League Baseball's first Commissioner. He sent a powerful message to all participants of the growing professional baseball sport when he banned the eight indicted 'Black Sox' players from the game of baseball *for life*! It was a terrible, terrible fate, especially for Shoeless Joe Jackson, who loved baseball more than life, and was arguably a true innocent among the eight accused, jury findings aside.

But in other matters of baseball lore, like the New York Yankee's George Herman "Babe" Ruth, Wallace Charles Phelan was adamant to his young son David. "The 'Sultan of Swat' is three bad fates, Davy: Italian, Catholic and now a Yankee pin-striper." Major League Baseball fans would remember the year 1919 for the 'Black Sox' scandal and Babe Ruth's triumphant march into the Major League Baseball record books and history.

David Phelan would most remember the year 1919 for this ongoing forced march down the Windsor waterfront with his mother Lulu Pearl Phelan, carrying her husband's fateful Ty Cobb chestnut-oak bat on her right shoulder.

But also, for the disturbing, underlying fear of some unknown consequence of what had happened so recently in the repressive

Winnipeg General Strike. The workers' protest that was so violently put down by the industrialist factory owners and their police proxies. The strike had come to underlie all other working-class fears across Canada, and had finally overtaken David's own family on this evening.

"May the Good Lord hold those working men and women of courage safe in the palms of His holy hands and preserve us from their fate," Lulu Pearl had added to their usual evening grace and thanks at their dinner after.

And now, marching doggedly along with his mother at eleven in this evening of Saturday, July 12th, it was clearly going to be a memorable day for David—but not, he feared, a good one. And David feared the same for his proud mother, pulling steadily at his arm, and for his absent father. A confrontation now seemed unavoidable. It was three bad fates in concert and no way glorious: his father's receipt of his weekly pay packet at noon; a much-anticipated contest between Ty Cobb and his American League Detroit Tigers versus manager Jim McGraw and his hated National League New York Giants; and not least, the marching fifes and drums of the Loyal Orange Lodges to once again rub Roman Catholic noses in the dirt of their defeat at the River Boyne, for the 229th time.

The Loyal Orange Lodges' marching was the reason Lulu Pearl had kept David home that afternoon, although he was desperate to attend the baseball game in Detroit with his father and Garrett Bryant, now married to Lulu Pearl's cousin Siobhan, with two girls of his own and another on the way. In a small defiance, David had spent the afternoon in the alley behind his older friend Roddy McCrae's house, a block away on Windermere Road, where Roddy had taught him gin rummy, and they had played for wooden matchsticks. David had lost them all, but enjoyed himself fully—until his mother phoned Mrs. McCrae to call him home to supper. But more worrying, Wallace Phelan never came home on time or called, as he always did, to alert his mother to any lateness or absence. A phone call to cousin Siobhan confirmed Garrett Bryant was also absent.

From Mrs. Lulu Pearl Phelan's point of view, it was enough that her husband had been in sympathy with these marchers who kept the old feud alive, though now sworn to have put aside his Loyal Orange sash and other regalia, and not march himself. And further, that Wally still regularly attended the low sporting contests at Detroit's Navin Field with their son. And, Lulu feared to think it, may even have partaken of the Devil's cup, though she could never catch it on his breath, and was reluctant to do so lest her fears be confirmed. David sensed her concern, but knew also that his mother was conscious of the unfairness of putting him in the midst of any serious argument between them over the matter—at least until this troubling night now. Didn't his father understand the consequences of his mother's position? "LIPS THAT TOUCH WINE SHALL NEVER TOUCH MINE," as her Women's Temperance marching signs warned.

Would Wally really take the risk?

Yet his mother *had* allowed his father to pursue a carpentry job with the American crew that built the new Detroit baseball park in 1912. Lulu Pearl was also a practical woman, about to birth her first child, and could not deny the decent wage the Navin Field work provided the new family. Not to mention the other carpentry opportunities on the Detroit side it would open up, as his father had successfully argued. But David knew it was much more than that to his avid sportsman father.

"Not less than a dram a day of honest Phelan sweat in those Navin Field boards, Davy, to help christen the grand new park!"

Thus did his father, Wallace Charles Phelan, bless and confirm the Tigers tradition among Phelan males and haunt the surrounding Irish Corktown neighbourhood, with all its spirituous liquor temptations, restrained by his son, his oath to his wife, and the promise of the Claddagh.

But as strong as these constraints were, more was expected of him as a fit winner of the family's bread and meat. And it was here in the spring of 1919 that the labour disputes in Winnipeg and other parts of the country, since May 14th and after, had so distressed his parents and made dinners uncomfortable for the family. Now the Great War was over, and the men came back to find a new conflict was brewing. "The wonder of it all is that we should have seen it coming and prepared ourselves," his father had said, after bringing home the newspaper the next day.

"And are we all seers and magicians?"

"Lulu, I only meant..."

"I know. I'm sorry, Wallace. That was not fair. I will say the grace." David had bowed his head and heard the additional prayer for a just labour peace for the first time, and knew his mother Lulu Pearl was more worried than his father. He longed for a return to the old Saturday dinners and the ritual presentation of his father's pay packet to his mother.

Hurrying now to keep up beside his determined mother, David could begin to appreciate the practical demands on Lulu Pearl of ensuring an income sufficient and steady enough to maintain a decent Christian home for her husband, lay a full table at each meal and provide a foundation of sound moral example for him, her precious son. It meant that Wallace Phelan would faithfully turn over his pay packet each Saturday week, so that his mother might dispense it providently, to their general benefit. This was customarily done at the start of dinner that same evening at six o'clock, when the family gathered and reviewed the week's news and experiences, large and small. It was also a time to determine the needs of the coming week for his father at Ford City, his mother at home and about her community works, and David at school. Both parents expected diligence and good reports in return for a measure of freedom to pursue the active interests of any boy his age in privacy.

The good things his parents knew, would bless him; the bad things they didn't know about—the inevitable fights, the small thefts on dares, the first trials of tobacco and what might have been *poteen*, rumours of Susan Whalen behind the school and the first inklings of sex. Not to mention the handing down of the forbidden "shite," "fockin," "right bastard" and "arsehole" from the older Irish boys, the careful omission or unavoidable lie—could not condemn him.

Now, one of the Wonders of the Age was there, on display, in the busy Windsor waterfront streets around David and his mother beside him: the universal success of the Electric Starting Motor in the latest gas engine automobiles. It eliminated the tedious hand cranking of the previous designs. "Soon see women in the driver's side and no man needed!" Wally had joked to David.

"And wouldn't *that* be an improvement to all God's green Earth?" Lulu commented. The look of honest disbelief on his father's face at the dinner table had caused David to laugh without really knowing why—and his mother to frown. Then there were the times when David had his own special news from school.

"Susan Whalen isn't coming to senior level any more," watching his parents closely. "William's her brother. He says she's going to have a baby ... but she's not married...?" It was a question, and all laughter fled the table. His father was about to say something, then stopped, and looked down the end at his mother.

"This is not a matter for discussion here, David. It is a sad thing for the family. And that little one too, at no fault of its own and innocent as a lamb, to be born into such pain. Now I don't want you talking anywhere about it, Davy, and increasing their burden. One small thing we can do."

"Yes, Mama," David had dutifully said.

Yet later in his bed, he had heard his parents having words, as he listened at the floor grate, and decided he would risk pursuing the question again with Susan's brother. But the following week

William's sister was dead. William would say nothing more about it. David didn't either, and no one he knew attended the funeral.

Each of these items had been offered up, received, and dealt with in its turn, as suited his parents. But since the 15th of May, two months before, the only talk at Saturday dinner, and every other dinner as well, was of the General Strike in Winnipeg and the effect the new movement of Revolutionary Industrial Unionism would have on his father's job at Ford City, and the family's prospects for a continued pay packet.

"Have good men and their families fought, sacrificed, and suffered for four terrible years in one war, only to come home to fight another? No jobs to support them, a starving crofter's wages that would make the Devil blush, and conditions that are as likely to make them cripples as make them their livings?" Lulu was in complete sympathy, and so was Wally. But now arguments with his foreman might carry a heavy price. His mother was torn.

David struggled still to keep up with Lulu Pearl Phelan as the July night turned humid and thick with automobile exhaust and the choking fumes of industry around them. Where might his wayward father be, David wondered, as he and his mother continued to investigate the many possibilities without success. It was a tiring process.

Underneath the enveloping atmosphere, David smelled the sharp odour of sweat and exertion from Lulu Pearl beneath the Ingram's Milkweed Cream and Body Lotion scent he was so accustomed to with his *decorous* mother, Siobhan's word. David no longer noticed his own boy's smell.

But tonight, he *did* remember the salty beads of nervous moisture on his father's brow the day he had brought home the smeared pamphlet that might cost Wallace Charles Phelan his job and their family's living: the new movement of "Revolutionary Industrial Unionism."

A swift brush of the hand told David his own brow was the same now. The tension between David and his mother felt the equal of that fateful evening and its unknown consequences.

The handbill was a smudged photograph on cheap paper and showed a gathering of the Great War Veterans' Association. Hundreds of men dressed respectably in hats, suits and ties, some with canes, some with crutches and missing limbs, as if on their way to Sunday worship rather than forming up to march in protest to the Winnipeg Legislative Assembly. Their message, printed in black block capitals on the wide cloth banner under which the leaders marched at the front of the parade, was equally respectful:

WE WILL MAINTAIN
CONSTITUTED AUTHORITY, LAW & ORDER
DOWN WITH THE HIGH COST OF LIVING
TO HELL WITH THE ALIEN ENEMY
GOD SAVE THE KING

"No one thought the Federals in Ottawa would side so completely with the factory owners and Citizens' Committee," Wally reminded Lulu Pearl.

"And why not? The patriotic Citizens' Committee of 1000—applications from press barons, factory owners, bankers, bent politicians and greedy landlords kindly solicited. Veterans, working men and women, trade unionists, Bolsheviks and European 'alien scum' are invited to remember Bloody Saturday and to kindly club themselves senseless so our famous Royal North-West Mounted Police are saved the trouble."

"One man died. Is that right, Mama?"

"It is. And more than a man died that day. Our Minister of Justice, the Right Honorable Mr. Meighen, did his just duty by making honest workingmen's complaints acts of criminal sedition and sent them to jail, where they languish still."

"What's sedition ... and languish?"

"It means they're considered traitors, Davy, and in prison they suffer a long time," Wally said.

"Men who fought for Canada and Britain, risked life and limb, and their poor wives and families fearing the worst—traitors in the country they fought to preserve and finding a new Hun at their backs and Federal troops confronting them in the streets of their home."

"But it may be the start of something grander, Lu. There're the new strikes from Victoria to Amherst in the east."

"Where are they?" David had asked.

"One's in British Columbia, the other in Nova Scotia. I'll show you in your atlas after dishes," his mother had promised.

"No, Wallace, though it grieves me to say it. It was all over with Bloody Saturday and the powers in Ottawa ordering the publics to take up their duties again or risk losing their jobs. Now the trains are back running on time, the post is delivered, the telephone rings, the lights light and the water pours out of our tap—a paradise for the capitalists and the boots of the bosses and politicians returned to our necks."

"At least they released the leaders of the One Big Union and the Central Strike Committee."

"Beaten dogs with no teeth, and Dixon and Woodworth still in jail. These two men is it, godless seditionists trying to overthrow the whole of the country? I'll retire to Bedlam with old Mr. Scrooge."

"What do you want me to do, Lu?"

David had waited, but his mother only shook her head and said nothing more. They had finished the meal in silence.

5 His Mother's Son

Now, once again, his mother Lulu Pearl had said nothing more since her last admonition to him.

His tears had stopped, but David was afraid of what he might see if he dared to look up at her face. "So now where are we going, Mama?" She laughed at that, and it was a terrible, bitter laugh.

"I fear no place we haven't been before, Davy, and not carrying our Temperance signs and handbills. This time I will confront the Devil in his own Den." Lulu squeezed his hand harder, and then they turned east on Niagara Street and headed for Walker Road, with the brighter lights and noise of Windsor's busy waterfront at eleven thirty p.m. on a Saturday night growing brighter and more strident by the minute.

"Sure, and this waterfront is more curse than blessing, my son. A 'precincts of Satan,' as any decent man would agree." Lulu Pearl had challenged his father Wallace Charles when she and David had returned from a Women's Temperance March, and himself busy "scouting."

"That may be, Lu. But scouting has given me a man's work, and us our house and living these eight years."

"And given other poor wives and their children drunken and abusive husbands and fathers for longer still."

"You say yourself each man must choose, Lu. Discipline is our Methodism."

"I do, Wallace. And what of the women and children who have the choice made for them by drink-sodden men? 'Thirst is the end of drinking and sorrow is the end of drunkenness.'"

Wally never won these arguments.

But David was Lulu Pearl Phelan's son, and she was Canadian first and Irish second in matters of history and allegiance. He had learned his letters early and the rest had followed. "You are four now, Davy, and it's time you learned who we are in Canada and where." His mother's birthday present had been a *Hammond's Modern Atlas of the World,* followed by the beautifully illustrated *Boy's Book of Canada and the New World,* when he turned five. On the cover of the *Boy's Book* was a reproduction of a painting by Frances Anne Hopkins, titled *Voyageurs at Dawn.* It showed men in colourful dress, smoking long white pipes, sitting under cover of a wide bark canoe, cooking breakfast over a log fire at the edge of a shady green river, and in the shadow of a great grey rock with the dense forest at their backs.

"Did they really sleep under that big canoe?"

"And why not, Davy, a fine bark house to keep off the rain and weather?" Lulu had confirmed when they'd begun reading it in his bedroom at night and tracing Canada's numerous lakes and rivers, and all the cities and towns laid out along them in his Hammond's atlas.

David soon realized it was his mother's way of answering his father's gifts of a new baseball mitt and a boy-sized bat Wally had turned on his own lathe for his son. David developed his baseball skills under Wallace Phelan's careful eye, and his knowledge of Canada's and Windsor's history under Lulu Pearl's careful tutelage. He knew more about Windsor, Ontario, Canada, than any boy his age.

Windsor's location at the heart of the New World drew European explorers, missionaries, armies, and settlers from St. John's in the east and on up the St. Lawrence River system. Lulu Pearl had put his finger on the city of St. John's and her own on their city of Windsor. "Now get into your great bark canoe like the Hopkins' voyageurs and find your way home." David slowly traced a route down the St. Lawrence, along Lake Ontario, then along Lake Erie to the Detroit River and Windsor—with Lake St. Clair and the three greatest of the Great Lakes, Huron, Michigan and Superior, farther north and west, and the Ohio and the Mississippi watersheds to the south, which he pointed out. "I did it!" He said proudly.

"Oh no! I'm sorry to say young David Phelan and his jolly voyageur friends all lost their canoe and drowned. It was a terrible grief for his poor mother." He looked at her, and she laughed at his expression. "Yes. It happened right here." David looked and then laughed himself.

"I forgot about Niagara Falls."

"A fatal mistake."

"I should have ... *portaged*."

"A fine French word and a good idea."

David learned that Jesuit missionaries had accompanied French explorers down that route in the 17th century, and that in 1701, Antoine Laumet Cadillac established Detroit, on the north bank of the Detroit River, as a fort and fur trading settlement to prevent further British expansion. "And that's why we have the names we do, not a day's drive in a Cadillac automobile." Lulu had pointed out Belle Isle, Belle River, Bois Blanc, LaSalle, Peche Island and Frenchtown. "Put your finger here, just to the east of Windsor."

"Puce?"

"Meaning?" David shrugged.

"Flea!" And she pinched him till he squealed. "Enough then. Time for sleep and church tomorrow.

"*Go n-éirí an bóthar leat!*" His mother turned at the door in surprise.

"And who taught you that, as if I'd need more than a single guess?"

"Father."

"Then may the road rise with you, too."

But Detroit's and Cadillac's and France's fortunes went steadily downward, according to David's *Boy's Book*. In 1780, English-speaking United Empire Loyalists left the newly created Thirteen Colonies, after the American Revolution, to join the French settlers; Napoleon was defeated by the British and Prussian forces at Waterloo in Europe; and the badly outnumbered but better prepared British and Canadians, with their native allies, fought the Americans to a stalemate in the War of 1812.

"History's better here with you, Mama, than at school where we copy from the board."

"It's always useful to know where we are and how we got here."

Heavy ferry traffic continued across the river between Detroit and the small village that grew up around the ferry dock across from it. The village had been called the Ferry or Richmond or South Detroit at various times, but in 1836 the Loyalist and British traditions prevailed, and the busy river port and gateway to western settlement and trade became "Windsor."

"I'm glad they called it Windsor. I like it better than Ferry or South Detroit."

"But enough of your father's Blarney. You've kissed the same Stone and us three thousand miles from Cork."

"I wouldn't kiss the stone if I were you." David confided, genuinely concerned. Lulu raised an eyebrow in question.

"He said I mustn't tell you."

"Then maybe I'll just kiss it and find out for myself."

"No, Mama! Before the visitors kiss it the Catholic guides pee on it ... especially if you're English or Protestant."

"David Charles Phelan!"

"I'm sorry, Mama. Please don't tell him. Father would ... if you were going to kiss it, I mean."

"He would if he wanted back into his own house."

The new automotive industries, Ford, Chrysler, General Motors, and others, and all the foundries and secondary industries to support them, provided steady work for a new influx of foreign labour from Europe, many young Irishmen like his father Wally with the others. It meant Lulu Pearl Connor and other women were outnumbered almost two to one, and their society eagerly pursued.

"So, you chose father out of all those men."

"With some pushes from Siobhan. And when he'd proved himself a disciplined man, an abstainer fit to be husband and father. But don't you be telling him that. His head's swelling in his bowler already. It's the work that praises the man, Davy, not the other way round."

"Yes, Mama."

By 1919, these events and outcomes were generally agreed to be blessings for the Windsor waterfront in the end, already on its way to becoming one of the most important commercial enclaves in the industrial world. But the curse, according to his mother, and Windsor's shame, was also well established—too well established and continuing to prosper, by this time.

It came with the arrival of a Massachusetts born businessman, who spent only five years in Canada but, in that short time, built a village, a railway and a world-renowned business: Hiram Walker and Sons Distillery—Corby Spirit and Wine Ltd.

His mother was adamant! "A scourge of our own making, sent to try us, as if the Four Horsemen of the Divine St. John were not enough, and we needed to create a fifth bearing Liquor's Poison Chalice. A weapon as potent as the White Bow of Conquest, the Red Sword of War, The Black Scales of Famine, or the Pale Sickness of Death."

For Lulu Pearl Phelan and the Women's Christian Temperance Union, Hiram Walker's legacy was the whisky that left a dark stain on the lives of sodden, weak-willed men who lacked Methodism and discipline, and dragged their wives, children and whole communities into a morass of indolence and despair. "Hiram Walker furthered the Devil's work, and Satan rewarded him handsomely."

His mother stopped suddenly, kneeled, and took David so roughly by the shoulders he began to squirm. "And this night, Davy, this very night, I fear the Devil has your father Wallace in his wicked claws, and your father has once again succumbed to the temptation of Liquor's Poison Cup."

David squirmed out of his mother's grasp and began to cry, his mind filled with cavorting shadow images, fierce and threatening.

6   Something Red

At eleven forty-five p.m. David's eyes, ears and nose confirmed the Devil's work was reaching its weekly summit. His mother tightened her grip on his hand once more. "Mama ... you're hurting me." Lulu stopped at that, bent down suddenly, and hugged him to her, the escaped hair, and the feel of the hard length of the bat across his back, scaring David again and drawing more tears.

"I'm sorry, Davy. This is no fault of yours. I'll call a cab, take you safe home and do this myself."

"No ... please. I want to be with you, Mama, and ... father."

"Then we must both be brave. 'If God sends you a stony path, may He give you strong shoes.' Are your shoes strong, son?"

"I don't know, Mama."

"Then I pray mine are strong enough for the both of us. I love you, Davy ... and your father, God help me."

"I know that."

Mother and son turned north from Niagara Street onto Walker Road and the commercial heart of the Walkerville city district. The Detroit River and the brown brick masses of the Walker's Distillery operation were in front of them, and behind those, the tall grain storage silos and the even taller buildings of the Detroit business district skyline, rising like a dark wall, uneven and indistinct. There were other points of light now visible, now lost in the evening's gloom. David finally realized the winking points were the lights of commercial ferries, moving between the two cities on the Detroit

River, or the commercial lake freighters moving between Lake Erie and Lake St. Clair. The Ford Motor Company's plants, where his father worked, were farther east. David had rarely been up this late, and the familiar streets and sights seemed to press like weights on his senses. The nighttime world was no longer familiar, and it was David that held more tightly to Lulu's hand as they walked.

Even at this hour on a summer Saturday evening, the distillery works continued to exhaust tall plumes of hard coal smoke from its square, tapered chimney stack, and the black plumes still managed to stand out against the night sky. Then there were the hissing eruptions of white steam from a half dozen relief valves in the boiler and steam lines, going grey where they mixed with the smoke. At four blocks' distance, yellow circles of streetlamps seemed suspended in the thick air, their cast iron stanchions almost invisible. They passed the Kerr Motor Company, then the Walkerville Brewing Company and The Walker Sons Lumber Yard and Planing Mill. All were in loud, vociferous operation.

"It's darker than I thought, with the lamps, Mama," David said in an uncertain voice. He sounded much younger, even to himself.

"Then may the blessings of the God's light within be upon us."

Toward the distillery and waterfront, the sour smell of the coal smoke underlay the higher, sweeter smell of fermenting barley and malt. Automobile traffic was surprisingly heavy, with private Hupmobiles, Cadillacs, Chevrolets and Fords, most, newer than the Phelan family Ford truck, parked at the curb.

David jumped at a sound like hammering metal.

"Easy, Davy. It's just one of those new electric starting motors your father was going on about." Next to him, driving lights flared, a throttle advanced, gears engaged and a large, stylish auto backed out into traffic with a roar that made even Lulu Pearl flinch. David recognized the model from advertisements in the *Border Cities Era*. "That's the new McLaughlin Big Six. It has sixty horsepower and carries seven people. It costs over two thousand dollars...." The recitation of these facts didn't help the pain growing in his stomach, but such expensive cars had strong appeal for David and his friends, Roddy and Gar, and it was automatic. They regularly scorned the cheaper, more numerous automobiles that were mostly open designs, like Henry Ford's Model T or 'Tin Lizzie', with just canvas-and-isinglass side curtains to protect driver and passengers. When it rained the canvas and isinglass smelled faintly of fish.

Lulu said nothing.

"Why so many trucks, Mama?" The stream of commercial vehicles dominated Walker Road, moving up and down with covered loads on open beds, or hidden behind wide double doors in the panel models. Some backed into side service alleys and others onto the curb in front of shops and small warehouses to unload their goods. A big open-bed truck, with wooden side and end gates and "H. E. Guppy & Co. Wholesale Grocers" in white letters on the doors, had backed right over the curb, and two big men were unloading huge crates of Leamington, Ontario tomatoes into a fresh produce warehouse, with much grunting and cursing in the close air. Their rough work shirts were marked by vees of sweat front and back, and stains under the arms. One of the men caught sight of David and his mother, about to walk into the street and go around, and surprised his Lulu Pearl by tipping his cloth cap.

"Sorry for the trouble, mum." Oddly, she didn't seem upset by the hard language and nodded back. The man hadn't noticed the bat.

"Those men were swearing…"

"Yes, Davy, men do when they must labour hard."

"But it's night … and Saturday?" They waited at the corner of Wyandotte for a long bus, like a grey beetle, to turn onto Walker Road. The Sandwich Walkerville and Amherstburg Street Railway seemed to have stopped running this late, as he hadn't seen the electric cars. David thought his mother hadn't heard him.

"The factories never sleep, my beautiful boy," Lulu explained. "The owners want the coal and wood and tin and hides to keep the machines supplied and their workers sweating at all hours of the day and night, while themselves lie up like kings in their beds." Lulu looked down at him. "The work praises the man, Davy, and we will not disparage their labours or curses."

They crossed the series of Pere Marquette and Grand Trunk tracks, polished bright by the steam trains that serviced the distillery, car plants, and other industries on both sides of the river. Like Walker's Distillery and Flouring Mills, each of the large auto plants had their own spurs for the offloading of raw materials and the carrying away of the finished products, bound for destinations across the continent.

"Hey, Paulie. Paulie!" Crossing the tracks, David shouted and waved up at the dimly lit, two-story rail switching tower cabin above them, with its white under-lights shining down on the tracks like powerful searchlights. From its interior, Paulie, the switchman, would watch for signals from the red, green, and yellow bulls-eye lanterns of the trainmen and conductors below, and pull or release the heavy levers that ground and groaned and shifted the tracks, as needed.

One of these switchmen, at least, was Irish, and his father had taken David up and introduced him to Paulie. The man smelled of oil and soot, but it wasn't unpleasant. Wally had let David pull on a tall lever in vain, until both men laughed, and Paulie added his burly strength to accomplish it.

"A nip of the *poteen*, Wally?" David had looked away in embarrassment, and his father politely refused. But Paulie was under no such constraint, and took his own nip of the clear mixture from a flat bottle concealed in a side pocket of his denim coveralls. The strength of the illegal spirits caused the switchman to squeeze his eyes shut, and he wiped his mouth on his sleeve and groaned like one his switching levers. "Ah! God's own nectar!"

Now David and his mother were beside the switching tower, and he was about to call out again, when he caught sight of something red under a white face staring down at him, before pulling back into shadow. It wasn't Paulie.

"Mama. I think there's a woman up there?" David waited, but his mother did not even look where he pointed.

"It's your eyes playing tricks. Nothing more, Davy." Lulu pulled him forward and they passed by the open doors of the Fire Hall, where a short man in suspenders and rubber boots with the tops turned down, was sitting on the running board of the big red truck and smoking. He stood up as they passed, and Lulu acknowledged him with another nod. Approaching Sandwich Street, they were surrounded by the bonded warehouses, with the fermenting rooms across the street and the main offices, malt house and grain elevators farther west, towards Devonshire Road.

They reached Sandwich Street, turned east again, and joined the streaming Saturday night crowds on this stretch of Windsor's bustling, Saturday night waterfront. Lulu Pearl occasionally peered through the doors and windows of the possible drinking and dance hall establishments where Wallace Charles might be lurking.

"See anything, Mama?"

"Just men deep in the Devil's cup and leaving their poor wives and children to languish at home, and fear the worst. Methodism, Davy! That is our only way forward."

Mother and son were heading towards the Ford plant, and it felt to David as if the entire populations of Sandwich, Walkerville and Ford City had joined Windsor's fifty thousand people on the same street.

Why had no one yet noticed the Ty Cobb bat on Lulu Pearl's right shoulder?

David looked back at the distillery across the road, and could clearly see the billows of steam and hear them hissing from a dozen different points on the brown walls and complicated runs of pipe, behind the noise and laughter of the crowds on the sidewalks and the traffic in the wide street. The chimney smoke and steam, and the sooty exhaust from the slow-moving cars and trucks, was acrid in his nose and mouth, and David instinctively slitted his eyes. But the racing of engines was nothing to the raucous sounding of horns by drivers impatient to move their goods, or others, mainly young men in summer suits or drab workmen's clothes, blowing off their own raucous steam on a humid Saturday night.

The sidewalk was no better. Everybody wanted the same space, and the crowd surged back and forth, moving as slowly as the road traffic and just as noisy. Again, it looked to David to be mostly men, and Lulu Pearl one of the few women in his limited sight. Soon he was being towed along in his mother's wake, as the men seemed to sense her unusual determination and moved to either side. Now David didn't like the looks he noticed some of the loudest men giving his mother.

Then he caught another flash of colour, standing out amidst the blacks and greys and dark blues, but this time he recognized it.

"*Orangemen*, Mama! Lots of them."

"The colour of hate. Ignore them, Davy!" Lulu ordered.

But it was impossible. The laughing men, young and old, including some boys not much older than David, travelled west in boisterous groups, dressed in blue serge suits, black bowler hats, and polished black boots, with orange and green collarettes draped down their fronts and orange loops of ribbon pinned to their lapels. Unaccountably, many carried furled black umbrellas.

One young boy was hoisted on his father's shoulders and waved a colourful banner that David remembered. When he was older, his father had quietly explained the meaning, after David's promise not to tell his mother.

"The Grand Man, with his plumed hat and long red coat, his high boots and spurs, on that fine white horse is himself, Davy: Good King Billy, William Prince of Orange. The red coat may be likened to the blood of Protestant martyrs on Catholic hands which he avenged at the Boyne on that blessed day, July 12th in the year of Our Lord 1690.

His sword is drawn as a sign to Irish Protestants, wherever they may roam, to be always vigilant to preserve their right to live and worship as they please, free from the threat of Popery. He fought for *us* that day, Davy, and we honour him still." Wallace Phelan's mustachioed face glowed with Irish Protestant pride.

Farther east along the crowded sidewalk, an old Orangeman in full regalia stood on an upturned box. Hands on his lapels, he gave forth, reciting in a strident orator's voice to a mixed audience of fellow Orangemen and ordinary citizens:

> *"Orangemen will be loyal and steady,*
> *For no matter whate'er may betide,*
> *We will still mind our war-cry 'No surrender!'*
> *So long as we've God on our side,*
> *And if ever our service is needed,*
> *Then we all like true Brethren will join,*
> *And fight like valiant King William,*
> *On the green, grassy slopes of the Boyne."*

"Pig's swill! Let us by!" Lulu Pearl Phelan manoeuvred them around the standing audience, using Ty Cobb's bat as a lever to force open the crowd. It was here that David noticed another group of cheering men among the masses, wearing Detroit Tigers baseball caps and jerseys, and waving team pennants. He remembered the big game between Ty Cobb's American League Tigers and the traitor, Jim McGraw, and his hated New York Giants of the National League.

"I think the Tigers won today, Mama. Father will be happy..."

"Yes, and I fear that's part of the trouble ... and this bat before it."

"But it belonged to Ty Cobb—"

"I know. It makes no difference."

She cautioned him. "Now be careful, Davy, don't stumble."

David was torn again and said nothing in his father's defence. But he still remembered that special day, in their basement workshop with his father, and the revelation of Ty Cobb's hand-carved, chestnut-oak bat.

David would never forget holding it in his very own hands—nor the unbelievable tale that his father recounted to him when he first held the vintage Cobb bat. He thought about it now as his mother pulled him through the bustling Windsor waterfront crowds late on a Saturday night. It helped distract him from his growing dread of what might be coming.

David still couldn't believe it.

7   Chestnut-Oak

"Here's what I've been waiting to show you, my son."

David had just turned six years old when his father had taken him downstairs to his wood shop, sat him on one of the tall stools and laid out something in an oil-soaked wrapping on the workbench.

"What is it?" Wallace Charles Phelan unrolled the object in the cloth with slow ceremony.

"A true sportsman's treasure, Davy." The boy saw a baseball bat, one that looked too long and heavy, made of yellow wood and much the worse for wear. It had taken too many dents and scuffs from baseballs.

"Did you make this? It's not very smooth." His father had turned many bats on his woodworking lathe over the years. Some to match David's size as he grew, but mostly for local teams and amateur players like himself. Wally laughed.

"I did not. Give me your hand, my son." His father ran David's fingertips along the length of the bat, and he could feel small grooves and unevenness. "Feel those?" He nodded. "Made by a knife."

"What do you mean?"

"This bat was hand-carved using a knife. Probably a pocket knife, a strong one like a Buck's."

"Why?"

"Ach, now. There's a question."

"What do you see here?" Wally rolled the bat and directed his attention to the area behind the sweet spot, where the bat manufacturer's stamp would usually go. But there was no black pattern and lettering, only something carved into the wood.

"Letters?"

"Exactly. What letters?"

"It's kind of hard to make out." David traced them with his fingertips while his father waited, smiling encouragement.

"W ... B ... C?"

"Try the middle one again."

"An H? W. H. C.?"

"Right you are, Davy. Now look at the pine tar the batter rubbed on the handle for grip." There were two blackened areas, each about six inches long, on the handle of the bat. One began at the roughly carved pommel, the other, two inches above the first. "Know any player who used to carve his own bats ... uses a split-hand grip ... initials W. H. C.?" David had an immediate idea—then wasn't so sure.

"Well, Ty Cobb ... when he was young. But then the initials would be T. R. C., Tyrus Raymond Cobb. After that old city you told me about."

"Right again. You're a smart boy, Davy. It *is* the initials that don't fit. Now what kind of wood is this?" David looked closely at the tight grain, felt the yellow wood.

"Ash?"

"Too yellow."

"Pine?"

"Too hard."

"Then hickory or oak."

"Hickory's too dark. But you're half right about the oak."

"How?"

"It's chestnut-oak."

David felt it again. "It's made from two different woods?"

"No. One wood. From one tree," Wally confirmed.

"I've never heard of a *chestnut-oak* tree."

"I hadn't either. But it turns out they used to grow in the southern United States—at least in one place—until a tree disease from Japan began killing them. A town in Georgia..." Wally smiled and waited for David to catch up.

"Royston! Where Ty Cobb grew up."

"My only son! You make a father, a sportsman and a Tigers fan proud." Wally ruffled his dark, reddish hair in a way David liked and always made him laugh.

"But the different initials?"

"Yes. Here's the story and a guess."

"Some years ago, we were just about finished our work on the new Navin Field in Detroit when one of the Tigers equipment men comes up and shows me this bat.

"Hear you're a dab hand at the woodworking, Phelan. Think you can mend this bat? It's important to one of the players."

"Who? I asked. But the man went sly and wouldn't say, Davy. So, I hammered the handle on a cement step—could tell by the sound she was cracked sure. Warped a bit too. I had to say no. Good for practice, but risky in a real game.

"Okay, he said, and took it away." Wally paused, picked up the bat and held it under the light. "You see, boyo, it was the strange wood, the hand carving I could feel and wanting to know who cared so much about an old bat, warped, and cracked.

"A week passes. I'm throwing scraps of wood into the burn barrel. Sure, and the very bat's right there, and I haul her out." Wally shows David a scorch mark on the end.

"Taking my half supper time, I show the bat and ask around. And old Buck Baton, a Frenchie from Louisiana, asks for a closer look, then starts to laugh and wheeze and carry on.

"Dis be chestnut-oak, *mon ami*," he says. "Be no mistake. But almost die out. Down Georgia, see. Where you get dis?"

"So, I explained, and showed him the initials. And he carried on again, laughing and wheezing like a torn bellows."

"*C'est le père! Le père!*"

"And that's when I understood, Davy."

"What?"

"*Le père*—the father. W. H. C. Not Tyrus Raymond Cobb. *William Herschel Cobb*. The father who gave him his name." David was stunned—not just a bat used by Ty Cobb, but a bat handmade by him.

"Can I try it?"

"Why not? Done so myself near a dozen times since." David stood with the bat and took a stance.

"Give it a rip." He did ... lost his balance and fell into a pile of shavings in the corner, to his father's loud amusement.

"Heavy." David brushed himself off then sat again on the stool and put the bat on the cloth. He traced the initials once more. "Why his and not his father's?"

"Another story, and a sad one for any young lad." David waited. "Times like this a man misses his drink to help the telling along." Now Wally did seem truly moved. "Betrayal, it was—or the suspicion of it, which can be all the worse for a man."

"How?"

"Pride, Davy. Betrayal can shame a man and whittle his pride to a nubbin."

David listened, and when his father began, didn't say a word for the next ten minutes.

"I got most of the tale from old Buck, and other bits from the newspapers and gossip, here and there. Seems it was a summer night in Royston, August of 1905. Tyrus Raymond was eighteen, living away and playing his first real baseball with a team in Augusta. William Herschel didn't approve of the game. A bit like your mother, against the drink and the travelling and the rough living. He wanted his son to be a doctor or lawyer, settled and worthy of the world's admiration. A man like himself, educated and a respected teacher.

"Now Ty Cobb's mother's name was Amanda Chitwood. Married her when she was just a wee thing, twelve years old. Had three children, Ty the first-born son. Twenty years pass. Then it seems there were rumours about Amanda and another man. And rumour rides a fast horse, then as now, Davy. The story persisted, and his father was so upset, he had to find out. So, William Herschel says he's leaving town on business for a few days, going to their farm where he and Ty used to work in the summers. Buck says that's where they became close, as a father and son should. Like us, boyo.

"But William Hershel, he had a plan. Doesn't leave town at all. Comes back to his house around midnight, he does. Supposedly a time when he knew Ty's younger brother and sister are away at friends or relatives or some such. He puts a ladder up to the porch roof outside their bedroom window, climbs up and begins to open it—

"BOOM! And then BOOM!"

David jumped off his stool in sudden surprise, and Wally laughed again and pointed to the locked case over the workbench, where he kept his rifle and twelve-gauge duck hunting guns, along with more than two dozen intricately carved and painted decoys on the shelves above. Since starting school, David had been after his father to take him along to the marshes around Windsor and Detroit, where he and his friends hunted ducks and geese each fall. But he was still too young, and his mother didn't fully approve of the hunting—although Lulu Pearl admitted the fresh fowl hung in the larder were not unwelcome.

"But what happened?"

"Shot. And shot again. It was her own self, Davy, his wife, Amanda. Two loads of buck right through their bedroom window. And with the man's own two-barrelled shotgun. First took him in the gut," his father poked a finger into David's stomach. "Second carried away part of his head," Now slapping the left side of his son's head. "Flipped him off the porch roof like he was no more than a child's wooden toy soldier."

David again sat with his mouth open and his eyes turned inward, trying to imagine it, and then not wanting to. He had watched Wally gutting ducks and geese, his hands bloody to the elbows with entrails.

"The man was killed by his wife's own hand. Died with a pocket pistol still in his coat, and never knowing the truth of the rumours. The son, Ty, was in shock, but stood by his mother all through the trial that followed. Amanda swore she thought his father was a thief or worse, and the whole thing a tragic misfortune." David thought he knew "worse" from the talk of the older boys at school, but kept quiet. "Jury must have agreed because the judgment was for her. Not guilty."

"An accident?"

"An accident, yes. Now here's the other thing, and strange are the ways of the world. Not even a week passes after burying his father, when doesn't Detroit call Ty Cobb up to the majors." David's mouth dropped open in disbelief. "Thirteen years later, he's setting records for the Tigers and making us both proud. How's that for a story?" His father slapped David's thigh.

"Is it really true?"

"As well as I can tell, it is." David touched the bat with awe, and its solid presence did seem to make it all real.

"Did he blame her?"

"His mother?"

"Yes. For killing his father. Even if it was an accident."

"Ah, Davy. Who can see into another man's heart and know the way of it?"

"I guess." David ran his fingers up and down the rough length of the bat while Wally continued.

"But I believe he *did* sit by her every day of the trial. I do know Cobb's mother never remarried and left Georgia to come up and live with him in Detroit."

Wallace Charles Phelan took the bat and laid it between them on the workbench. "Buck swears that one of the last things his father said to Ty, before he first went off to the baseball, was, 'Don't come home a failure.' So maybe the initials are a tribute and a proof to a dead father."

"But he threw it away?"

"He did. And that's a mystery." David waited while his father sorted out his thought. "But Ty Cobb plays hard and fierce. Hard and fierce, Davy. And maybe William Hershel is looking down over Heaven's wall and knows it." Then Wally had put his hand over David's, and they touched the bat together in a shared moment of silence.

Cobb's bat, for David, had become a Holy Thing.

"Now look at this." Wally went to a large cupboard behind them, returned and placed a long case on the bench. "Every treasure needs a proper chest, Davy, and this will be ours."

They mounted the bat in clever receivers on the back of the white pine case. David could smell the tung oil used to seal the wood. Then his father slid the long glass cover into its waiting grooves, and let David turn in the two screws that secured a wedge to hold the glass in place.

"Now this is one treasure we won't bury like Long John Silver. Where should we put it, Davy?" David thought a moment and pointed to their special memorial wall. It was covered with Tigers pennants, caps, small souvenir bats, Cracker Jack cards of their favourite Tigers players and more, dating back before the turn of the century. "Well now, I was thinking of some place else. A place where it could be admired every day and no effort..."

"At dinner? In the dining room?" His father seemed to consider it, but shook his head. "Then maybe upstairs. In your bedroom."

"No, boyo, I'm afraid your mother would never allow it. I was thinking of another bedroom." It took a moment, but Wally's smile made him certain. David cheered and ran around the basement yelling his pleasure, while his father roared and Lulu Pearl at last called down to question the commotion—causing further laughter.

"Daft as drunken leprechauns, the pair of you!"

Together, David and his father went up to his room and carefully mounted Ty Cobb's bat on the wall opposite the end of his bed. The bat was the first thing David saw in the morning, and the last when his mother tucked him in bed and turned out the light at night.

"All this fuss over an old piece of wood," Lulu had said.

"*His* wood, Mama. Chestnut-oak. Ty Cobb carved it for his father, W. H. C., William Herschel Cobb."

"Then may Saint Peter preserve us from the follies of men at their games."

"Oh, Mama." Lulu Pearl's look softened, and she bent down to kiss David again.

"And the Holy Peter preserve you in His Grace until morning, my lovely, lovely boy."

8   Mulvaney's

The further sudden increase in men's shouts and strident, drunken laughter yanked David back to himself.

"Where are they all going, Mama?" David meant the Orangemen. They had finally pushed a full block to Montreuil Avenue and were approaching the Ford Motor Company plants, and the drinking houses and *shebeens* that had grown up around them to service the thirsty auto workforce. David had marched with his mother and the Temperance women here before. Lulu Pearl reached the corner, but they didn't cross. Small clumps of Orangemen moved in both directions around them, some tipping their bowlers to acknowledge her. She gave them back such a look of contempt, that their greetings died on their tongues.

"Out of the mouths of babes and madmen. I've been as blind as Paddy's Pig."

"How, Mama?"

"Mulvaney's! It's Mulvaney's *shebeen*! As sure as Satan's Precincts spawn sin and drink-sodden reprobates neglecting their families."

The sound of contempt in her voice was even more severe. "We must cross and go back, Davy. Stay close." Lulu Pearl turned them left, held the bat in front of her, and stepped boldly into a small break in the heavy traffic. The cars stopped, but the driver of a huge black freight truck, loaded with oak boards for Walker's cooperage works, leaned on his horn and kept slowly coming.

"Mama!"

Lulu Pearl dropped David's hand, turned quickly to face the driver high behind the wheel, and swung Cobb's heavy chestnut-oak bat against the front headlight with a sound of breaking glass and crumpling sheet metal. David stood amazed at his mother's strength and determination.

"Mama!" he shouted and jumped back.

The truck driver, in turn, stood on the truck's brakes till they screeched in their own alarm, and took the black freight truck out of gear. In the next second, he had pulled the handbrake in another screech, and jumped down from the cab, growling like a British bulldog.

"Crazy bitch! What d'yer think yer doin'? You bleedin' insane? The big overalled man advanced on his mother, and Lulu Pearl Phelan swung Cobb's bat again, wide this time, only missing his reddened nose by inches—but connected squarely with the thick filler neck of the radiator. Another sound of bent metal, and white steam began to erupt in a thick whisper. The freight driver stood rooted, speechless, and David peeked from behind his rigid mother. By the look of the man's red face, David expected more steam to erupt from both his ears. "I'll teach yer..."

Lulu Pearl Phelan again cocked Ty Cobb's heavy chestnut-oak bat when the angry driver started for them once more—but the enraged man was stopped by one of the biggest, Loyal Orange Lodge men David had ever seen in full regalia. He stepped in front of Lulu Pearl and beckoned the man forward.

"Come ahead then, boyo..."

"That damned bitch knackered my light and rad work!" A crowd had gathered and began to laugh and jeer at the man. Horns blared around them, some impatient, others sounding enthusiastic encouragement.

"Could have been your thick head, bucko," said the Orangeman. Lulu took back David's hand and pronounced her verdict.

"A deluded servant of the Devil, not worth the effort," she said.

"Always pleased to help out a lady, and do the Lord's work, then." But if their new Loyal Orange saviour was expecting gratitude, he was mistaken.

"Your help was not needed, nor asked for. The good Lord looks after his own. And you and your Irish lot there, with your ribbons and marches, stirring *Na Trioblóidí*, the old Troubles and hatred, while invoking *His* name. May you all swallow brimstone and burn with Satan your own selves."

Before either man could react, Lulu Pearl Phelan parted the crowd again with the bat, and they stepped onto the far sidewalk and started back toward Mulvaney's Tavern.

The laughter, hooting of horns, and curses that broke out behind were still echoing in David's ear when they reached Mulvaney's some few minutes after the clock of the Windsor Town Hall nearby had sounded its twelve midnight chimes.

David Charles Phelan felt the same eerie sense as when his father had read Mr. Poe's story "The Tell-tale Heart" to him, and incurred his mother's displeasure. David didn't understand all of Poe's references, but enough. "It's only stories, Lu. I enjoyed them myself as a lad." Now each stroke of the midnight hour from the Windsor Town Hall clock was like the cuts from Poe's "The Pit and the Pendulum" in David's stomach's own pit....

The feeling of unease only got worse.

When they passed right by the line of the distillery this time, David could hear sounds of giant pumps behind the smoke and steam, like the tell-tale heart of a monster, crouched and waiting to pounce. Lulu Pearl had said nothing since the upsetting incident with the truck driver and big Orangeman in the street, but her walk was even more upright and stiff, and she carried the heavy chestnut-oak bat gripped tightly by the middle at her right side.

They were walking fast and now overtaking more and more Orangemen, laughing, and singing bits of song—

"Sure, I'm an Ulster Orangeman, from Erin's Isle I came,
To see my British brethren all of honour and of fame,
And to tell them of my forefathers who fought in days of yore,
That I might have the right to wear the sash my father wore!"

David saw a few colourful Detroit Tigers baseball pennants waving among their Loyal Orange banners.

They soon passed the Hiram Walker and Sons Ltd. distillery dock by the grain silos and reached the Walkerville and Detroit Ferry Docks. The park, with its trees and benches and lawn bowling green, was just to the east, at the foot of Devonshire Road. Mulvaney's could not be far.

But, as Hiram Walker built up his businesses on the south side of the Detroit River in Windsor, he found he was making the trip across the water to Windsor more frequently. He had no choice but to cross by the Windsor and Detroit Ferry service farther west, at the foot of Windsor's Ouellette Avenue, and then take Sandwich Street back east to his distillery and flour mill. In 1890, the street was not completely paved or macadamized. It was dusty in summer, muddy from the rains in spring and fall, and frozen and rutted in winter.

Walker's solution, to save himself time, discomfort and ultimately money, was to secure a charter and establish his *own* ferry service beside his distillery. And being progressive and civic minded (also good for business), he planted the area around his ferry dock and even built a large pagoda where Walkerville residents could sit and watch the river, the ferries and the men at lawn bowling, in their white outfits and wide-brimmed hats. David and his parents had sometimes taken the steamer *Ariel* from there to Belle Isle for a picnic lunch and games of pitch and catch with his father to hone his boy's baseball skills. Then on to Detroit for the view back to their side of the river, before returning to the park at the Windsor-Walkerville dock.

"This must be where the Orangemen are marching," David said. Lulu stopped and finally spoke.

"No. Their little parades are done, Davy. They're up to other mischief. Why else would they end at Mulvaney's *shebeen*." Now David and Lulu passed the park, crossed the Grand Trunk Railway tracks again and stood across the street from the wide ramshackle hotel and saloon at the foot of Victoria Road, just seven blocks north of his King Edward Elementary School. Mulvaney's.

The saloon was full to overflowing with laughing Orangemen of all ages from the riverfront communities. David saw banners for Loyal Orange Lodge No. 584, No. 2335, No. 2552, No. 535, Wally's old lodge, and others besides. The crowd had spilled out into the street and circled the entrance to the grey weathered building and were periodically laughing and cheering at some performance or activity they couldn't see. Others inside Mulvaney's crowded up against the series of tall, brightly-lit windows that fronted the saloon. "Hold tightly, Davy."

They circled along the west end of the block, and Lulu Pearl Phelan again used Cobb's bat to part the crowd of men. His mother ignored their upset and then surprise at the presence of a lady and a boy making way through their midst. And a hostile lady, at that. Until Lulu finally wedged herself and David into the row of men in front of the tavern's wide windows.

Inside the tavern and out, flasks of liquor, large mugs of ale and beer, and bottles of clear liquid that David guessed was *poteen*, were in plain view. The crowd around them smelled of sweat, engine oil, musty clothing, and beer. Periodically, the sharper smell of coal smoke drifted down on them from Walker's and other factories. Backs to Mulvaney's windows, David and his mother watched the moving tableau playing out on the wide sidewalk in front of them, and the crowd booed or cheered at each round of activity.

"What are they doing, Mama?"

"What the Orange do best—baiting and hating the Catholics."

Amateur actors were re-enacting the Battle of the Diamond, a crossroads near Loughgall, that took place in the fall of 1795. It was out of this civil battle between the Irish Catholic "Defenders" and the Irish Protestant "Peep o' Day Boys" that the basis for the Loyal Orange Institution of Ireland evolved, more than one hundred years after the Boyne. The Peep o' Day Boys evolved into the Orangemen. Legend has it the Protestants were waiting and killed forty-eight Catholics with no loss to their own, and the Defenders' bodies were only found days later, when they harvested the corn.

David guessed the short man in a red blanket, with his clothes stuffed full of rags to make him appear fat, and wearing a ridiculously tall paper hat with the words, "Roman Oppression" printed in crooked letters, must be the Catholic Pope. He carried a rough wooden staff that was taller than he was, with a crudely made crucifix at the top—from which something furry and brown dangled. "A rat, Mama! A dead rat!" But Lulu was watching the crowd, not the performance.

The pope led a group of Catholic Defenders, a dozen men in red scarves who were exaggeratedly sneaking up on the saloon, while the crowd hissed and booed loudly and began to throw bits of trash.

"For Ulster and King Billy!" Orangemen and the Peep o' Day boys cried, bursting out from each side of the building to "ambush" the bewildered pope and his followers, who cringed and groveled in the dirt, the Prods beating them with furled black umbrellas to the raucous cheers of the audience.

After a few minutes of this, the performance ended, and the actors stood up and bowed to the applause of the audience. The pope held his staff high overhead and pretended to bless them all with the dangling rat. Each performer was handed the drink of his choice, clapped on the back, and ushered into Mulvaney's raucous *shebeen*. The crowd followed, as many as could, trampling the pope's staff, the dead rat, the red blanket and scarves into the dirt.

David wasn't sure in the crowd and confusion, but he thought one of the Peep o' Day boys was wearing a Detroit Tigers baseball cap.

"Now listen to me, Davy, listen. I must leave you for a few minutes. I *must* and no choice." David had never seen his beloved mother Lulu's face so pale, in the glow of the street lamp against the vivid orange of her hair, escaping the neat straw hat. And her words reminded him in the moment of the mechanical voice of his bedroom alarm clock, the stroking midnight chimes of the Windsor Town Hall clock, and Edgar Allen Poe's pendulum biting so deeply. They all combined in his boy's imagination, and David doubled over in a new agony and began to cry.

"No, Mama! No-o-o-o! Please..." Lulu Pearl knelt in front of him, put down the bat and took David's teary face between her stiff hands. David could smell her Ponds Cold Cream, but it was anything but reassuring in this circumstance.

"Strong shoes, remember, Davy? Strong shoes. This is none of your doing, but still must be done." His mother spoke her words with a fond emphasis.

> *"For every storm, a rainbow,*
> *For every tear, a smile,*
> *For every care, a promise..."*

"I promise I will never again, never, leave you like this, my beautiful boy." His mother held him closer than he could remember for long seconds. "Know you are forever in my heart, my only David. Forever!" Then Lulu Pearl Phelan picked up Ty Cobb's heavy chestnut-oak bat and pushed her way determinedly through the big batwing doors, into the raucous confusion of Mulvaney's *shebeen*.

Cobb's Journey was done.

But Fate would intervene, and in time, David's mother might be unable to keep her promise.

9 White Angel

David Charles Phelan choked back his tears and stood a few moments in agony.

Then he pushed his way forward through the crowd around him, until he could reach and climb the wide, black iron lamppost nearby. Now he was standing on the thick topmost ring of its decorative pedestal. There he wrapped both his arms around the ribbed iron and clung tightly, looking over the heads of the restless sidewalk crowd and through the tall west side windows, into the garishly lit interior of Mulvaney's Irish *shebeen.*

What David saw and heard next, would come to be make-believe, a fanciful story whose words and unfolding images were half-remembered years later. Between the doubtful witness of his own senses, and what he could piece together from the little Lulu Pearl and Wallace Charles Phelan would say about it, David learned the story....

The late night's humidity and gloom; the hard edges of the fluted iron column against his face; the noise of the drinkers and shrill whistles of trains from the Grand Trunk Railway tracks behind him; his mother's white linen blouse moving slowly through the crowded tables and tobacco smoke toward the bar, with its line of men in bowler hats hoisting mugs of beer, waving umbrellas and laughing; the harried barmen in shirt sleeves and silver arm garters pulling tall beer handles that streamed and foamed dark liquid into the mugs below; and the great wide expanse of mirror behind that reflected his mother Lulu Pearl's advance in its wavy, imperfect glass.

Lulu Pearl Phelan halted and shouted.

"WALLACE CHARLES PHELAN!"

His mother's sharp voice carried high and strong, and cut through the din. The words hung heavy in the smoke-filled air in black printed capitals.

David could pick out his father Wallace Charles standing tallest in the middle of a tight group at the right-hand end of the long, polished wood bar. Wallace Phelan had an Irish Orange collarette draped around his neck and a foaming mug of beer halfway to his lips, when he turned to confront Lulu Pearl.

His father's flushed, laughing face leaked all colour around the thick walrus moustache—went confused, both terrible and sad at once. His father was a stranger David Charles Phelan didn't recognize. But his boy's mind could register Garrett Bryant, in a Tigers ball cap and in Loyal Orange regalia, standing beside him, and confirmed it must be him.

Wally moved away from the bar...

A smirking woman in red was holding his father's arm beside him. The young woman had long red hennaed hair and rouged cheeks. And she slowly disentangled her arm from his father's. Oddly to David, she was wearing Wally's Detroit Tigers ball cap with its distinctive brass pennant pin.

Lulu Pearl recoiled at the sight, appeared to lose her balance, and reached out a white hand to the bar for support.

The woman in red smiled at her, and after a moment, his mother pushed away from the dark polished wood and stood straight. Now her face was as blanched white as his father's had become in her presence.

"Lu ... Lu, I..."

"The very one, Wallace! And your only son David waiting outside and knowing my shame."

"I..."

"And you, Garrett Bryant, with Siobhan at home and carrying your third babe in her belly." Garrett reddened, looked down and said nothing. All laughter, all movement, all drinking, all talk in the saloon had stopped, and seemed to wait with David as the drama unfolded.

Then a large Orangeman in his regalia at the mug-crowded table beside his mother stood up. It might have been the man from the incident with the freight truck driver. He raised his own foaming mug of beer in an old Irish toast—

"Here's to our wives and girlfriends! May they never meet!" The silent witness of Mulvaney's broke into huge laughter and an answering cheer, with the clinking of mugs in agreement from the onlooking Orangemen.

Before Wally could bring his beer mug to his mouth once again, Lulu Pearl Phelan shattered it to glittering shards in one violent blur of Ty Cobb's chestnut-oak bat!

It was no longer Ty Cobb's bat. It was Lulu Pearl Phelan's bat now.

Even the big Orangeman recoiled in panic. Wicked shards of glass mug exploded against the wide wavy mirror behind the bar with a sharp sound like gunfire! Cracks raced out from the points of impact. Jagged sections of the huge mirror separated and fell in slow motion, one by one, out of the ornate gilded frame and broke into smaller pieces that rained like falling stars onto the rows of different coloured bottles of liquor below, and carried them to the floor in succeeding crashes.

All laughter stopped. All voices quieted. Awed silence reigned—

Then it was heated curses and blood. Blood on his father's fingers still holding the broken glass handle of his mug. Curses from Orangemen across the wide expanse of Mulvaney's. All of them rising to their feet in unison to take in the continuing drama.

Red, flushed faces were everywhere. David clung to the black ribbing of the iron lamp post and cried out for his mother.

He saw a fat man in a dishevelled grey undershirt and dark blue suspenders and pants coming down the long winding stairs near the other end of the bar, shrugging on what must be a matching blue policeman's tunic as he did. The Windsor constable was followed by a second young woman in red, with dark blonde hair, bare shoulders, and half-exposed breasts. The two hesitated at the bottom of the stairs, and despite himself, David was distracted. He had never before seen a woman's naked shoulders and breasts, and she seemed to be lacing up the front of a ... a corset! The mass of drinkers all looked to the constable in one accord, silent and expectant. But he was as dismayed by the disordered scene presenting itself as the rest of Mulvaney's.

Then Garrett, the woman in red, and the assembled men by the bar slowly retreated from Lulu Pearl and looked instead to David's father, along with all the other drinkers in the room.

From the bottom of the stairs, the Windsor Police constable and the young woman in red did the same.

Silence.

Wallace Charles Phelan at last drew himself up to his full, manly Irish height to answer. His determined voice carried across Mulvaney's to David's own ears beyond the tall window.

"Sure, and if you want criticism—marry! Be off home, woman!"

Laughter broke out again and spread across the *shebeen* once more. But it was uncertain, nervous. "And I'll pay all damages!" Wallace Charles Phelan assured the crowd, the broken mug handle still in his hand. "And another round of drinks for my friends here, barkeep!"

None of the bartenders moved, and one backed away. David thought his mother, Lulu Pearl Phelan, may have nodded, her worst suspicions confirmed. In the interval, her colour blanched further, if that was possible.

Then his mother reached deliberately down into the blue cloth purse at her waist and brought out his father's own carved wooden White Angel from the Christmas Nativity Scene at Lincoln Road Methodist Church. David well knew the face of the angel was Lulu Pearl's own. His mother held it out, right in his father's face. David watched in dread.

In slow stages, Wallace Charles Phelan's face broke like the mirror beside him, blanched, drained of all colour, until it matched the bleached pine whiteness of the wood.

"Lu ... I ... I..." His mother laid the White Angel carefully on the bar between them, yet another silent witness to her shame.

"Home? Oh yes, Wallace, I'll be off home, all right..."

Then, and for long years after, the ensuing sound would be David Charles Phelan's most vivid memory of that disturbing night at Mulvaney's. But try as he might, he could never describe it fully, adequately, even to himself, in words that would capture its simple uniqueness. It wasn't the sound of shattering glass, or crushing wood, or a Louisville Slugger connecting fully with a hard-thrown baseball. It was a broader, softly solid noise of hardness meeting a softer resistance. Yet David fancied Mulvaney's, the whole of the wide saloon, hundreds of milling people in the streets around him, the whole of the combined populations of Windsor and Walkerville must have heard it—the sound of Wallace Charles Phelan's treasured Ty Cobb chestnut-oak bat hitting the side of his very own head.

"...but you'll be coming with me."

David's father didn't collapse slowly, in stages against the polished wood bar; nor was he driven back into the welcoming arms of his drinking companions. To David's wide eyes, he was simply—*gone*. Did he still have a father at all? And his boy's warm tears began in earnest, until strangers' willing hands lifted him down to the rough pavement, and a multitude of voices he tried shut out began trying to console and question him. But how could David even begin to explain it all to a handful of strangers, when he wasn't the least bit sure himself about all that had just transpired?

When David tried to shake them all off and looked down at his feet instead, he found he was standing on the soiled red scarf from the recent Irish Loyal Orangemen's anti-Catholic performance, the dead rat still tied to the stick beside him.

10   From the Sea

"Mama wants you to read this. Out loud. She says I should hear it from your own lips."

David held out the Phelan family Bible to his father, Wallace Charles Phelan, sitting in one of the brown wicker chairs on their back stoop, occasionally touching the patch of dried blood on the cloth bandage Dr. Kirsner had wrapped around his head at two in the morning. David had been too upset to go to sleep, and his mother, Lulu Pearl Phelan, had let him help with the bedclothes for his father's exile, and then sat him at the kitchen table nearby with milk and an oatmeal cookie. David anxiously watched and listened through the screen door while Dr. Kirsner attended to his father, with his mother taking instructions for care. And Windsor Police Constable Carrick stood looking on, still dishevelled in his blue policeman's tunic from Mulvaney's Tavern and his parents' violent confrontation there.

Almost an hour and three cookies later, when his mother had finally dealt with them, Lulu Pearl took David up to his bedroom and tucked him in. "Truth to tell, Davy, I would not have done differently with your father—yet I am sorry you had to bear witness to our family's shame. For that, I blame my own spitefulness, my want of Methodism in the matter, and for not returning you home, knowing it might come bad. And now you're left fearful and overtired, my beautiful boy. But sleep, sleep well, and we will sort our troubles out in the morning. Together. As a family."

"But, father..."

"Hush now, Davy. I will wait and watch with Wallace Charles as Dr. Kirsner instructed. And you and I both will be attending the two o'clock church services tomorrow." The Phelans now belonged to the Lincoln Road Methodist Church, near the corner of Lincoln Road and Wyandotte Streets, five blocks north. But it was the nine thirty a.m. Sunday school and the ten thirty a.m. service they usually attended as a family.

Lulu Pearl bent lower. "May God lighten the darkness and hold you in the palm of his hand until morning, my lovely boy." His mother softly kissed him and hugged him and left him, turning out the lamp and closing his door soundlessly. David had the sudden thought that she must have cleaned up the broken glass from the Ty Cobb bat case before taking him up. But he didn't remember her doing so, and now felt as hollow and broken as the empty pine case in front of him.

David Charles Phelan eventually slept, but woke up at eight a.m. feeling exhausted and confused, then panicked and rushed downstairs to find his mother in the kitchen making their butter breakfast biscuits and brewing their coffee. Lulu Pearl Phelan's auburn Irish hair was perfectly done up and her clothes neat and fresh, but his mother's eyes were red and bruised. The heavy brown leather Phelan family Bible, a King James version with stiff yellowed pages, was open on the kitchen table, and Lulu's straight pen, black ink bottle and blotter beside it. David saw Ty Cobb's former chestnut-oak bat resting in the corner of the kitchen nearest the new Battle Creek Gas Stove Oven that was his mother's pride. The cracked bat Ty Cobb had discarded and David's father had retrieved at Detroit's new Navin Field he was helping to construct didn't belong there, but in a new, uncomfortable sense David found hard to express, maybe it did.

The Phelan family kitchen and all Lulu Pearl used in it were his mother's domain. He could see no sign of blood on the bat's end, as if its final exercise against his father's head by his mother's hands were a disturbing dream or waking nightmare—almost. But David saw his father asleep in the wicker recliner with the grey blankets and pillow they had laid out on the back stoop, Wallace Phelan still in his dark suit from Mulvaney's. Even Garrett Bryant and Constable Carrick had not persuaded Lulu Pearl to let him into the house, and Dr. Kirsner the same.

"Wallace has made of himself a stranger to me, to his son and to our Methodist Christian home," Lulu had said, in an echo of David's own thought the night before, marching on their way to Mulvaney's, and that was an end of it.

"Then, Mrs. Phelan, you will have to sit with him here and wake him again on every hour," Dr. Kirsner said. "If he goes unconscious, you must call me immediately. Otherwise, I will return at one this afternoon to check on him and change the bandages. It should be safe to give him something for the pain by then."

"Thank you, Doctor." His mother had brought out her purse.

Dr. Kirsner held up his hand in refusal of any payment. "That won't be necessary, Mrs. Phelan. My wife and the women of our Windsor Jewish Synagogue have the greatest respect for you and your Methodist temperance cause. And I must say, for the work you did at the temporary infirmary at the African Church. You attended there during the worst of the Spanish Flu, when the coloured in that sanctuary were spurned by most in the Windsor community. I would never hear the end of it from them."

"And did I not see yourself there more than once, doctor? And at the Home for the Friendless, not two months gone, easing the pain of men who are destitute?"

"Well, my Jewish community understands ... isolation."

"One God, many paths." The doctor bowed slightly to his mother Lulu Pearl. "Please thank Mrs. Kirsner kindly for her thought, but Phelans always pay their debts and are beholden to none. If not for your services, then for your Jewish charities."

"As you will, Mrs. Phelan, eight dollars will suffice for both visits." His mother counted out the money; the doctor tipped his hat and started for his car. "Remember, every hour."

It was Garrett Bryant who, with the help of Constable Carrick, had gotten David's father Wallace Charles out of Mulvaney's to their big Ford truck and driven them home, with the constable following in his Windsor police wagon, "to discuss the charges." Garrett drove, with Lulu in front and Wally sitting limply between. David climbed into the open box behind, with its bits of wood and the smell of fresh shavings on the heavy air. Wally was conscious and moaning by the time they parked in front of their house on Gladstone Avenue.

Garrett had tried to speak, but David's mother cut him off.

"Was the shame of Siobhan and yourself at your wedding not enough, Garret Bryant? Save your pathetic man's excuses for the fools and the weak-willed who may care. You will help Wallace to the back stoop. I will ring Dr. Kirsner; you will ring Siobhan. Then you will leave my house by the back door and go home to your wife and children—if they will have you."

Garrett could only hang his head in shame at the justice of Lulu Pearl's reprimand. He too, had solemnly sworn the Temperance Oath before Siobhan and his two girls.

Following that stressful exchange, David was too afraid to say anything. And Garrett Bryant did as he was told, after the doomed attempt with the others to get his father into the house. That had left only Windsor Police Constable Carrick, arguing with his mother in the dim yellow light of their back stoop.

"Now, Mrs. Phelan, there're the serious matters of the unprovoked and violent assault on your husband, and the extensive damages to Mulvaney's, not to mention your upsetting the civil order and peace of the community." At that, Lulu Pearl Phelan had leaned back and laughed in a long and reckless way that made David afraid for his mother. This was a Windsor Police Constable.

"Sure, and with upstanding officers such as yourself on duty, Constable Carrick, the community peace and civil order is safe and secure as the graven armour of St. Patrick that bears the holy words! Surely, a fine upstanding man as Christian and observant as yourself can recall them?" And Lulu Pearl recited the words graven on the armour of the holy St. Patrick aloud in her clear Irish cadence—

"Christ be with me
Christ before me
Christ behind me
Christ in me..."

"Mrs. Phelan, there is no need to add sarcasm to your list of offences."

"Is there not?" Now his mother went cold and rigid, stepped nearer to the fat Windsor Police Constable until she looked directly into his broad red face and coarse features. "*My* offences, is it? And what of *your* offences, Constable Carrick, on this fine evening in question?" Here the man seemed suddenly, deeply uncomfortable. He knew what was coming.

"My offences?" he said.

Lulu Pearl Phelan laughed again and picked up his father Wally's water glass from the small wicker side table, there on their back stoop beside his still form. "An old Irish toast I had the honour of receiving from such as yourselves, Constable: 'To our wives and girlfriends! May they never meet!'" She stopped with the glass almost to her lips. "But wait a bit, now. Do we not have to modify that fine wisdom somewhat in your own case Constable Carrick? 'Here's to our wives ... and wee whores! May they never meet!'" Lulu Pearl drank and then smashed the glass to pieces on the wooden floor of the stoop, splashing his boots and blue pant bottoms.

Windsor Police Constable Carrick jumped back and then seemed to shrink, like a Raggedy Andy doll that had lost its stuffing, before the force of his mother's withering anger and disdain. David Phelan had heard the term "whore" used at his King Edward Elementary School, about Susan Whalen, going with the older boys into the woods behind it. He had not risked asking even his father Wally about it at the time. He knew it was bad, a shameful thing. Now David almost felt sorry for the red-faced Constable.

"Or was it your own wee daughter, Constable, you were having a drink and a cuddle with upstairs at Mulvaney's?"

"You dare to...?" Carrick tried to stand taller and recover some dignity in his feeble outrage.

Lulu Pearl Phelan stepped in again, even closer this time. "Well, Carrick, she was *somebody's* daughter once. Or a wife, or a mother, more's the pity. So, when I again serve your own good wife and daughter in Dumfries Fine Ladies Wear for their intimate needs, I'll be sure to advise them to take your opinion, Constable Carrick, you having such wide experience in the matter of female underthings."

"You would do well to think about that rash course of action, Mrs. Phelan." Now Carrick's fat face was suffused with even more blood, his fleshy fists clenched and raised in threat.

"Would I now?" Lulu Pearl Phelan remained unmoving, rigid with barely suppressed indignation and even more withering disdain. "Then maybe I should just speak to Mrs. Griffiths, at Lincoln Road Methodist's afternoon services today. Yes. I'll tell her how fortunate it was that you were upstairs at Mulvaney's and so handy to the situation to preserve 'the civil order and peace of our community.' Will Windsor Police Chief Griffiths not be pleased to learn one of his constables is so vigilant? And of course, there's Alderman Keogh, whose wife is active in my Lincoln Temperance Union chapter, not to mention Reverend Winthrop and his wife and daughters. Yes, that might be better...."

David watched Windsor Police Constable Carrick's face shade down from angry red to chalk white, to an unhealthy green, and his shoulders sag. When he spoke at last, his voice had faltered to a tone of pathetic pleading and beseeching.

"I might ... I might talk to Mulvaney.... Your husband *did* offer to pay the damages, especially to the big mirror. I could ... do that." Lulu Pearl Phelan fixed Constable Carrick with her eye until the weight of it bowed his head. His mother's tone was dead stone with its chill cold.

"Mr. Mulvaney can tally up his list of charges. And no exaggeration, mind you, Constable. Nothing added. I will bring the cash payment round myself each week, until the debt is retired. And add something for his trouble."

"And Wallace *is* your husband. If he didn't press any assault and battery charges against you...."

"Yes, Wallace, is still husband, for all that. When Wallace comes to his senses, I'll be sure and discuss it closely with him."

"And you'd have to agree, in writing, to stay out of Mulvaney's Tavern in future, Mrs. Phelan. You and all your Temperance women."

Lulu Pearl laughed in acerbic sarcasm. "And is your own good wife, Phyllis, not one of them, Constable?" Carrick looked away, but said nothing. David watched from a short distance as his mother laughed once more. "And, in writing, is it? Sure, and a wife must accompany her husband, must she not?" David thought of the dry caustic soda his mother used to scrub the stains from her pans, sinks, and water closet.

"Wallace too, then," Mrs. Phelan."

"Agreed, Constable Carrick! Agreed—in the interests of civil order and community peace. We Phelans never forget a service—or an offence. You have my solemn promise to repay each in kind. Fully." David thought the fat Windsor Police Constable wanted to say something more. Maybe a lot. Instead, he turned awkwardly, pant cuffs still dripping, and stepping carefully to avoid the broken glass, clumped loudly down the back stoop's steps and out around the house to his police wagon parked at the curb in front

Now Lulu Pearl looked at David gravely. "I'm so very sorry you had to witness that, Davy. So very sorry. But my son, sometimes important things need the saying of out loud, and you're getting old enough now to learn it."

David Charles Phelan had watched the whole of it unfold with the constable, and noted it carefully for the future, painful though it all was. "Yes, Mama, I understand. I won't forget."

David promised himself in that moment, he would never again, never, do anything in his life to cause his beloved mother Lulu Pearl to look at *him* the way she looked at Constable Carrick as he departed their back stoop.

"Mama marked the page. Her writing is on the back of the picture," David added. Wallace Charles Phelan sat up slowly with a groan and accepted the heavy weight of the King James Phelan family Bible.

"Would you fetch me a glass of water, Davy?" Wally drank it down before opening the heavy book on his lap. "I could use another." David filled the glass again at the single tap and returned.

"How do you feel, Papa?"

"Like Ty Cobb himself played nine long innings with my head for a baseball." He tried a smile, and David felt better. He knew the situation was serious and struggled to hold down his dread. Maybe if his father could joke about it, there was hope. "Lu said to read it out loud? To you, Davy?"

"If you had the ... the courage. And to explain that picture and some of the words." David sat at the end of the recliner and waited for Wally to begin. He knew his mother was in the kitchen, seated at the table, but no sound came from it. Lulu Pearl was listening too. Wally took a moment to look at her words, and the pain in his expression was so severe, David had to hold his breath against the urge to cry out in sympathy and grab the Bible away. But his father began in a voice that was drained of all feeling—

Wallace Charles Phelan:

I write this in an extremis of pain and foreboding greater than any that God has seen fit to visit upon me to this hour. Why I must deserve it, our Lord only knows. I confess the burden is one my woman's spirit may not endure.

I fear for your immortal soul and our nine years' marriage. I fear for the child we have together brought into this uncertain world.

It shames me to name you husband and father to my son. I fear you have betrayed your solemn vow of faithfulness in the holy bonds of matrimony, as I am certain you have betrayed your bounden duty to us, your family. I no longer wear the Claddagh ring.

I fear too, you have betrayed the larger trust of those young men, some from our own congregation, who were sorely tested, maimed, and killed, far from loved ones in that cruel war just ended, when you dishonour the God-given skills that kept you safe and home with us to practice your carpentry profession in support of their struggles and our country's freedom.

Do you become womanish, become the weak-willed wife of Lot, when our hope in marriage, our son, and our nation's prosperity demand that same obedience to God's will and dedication to His purposes that was Lot's severest trial and only salvation?

We are not of the Roman faith, but this very porch and exile are your Purgatory. And as you are in the Devil's sway, so are you also, rightly, put behind us.

For if Mulvaney's, that Den of Iniquity, is not Hell, it is certain Satan's precincts, and the men and women there more to be pitied than condemned. I pray for their souls' recovery, as I pray for yours.

If the home I have laboured with good cheer to make for us and our child is not Eden's paradise, it is at least God-fearing and clean. Though with your wilful fall from Grace, I may no longer say respectable.

If not the Mark of Cain I have put against your brow, the wound is yet a scarlet badge of shame. As with Cain's curse, I do not know if it may ever be removed.

But I remain a Christian woman, wife, and mother for all this.

Our Saviour's example to us holds out the choice for sincere repentance, and the gifts of divine forgiveness and redemption in a joyous return to God's favour. Our Lord endured his passion for three days, died and was reborn to new life and the Hope of All the World.

I allot you these same days and nights to examine your own soul's peril. The chance to be born anew to the responsibilities of a Christian husband and father, a man of Temperance, or make of your life a Gehenna and live outcast and apart from us forever.

As the Lord is my witness, I do not say I can forget. But I may forgive.

L.

"Don't cry, Papa. Mama will forgive you."

David had never seen a grown man cry. But by the time his father had finished reading the letter, his voice was shaking, and now he held his head in his hands and quietly wept. David felt tears coming too, but fought them back. They wouldn't help. So, he moved to embrace his father, who hugged him fiercely back. After a minute, Wallace Phelan spoke into his ear.

"The child is father to the man. And now the son is father to the child. Your mother may forgive me, Davy. But can I ever forgive myself, doing what I did and knowing what I know?"

"What's that?"

"It's this." His father wiped away his tears and positioned the King James Bible in his lap so David could see it, and showed the front of the page on which Lulu Pearl's letter was written. David saw again the faded but still lurid black and white picture of a man and woman on a hillside in old-fashioned Biblical robes. They were turning their backs on the walled city below them, where the inhabitants were in some kind of agony of destruction and fear, with stern-faced angels bringing down heavenly fire upon them from above.

"I can't read all the words." David pointed to the large printed black letters under the scene.

"The words say: GOD'S JUDGMENT ON SODOM AND GOMORRAH. The people of those cities had fallen into sin and wilful ignorance of the Lord's Commandments, and God destroyed them with fire and brimstone."

"What about those two?" David pointed to the retreating figures.

"That's a man named Lot and his wife. They remained faithful to God and His Word, and the Lord spared them in His mercy and let Lot lead them away from the fallen." David looked more closely.

"What's wrong with the woman?"

"Ah, you've a sharp eye, my son. God warned Lot and his wife to go and not to look back. But Lot's wife gave in to Temptation, and the Lord turned her into a Pillar of Salt as a punishment and lesson to us all."

"Real salt?"

"So, it goes. It's the lesson your mother thinks I need the reminding of."

"You're Lot?" Now Wallace Phelan's laugh was bitter and held no humour.

"No, Davy. No. I'm a great Pillar of Salt, with a walrus moustache and a bowler hat. I gave in to temptation. I looked back. I gave your mother my solemn promise in good faith. I took the Temperance Oath against consumption of all alcohol. And when I broke my word, violated my solemn oath, Lu cast me out. She put me behind her. Behind you. This stoop is my Gehenna, my Purgatory, my Hell. It was the Orange, the drink, the..."

"The woman in red? Was she a ... a whore?" Now his father looked away, and his face held the greatest pain when he looked back.

"Where did you hear that word, Davy?"

"First at my King Edward Elementary School, with Susan Whalen. Then last night, when Mama talked to Constable Carrick. I think it really scared him. Mama's not going to be arrested and go to jail. We'll give Mr. Mulvaney some money each week. And you can't go back there. Ever."

"Well then, I don't know who I fear most, Davy—God, the Devil or Lulu Pearl."

"I think so too, sometimes. But I still know Mama loves me. And when we were walking last night ... she said she loved you too." His father's eyes brimmed with tears again. David waited, but he had to ask. "Did you go upstairs at Mulvaney's? Like Constable Carrick?" Wallace Charles Phelan raised his face to the Heavens, said something unintelligible, then took David by the shoulders so hard it hurt.

"Look at me now, Davy!" It was hard, but David did. "By the Grace of God, your mother and all that's Holy, I swear I did not. I did NOT!" Then Wallace Charles Phelan paused, and did seem to work up his courage. "But I might have, Davy. I might have—to my lasting shame—and Lu's." His father released him and sat back heavily in the wicker recliner, making it groan. "Yet there's more to it than that. You're only seven, but maybe it's time the truth about your mother was told you." Now David was afraid again. "Go up to our bedroom and bring down the picture of Lu with your Grandfather and Grandmother Connor. Then ask her for the picture from her special box. She'll know the one I mean."

"I'm not allowed…"

"It'll be all right, just this once. But ask your mother for me. She can decide."

David went upstairs to their bedroom door and knocked. In a few moments Lulu Pearl opened it. His mother's eyes seemed even more red and bruised. She was dressed in her light green housecoat. The room smelled of Ingram's Milkweed Cream and Body Lotion and Velveola Souveraine Face Powder, comforting smells that lingered in David's room after her bedtime kiss or reading to him, and had always meant his mother.

"Father read the letter to me, Mama. He explained about the Pillar of Salt and being in Hell on the back stoop. He swears he didn't … go upstairs at Mulvaney's, like Constable Carrick. I believe him." Now his mother hugged him. Would his parents ever again do the same with each other?

"Oh, Davy!"

"He asks if he can have the picture of you and Grandfather and Grandmother Connor? And can he have the other one? From your special box? He said you'd know. You'd decide." Lulu Pearl considered a long moment, like visiting the distant past and returning, then said the same thing as his father. It was strange.

"Yes, Davy, it's time. I should have explained it myself, but I was wanting you to be a bit older. Like you being older before explaining to you what you saw pass between me and Constable Carrick, after we brought your father home from Mulvaney's."

His mother took the framed photograph from the wall hook and gave it to David. Then she produced a small key from somewhere and unlocked the bottom drawer of the dresser, and took out a fancy chocolate box from N. M. Meisner's Confectionery. She opened it slowly and reached in for a square of white lace, tied with pink ribbon.

Lulu Pearl undid the ribbon and folded back the lace to reveal an unframed photograph. David waited again while his mother looked at it, so long that he thought she would change her mind. But she came over and handed it to him where he waited by the door, still wary of entering the forbidden space of their bedroom. "Be careful with it, Davy. It's the only one I have." He looked at the woman in the worn photograph, but didn't recognize her.

"Who is it?"

"A person with strong shoes, my beautiful boy. Let your father explain. And I'll talk to you later if you wish. But not today. I'm going to lie down for a little, before Dr. Kirsner comes." His mother touched his cheek. "You make me very proud, Davy."

Lulu Pearl Phelan closed the door slowly behind him, and a few seconds later, David heard the strain of the bedsprings taking her weight.

The heat of the Sunday afternoon was growing uncomfortable, even in the shade of the back stoop. His father took the pictures and asked David to fill two water glasses and then pull the other wicker chair to the table beside him. Father and son stared at the faded brown photographs for a long time. David could read the name in fancy gold letters in the lower right-hand corner of the larger, framed picture of his mother and grandparents: 𝕿𝖍𝖔𝖒𝖆𝖘 𝕸𝖆𝖞𝖍𝖊𝖜 𝕱𝖎𝖓𝖊 𝕻𝖔𝖗𝖙𝖗𝖆𝖎𝖙 𝕻𝖍𝖔𝖙𝖔𝖌𝖗𝖆𝖕𝖍𝖞, 𝕳𝖆𝖑𝖎𝖋𝖆𝖝 𝕹𝖔𝖛𝖆 𝕾𝖈𝖔𝖙𝖎𝖆, 1890.

David's Grandmother Connor was seated in front of his Grand-father Connor, who stood at her side, a solid-looking man with a trimmed black beard ending in a point and a curling moustache above. He was wearing his dark blue, tightly-buttoned ship's captain's uniform, with his round peaked cap and gold trim held in one hand across his waist, and the other hand resting on his wife's shoulder. There was a fancy, painted curtain scene behind, showing tall sailing ships heeling over in the wind, sails billowed and colourful pennants streaming from the tops of their masts. The words, "HALIFAX HARBOUR," in large ornate lettering, curved across the top, above Captain Connor's head.

David's Grandmother Connor held her baby, in white swaddling clothes, in the crook of her left arm, with what must only be his mother Lulu Pearl's small face peeping out and her eyes closed. His grandmother was a slight woman, like her now-grown daughter, and her thick hair hung carefully across her shoulders in large curls. David knew it was red, like his mother's. Her long dress was some lighter colour, trimmed with white lace and wide ribbons at the neck and sleeves. She was smiling and pretty and looked very young. The only jewellery David could see was a round watch on a short length of ribbon, pinned to her left breast.

"But how can she tell the time?" he'd asked his mother once, and Lulu Pearl had laughed and explained.

"The watch is worn upside down, Davy. When my mother lifts it on the ribbon to look, it appears right side up." David tried to imagine it, but couldn't.

"Where is it now?"

"Lost." His mother had stopped smiling, and David couldn't interpret the look on her face, before she took the picture upstairs again. But on the back, David knew, Grandmother Connor had written, "Christening, Lulu Pearl Connor, 7 mos." in spidery black ink strokes.

Now Wally took a long drink from his water glass, then pointed to Grandfather Connor. "You remember him?"

"He was captain of a trading ship, with sails like those. But there was a big storm near Boston, and he died. Grandmother Connor had to open a boarding house near the waterfront in Halifax. For sailors. When Siobhan's aunt was dying, she sent Siobhan away to help Grandma Connor and Mama at the boarding house. Later Grandma was sick, and she died too. That's why mother and Siobhan stayed."

"Well, the dying is true. But most of the rest is not."

"Then why...?"

"Shame, Davy. Shame. It was your mother's wish to protect you, at least until you were older and could better appreciate the truth. We agreed on that before you were born."

"But I'm almost eight."

"You are, boyo!" Wallace Phelan leaned forward and winced at the pain it caused. "Now look at your Grandfather Connor, so proud in his fine captain's uniform. Sure, it's fine, but it's *not* the dress of a ship's captain. It's the uniform of a Halifax Customs Officer." David looked again and didn't want to believe it. His grandfather had been a brave ship's captain for as long as he could remember.

"What's a customs officer?"

"Customs are taxes, money the owners of a ship's cargo have to pay to use the Halifax Harbour, load and unload their goods. Halifax was an important Canadian seaport back then, still is, especially with the war. Before, as now, plenty of trading ships are coming and going in the harbour. Your grandfather collected the money, the custom's duties, for the port of Halifax and the government, and earned himself a good wage doing it. He was a seaman once, but never a captain. Your Grandmother Connor wanted him home and in one place when they married."

"Then ... how did he die?"

"Badly, Davy, and sadly. His weaknesses were the gambling and the drink. Serious weaknesses. Wherever there are ships and sailors, there is sure to be both in abundance."

"Like gin rummy?"

"How do you know about that?"

"Some of the older boys at school."

"But not you?" David hesitated, and his father ruffled his hair, and his spirits lifted a bit. "I won't tell your mother."

"Like the gambling and drinking at Navin Field and Corktown? With the alcohol and the swearing, the Orangemen marching and the fights with the Catholics?" Now Wallace Phelan looked pained once more and bowed his head.

"Yes. But temperance, Davy, temperance is safest. And if not temperance, care and moderation. Or this is the result." His father touched the bandages around his battered head and spread his arms to acknowledge his exiled state, let them drop, then fell back in the recliner and was quiet. David gave him time.

"I think, for your Grandfather Connor, it was stud poker, and the Irish weakness for the horse racing and the betting. And these combining with the sad tendency to drink himself insensible and bet too much money on both. Soon your Grandfather Connor was deep in debt and then caught stealing from the tax money he collected. The man lost his job and spent time in the Halifax City Jail with others like himself and worse."

"What did Grandmother Connor do?"

"What any wife does. She suffered for her husband's sins and your mother with her." Wally looked up to their bedroom. David saw his guilt, pain, longing and the regret that accompanied it.

"Did he die in jail?"

"It would have been a blessing, but he did not. Grandfather Connor came home with a great anger in him, and mother and grandmother suffered more. No job, no money, but more of the stealing, the drink and the gaming. And every day, somehow blaming his wife and daughter for his troubles. It is the worst kind of coward, the worst, Davy, that would raise his hand against his own wife and child, and punish them for sins that are his own. Never forget that, my son."

"But you punished me last winter."

"Oh! And was it three other boys, and not yourself, Roddy and Gar Langlois, who set the fire in the alley that almost took down the McCrae's garage?

"It was an accident!"

"Right, boyo. But my hand five times on your backside was not, with your mother beside me to keep to the count, then give you the rough edge of her tongue and your own wee exile in your room for the weekend."

"Mama's talking made me feel worse than your spanking did."

"I'll not disagree with you there, Davy. The trouble was, back then, there were none to stay your Grandfather Connor's hand. It took a drunken brawl on the waterfront to end his life, maybe over money, maybe with the Orangemen and the Catholics. No arrest was made. Lu was only twelve when they buried your Grandfather Connor." David thought about this.

"They had no money." Wally nodded and looked grim.

"Not two dimes to rub together, Davy, and money still owing on the mortgage. Your grandmother had to take in boarders, mostly seamen, and live with your mother in a single room in her own house, Lu going to school in the day, and doing cooking and cleaning and laundry at night. She was fifteen when your Grandmother Connor was failing from the sickness that would kill her. She sold the house for the little money that was left, so she could send Lu here to Windsor Ontario with Siobhan. Grandmother Connor had hopes of a better chance at a good life for them both, away from the Halifax waterfront and that too often violent and criminal population."

"Was it the influenza like last year? Did they close Mama's school too? Make her wear masks?"

Siobhan and her oldest daughter had caught the Spanish influenza, but David's mother had nursed them through it at home, then volunteered at the African Church, which was set up as a temporary infirmary on the orders of the Board of Health, like David's King Edward Elementary School and the other schools and churches. The Contagious Disease Hospital and the big Hospital Hôtel Dieu of St. Joseph, on Ouellette Avenue, had been completely overwhelmed. David thought of the two students, the older Joseph Renaud, and little Mary Cade, from his junior school. When King Edward Elementary School reopened, they had not come back. The principal held a special assembly to remember them.

Now their photographs hung on the wall, apart from all the ribbons and the plaques and the trophies for victories in sports or academic achievement. They were draped with black ribbons, and below them were the words *In Memoriam*. The red fire axe was also on the wall nearby, and when David thought of one, he thought of the other—and of his mother's face the night before. David waited, and the silence from Wally was uncomfortable. "So, it wasn't the same?"

"No. Not the influenza."

"Then what?"

"It was the sailors," he said at last. You'll understand when you're older."

"Mama said I could ask her questions."

"Not that question, not now. You must promise me, Davy."

"But why?"

In answer, his father picked up the second photograph and held it up to him. "Who is this?"

David looked closely again. "I don't know. I've never seen her before."

"But you have." He placed it above the image of Grandfather Connor and his customs uniform. It took time, but his father was patient.

"They're the same?" David couldn't believe it. The woman in the second picture was old, shrunken, her hair almost all grey, and all the lines of her face turned down. Her grey dress was tired and shapeless, like her hair. David thought he could see a deep sickness in the dark wells of his Grandmother Connor's eyes.

"Eighteen she was when she married, and dead at thirty-five, with not half a life lived."

"Then where is she buried? We could visit her grave some day and bring flowers."

"That's the worst of it, Davy. Your mother doesn't know."

"But—"

"Grandmother Connor's final letter to Lu said only good bye, that she had used the last of her money to take ship's passage back to Ireland."

"Then somewhere in Ireland. We could go. We can find out."

"No, Davy, no. Weeks later your mother received a notice and a small packet from the ship's owners, confirming your Grandmother Connor had taken third-class passage, but never arrived in Ireland. They found only those few belongings—the letter, the picture, and her handkerchief of Irish lace in a cloth bag—and her … her Claddagh ring, tied with pink ribbon."

His father paused here, his expression pained, and then raised his eyes heavenward to the overcast skies. David was certain he was thinking of that very Claddagh ring, now on Lulu Pearl's finger, with its crowned heart she'd turned upward at Wallace Charles Phelan's sworn promise of faithfulness in marriage and the end of drink with his Temperance Oath of Sobriety in their future lives together as man and wife.

"What happened to Grandma Connor then?"

"A mystery, Davy. But the notice said 'Lost at sea and presumed dead.'" Wallace Phelan took another drink of water, and David realized he was thirsty himself. Once he started drinking, he drained the glass.

"Was there a bad storm?"

"No. There was no storm, Davy. Or if there was, it was the storm and pain inside herself, and for an end to it all."

"I don't understand."

"I know, boyo. We believe Grandmother Connor took her fate in her own hands, and that her death was of her own choosing."

"She … drowned herself?" It took David a moment to remember the word. "Suicide?"

"More a sacrifice, I would say. Even in illness and pain, your Grandmother Connor was a strong woman, Davy, as her daughter after her. Her name before marriage was Hannah Virtue. She sent her only daughter to a new life here in Windsor and took the heavy burden of their old one alone. Wally turned her picture over and read

David the words his grandmother had written in faded black ink on the back: "*There is hope from the sea, but none from the grave.*"

"What did she mean?" David's father became thoughtful.

"Maybe it's different for different people and different times. For those like many of our families who left Ireland in those hard famine years, their country was a grave, and across the sea lay the chance of a new life in a new land, the promise of better times for their children. We can none of us escape death, Davy, but some have the courage to seek it out, to go to it for a better good. Your Grandmother Connor was dying, her life and sickness a burden on her daughter. The sea was her grave, her chosen resting place, but her hope was your mother, Lulu Pearl Connor. God gave them 'strong shoes,' my son, strong shoes."

David looked at the pictures again and tried to make the two different women the same woman. And that woman, his own Grandmother Connor, planning her passage alone, *knowing* she would jump to her death from the high deck of the steaming ship and into the relief of the sea, and her body into its peaceful rest below. David had never seen the ocean, only pictures with his mother in books. It was huge. His Grandmother Connor's falling body was the tiniest of drops added to its immensity.

"She probably waited until it was dark, and everybody was asleep."

"Yes, that would have been ... surest," Wally allowed.

"I guess it's not easy to understand. For Mama too, maybe." His father moved the photographs aside and turned the Bible so they could both look again at the image of Lot and his wife, a Pillar of Salt behind.

"No, Davy. I think Lu knows it was an escape, for the two of them. Her into life, her mother into death. Like Lot and his wife. Seeing this last picture of her mother is like looking back. Who knows what might happen? What storms it could raise? I think it makes your mother afraid. For herself and for us. So she keeps it locked in her box. Through all their times of suffering, your Grandmother Connor took them both to church, and they took a measure of comfort there, when none was around them at home. Now Methodism is your mother's shield. And ours.

"Like the armour of St. Patrick, God all around her."

"How did you come to that?"

"It's what Mama said to Constable Carrick, and made him go away."

"Yes. That is my lasting burden and shame, Davy. The Orange, the drink, the brawls ... her sight of the woman in red beside me last night. Lu warned me against it. But I made her look back...."

David's Grandmother Connor, born Hannah Virtue, had chosen to sacrifice herself, alone and far out to sea, so her daughter, Lulu Pearl, David's strong, loving mother, could "hope," could find a "better good." It would take another thirteen years, but young David Charles Phelan would find his own better good, his own hope.

Her name was Norah McGee....

Part Two

Cobb's Love

Windsor, Ontario—1931

11 Shillelagh

Nineteen-year-old David Charles Phelan passed his father the last of the hand-carved decoys in their duck boat. Wallace Phelan looked back at their duck blind of brush and cattails on the north shore of Lake Erie, in the extensive marshes of the Point Pelee peninsula, and motioned for David to row them farther out. When Wally judged they had reached forty yards, the outer range where a duck or goose could be taken down by shotgun, he motioned again. David skilfully held the the open, flat-hulled mahogany boat they had built together steady in the early dawn breeze and rising mists. His father placed the mallards, a drake, and a jenny, and dropped the weighted anchor lines that kept each in place.

The entire naturally-detailed set, twenty-two blocks of Mallards, American Blacks and Canada Geese, was perfect. His father's art with carving tools and fine paintbrushes was unsurpassed, and made each decoy come alive in the light wind and rippling water this first Saturday in November. On one occasion two years before, three other hunters, arriving late and invading one of the Phelans' most productive duck hunting locations, had blasted a pair of Wallace Phelan's decoys to shell smoke and painted splinters, and exclaimed in confused disbelief at the result.

It was all David could do to prevent his father from storming their boat and taking them all on single-handed, in his outrage at this violation of two precious decoys and another duckman's exclusive precincts. Effusive apologies, all the cash the three could put together, and a disordered retreat, looking back in apprehension as Wally continued to threaten them, finally settled the matter somewhat. From that day on, David's father scrupulously sought out the more isolated locations around the Detroit River and the marshes and inlets of Lakes Erie and St. Clair. Phelan father and son hunted together, after the major leagues baseball season and World Series were ended, often enduring late fall and winter weather so miserable that other sportsmen retreated to the dryness and warmth of their living rooms. At first, David had wondered at Wally's ability to lay their set and build their blind in bare hands, but after eleven years, he was able to do the same without thinking.

Their shallow-draft duck boat, the *Lulu Pearl*, was a beautiful skiff, twelve feet long, squared at the bow and stern, with three keel strips and a slight rocker to prevent sideslip and help it make straight way with oars or their Evinrude outboard motor. Wally had waited until he found just the right African mahogany—clear, straight-grained, and perfectly seasoned so the planks ran clean and true. Father and son had built it together, working from Wally's precise drawings and dimensions, based on his long years of experience as a hunter and waterman. David did the finish carving, shaping, smoothing, and fitting of each stage of the port side, after watching his father's masterful work on the starboard. In the end, the two halves were mirror images and gave to both a rush of Phelan family pride. It drew them into knee-slapping laughter when Lulu Pearl Phelan adamantly refused to take a seat in her namesake and pose for a photo—but could not suppress her smile and pleasure as she stood before it and pointed at her name.

But David would never forget the look on his father's face when he presented him with the shiny, machined brass fittings David had turned on his metal lathe after his regular shifts at South Windsor Machine and Tool. It ended in shared laughter and manly hugs.

"Ah, you've the fine Phelan eye and touch, my son, and will never be without work to put food on your table."

It was at his father's urging that David became a machinist and metal-worker, exchanging the woodworker's lathe for a precision tool bench at which he'd excelled. After the demands of the Great War, fine metalwork was the future and woodworking becoming more and more the past, as automatic machines and mass production did the jobs of a hundred skilled carpenters in less time and more cost-efficiently. But someone would have to design and make these new machines where precision and close tolerances were crucial. David had graduated from high school, secured an apprenticeship at sixteen, and earned his journeyman's ticket just three years later, at nineteen.

David rowed them back to the duck blind and knelt to give their gun dog, Navin, his biscuit reward for sitting patiently in his place while they laid their set of duck blocks. "Good boy, Navin! Good boy. Down now." The six-year-old black Lab was approaching his prime as a pointer and retriever. He made no sound or movement in the blind, as he was trained, and settled on his canvas groundsheet to enjoy his treat. His father had relied on Garrett Bryant's hounds in the beginning, but decided that the Labrador retriever, with its water-resistant coat, soft mouth, biddable nature and quick intelligence, made it the best foul-weather and water dog. The breed was English, brought to Newfoundland, not Labrador, by fishermen at the beginning of the 19th century, so water was its element. Wally allowed Garrett's hounds were good in the field for rabbit, pheasant, and similar prey, but his father's love was the waterfowl, and now David's too.

"Andrew Williams!" his father stood and announced, handing David one of the cups of steaming, sweet black coffee, enhanced with a dollop of whisky, that he'd poured from the thermos. David stood beside him and faced the decoys and waited for Wally to begin their ritual incantation and toast. Soon even Navin had come to sit up beside his masters for the ceremony. In the beginning, when his father had first taken him duck hunting with Garrett Bryant, the two of them would alternately recite the lines. But Garrett had taken Siobhan and their family to British Columbia seven years before, to work in the sawmills of Port Alberni. His family of five girls was large, and the better pay and temperate climate, barely touched by deep winter's cold, combined to persuade him. His father missed Garrett, but David missed Siobhan and his older cousin Mare the most. Now David had inherited Garrett's part.

Wally raised his cup high and his fine Irish tenor carried strongly above their extensive set and out across the restless waters of the sheltered bay, with David's the same, in an alternating lines, harmonious recitation:

Andrew Williams

"Here lies the Decoyman who lived like an otter,
  Dividing his time betwixt land and water;
His Hide he oft soaked in the waters of Perry
  Wilst Aston old beer his kept cheery.
Amphibious his life, Death was puzzled to say
  How to dust to reduce such well-moistened clay.
So Death turned Decoyman, and 'coyed him to land,
  Where he fixed his abode till quite dried to the hand.
He then found him fitting for crumbling to dust;
  And here he lies mouldering as you and I must."

Together father and son raised their cups and saluted the old Decoyman of legend, the breaking dawn and the profound magic of a day spent hunting elusive, fast-winging fowl on pristine waters. Each drank his cup down, but for a last swallow, which he poured onto the rippling waters to give Andrew Williams his due. The poem was from Wally's favourite book on the early history of the Decoy in Europe—not a carved wooden lure, but a special trap-pond into which ducks were driven during the moult, when they could not fly, to be netted and killed by the thousand, and not a shot fired. His father had handed down Sir Ralph Payne Galloway's 1886 volume,

The Book of Duck Decoys, to his only son, and David had a new respect for the small class of secretive, solitary Decoymen like Andrew Williams. Williams had faithfully managed the private trap-pond on the lands of the Lloyds of Aston, in England, until his death in 1776.

Whether kept or sold, the large harvest of wildfowl had been an important source of food, income, employment, and prestige in the lean times of fall and winter for hundreds of years, until declining duck populations finally demanded lawful control and regulation. Although poaching and abuse continued, then as now, David knew.

Lately, the poem's final lines seemed to take his father more inside himself, deeper, and David had come to arrange their ritual so the last line was his own, not Wally's.

Father and son sat in quiet contentment in the blind, together now in body and spirit, under heavy canvas coats and wool caps, on two camp stools. The hand-carved, polished wooden duck calls hung from their necks on rawhide cords, and their cherished shotguns rested lovingly under waxed cotton sheets, easy to hand at their sides. Navin sat like a sleek stone idol on Wally's left. The Lab stared toward low treelines on either side of the small bay and then at the grey horizon in front of them, his ears forward, scanning and alert to any sights or sounds of approaching birds.

After ten minutes of wordless communion with the slowly waking world around them, David sensed the slight tensing of his father's shoulders and anticipated the question David knew Wally had been waiting to ask.

"Who is this Norah, then?"

"Norah McGee. She's finishing her nursing training at the Salvation Army Grace Hospital, where Roddy's oldest sister, Deirdre, works."

"But Protestant?" David hung his head and sighed. Would the old Troubles never end for the Irish in the new lands of Canada?

"Very. Ulster on both sides of her family."

"How recent?"

"Great grandparents. And like me, no noticeable accent." Now Wally sighed. David knew his father regretted this loss of Irish lilt in his son and other third-generation Irish Canadians. "Unless she's ... upset and challenging you."

"How is that, boyo?" his father inquired further.

David pointed to the inside of his right thigh. "Norah did most of the repair work."

Two-and-a-half months before, a piece of flawed steel had begun to break up on his high-speed lathe. David had instinctively turned away, but a sharp sliver of the metal found its way under the edge of his leather apron, penetrated the heavy denim of his coveralls, and sliced his thigh. The wound was long and not that deep, but giving forth plenty of blood.

"Well, here's the little bugger!"

David had stared stolidly at the grey name tag above the pocket of the Grace Emergency doctor's white coat during the painful probing and removal: WICKHAM. The thin-haired young resident held up the black steel sliver in the tip of his forceps. It looked too small to have done the damage. "Souvenir? Tie pin, perhaps?" David gritted his teeth and shook his head, drawing a laugh from the doctor. "Missed the artery, so not quite as much fun. I'll clean the wound and disinfect it." The burning sensation brought tears to David's eyes. Wickham pulled down his white surgical mask revealing narrow facial features and a thin line of blonde moustache above his equally thin mouth. "Now I think we can trust Nurse here to stitch you up, and back in two weeks for suture removal. Just keep the wound clean and change the dressing regularly, or next time we can take the whole leg. Jolly fun! Ta-ta." Wickham showed his small pointed teeth in a smile and left.

But the smile was for Nurse, not David.

"If you'll just lie back and spread your legs, Mr. Phelan?" In his pain and his annoyance with Dr. Wickham, David had paid no attention to Nurse. He was abruptly embarrassed at his bloody undershorts on the table beside him as he lay on the gurney and only a white sterile cloth covering his private parts. His undershirt probably smelled of milling oil and sweat.

"Uh..."

"I've always wanted to say that to a man." Nurse put down a narrow, stainless steel tray between David's legs and pulled on thin rubber gloves before picking up the curved silver needle and surgical thread. "Now don't worry, sir. I'll do all the work. And I promise it will only hurt for a moment. That's a lie, of course, but just keep still, look away and think of England."

"Uh, it would be Ireland for me."

"Well then, sir, if you have your shillelagh handy, you might want to take it between your teeth and bite down hard." Despite the impending pain, David still noticed the attractive pattern of fine black hairs at the nape of Nurse's neck, where she'd pulled the thick waves up under her starched white nurse's cap and held them with a tortoiseshell comb. "Just a little prick."

"Ow-w-w-w!"

"And another. Another. Another. And another.... Now one more for the luck of the Irish—and a beautiful love-knot to finish it off." David concentrated on the bright light overhead in its round polished steel reflector.

"Ah, Jesus!"

"No. Just a worshipful nurse. Our blessed Saviour has gone on to redeem other wayward souls with his wit and wisdom, and we poor sinners are left to struggle on alone." Another dose of disinfectant followed, with more grimaces in silence. Nurse finally laid a gauze pad over David's stitches and taped it in place. The sharp pain receded to a dull steady ache.

"Nurse...?" Now the eyes of the two engaged fully above her surgical mask. Hers were a bright obsidian, widely spaced, and seriously considered the man prostrate before her for a long enough time to make David Phelan squirm with unaccustomed discomfort. Then she pulled down the mask, revealing her beautiful dark features in a perfect symmetry with her hair and eyes, her shapely mouth quirked with slight amusement. It took a few seconds of careful scrutiny of David before Nurse announced her decision.

"Norah McGee."

"Ah ... any relation to Thomas D'Arcy?

"And he would be...?

"Thomas D'Arcy McGee, one of the Canadian Fathers of Confederation that established Canada as a Dominion. He was Irish."

"Ah yes, now I do seem to recall. But say, didn't they shoot the poor bugger for his trouble?"

"Uh, I believe so. Right at his own front door. A member of the Fenian Brotherhood probably."

"Then if I *am* Irish, Mr. Phelan, I'd best not admit it." Nurse bent her head and added a few further lines of information to David's medical record on her clipboard.

"I'm David Phelan."

"That I know, sir. I have your admittance record." Then, unexpectedly, Nurse McGee dropped her gaze to her patient's chest and paused in concentration. "Is that not a Claddagh?" David touched his mother Lulu Pearl Phelan's Claddagh ring on its silver chain around his neck.

"It is, Nurse McGee. My mother's."

Then Nurse McGee's eyes dropped lower and she smiled mischievously, looking back up into David's face, now shading brick red at the embarrassing realization of the source of her amusement. David felt the white sterile cloth rising with the beginnings of his erection.

"Well, Mr. Phelan. I think you'd better do something about that, so I'll leave you to get on with it in private. But please, sir, try not to stain the bedclothes." Then Nurse McGee was gone with her tray, trailing quiet laughter behind her. David didn't know if Nurse McGee meant the Claddagh ring or his erection, but guessed it was the latter. "I am an idiot." He slid carefully off the gurney and eased on his shorts, socks, coveralls and work boots, trying to suppress his groans at the sharp twinges of pain.

And at his embarrassment in front of Nurse Norah McGee.

Two weeks later, David Charles Phelan was back at Grace Emergency. He'd gotten what information he could—well prepared, he thought, but nervous too. He could not have known that Roddy's sister, Deirdre, had fully exploited the opportunity for her own entertainment.

12 Triple Mother Goddess

David had tried twice to speak casually to his friend Roddy's sister, Deirdre, about Nurse Norah McGee. But Deirdre only laughed, shook her head at his inquiry and teased him mercilessly. *In extremis*, the frustrated young machinist was finally forced to plead with her specifically and directly about Nurse McGee's status and her working schedule at Salvation Army Grace Emergency that second week he was due to have his sutures removed. Deirdre looked at his blushing face, laughed, shook her head again and thoroughly enjoyed his embarrassment.

"Her status, is it?" Deidre tossed her red curls in amused wonder again, and it only went on longer as she took in David's deep, self-conscious unease. "Oh, it's *Miss* McGee, all right, if that's your interest? But boyo, if you have any great ideas, you'll be standing in line behind the Prince of English Lack-Wits, and any leftover orderlies whose manhood Nurse McGee has not surgically removed without the blessing of anaesthetic."

"Nurse McGee did seem a ... a bit bold?"

"Bold, is it? That, and more than a bit about it, me old son!" Deirdre smirked in anticipation at the entertainment to come. "Well, David, I *can* tell you that she was the first novice nurse to absolutely refuse to perform her deep curtsy before his majesty, 'Peter the Great.'"

Deirdre waited, laughter still sparkling in her green eyes, thoroughly enjoying his confusion.

"Uh ... Peter the Great? The Russian tsar from our history study in school? St. Petersburg named after him and all that?"

"No, boyo, Peter the Great, the 'great' pickled penis from our Grace Emergency surgical specimens lab in the basement." More unease, more sparkling and more laughter. "Floats majestically in his pickle jar, His Royal Majesty does, standing proudly between the four diseased kidneys and a sad ectopic pregnancy. We nurses hold the obeisance as part of our Grace Emergency initiation ceremony to welcome and recognize the new nurse trainees." David felt sick to his stomach, but couldn't help envisioning pickled Peter. "No one remembers how the Great Peter died or when his penis met its abrupt end, but we all agree they kept the best bit." David could only roll his eyes in his unease and look away at her amusement.

"Deirdre ... Deirdre ... please." Then Roddy's sister shook her red curls in amused pleasure again, but must have taken pity on him.

"In certain truth, David, I think our good Dr. Wickham, our Prince of English Lack-Wits, has lost his place with Nurse McGee—if he ever had one.

"How can you be so sure?"

"I had the whole story from an orderly who was there to witness it."

"One with his manhood still intact?"

"Alas, no, boyo. Maybe a wee stump. But that was my own fine surgery."

"So?"

"So, at the end of August, the young lady in question was one of two surgical nurses assisting Wickham with an extreme amputation. It was the entire right leg of a young French-Canadian lad. He'd cut his right foot deeply on something metallic and sharp while playing soccer with his friends in one of the poorer Sandwich East neighbourhoods by the Detroit River. Barefoot the lads all were, of course, and his parents living deathly poor and not bringing him in until the sepsis, the blood poisoning, had become critical. Wickham took off the leg, and with a wicked smile on his thin-stretched lips, the cruel bastard turned right around and handed it to Nurse McGee instead of the waiting male orderly beside him. One of his 'harmless' little jokes to amuse the attending staff looking on. Said Nurse McGee should 'kindly dispose of it.' That the unconscious boy 'would be unlikely to need it since he didn't know of any one-legged soccer teams.'"

David tried desperately not to imagine the scene unfolding in the Grace Emergency operating theatre, but could not. The insistent image of the anaesthetized boy's newly severed leg, welling its blood supply in Nurse McGee's arms, made him go nauseous and faint to the point vomiting. It was due to occupy a place in his nightmares for the rest of his life. He wanted to step back from the harrowing vision, but could not.

"Exactly, boyo." Deirdre's expression drained of all humorous emotion. She pulled herself upright with a wilful effort and continued. "But our Miss Norah McGee did not flinch, did not step back, did not move, according to the tellers of the tale who witnessed it play out. Stood holding the poor lad's bleeding right leg in her arms, she did, and stared only and ever at Wickham. Stared and stared, they said, until the sadistic wee bastard was forced to take his full notice of her.

"The male orderly that should have taken the leg said the look from Nurse McGee's black Irish eyes was so scathing, so loathing, so damning, it caused the cursed little prick to step back like he'd been struck, his face matching the colour of the boy's own blood. And Wickham dropped the hemostat he was holding to the floor with the whole operating theatre hearing it. The second nurse said you could practically hear what manhood Wickham might have had slowly drying up and shrivelling to a crisp pizzle between the bastard's legs. And I'm guessin' it was not much to begin with." All humour, all pleasure Deirdre had taken in David Phelan's hesitant inquiries about Nurse McGee were gone in their shared disgust with Wickham and deep sympathy for the boy. She reached out and put a reassuring hand on his shoulder until he finally met her eyes, and nodded.

"But listen now, me bucko. When that poor lad was dying from the blood-poisoning and shock a few days later, our Miss McGee came to him directly after her shift. She sat with his poor sorrowful parents at his bedside until he slipped away at last into the peace of God's promise and grace, and his ordeal ended. I don't know how long, but it was hours. His parents returned the next day, along with their neighbours who knew him, and couldn't thank Nurse McGee enough for supporting them through their ordeal and grief. The whole lot of them ended weeping."

Now David's thoughts carried all the way back to Mulvaney's Tavern, years before. The look he had seen his mother, Lulu Pearl Phelan, give the red-faced Windsor Police Constable Carrick, married but with a young whore beside him, on that unforgettable night of his father's lasting fall from grace. Of the hours that night a stoic Lulu Pearl had sat with his father on their back stoop, his Purgatory, to wake Wallace Phelan again and again following Lulu's blow to his head with Ty Cobb's carved chestnut-oak bat, in case of concussion and blackout. And all this after the shameful, painful ordeal Wally had put Lulu Pearl through earlier that very evening at Mulvaney's, with his own woman in red standing at the bar beside him and wearing his Detroit Tigers baseball cap.

Now, in Grace Emergency, David Charles Phelan resolutely promised himself he would never do anything to incur such a damning look from Miss McGee as she had given Wickham that sad day—and would do everything in his power to invite from her such care and affection as his mother had bestowed on him, David Phelan, her loving son, while she lived.

Wallace Charles Phelan was not a bad man, not really. But he had made his faithful wife "look back," after swearing an oath to never commit such a shameful betrayal of his marriage vows and his Temperance Oath of Sobriety. David was his father's son, and his mother's. He was blessed in both. He hoped deeply his own human faults were less than his father's that evening at Mulvaney's. And that Miss Norah McGee would recognize that solemn commitment in him—if she ever gave him the chance to demonstrate it.

"Good luck, boyo," Deirdre had said, after hugging him, giving him Nurse McGee's shift schedule for the coming weeks, then retreating into her own house with just a shade of wry humour hanging in the air behind her.

Now the young woman in question briskly parted the Grace Hospital Emergency Ward's curtains screening David Charles Phelan from the nearby patients and consulted her clipboard. "And you would be—?"

"Isn't it on the admittance record?"

"—Mr. Phelan."

"Miss McGee." If she was surprised at the use of her name, nothing showed on her face.

"It's Nurse McGee, if you please, sir? We try to be thoroughly professional here in keeping with hospital standards of practice. Now, if you will just—"

"Lie back. Spread my legs. You'll do all the work. It will only hurt for a moment. But of course, that's a lie." Maybe just the start of a smile, but immediately suppressed.

"Wise words, if I ever heard them, Mr. Phelan."

"And were they not your very own, Nurse McGee?"

Nurse gave David a pointed flash of her black eyes and put on surgical gloves, neatly removed the gauze bandage concealing his wound and sutures, swabbed the area with the same stinging disinfectant as before, and turned for her scissors and small silver forceps. "So, sir, just a wee snip and a pull this time. And pray God the scissors don't slip too far."

When Nurse McGee turned back, instruments poised and ready, the stunned expression on her lovely Irish features was worth all of David's effort.

Grace Emergency Nurse Norah McGee froze in mid-operation, with her inviting pink lips shaped into an O of surprise, as David removed the dark wood shillelagh, bitten crosswise, from between the teeth of his own grinning mouth. He had turned the shillelagh lovingly on his father Wally's fine woodworking lathe over the course of three days. David then carved the intricate Celtic cross near the top:

And below it, was the Tree of Life, with its curled branches in the Upper World turning back on themselves to entwine with the curlicued roots in the Lower World, to form the Celtic Circle of Life:

David had next added circling torcs and wide, sacred cauldrons in between them, finishing the mythic image with a flourish in the long, elegant outlines of a Celtic horse, as if racing its way to the smooth-knobbed top of the shaft.

The whole of the shillelagh was a perfect two feet in length. He'd sealed the traditional Celtic designs with soft wax, and stained the oak to near black. When he carefully warmed and teased away the wax, the lovely designs were revealed and just visible in a denser and darker black enamel, and textural to the touch.

Wally, the expert carver, had advised David on small matters of technique and raised a bushy eyebrow, but his father sensed the private nature of this artistic endeavour and never questioned David's frantic work those nights in their workshop below. Deirdre was sworn to lips-sealed secrecy at the cost of more amusement at his plight and plan.

Though stiffly nervous, David tried to keep the tone and expression of his voice light.

"I took that wise medical advice to heart, Nurse McGee, and remembered to bring along my shillelagh this time."

Now Nurse was slowly shaking her white-capped head in amused and growing denial of the sight before her.

"I will bite down hard you may be certain sure. But please, I humbly beg of you, be gentle. And maybe afterwards, if I survive this lifesaving surgery, we might share a cigarette?" David showed Nurse McGee the bright white package of children's chocolate cigarettes he had bought at the old N. M. Meisner's Confectionery—and heard Miss McGee's open laughter for the first time, and warm and genuine it was.

"Oh, but maybe afterwards, you won't want to, Mr. Phelan."

Nurse McGee did up her mask, bent to her scissors and forceps, snipping, and teasing each suture out. David felt almost no pain, but groaned dramatically around the wood in his mouth. Nurse pulled the last stitch with calculated intent, and his mock groan turned sharply real. More disinfectant, more pain, and a fresh dressing, but no further groans. "I think that will suffice."

Nurse McGee pulled down her mask, then winked and took the package of chocolate cigarettes and neatly snipped it open to extract one of the tissue-wrapped tubes, with "N. M. Meisner's" in fancy script along its white length. "Don't mind if I do."

"My pleasure," David managed.

"Yes, it sounded like it, sir." Norah McGee stood at the white emergency room curtains and looked back at him. "Maybe you should put on your pants before you trip over that."

"My shillelagh?"

"If that's what you call it." Nurse McGee laughed and nodded at his lap. David was amazed to find himself half-erect, in the midst of pain and embarrassment. Again!

"Uh, Nurse ... Miss McGee?"

"Everything seems well to hand, so I'll bid you good day, Mr. Phelan."

The curtain closed behind her, and David felt a right fool. Still, he decided to leave the shillelagh and the package of chocolate cigarettes on the instrument table with a note on his admittance record:

Miss McGee.

I would be pleased if you took my shillelagh into your capable hands and enjoyed the cigarettes. I intended them both for yourself alone.

Sincerely, David Phelan.

13 Where All Ladders Start

Three weeks had passed before Deirdre telephoned him before supper on the Friday evening. "Get yourself down to the Dominion House Saloon by one o'clock on Saturday, boyo, and mind your cheek."

"The saloon on Sandwich Street? Near the Ambassador Bridge?"

"The very one."

"But Wally and I are going to a big Tigers game in Detroit, against the New York Yankees, tomorrow afternoon. Is this about...?"

"Then you'll have to make a wee choice, won't you, bucko?"

"And what if I do arrive?"

"Find where they keep the lost and found, and stand to attention there."

"Is this about...?" But Deirdre laughed her annoying laugh and hung up. David thought about it over supper and decided to phone back and ask Roddy. His friend knew nothing but, curious too, offered to accompany him. David was tempted, yet declined Roddy's offer. And Wally was surprised and very disappointed, but David left his reasons vague for backing out of a Yankees game, exciting still more curiosity. Then, of course, he could have asked his father to drop him off by the Ambassador Bridge, before Wally drove across to Detroit and the Tigers' Navin Field—but again, he would have had to explain.

Instead, David walked the five blocks north to Wyandotte Street and caught the electric street railway's crosstown trolley all the way west, through the heart of Windsor's downtown district and on to Sandwich with the Ambassador Bridge overhead, before getting off and walking the short distance north to the Dominion House. Because of the busy Saturday, the only seat on the trolley car had been in the stuffy smoking cabin. Now David's freshly laundered clothes carried the stale smell of tobacco and his own sweat under his white cotton shirt and tie.

The Dominion riverside saloon was always noisy and crowded on weekends, being so handy to the bridge and popular with people going both ways between the two busy cities of Windsor and Detroit, not to mention regulars from the neighbourhood. Just before one o'clock, David readied himself and walked as boldly as he could manage through the Dominion's main entrance, was immediately engulfed in more smoke from assorted cigarettes, cigars, and pipes, but fought his way to the bar and ordered a mug of beer. The jostling on the way sent new stabs of pain radiating from the newly healed thigh wound, and the room was so crowded, he was finally forced to stand on a small patch of oiled wood floor in one corner. A vivid splash of red hair and Wallace Phelan's white face at Mulvaney's, that fateful evening past, drifted up from somewhere in memory. David took a long swallow of dark beer and let its bitter bite wash down the association.

Instead, he concentrated on craning his neck and scanning the crowd, coming and going and milling about, but saw no recognizable face—until at one twenty p.m. he had an anxious feeling and then an odd inspiration. David struggled back to the end of the bar and managed to catch the eye of one of the barmen over the din and crush of thirsty patrons.

"Another beer?"

"Yes, and would you be having some kind of lost and found I could look at?" The man pulled his foaming mug of beer then reached under the bar and shoved a beat-up wooden box along the floor to the end, where David stooped and ignored the various hats, work gloves, ties, old pocket knives, stained handkerchiefs, and reached down in surprised wonder.

"You prove that's yours? Had my eye on it if it wasn't claimed." David was holding his two-foot shillelagh in front of the bartender's suspicious eyes, sparked with anticipation and envy.

"Yes. I made it myself, for someone special. An Irish shillelagh. Carved the Celtic cross, the torcs, the sacred cauldrons, the Celtic horse, the Tree of Life. Stained the oak near-black over lost wax to get the slight contrast in darker black for the images."

"Don't know nothin' 'bout that. Girl found it a while ago. A beauty she was. Guess it's yours, then."

"Where is she? The girl?"

The bartender was back at the taps and almost sneered at his ignorance. "Where do you think, lad?"

A second inspiration, some embarrassment, and David was out the heavy front doors as fast as the crowded room allowed, leaving his full mug of dark beer on the bar, and then making his way around to the wide-open door on the east side of the Dominion saloon: LADIES AND ESCORTS.

"Paddy's blind pig sees better than I do!" This side of the Dominion House Saloon, with its smaller round oak tables and chairs, was only marginally less confused than the men's area. One of the servers behind the bar was a stout woman with hennaed hair and the biggest arms David had ever seen on a woman. As soon as he walked in, solitary and alone, she had a wary eye on him. But he threaded his careful way among the tables and seated patrons to the polished wood bar in less time and with less pain to his thigh.

The big woman was not welcoming.

"Here, what are you planning to do with that great club?"

"Uh, it's a shillelagh. Irish..."

"And I'm the Virgin Mary! It's a club."

"Please, I'm looking for a woman."

"Well, I'd oblige you, dearie—if I didn't think you'd bash my brains in with it. I'm no lady, and you're no escort. Out with you before I call my bruiser."

"Mr. Phelan! Sir!" The clear steady voice pierced the low buzz of noise and activity, and David and the big woman looked to a table right across the wide room, under a huge portrait of equally huge assorted dogs—seated, smoking, drinking and gambling—around a long table filled with cards and beer. It was a copy of C. M. Coolidge's *Dogs Playing Poker*.

"Uh, that's who I'm looking for, ma'am. I'm returning the club ... the shillelagh to her."

"And she could well use it, lad, the way the local bird-dogs keep barking at her and offering to buy her a drink and more. She keeps telling 'em all to stick it where the sun don't shine. You'd do well to hold on to that fancy club for your own protection, lad. That one's trouble and no mistake."

"Yes, I know, ma'am. I've already taken some sharp words, sharp needles, and punishment. Two beers, if you please, and one for your kind self." The stout woman laughed, shook her henna orange head, and turned to pull the beers. David paid, put the shillelagh under his left armpit, and lifted the two foaming mugs.

"Then loosen your belt buckle and get ready to bend over again, dearie. Can't say I didn't warn you." A minute later, when David carefully approached Miss McGee's table, a very big man, with black beard and shaggy hair, was leaning over it with a hand on a chair opposite.

"...sorry, sir, but my husband would surely not approve of you seating yourself," Miss McGee said, all modesty and mock innocence.

The man turned abruptly, and David immediately saw the violent potential in his narrowed black eyes. He deliberately put down the mugs of dark beer in front of Miss McGee and stood stolidly upright with the shillelagh in his right hand and slapping into the palm of his left. Immediately, the big red-haired woman came from behind the bar, and David saw she had a club of her own—a heavy old baseball bat. A sudden reminder of Ty Cobb's hand-carved chestnut-oak bat, now back in its new case, and hanging on the wall of their Phelan family dining room, after Mulvaney's. And of his beloved mother Lulu Pearl Phelan's tragic death, some months later from the Spanish flu. It had ever after become Lulu's bat, a loving memento and symbol of his mother's strict but kind and progressive values.

David had felt so helpless then. But he was not helpless now.

He suspected the Dominion House "bruiser" was her hennaed-haired self, and probably the owner of the Dominion House Saloon as well, and that the dark stains covering the end of her bat *weren't* pine tar. Now David felt the adrenalin and testosterone swell his own muscles and harden his will, as he continued his steady stare into the thuggish patron's black eyes.

"My wife's right, bucko. I don't approve and never would." The big man was wary of the polished wood shillelagh, but also David Charles Phelan's wide shoulders and narrow waist, the work-hardened machinist's hands, and his quiet readiness to answer whatever might follow with his own violence.

"Your loss, sweetheart," the man sneered and made his heavy way back to the men's side of the Dominion House through a crowded doorway David hadn't noticed. The expectant male audience, watching from the doorway, was disappointed.

"Are you trying to get me killed?"

David couldn't help the exasperation in his voice at the potential violence Miss McGee's words might have triggered.

"But I'm a nurse, remember, Mr. Phelan?" Miss McGee smiled with an amused twinkle in her black Irish eyes.

"But aren't you supposed to be saving lives, not risking them—especially other people's?"

Miss McGee must have seen his upset, and nodded slightly.

"You're right. I apologize, Mr. Phelan. Sincerely. That was stupid and very unfair. Sometimes I feel like nothing but a raw meat bone men gnaw on and worry. At the hospital, here.... But please, won't you seat yourself and have a drink?" David now felt the eyes of the whole Dominion House Saloon and its owner on them. He sighed, turned, smiled, showed the owner the shillelagh once again, and presented it to Nurse Norah McGee with some ceremony in both hands and with a slight bow.

The big henna-haired proprietor shook orange curls and turned toward the bar with her own club. "Didn't I warn you, lad? That one's trouble and no mistake," she tossed over her left shoulder.

"I heartily agree, and yes, ma'am, you did warn me." David bowed to her retreating back, as well.

"Did you really?"

"Really what, Miss McGee?"

"It's Norah, please. Object to that man buying me a drink?"

"And if I did? Really?"

"I'd be glad, Mr. Phelan."

David nodded and took a sip of his beer, but said nothing. Norah shook her head, sighed, and held up her own mug of beer. "Pax, Mr. Phelan?" Norah smiled that bewitching Irish smile David couldn't resist, and his own Irish smile finally broke free, despite his intention to remain stern over the incident.

He shook his head in exasperation. "Well, you do have a lovely smile ... Norah." He let the tension and upset seep slowly out of him and touched his mug to hers. "Pax. Call me David."

"I like the name. It makes me think of that beautiful statue in Florence—the big nude one. Michelangelo, I believe." David blushed, and Norah laughed. "I truly am sorry, David. About the husband remark, not the nude statue."

"Apology accepted. You know you do remind me of her." David picked up the shillelagh and pointed to the carved heads of three Celtic women that circled the top."

"Don't you mean *them*?"

"No. It's one woman. But she has three heads."

"Are you saying I'm a freak, Mr. Phelan?"

"Maybe the opposite. This is the 'Triple Mother-Goddess' of the Celts. Abundance, Fertility, Nurture. She's found in sacred places, like the Suleviae, the water goddesses, at the springs near Bath or Aqua Sulis."

"O-o-o-h! I do like springs. My parents have a cottage on Buckhorn Lake, near Peterborough, where I swim like a fish—or maybe a water goddess. I'm flattered, sir. And with three heads, all the better to resist having them turned." David smiled slyly.

"Ah, Norah! But it's not all baths and babies. For the Irish, their Goddess of Fertility was the same as the Goddess of War."

"I know a wee bit of Irish legend, myself, sir. Now you're saying I'm Medb? The one who slept in turn with each of the nine Kings of Tara?" David covered the wound of her counter-thrust with a deliberate sip of his beer. The bar mistress caught his eye and smiled her triumph. But David went back to the fray.

"Well, my father did say none of them could be crowned unless they touched the Stone of Fal there, and it cried out for him as the rightful king—and coupled with the goddess Medb."

"Coupling, sir? A quaint word for it. I'm not surprised you had it from your father then. It's the kind of myth of entitlement Irish men are fond of handing down to their sons in matters of the intimate sort. I judge it to be about as effective as whistling in the dark, a comforting illusion, until real intimacy rears up before them and they befoul themselves."

David didn't blush this time, but looked straight into Norah McGee's Irish black eyes."

"I feel no need to whistle and no intention to embarrass myself—in that specific fashion. If this is the Valley of the Shadow of Intimacy, I'll follow humbly wherever you lead, Miss Norah McGee."

"Well, now, Mr. Phelan, I do admire a bucko who's up to that challenge."

Whatever the look Nurse Norah McGee had given Wickham that day in the operating room, David judged this must be its opposite. She returned David's stare and deliberately reached behind her head to remove her tortoiseshell comb and shook out her deep fall of raven hair. All trace of the nurse-in-training, any clinical restraint and formality, were banished by that simple action. The full effect of the warm, engaging, mischievous, utterly desirable young woman underneath breached any vestige of foolish male pride and posturing, any sense of entitlement.

"Thank you for that, Norah."

The phrase seemed too common. But the loosing of her hair was a gift from the Triple Mother Goddess, freely given in this unlikely setting. David raised his mug of dark beer in honour and gratitude of this rare gesture for him alone.

"You're welcome, David."

Now Miss Norah McGee stood up and put the tortoiseshell comb in her purse. "Maybe we should leave this stuffy alehouse? And your shillelagh was a beautiful gesture. Thank you." She saluted him with it and slipped it into the belt of her shirtwaist dress like a sword. The effect should have been comical, but was the opposite. "So, thank you, too."

David stood, smiled his pleasure, and bowed his head slightly in response. "Then I would enjoy it very much, Miss McGee, if you would join me in a stroll along the riverfront?"

"Ah, sir. And might we be discussing these quainter aspects of Irish history and myth at more length?"

Now David *did* redden and look away.

"Don't you find it interesting, Mr. Phelan, how the past is always intruding on the present with the Irish?" The accuracy of Norah McGee's observation, its relevance to David's own life, stunned him.

When he finally replied, it was with his own considered opinion on that very issue.

"The past is a ladder on which we stand and must climb in the hope of a better life to come." The atmosphere between them was abruptly serious, and each consulted the face and eyes of the other, neither one dissembling now, nor looking away. Norah finally spoke:

> *"Now that my ladder's gone,*
> *I must lie down where all the ladders start,*
> *In the foul rag and bone shop of the heart."*

"A very Irish sentiment," David agreed. "Yeats?" Norah nodded, also impressed.

"'The Circus Animals' Desertion.' You've had some education, Mr. Phelan."

"My mother. And you, as well, Miss McGee."

"What? You think I spend all my time in examination rooms making and removing stitches from interesting places?"

"No, Norah. But I judge when you're there, it's done right. And what I think, is that *people* are the best ladders—if you are fortunate enough to find one."

"Also, a very Irish thought. I think I agree."

As they headed out the saloon door, and Miss Norah McGee took his proffered arm, David Charles Phelan knew the past *did* intrude, though not always for the better. For the Irish, getting too caught up in the past was as easy as falling off a ladder ... and as dangerous.

Wallace Charles Phelan, looking over the quiet waters of the the Lake Erie marsh touched with late morning mist, and their set of duck decoys floating placidly without a hint of breeze, considered the matter of Norah McGee for long minutes while David waited. He finally turned to look his son in the eye. Navin stood up from his lunch bone attentively, as if he knew a serious matter was being decided.

"Would your mother Lulu Pearl have liked her?" David knew the question was inevitable, just as his father insisting on hearing Norah's story and Irish pedigree.

They'd had a fair morning, calling in a flight of Canadas and three pairs of mallards. Each of them had taken a goose, and Wally had two drakes to David's one. Both Phelans were careful with their shooting, taking them cleanly and avoiding the shots that might leave cripples to die a slow death in the cold Erie waters. After his wife's death, Wally took males as much as possible, and after a few years, David did too. Sometimes Navin would point and sound his low warning growl, then stare at them in bewilderment as they signalled him quiet and let females sail by.

So, the reason had to do with his mother, Lulu Pearl, yet his father had never fully explained it. Somehow, his loving mother had become associated with the female ducks, the 'jennies,' and their care and nurturing of the precious chicks.

In the previous thirty minutes, Wally had listened to David's account of Norah McGee with brief smiles but not much comment. Now, after lunch, his father had asked the question David had been expecting, and he marshalled his answer.

"Like Norah? Yes, I believe mother would like her a great deal. She's a suffragist and a great admirer of Dr. Emily Stowe in her fight to become Canada's first female physician, and to win the vote for women. Right now, Norah's angry that women in Quebec have the federal vote, but not the provincial."

"Not an abstainer?"

"No. But why should she be? I drink in moderation." Wally was silent on that subject, as usual. "Norah wants to meet you." His father stared into the remains of his coffee, then threw the dregs down on the marshy ground and startled Navin. The dog raised his head and looked at them both. At a nod from Wally, he quickly went back to his bone.

"She knows?" Wally said.

"Yes. After a while I couldn't really keep from telling her. And once I was certain of my feelings for her, I didn't want to."

"All of it?" Wally was looking out across the flat Erie Bay. The wind had fallen in the late morning, and the water under the decoys was the colour of sheet steel. David knew he meant Ty Cobb's chestnut-oak bat, and Wally's shaming of his proud wife Lulu Pearl, in front of the whole crowd of Orangemen at Mulvaney's. The breaking of Wally's Temperance Oath of Sobriety had triggered the just punishment his mother had so violently meted out to him, with Wally's own carven White Angel on the bar at Lulu Pearl's side in solemn witness.

It was now Lulu's bat. And always would be.

"Yes, all of it," David confessed.

"You're serious about her."

"Yes." Wally still didn't look at him.

"Well, David, we all knew this day would come. It's right, and the natural way of things. If you feel this strongly about her...."

"I offered her the Claddagh." Now Wally did look at him. No matter what his father said about rightness and naturalness, it was this offering his mother and grandmother's heavily symbolic Claddagh ring that made it real to David. And now to his father.

"So soon?"

"I'm sure." Wallace Charles Phelan nodded at last, and looked to some point above the horizon. David was aware of their lives separating, branching. It was almost physical.

"That can be the way of it sometimes." Wally examined his empty cup, holding it with both hands. "So that's it then. My best to you both, Davy." When his father called him by his boyhood name, David knew the past was still with him—with them both, really. How could it not be?

"Thank you. But Norah won't accept the Claddagh without your consent." David put his hand on his father's shoulder, until Wally would look at him. It felt like pulling his father back.

"You're not needing my permission."

"It's more you're blessing we want." His father reached for the thermos and poured them both a second cup.

"My blessing, Davy? I no longer have the right. I haven't for years." Wallace Charles Phelan sat motionless for a moment, and they both ignored their coffee. David started to say something without knowing what, but his father's hand on his arm stopped him. "You don't know it all, David. There's one thing more I need to tell you about your mother. I had it from Siobhan just before Garrett took their family west to Port Alberni British Columbia, for the logging mill job. "Your cousin Siobhan waited all those years to tell me.

It almost killed me."

14   A Child Lost

David's father shook his head at himself.

He sent his gaze far out over the calm Lake Erie waters and his bobbing, hand-carved duck decoys, and seemed to embrace the thin horizon and this painful moment of Siobhan's revelation to him, not long passed.

It was a Tuesday, the third and maybe final day of Wallace Charles Phelan's exile on his own back stoop, his Purgatory. David brought Wally his breakfast and the lunch Lulu Pearl had put in his pail for work, and later, his supper on a plate when his father returned from his day shift at the Ford Auto Plant. His parents had not spoken since that Saturday night after Mulvaney's, and Lulu Pearl's shame and her swift, decisive and painful retaliation that left his father unconscious on the floor of the saloon, with David and the members of Windsor's Loyal Orange Lodges witness to it all.

Sunday afternoon, Dr. Kirsner had changed Wally's head bandages and checked him over carefully, especially his visual function, level of awareness, alertness, reaction time and mental acuity. He then gave Wally his stern physician's look and instructed him to get more rest and to not go into work on the following day if he was the least unsteady on his feet or experiencing even mild dizziness and balance problems. "In the midst of those assembly lines and working industrial machinery, you could do permanent injury to yourself and your family's income and well-being, Wallace."

But Wallace Charles Phelan was determined to provide for his family. "My cross to bear, Davy, my cross of shame." He had confided to eight-year-old David.

That Sunday, the first day of his father's exile, young David and his mother had walked briskly to their usual afternoon services at Lincoln Road Methodist Church. He was immediately and uncomfortably aware of the stares and whispers of the congregation as he and his mother walked up the centre aisle of Lincoln Methodist and took their usual seats, three rows from the front, in the right-hand pews. The stares were furtive, but still intense and lingering. Lulu Pearl said something briefly to Mr. Wigle on her right, who listened with the same level of intensity. David forced himself to stare straight in front of him and tried his best to ignore the empty space beside him on their pew, where his father usually sat. But of its own accord, his left hand slid over the varnished maple to confirm the emptiness beside him and within him. David was suddenly angry, but his anger had no focus—not his father, not his mother, not himself. David desperately wanted to leave.

"I'm late for Sunday school, Mama?"

"No, not today. Today I want you beside me, Davy." Ten minutes later, Reverend Winthrop began the services, but David remembered nothing of the sermon, prayers, or hymns. An hour later, in a mindless daze, Lulu Pearl led him out of the church and paused with the other members of the congregation to shake hands with Minister Winthrop and his wife.

"You know Sophie and I are always at your service in times of direst need, Mrs. Phelan. Always. And together we might pray for God's strength and the benevolence of his loving mercy." David felt the tension.

"Yes, Reverend, I'm grateful." Then Sophie Winthrop took his mother's hand for a moment between both of hers.

"The Lord sends us trials, Lulu Pearl."

"That he does, Sophie." Before either one could say more, his mother led David away through the crowd on the sidewalk, her head up, nodding to people they knew, but not stopping to exchange news and pleasantries, as was her usual habit.

Thus began the ritual of David taking his meals out to his father on their back stoop. When Wally had left for the Ford Auto Plant plant that Monday morning, his face was as white as the bandages showing beneath his grey cloth cap, but set in determined lines. Looking for his mother, David found her by the front door, watching his father get into their Ford truck and drive off. "He still looks really sick, Mama."

"Yes, I know. But it is a necessary part of his trial and penance, Davy." Yet he saw Lulu seemed in a state of similar pain, and a matching determination.

"I hope he's not sick at work."

"The Good Lord is stronger than hope, Davy. Our Saviour was three days in the Valley of the Shadow and rose again in glory. We'll know God's will in this—and your father's—on Tuesday.

Now, young David Charles Phelan sat on his front porch and waited for his father's return from work. He heard the familiar engine sound of their Ford pickup before it turned the corner onto Ottawa Street and was waiting at the curb. When Wally got slowly out of the truck, David ran to his father and hugged him around the waist, his silent plea for reassurance.

"I'm scared, Papa." Wallace Phelan held him tightly, and David thought he could hear his father's stout Irish heart beating behind his chest. He smelled of wood and varnish, oil and sweat, and David felt a slight return to normality.

"I am too, my son. I am too. But this uncomfortable bed of pain is one of my making, no one else's. My selfish, thoughtless actions, the breaking of my solemn Temperance Oath to Lu, the woman I swore to love and value, have brought pain and shame upon you and your mother, upon our family and Phelan reputation, in a measure I could not have before imagined. Learn from it, Davy. Never forget."

"Mama's waiting for you on the back stoop."

His father's arm was a heavy weight across David's shoulders. They walked along the side of the house, through the gate and climbed the five steps to the back landing. Lulu Pearl Phelan had been sitting and stood when she saw them. David saw the tenseness in the stiff manner of her posture and set of her mouth. Lulu's face was washed of all colour, and she said nothing and waited, while David stood anxiously between them and looked from one to the other of the people he loved most in the world.

The ensuing silence made his fear for them, for their family and for himself, too real. He wanted to say something, to offer some comfort to them both, but didn't know what. Wally finally took off his grey cloth cap and spoke first. David concentrated on a spot of dried blood that had seeped through the gauze head bandage some time after he'd left for work that morning.

"Lu ... that woman in red, I want you to know..."

But Lulu Pearl Phelan held up her hand and silenced him. She went into her kitchen and returned with Ty Cobb's heavy, hand-carved, chestnut-oak bat, fully *her* bat now. While his father fingered his cap nervously, round and round, she lifted the Phelan family Bible from the small table and held them both out to him, the bat and the Bible. David marvelled again at his mother's sheer strength, and it wasn't just physical. He knew the weight of each.

"You must choose, Wallace, before God, your son and your family, the one or the other. I cannot endure such heartbreak and doubt again, and remain a dutiful Christian wife and mother, in keeping with the Lord's plan for us all. Your only son cannot follow such a father's example and still grow into a man of faith, substance, and integrity." His father hung his head for long seconds, took a deep shaky breath, and David Charles Phelan watched in amazement as Wally sank slowly to his knees on the rough wooden floor boards, held his cap in his left hand and took and held the heavy Phelan Bible in his right.

"The Sins of Omission, wilfulness and broken faith are solely upon my head alone, and I am justly rebuked. These three days past, in a Purgatory of my own making, I have witnessed the precious life and loves I may lose, and tasted the bitterness, the despair their absence would bring me—a living Purgatory. I want you back Lu. I want my son back. I beseech you, beseech you humbly to grant me a second chance." His father bent his head and kissed the Bible, with the tears beginning in his eyes, then leaned slowly forward to put his face against his mother's abdomen.

Lulu Pearl Phelan's resolute sternness drained slowly from her stiff, determined posture and her own eyes came to tears.

"Oh, Wallace ... Wallace Charles Phelan, my husband and father to my child..." To David, watching his mother, it was as if the carved White Angel had returned to life. The hardness went out of her, and the blood seeped back into her face, erasing the lines of tension and pain. Lulu Pearl extended both hands, lifted his father up and came into his arms. They kissed, and kissed, and kissed, murmuring words David couldn't make out, and wasn't intended to. Wally held his his mother's head in the hollow of his neck, and his parents rocked back and forth, both crying steadily, so that his father's tears fell into his mother's tightly bound red hair and hers onto his grey work shirt.

"Forever, my darling, darling Lu, forever." His father looked down and saw David crying with them and picked him up, and he was held secure and safe in their loving embrace, and all his fears and doubts running away with his tears, as he felt his own on his cheeks.

But the "forever" was barely two months.

Even more than during the "War to End All Wars" and his family's intense closeness and shared love, these were the warmest, happiest, most loving months of his boy's life. David couldn't know the end of the First World War would be the beginning of something equally terrible, and far, far more personal for him.

"War is many things, but at its root is change, Davy, change and insanity. This 'Great War in Europe' has changed everything," his mother said.

In 1918, as the war was winding down and David was a King Edward Public School boy, six years old, Lulu Pearl had tried to explain the source of his anxieties to help him put it behind him and behind them all.

Before bed that fall, David would bring up their *Rand McNally World Atlas* and Lulu's heavy scrapbook from the parlour, and mother and son would work their way through the large scrapbook while Wally carved and painted his duck decoys in his basement workshop below. It was all there in clippings from the local Detroit and Windsor newspapers—Toronto's *Mail and Empire* and *The Globe*, Canada's self-declared "national newspaper"— and from weeklies like *Saturday Night* and the new *Maclean's* magazine: graphic pictures, stories and three-inch headlines that insinuated themselves permanently into David's imagination. Some were so horrific and troubling that he wished he had never looked at them as closely as he did, even under his mother's supervision.

"This is us, the world and its peoples in the worst of times, Davy. But looking away will only make them more likely to occur again."

Change and insanity. Strange terms and names and places. His mother continued to say it was important. David struggled to understand, and didn't look away.

"An obscure Serbian nationalist is driven by the fervour of his cause to assassinate the symbol of his oppression, the Archduke Francis Ferdinand, heir apparent to the Austro-Hungarian empire. Humiliating demands for reparations are refused. War is declared, Davy. More declarations follow quickly and within months the

'Central Powers'—Germany, Austro-Hungary and Turkey—are ranged against the 'Allies'—France, Britain, Russia, and the United States—across a great Western Front, to redress their perceived grievances. And ourselves, Davy, the great Dominion of Canada, a wide ocean away, are there with our Great Mother Britain."

David tried to picture these scenes in his boy's imagination, and to understand the new terms and language with his mother speaking so formally. But it was her way of talking, whether of war or the Windsor temperance movement she championed, with David at her side and carrying his signs. It was Lulu Pearl Phelan who rallied Sandwich West's support of the Ontario Temperance Act of 1916, banning the sale of alcohol. But liquor could still be produced or imported. Lulu had worked on the religious front as well, with the co-operation of the other Methodist Churches.

Lulu went on to describe how the Germans would overrun Belgium and advance on Paris, driving for the English Channel. But after the great battles at the Marne and Ypres, the whole affair bogging down in a new kind of warfare fought in great mud-, water-, and rat-infested trenches. "Six thousand young Canadians died in their first great battle at Ypres, Davy, under waves of the new German terror weapon, chlorine gas. But our brave Canadian boys held. They held, Davy, and we are forever in their debt".

"So that's ... Remembrance Day!"

"Exactly so, my son. Exactly so." His mother paused and looked away for a few moments, and the corners of her eyes teared.

Together, they turned the troubling pages with their images of mass slaughter, death, and endless suffering. His mother quoted from an article in *Maclean's* magazine in her solemn voice:

"'...war is ribbons of barbed wire; the grinding forward of strange metal tanks; week-long artillery barrages cultivating the mud and dead bodies; doomed charges into the streams of deadly fire from

Maxim and Vickers machine guns; sudden shifts in the fitful winds that blow the yellow billows of the new "mustard gas" back onto the very ones who deployed it; nascent national air forces flying their fragile, wired wood and cloth Sopwiths and Fokkers, bringing a different death falling from the shell-smoked skies above—three endless years of slaughter, shell shock, atrocity and heroism, then more of the same at Verdun and in the Somme offensive.'"

Lulu Pearl paused a moment as the emotion overwhelmed her and tears edged her eyes, then continued in her own words.

"Yet more brave Canadian boys died or were maimed and wounded for life, with little hope of a future, Davy, little real hope. But their pain, their early death, spilled blood, and sacrifice wins our beloved 'Dominion of Canada' new independence from Britain. We are now fully and independently Canada, one nation unto ourselves, from sea, to sea, to sea."

Again, Lulu Pearl Phelan paused her narrative, and this time David saw the lines of tears on her cheeks, but these, at least, were tears of pride in her adopted nation of Canada.

"The 'War to End All Wars' they've been calling it, Davy," his mother said, and laughed bitterly. "Don't believe it, my beautiful boy, not for one second. Ten million men killed, twice that more wounded and maimed and filling our hospitals to overflowing. And the resolute nurses who shared their pain and too often gave their own lives at men's sides for the succour of our fallen soldiers. And what of that same number of sinless women and wives and children uncounted, left alone, bearing the pain and poverty of such a loss? A great victory indeed!"

More bitter laughter. And David thought a moment before offering his own contribution.

"Well, Ty Cobb joined up. And one of his family was a general in the American Civil War. A hero." David countered.

"Did he now?" His mother didn't seem at all impressed by Ty Cobb, in war or in peacetime. But the Great War in Europe had changed baseball forever too.

David and his father followed the developments avidly, but in private, in the workshop below, while Wally carved and painted his blocks, and David practiced with his father's polished wood duck calls. "Work or Fight!" had been the U. S. government's edict to men of fighting age. In such times, playing baseball was not considered work, but an "unuseful" occupation, Wally explained to him.

David tried again with his mother.

"Yes, Papa told me Ty Cobb was a captain in the ... the Chemical Warfare Service." He smiled proudly at remembering the name, but Lulu only shrugged it off. "And Tris Speaker, and other players too." David didn't tell her about Shoeless Joe Jackson or Babe Ruth. Their "war essential" jobs were not "real" jobs, but special paid positions made only for them and a handful of others on shipyard baseball teams. His father was upset and ashamed at the scandal. "And the teams had to end their season early, in September, the same month as school started." This seemed important to David.

"'Tis little enough, boyo," Lulu said. "Insanity in war means huge sacrifice, Davy, huge sacrifice for all people, at home or in those hellish trenches, up to their knees in mud, filth, and scrambling rats. I won't say the cause was not just in the end, once the insanity had taken hold across the world. But was the cost of it all, the severe cost, not a price too dear, and paid as always by the blood and sweat and tears of the humble working men and women of this world, and their families? All while the rich, the powerful and the privileged remain safely in their soft feather beds at night, gather up their war profits and cheer them on to their sufferings and deaths. Ty Cobb and the baseball have survived, when many deserving innocents have not. In that way, Davy, we are none of us, none of us, innocent."

And long years later, remembering the "innocents," trying to explain the spirit and complexity of Lulu Pearl Phelan to his beloved Norah McGee, David knew his mother could have been talking about herself.

And about him....

15   Men's Stew

The third week of September, 1919, began and ended in rain, constant beating rain, and no blessed relief in sight.

David and Roddy and Gar wore their heavy black rubber boots and walked in the swollen gutters, splashing, laughing, and jumping up and down with both feet, to and from King Edward Public School, enjoying the sound and feel of the water rushing along the curbs and disappearing in gurgling streams down the curb drains. Gar had the sudden idea to plug the drain in front of Roddy's house with the accumulated leaves and trash, and the three laughed and jumped, splashed and cavorted, as they encouraged a great grey pond of leaves and debris to build yet higher and flow across the wide asphalt road of their Gladstone Avenue neighbourhood.

To their immense pride and delight, the passing cars launched increasingly monstrous sprays of filthy water that reached them on the sidewalk and splashed against their yellow slickers like grey liquid hail. They doubled over with glee and screams of mock outrage at their boy's cleverness and repeatedly punched one another's arms. The passing drivers laid heavily on their horns and shouted their curses at them, sometimes stopping and threatening to take after them, and it was wicked and fun. One huge, blue-black moving truck with St. Michael Bros. Carry and Cartage in fancy, yard-high script, braked heavily and the driver was about to jump down and come at them in his outrage—but saw the depth of the rain-riffled muddy water below, and him with no rubber boots, so settled for shaking his fist at them and cursing mightily.

Until Deirdre spied them and, in great glee at this opportunity for further mischief, ran for Roddy's mother, Mrs. McCrae. The stout woman stood on her high porch, took one look at the three bois-terous neighbourhood lads, and came charging down on the three of them like a fearsome, screaming-mad Irish banshee. She waved her wide straw broom vigorously over her head and laid into all of them until they scattered like panicked young leprechauns, before sweeping aside the blockage and dragging Roddy inside, crying, and begging relief at what he knew was coming.

But not before Mrs. McCrae shouted over her left shoulder at Gar and David to "Get off home with ya!" where they belonged.

Lulu Pearl Phelan was waiting for her own wayward son on their own front porch, hands on her hips and that stern expression on her face that belied her love and disappointment in him as she slowly shook her head, telling David he was to suffer the same painful fate and punishment as his friends. A disgusted Mrs. McCrae had immediately phoned her, and Lulu gave David the rough Irish edge of her tongue for more than a minute, soon putting him on the verge of tears he tried desperately to hold behind his eyes, but couldn't.

Lulu Pearl took her only son by the shoulders with both hands and shook him. "Never again, me bucko! You understand me, now? Never! Don't you dare upset the peace and goodwill of this neigh-bourhood, threaten our Phelan family reputation, and endanger the poor drivers trying to get through it to pursue their business." Lulu Pearl let go David's shoulders, lifted his chin, and brought her stern face close, red hair escaping its pins with her anger.

David knew she hated such escapades. Now he was the one who was shaking.

"Look at me now and understand. Understand well. You embar-rass yourself, bucko, and us, your loving parents with you." David blubbered and shook and hung his head, while the tears rained down on the black, red, and tan-patterned Axminster carpet and his wet, stockinged feet.

Wallace Charles Phelan stood back a safe distance and watched as his wife took their son to hard task. Listened to David's mumbled attempts at explanation and shook his head at his son's antics. Neither noticed the hint of a smile below his wide black walrus moustache,

Wally only smiled at the story and tried to soften Lulu's upset and reprimand. "I know. I know. But please, they're boys, Lu, just young lads like I was once myself and getting into me own mischief. They like the water more than the Dabbling Puddle Ducks."

"No, Wallace! Not this mischief! Not this time! David Charles is my only son and a boy of this, our neighbourhood. He and Roddy and Gar were this very afternoon responsible for a very dangerous mischief, dangerous to themselves and others, that might have had serious and painful consequences for us all. Drivers losing control of their vehicles in a quiet neighbourhood with children playing. The wide world and this house have enough of both, thank you, Wallace. It's the company and pleasure and civility of sensible young girls, and their dolls and dresses, I'm missin', not the thoughtless antics of boys. Until such time, our dripping young Dabbling Puddle Duck here can waddle his way down to your workshop and await the discipline it is your father's solemn Christian duty to deliver, and me standing mother at the top of the stairs to ensure he receives it as the Lord's witness."

Lulu Pearl Phelan's implacable look at her husband and son gave David's father no choice.

Wally hung his head in strict Methodist shame and acquiescence to the will of God and his formidable wife, nodded, and took David by the hand to the cellar door, with Lulu Pearl standing at the top of the stair above them, arms crossed. David had the sudden and surprising insight that this was his own Purgatory, that of a wayward son, a "Prodigal," and he vowed not to cry further.

He almost didn't.

Until his mother shouted down, "Enough, Wallace!" and his father stayed his hand from his bare backside. Then the tears burst forth again like a muddy spray of water. His mother pointed his way up the stairs to his bedroom on the second floor, and David went, trailing his tears of shame behind him. "And I don't want to hear a single quack out of our Dabbling young Puddle Duck until I call it down for its supper—or not!"

But the next morning, Wallace Charles Phelan, secretly, solemnly and with great ceremony, placed a special package in David's King Edward Public School lunch pail. "For you, my only son, and for the rest of your chastened flock. And not one word about it to She Who Must Be Obeyed." His father winked, squeezed David's right shoulder, and drove off to his shift at the Ford Auto Plant.

David couldn't wait for lunch and opened the brown paper wrapping as soon as he got Roddy and Gar together before class. His father had speedily carved and gaudily painted three miniature boats, with their stick masts, out of basswood, and printed each of their names in India ink along the sides.

Later, the three Dabbling Puddle Ducks shouted their boy's mirth, floated them in the puddles and the gutters to and from school, fought small naval battles against the hated German foe and each other, and were twice late to King Edward Public School, and sternly reprimanded. When David finally showed his boat to his mother, Lulu laughed, hugged him in the familiar manner he loved, and shook her head at his father. "And do men never grow up?"

"They do my marvellous Lu, so to bask in the pleasure of formidable women like your lovely self." They embraced for so long again, that David grew self-conscious, but also warm and contented in their loving presence beside him.

Thursday evening David was sitting down, worried and waiting, for his father's arrival on their front steps, when Wally at last arrived home from his interior carpentry work at the Ford Auto Plant. He parked the old Ford Model T truck and came trotting up the walk, smiling despite the continuing rain. David was wearing his rubber boots and slicker and eating a peanut butter cookie, trying to allay his anxiety.

"Spoil your supper, boyo! Your mother won't be pleased."

"Mama's gone back to bed, Papa. She says you're supposed to go up." His father stopped abruptly, then suddenly spun on his heel and raised his arms like a dancer, so that drops of water flew from his cap and lunch pail.

"Got a bit under the weather, did she, my son?"

"I don't know, Papa. I don't. But she said she felt tired after coming back from the Friends of the Homeless place where she helps out."

"Well, Lu *has* been putting a lot of time in there lately, giving a needed hand to those in difficult circumstances, so it's little wonder. I'd better see to her then, lad. Let's go inside." Wally took his hand and led him around to the stoop where they hung their wet jackets. "Put on the kettle for tea, Davy. And get out the lemon and honey, you know where." His father disappeared upstairs for ten minutes, returned and wet the leaves in their vintage Brown Betty teapot, sliced the lemon onto a small plate, and arranged them on a tin tray with two cups and the honey. Wally's brow was creased with concern, making David yet more anxious.

"How is she, Papa?"

"Just a bit tired, it seems, boyo. I think she may be taking too much of a burden onto herself with her work at Dumfries Fine Ladies Wear, her Temperance Union women's group and volunteering at the Friends three times a week. But you know how dedicated to her causes Lu is, boyo. David nodded.

"Mama doesn't like to change her mind." His father laughed and lightened the mood a bit.

"Don't I just know it! And makes you pay a dear price for trying to." Wally poured David a rare cup of tea, with honey and milk, and gave him another cookie. Before supper. "Our secret."

David checked their kitchen clock more than once, and judged his father was gone for more than twenty minutes this time. David began to wonder about their supper as the dinner hour approached. It was getting close on seven p.m. when their phone rang and caused him to jump. Their cousin Siobhan wondered why Lulu Pearl hadn't called about making the secret arrangements for the birthday party for her eight-year-old daughter, Mair, on Saturday afternoon. David explained she was not feeling well.

There was a pause. "Then be sure you and Wallace are taking special care of her, Davy, very special care. Plenty of rest for Lulu Pearl and no worries from either of you. I'll call again early tomorrow morning if there's something I can do."

David told his father about Siobhan's call after he returned to say Lulu Pearl was resting and would come down when they'd made supper, a rare event in his Phelan family and his mother's kitchen. "Siobhan sounded worried, Papa."

"Siobhan is Lu's close cousin and best friend. It's understandable." David worried more.

Wally cut up some leftover lamb, while under his watchful eye David chopped potatoes, carrots, and onions for a stew with plenty of broth to help build his mother's strength. The stew was done at seven forty-five, and David had carefully set the dinner table, placing each bowl and utensil precisely as his mother had instructed him, with her crusty bread evenly sliced and stacked. The familiar ritual made him feel a bit better. Then he heard Lulu Pearl's careful footsteps on the stairs, and placed himself on the landing below with a brave smile, trying to master his worry. Lulu had dressed carefully in muted blue, as usual, but a strand of her lovely red hair had escaped the pins. Again.

"I cut up all the vegetables and set the table for dinner, Mama. Father said we should use your good white china because it might cheer you up."

His mother managed a warm smile at the sight, and David took some heart at the familiar expression. "Then will we be having the peanut butter cookies in your lamb stew on my best china, my lovely boy?" David looked down and nervously brushed the cookie crumbs from his shirt. Lulu Pearl laughed and hugged him. "My little man! Thank you, Davy." But her voice and embrace lacked their usual energy. Then Wallace Phelan was there and leading his wife gracefully by the arm to the table. There, he pulled out her chair and offered her the napkin beside her bowl with such great ceremony that it brought another laugh.

"Are you really sick, Mama?"

"Tired, Davy, just tired. I'll go back to bed and lie down after the dishes are done, and be right as this rain tomorrow."

"Siobhan called about Mair's birthday party. She'll call back in the morning."

"I haven't forgotten, Davy. If there are still enough peanut butter cookies left…?"

"I only ate two. I'm sorry." Lulu gave David her fond mother's smile and caressed his cheek in the way that always filled David's entire being with warmth.

"I believe the circumstances might allow an exception." Then his father motioned for her bowl.

"Now, Mrs. Phelan, I offer you our famous Men's Stew, exceptional as the name suggests, because no female hand came near its preparation, but no less delicious for that omission, if we do say so ourselves, right son?"

"Very exceptional!" David liked the big word. "And Siobhan said we must take special care of you. We'll do the dishes and put them away." His mother nodded her gratitude and tasted her bowl of stew, while he and his father waited for her verdict.

"Well, Lu?"

"Ah yes, the famous Men's Stew! I believe I have heard of such a rare and unlikely phenomenon." She closed her eyes in mock concentration, then opened them and delivered her verdict. "If I might say just a single wee word, sirs?"

"What, Mama?"

"Salt." The Phelan family all laughed, and David passed his mother the saltcellar. Lulu added a measured amount and took a second spoonful. "Exceptional—for a couple of men." More laughter. "Thank you both, my Phelan stalwarts. I don't suppose I can count on this to become a regular practice of the stout men of this household?"

David looked at Wally and his father looked back. "Well, Lu, uh..." His mother only laughed and shook her head.

But most troubling for David, as he watched with careful attention and concern, was that his mother ate only a little of their Men's Stew, and took only a small glass of water. David now observed that Lulu Pearl's fair skin showed a distinct bluish tinge he was certain could not be good. His beloved mother quietly excused herself after barely more than ten minutes at table, and his father helped her slowly upstairs while he finished his stew and began to clear the table. David was especially careful with his mother's precious fine china, her great pride before dinner guests and on special occasions in their Phelan household.

The following morning, Wally made Lulu Pearl take breakfast in bed. His father packed their lunch pails himself and tried to reassure David as they departed for school and his own work, in the rain that continued unabated, adding a sharp edge of chill to the air.

And David thought he heard coughing coming from Lulu Pearl's bedroom.

More troubling still, Siobhan was waiting for David on the front porch rocker when he got home from school. Their cousin stood up abruptly as soon as he saw her, and his stomach went as cold as the chill falling rain on his face. He began to run.

"I want to see her! I want to see Mama! I need to right now!" It was the stiff white surgical mask hanging down around Siobhan's neck that instantly alarmed David. Siobhan stopped him with her hands roughly on his shoulders and bent down to him. Hugged him. The desperate fierceness of that embrace panicked David further.

"Now listen to me, boyo! You must listen! I called Dr. Kirsner, and he's attending to Lu now, so she's in the best of hands. I spoke with Wallace at the Ford plant, and he's immediately on his way home to us. You can both of you see Lu then. But we must wait just a wee bit, Davy. It's for her own good. So Dr. Kirsner can complete his examination and we can better know her condition."

"But..."

"Hush now, hush. I know, Darling. I know you're very worried. We all are. But we will face whatever comes together, together, understand? Care for, love and support one another as a family, as we always have in our times of peril and uncertainty. For now, it's best we take some comfort for our own selves. We'll share a measure of fresh, steaming-hot, Irish black tea to warm our bodies, and with your mother's fine peanut butter cookies on our tongues in Lu's own kitchen. Together, we'll await Wallace and Dr. Kirsner."

"The cookies are for Mair's party tomorrow." Why had David said something so stupid at a time like this?

"Sure now, me bucko, and won't we all enjoy them together?" Then Wallace Charles Phelan arrived with the sound of squealing truck brakes, still dressed in his heavy work coveralls and a few curls of white wood clinging to one shoulder.

David ran to his father and hugged him wordlessly around the waist. Long minutes later, Dr. Kirsner joined them at the kitchen table. He pulled down his surgical mask, sat, looking weary, and took a deliberate sip of the tea to wet his lips. He began to share his diagnosis. The skilled family physician looked at David for a long moment before speaking, and David's agitation and dread increased, but he didn't look away. Wallace Phelan placed both arms on the table encircling his steaming teacup and solemnly inclined his head in invitation. "Now, we'll all be needing to know the hard truth of it, Doctor."

"Very well, sir. I will explain as directly as I can. I'm very sorry to say that Mrs. Phelan has undoubtedly contracted the Spanish influenza that has been ravaging the wider world since the war's end in 1918, and come to our own shores these last months, as you all know. I've given her something to slow the cough and ease her breathing, but her lungs are filling with fluid and Lulu Pearl labours mightily to draw breath. It is imperative that she have extended rest and care, and plenty of fluids from your own hands to keep her hydrated and resist the fever. She must at all costs retain as much of her strength as possible. Give her strong meat broths to help restore and maintain that strength and her own will, and all the soft foods she can take to keep up the vital nutrients her body needs, especially fresh fruits, greens, and vegetables."

Wally and Siobhan looked at each other with serious expressions of concern, nodded, but said nothing. Dr. Kirsner took another sip of his tea and gathered himself to continue.

A feeling of slow dread began overtake David.

"Now, this is vitally important for you all in this household: Mrs. Phelan must have no other visitors, absolutely none, if you are all to survive this crisis without yourselves falling ill. Lulu Pearl's close family only, and each wearing one of the surgical masks I will give you all for your own protection, and Mrs. Phelan's own peace of mind while you are in her presence. I shall return tomorrow morning to monitor the fever, her lung congestion, and her progress."

Dr. Kirsner opened his black leather case.

"You may see her now, for a few minutes only, but you must wear these masks without fail. An important precaution for you all in the presence of the contagion." The doctor took out the package of white surgical masks, and the adults exchanged another look above David's head as Siobhan took it. "And this is very important: handwashing.

Wash your hands constantly during the day, especially before entering and immediately after leaving Mrs. Phelan's room. Now, do you have any questions?" Again, the look between his father and Siobhan.

But in that moment, in that look, David knew, knew it in every fibre of his body and being—but resisted, denied it, and denied it, and denied it with all the strength of his loving young son's will.

"And I'll be staying the night to be immediately available to Lulu Pearl then, Doctor," Siobhan said. "Garrett can look after the girls. And I'll be home in time to manage Mair's birthday party, Davy, don't you worry."

"That would be most helpful, Mrs. Bryant, most helpful." Dr. Kirsner agreed.

"Most helpful? And you, kind sir?" Siobhan said. "What of your labours on this fateful day of days in Lulu Pearl's own care and service, and with more days to follow, no doubt. Our Good Lord knows we are blessed, sir, blessed in your presence, Dr. Kirsner. Phelans will never forget this debt. Your own road is hard in these perilous times, sir, but your Lord and Jewish faith have surely given strong shoes. Phelans return your generosity in kind and more besides, and let others know the value of your blessed presence among us."

Dr. Kirsner bowed his head, nodded to them all, and with his weary smile and a further downward glance, left the household. Siobhan went to phone Garrett.

Wallace Charles Phelan had said almost nothing, the whole of the time. Now David hugged his father fiercely, his tears dripping onto his Ford Auto Plant coveralls, as if his mother's very life depended on it, which he knew it did. Then he pulled back and slipped his hand into his father's, for its reassurance and strength. "Can we see her now, Papa, please? I can't wait."

"Yes, we can, boyo. Yes, we can and we must. Lu wouldn't want us to be worryin', now, would she?"

David and Wally each put on their crisp white surgical masks and climbed the stairs to her bedroom with heavy footsteps. But when they silently approached her bedside in the dim light, David saw his mother, Lulu Pearl Phelan, was already asleep, her breathing audible and uneasy.

16   Dance with 'The Lady'

On Wednesday morning, at her request, David spoke with his beloved mother alone, sitting at Lulu Pearl's bedside and weeping quietly.

He didn't recognize the much diminished and weakened woman in her bed before him now, less than a shadow of the once energetic and forceful mother he knew, who had lavished him with her love and guided him all his short life. David reached out instinctively for the reassurance of Lulu's hands in his, as he had always done at such painful moments in the past. "No, Davy, no my beautiful boy, you must not. It would be too risky with this influenza's easy contagion and spread." Lulu, as if resigned to a fate she judged certain, had firmly refused to go to the hospital and take up a much-needed bed, and the precious time and energies of the harried physicians, nurses, and staff there.

David would always ever after remember that tragic fall and winter of 1918 as "the time of madness, masks and mourning." The beleaguered and exhausted Windsor doctors and nurses, and their medical support staff, reported in excess of thirty new flu infections every day in mid-October. And the ninety-five new influenza cases diagnosed on November first alone so alarmed Mayor Charles R. Tuson that he banned by strict edict, costly fine, and even threatened jail time, any event that involved more than twenty-five persons: All theatre shows cancelled; all dance halls closed; all churches without services. David's King Edward Public School closed for a full month, along with all the other schools across Windsor.

David was old enough now to know it was a far from normal holiday, and all his accustomed antics with Roddy and Gar, no matter how energetic, were overshadowed by the grave atmosphere that hung over their neighbourhood like a heavy grey cloak, smothering what cheer might remain. The adults around David kept their children close, checked on them more frequently, hugged and spoiled them with small treats and praise of their courage in the face of the crises surrounding them daily. At the end of that most troubling November month, his school re-opened—but with two desks empty of their students, and with long black ribbons draped solemnly around the photographs of Joseph Renaud and Mary Cade by the principal's office, after their tearful and prolonged memorial assembly in the dank, stuffy school auditorium.

From Principal Bernard Riley's lengthy and grave address to the students, to David's own parents' avid reading aloud of the newspapers, and Lulu Pearl's insistence on volunteering at the Veterans' Memorial Hall, turned abruptly into an emergency hospital in the face of an epidemic that completely overwhelmed all medical and social services, David learned more than any child his age should know of the influenza. It soon after came to be called the "Spanish flu" or the "Spanish Lady."

Spain had been completely neutral in the Great War, but the warring nations had initially censored any news of the spreading influenza epidemic. When Spain did not and made it known to the wider world. Once the Spanish King, Alfonso XIII, came down with a nasty case of it in late May, 1918, the news spread worldwide from that point onward and dominated all media. For those three fall months in Windsor, in late 1918, and the two weeks his mother spent away, nursing Siobhan and Mair through their time of crisis with it, David felt like a high-strung soldier must feel when he knows his enemies are out there, edging closer around him on all sides, but he is powerless to guess where and when that enemy might attack. So this lethal, insidious epidemic conflict was its own "World War," and unlike any boy's game of soldiers David had played with Roddy and Gar. The deadly serious looks emanating from the tired eyes of the white-masked adults all around him made that abundantly clear.

It was the soldiers who spread it.

Sick and wounded troops were continually shipped back home, and new supply ships travelled again and again between Europe and far-flung parts of the globe. The men left pain and death on the battlefields, only to bring a new death to their families and communities who should have been safe at home. The infection landed heavily at the ports of Boston, Chicago, San Francisco, and Quebec City. Then the Spanish Lady migrated, took to the highways, railways and the waterways, north, east, west, and south to all parts of the North American continent. In the month of October alone, two hundred thousand Americans died. In Quebec, whole villages around the province simply disappeared. In Ottawa, Canada's capital, the poor— mainly Irish Catholics and the French—were most affected, living and working as they did in the crowded industrial neighbourhoods around Ottawa's main railway and shipping depots. Fifty thousand Canadians succumbed.

But the source of the dancing, energetic Spanish Lady remained a mystery to the doctors and researchers working to discover it. And there was no cure, no certainty, only endless precautions, and measures to try and contain it. Lulu Pearl Phelan had cut out the notice from the November 2, 1918, edition of Windsor's *Border Cities Era*, and pasted it into her scrapbook:

Spanish Influenza

Is an extremely contagious disease.
It is caused by the Influenza germ.
The Influenza germ enters the body through the mouth or nose.
It comes from the mouth or nose of a
     person ill with the disease.
Sneezing, coughing or expectorating
     spreads the germs into the air.
Therefore, if you wish to avoid the Influenza,
DON'T go near anyone who has it.
DON'T go in crowds anywhere.
DON'T ride in the street cars.
DON'T go to visit your sick friends.
DON'T go to theatres, public meetings, lodges or dance halls.
In all these places you will come in contact with
     people who have the disease in its milder form.
If you have the Influenza,
DON'T get excited or alarmed, 98 per cent of cases get better.
Stay at home and go to bed.
DON'T make yourself a menace to your
     friends by mixing with them, and
DON'T let them come to visit you.
Call your family physician and put yourself in his care.

Windsor Board of Health

Lulu Pearl was relentlessly strict with David and Wally, alert to the least sign or behaviour that might indicate a symptom of influenza. But Lulu was not so strict with herself, when it came to her providing care and service to others in dire need of it. David's immediate Phelan family, at the beginning, had been spared the influenza's ravages. But Garrett Bryant and his two youngest girls had needed to stay with them for two weeks in January, while Lulu Pearl lived at her cousin Siobhan's and nursed her and oldest daughter Mair back to reasonable health. David made his mother promise to phone him every morning to reassure him she was all right. He was up, sitting by the phone, before the rest of family was awake, even Garrett and the girls in their full distress. And when Mair and Siobhan had recovered, Lulu Pearl even then, could not be dissuaded from attending the victims of the influenza at the African Church situated in Windsor's poorest community.

David had never missed his mother so much, nor loved her so possessively.

And he had thought this World War was over. One war was. But a new World War had exploded across the globe, and this foe was far more deadly, more unforgiving, and more costly.

Bullets would not stop its depredations.

Good Dr. Kirsner, their expert Jewish physician, came and went on Saturday morning, but his tired face was a closed book. From her sickbed, Lulu Pearl Phelan insisted that David take the peanut butter cookies and accompany Siobhan back to her house and Mair's birthday celebration. "It's of greatest importance to Mair, Davy, offering a few hours joy and celebration, and some relief to our whole family in these troubling times. And you must be there, my lovely boy, and represent our branch of the Phelan family with at least a wee smile on your face."

Wallace Phelan agreed and drove them over, with David sitting between Siobhan and his father, and the bag of peanut butter cookies and Mair's present in green tissue and a red ribbon on his lap. Lulu had picked out a lovely pink and white lace camisole from Dumfries Fine Ladies Wear. Mair thought she was now a young woman and old enough. So David went for his loving mother's sake, when she could not, and yes, for his cousin Mair's too, and tried his best for them both. But there was no joy in it for him, and his cousin was bright and observant and must have sensed it.

Mair took David aside and held his hands in hers, looking serious. "Your mama will be okay, Davy. I'm sure she will. Remember, I was very sick and weak and bedridden for three days. Our cousin Lulu Pearl took such constant care of mother and me, day after day and at all hours for those two weeks, that we got steadily better. Now I hardly think about it. But I do think of her every minute of every day, as does Siobhan. We'll do all we can, I promise, Davy." Then Mair hugged him close and kissed David on both cheeks, like she was herself his mother.

But a masked and exhausted Dr. Kirsner came and went again on that Monday, and would speak only to his father and Siobhan, out of David's presence and hearing. "What did he say? What did the doctor say?" It was Siobhan who answered him. Wally hardly spoke anymore, and took a leave from the Ford Auto Plant to sit in their bedroom and carefully attend to the trays of beef broth and toast and soft eggs Lulu Pearl needed if she was to recover her strength.

His older cousin Siobhan carefully seated David in front of her at their kitchen table, while his father returned to his duties above them. Siobhan held David's eye and, as much as he wanted to, he could not look away. "I'll not lie to you, boyo. Your mother's condition is serious. Lulu Pearl still has her constant cough and high fever, and her breathing is very heavy at times, Davy. The whole of it together tires her, weakens her, and she needs her bedrest and our constant care. The good Dr. Kirsner has done all he can every visit. Lu is blessed in his care and we will not forget it, will repay it in any way we can. He has left some soft lozenges to help soothe your mother's throat, and we're to give her plenty of ice-water, as well. You must help, Davy, and make sure we always have a good supply of that ice." David nodded solemnly and vowed to make sure the ice never ran out. Siobhan hugged him close and long, and they were both in tears—family together, sharing their pain and hope.

His loving mother's eyes smiled at him above her white surgical mask when David, wearing his own surgical mask, visited her Monday afternoon. But Lulu Pearl Phelan had a sudden fit of coughing, and Siobhan, against his pleading protests, took him out of her bedroom before he could talk to her. "I'm so sorry, Davy, but no, you must leave for a bit. Wally and I will tend to her. You know we'll both do the very best we can. Off you go downstairs now and bring up a glass of ice water to the door. I'll be down there soon enough, boyo, and you can help me with the supper and Lulu's broth."

David was frustrated, but did exactly as he was told and had promised. Yet he absolutely refused, repeatedly, to go to school on Tuesday morning. Wallace Phelan was finally forced to sit him down, take both his hands, and speak seriously to him then, eye to eye, man to man. "Lu has a great respect for the learning, boyo, and you know that well. You're doing your Phelan family part, helping us with the ice water and the food, but you can do even more for your mother. Lu would want you in school every day, Davy, want you to take up the learning, do well on your assignments and homework. I know it's hard, bucko, I do, but God has given you strong shoes, as she well knows. You must do this for your mother's peace of mind and not distress her further."

"But this is too important, Papa." David said, his chin stiff, his eyes tearing up and the surgical mask still covering his face. Siobhan came in and stood quietly by with her hand on his shoulder, and David felt her deep sympathy for his father. Wally managed a smile at last, but still, David sensed the deep weight of the pain that was exhausting him and lining his face with worry.

"You're right, Davy. It *is* important, but so is following your mother's wishes, even in such troubling circumstances as these." His father squeezed his shoulder, and Siobhan inclined her head in agreement. "Now, you move quick, boyo, and help Siobhan with Lu's breakfast. Then you must be off to King Edward Public School, do your best there and make Lu proud. We'll take the tray up to Lu together. But that's it." His father hugged him, and David nodded, stifled his tears and did exactly that.

Yet Lulu Pearl was asleep again, and Wally told him through his mask that he would sit by his mother's bedside to feed her when she awoke. He took David to the door. "Strong shoes, boyo. We're the Irish." Wally squeezed his shoulder again and closed it quietly behind him.

After his too restless day at King Edward Public School, David had to rush upstairs and spoke briefly to his mother to reassure himself. Her warm eyes looked bravely back at the sight of him for those few minutes, so David tried his best for her. But still agitated after dinner, with little real conversation among the three of them, he wandered down to their workshop in the basement, and practiced with the pol-ished wood duck calls he and his father had made together, blowing softly to himself and not thinking about anything he could later remember.

That was David's routine on Wednesday, until after their supper together.

17   Memento Mori

"Your mother would like to speak with you, Davy." Siobhan retied her mask and waited.

If he hadn't known before, David knew it then.

He almost refused to go, but the objection never left his lips. This was worse than going into any battle. The mask his hands pulled up around his mouth was moist and stifling.

Siobhan led David up to his parents' bedroom like a stranger who didn't know the way. The door was open for him. His father's mask was down and, against all warnings, Wallace Phelan was holding his mother's hand. Lulu Pearl Phelan squeezed it, and his father nodded, and got up, and left with Siobhan. The door closed behind David without a sound. He thought weirdly of the mechanical clock in his own room. It must be ticking, but he couldn't hear it. Or maybe no one had wound it, and the hands were stopped. That was his responsibility. David had to stifle the urge to run to his room and see.

The woman in his mother's bed was not Lulu Pearl Phelan.

This woman was too small, with the bluish skin darker around the eyes and below the cheekbones, where it drew in. The red hair was spread out on the pillow but had no sheen. The face it framed was too thin, the lips without colour. The woman reached for the water glass on the table beside her, but the hand fumbled and almost upended it.

That broke the spell.

"Mama!" David rushed toward the bed until her voice stopped him.

"No, Davy! No! You must not come near me." It was his mother's voice, weak, but still pure for all the strain in her expression.

"I don't care! I don't! David threw himself into her arms and cried into his mask as they held him with some of their old strength. "You can't die! You can't!" He felt her shudder.

"Sit with me, my beautiful boy." He sat on the bedside and took her hand in his. She tried to pull it back, but he wouldn't let go of her. It was in the pulling that David felt her weakness. "Help me with the water, Davy."

He put the glass to her lips, and Lulu took small sips. After David put it back on the table, his mother looked at him with eyes that burned overbright. "Everyone dies, Davy. You know that. We are born in the shadow of the True Cross, live our lives in an imperfect world with the pain and suffering all around us, and long for the promise of the light beyond. In the space between, some, like Wallace and me, find that rare gift of love and devotion that balances the pain, makes it bearable, a burden we share."

His mother paused, in weakness and tears.

"We make a loving child together and leave him as the proof of that love and the greater creation. A child to continue the gift and keep us a little alive. The way of the world is a part of God's plan for us all, Davy. Without death, there's no hope of the Resurrection. We must believe in our true hearts that we wake into the grace of life everlasting. All who believe will be welcomed. I believe, Davy."

"No, Mama, no. You're not like Grandma Hannah. You're still young!" His mother motioned toward the glass, and David gave her another sip of the water. Lulu Pearl tried to sit forward a bit, but soon sank back.

"Youth is no defence, Davy. Hasn't the war and this plague taught us that hard lesson? And will we never learn it and live accordingly? I fear not. But I have my faith, and the Saviour's promise and sacrifice."

"It's wrong."

"No, my darling boy. But it is often hard. Strong shoes, remember? 'If God sends you down a stony path, may He give you strong shoes.' That's why the time allotted us is so precious. The whole of your life is waiting to be lived, Davy, and you must live it fully and well. No matter what happens, will you promise me that?" His mother waited, but David looked away and wouldn't speak. "Ah, love, I know you will." Lulu rested a moment, then took more water by his hand. "We need to talk about your father."

"He hardly talks to me at all." David turned aside. She took his face in her hands and, with gentle pressure, insisted he look at her. Then David couldn't look away.

"That's why you must understand, Davy. Wallace Phelan takes the whole of the burden of blame for this on his own shoulders. As if his actions that night at Mulvaney's had called up our own Irish *banshee* and started her to wailing. He talks of nothing else. Nothing. It's himself he wants in this bed, Davy."

"Then maybe—" But Lulu Pearl Phelan grabbed his hands with fearful strength and spoke with all the fervour a loving wife and mother could still command.

"No, Davy! No maybes. Never. I loved Wallace Phelan even then, in that very moment of the violence I did him with Ty Cobb's bat. I love him now. There is peace between us, and harmony. I forgave your father, and so must you. The great trouble is, he won't forgive himself. So, your father will need you, Davy. More than ever. Find the means to forgive. You must, my son. 'The hard heart will know no peace.'"

The effort cost Lulu and she closed her eyes for a few moments.

"You can't die..."

But his mother seemed to ignore his own order and reached under the sheets for the N. M. Meisner's Confectionery box and opened it. David had heard his father speak of some of the items it held, but not all.

"These are my remembrances—for you, now, Davy. My *memento mori*, my reminders that death comes to us all."

Lulu placed the items, one by one, on the bedclothes between them, with great reverence. The picture of Hannah Virtue was wrapped in lace and ribbon again. There were his grandmother's old letters, a beautiful set of little silver spoons with enamelled crests and gold lettering too fine to read, assorted small pieces of jewellery, a larger white and pink cameo brooch he had never seen his mother wear, and a heavy tarnished brass button Lulu was reluctant to touch, and put apart from the rest.

"Keep the photograph in respect and reverence, and see a bit of your own face in Grandmother Hannah's. Wait until you are a few years older, Davy, then read the letters. They recount a bit of our Phelan family history in Ireland, before we emigrated during the Great Irish Potato Famine almost a century ago now. The spoons have been in our keeping for many years. The jewellery is your grand-mother's and my own. This beautiful old cameo brooch is Grandma Hannah's favourite piece. I stopped wearing it after she left me and died at sea, because the sight of it in my mirror was too sad, too much to bear, a great weight against my chest."

His mother paused, closed her eyes, and took shaky breaths. Her tears were still there, and David felt his own on his cheeks and let them fall.

David did remember his Grandmother Hannah Virtue's upside-down watch that was long lost, and had the sudden thought that the sea had taken them both. Lulu Pearl continued.

"Of all of these, Davy, this is the most important, the most precious. I want you to wear it now, on this chain around your neck, above your heart. I had dearly hoped to give it myself to your ... but that will not be." David was about to ask, when his mother moved quickly on. "You remember its meaning?" Lulu held up her Claddagh ring on a silver chain.

"Love. And faithfulness. Always."

"Yes." His mother smiled her wan smile. "And my own love and faithfulness go with it, my beautiful boy. Your father Wallace found me, and Our Lord blessed me with a loving husband and a fine son. I'm proud of you both. When you find someone worthy, Davy, give her this with all my love and wishes for your happiness and a long life together, as my mother Hannah Virtue gave it me with hers." Lulu hung it around David's neck like a blessing, which in a way it was, and her whole face was radiant in that moment. "I will always be near you, Davy, and bring my love." Lulu Pearl Phelan looked at him with a mother's deep pride, then hugged him to her and whispered. "Now go to your father. Go to Wallace, and give him the comfort and reassurance he needs in this time of pain. Share his burden, and his love for us both."

Lulu Pearl Phelan took a shaky breath, smiled a little, settled against her pillow and closed her eyes for a moment before nodding to him in encouragement.

David didn't want to leave his mother's side. Not ever. But at last, he nodded.

He began to go, then turned back, his tears now streaming into his white mask, staining it with his care for her, and hugged Lulu Pearl Phelan, his dearest love in life and the world, with a fierceness he feared was more than she might bear. His mother returned his embrace with her own fierceness, kissed both his eyes with a reverence that seemed almost holy to David.

It was the hardest thing he would ever do in his life, but he obediently left her side for the last time.

And like Lot and his wife leaving Sodom and Gomorrah, like Wallace Phelan leaving the temptations of Mulvaney's *shebeen* behind him, fighting the urge to look back, David departed his mother Lulu Pearl Phelan.

There was the salt, but it was in his tears.

As he slowly closed her door behind him forever, David heard a sharp metallic impact and skittering on the polished wood of the bedroom floor. His mother had cast away her drunken, abusive, delinquent father's brass Customs uniform button in anger and disgust, and it was lost under the heavy dresser.

Lulu Pearl Phelan's Spanish Influenza got worse, and her breathing more and more laboured. In her severely weakened state, she soon developed a serious bacterial pneumonia and died of that complication early on Saturday morning in the presence of David's father and the Reverend Winthrop, while Siobhan and Mrs. Winthrop kept a silent but tearful vigil with David in their kitchen below.

By Saturday noon, against the vociferous protests of the Reverend Winthrop for the established customs of their Methodism, Siobhan decreed a traditional Irish wake for Lulu Pearl. Their cousin set about organizing the participation of the Lincoln Road Methodist Church, the Phelan household, their Sandwich West community, and Wallace and David's specific roles and responsibilities. The Reverend Winthrop tried religious reason and solemn argument: "I know it is a grave time of grief and some understandable confusion for you all, Siobhan, but this is not our way and a popish Catholic practice…"

Siobhan Bryant launched herself abruptly forward from her chair to confront the Reverend Winthrop with a violent, murderous look of a kind David had never seen before contorting his cousin's gentle features. She slapped the Reverend's broad face with the sharp sound of flesh striking softer flesh at the speed of a rattlesnake.

Winthrop pushed clumsily back and away in such alarm that his chair's front legs rose six inches off the floor. Siobhan leaned even closer into his reddened face. "The confusion is your own, Reverend! No-one else's! It is an Irish practice, and Lu is my dearest cousin, my intimate friend, my loving nurse, and a greater soul under Heaven and God's grace than us all. You will *not* fail to announce the wake from your pulpit tomorrow morning and may yourself visit Lu in state with others of the congregation, who will surely attend in numbers not seen before. I shall do all the rest required to be sure it is done right, and with the reverence and respect Lulu Pearl is worthy of."

But the Reverend Winthrop still blustered at this challenge to his authority, was still reluctant and about to continue his protestations.

Siobhan's hands flashed abruptly forward in an Irish banshee's assault, gripped both Winthrop's wrists, and sank in her witch's claws with a violence that made the Reverend cringe and cry out with the agony.

"Reverend Winthrop, I advise you sincerely and deeply, do not dare to set yourself against me in this, now or at any time in the future, or you will most seriously regret that opposition. Do I make myself perfectly clear? Am I crystal?"

The Reverend flinched back, cried out again in pain and alarm, and looked to Mrs. Winthrop for her intervention and support. There was neither. Her own face set in solemn agreement, his wife nodded once, and Siobhan slowly relaxed her grip and released the Reverend Winthrop to begin his assigned part in the process of the Irish wake with his Lincoln Road Methodist Church congregation.

Through it all, David's father sat beside him, sat in silence, observed it unfold and let his tea go cold. He did reach down to hold David's hand in his lap.

"But the funeral arrangements?" the Reverend spluttered. "The service? The preparation of the body? The burial? How long will it all last?"

"You'll not involve yourself, sir, apart from your religious duties and ceremony. I'll be dealing with the interment men and all such," Siobhan declared. "And Lulu Pearl's laying-out and her wake will last as long as it takes for those that have the need and want to attend her, and bless themselves in Lu's presence."

"But ... but surely you see that the remains must be properly attended to and prepared by those whose job—"

Siobhan thrust herself forward again and the Reverend Winthrop blanched and drew back. Again.

"Remains, is it? Remains?" Siobhan Bryant stared the man down with a disdain tinged with pity and utter disgust. Even David started back at the dripping acid in his cousin's tone as she spoke. "There are no remains here, Reverend. None! And all company present and to come would do well to remember it. Lulu Pearl will not lie alone, naked and revealed before strangers, in a cold grey basement, and them filling her veins and body with their poisons. Her place was here, with her family and friends who loved her in this life, and it's here with us still who love her in death. I will now speak with Mrs. Winthrop."

Again, the Reverend's wife nodded at him, an abrupt dismissal that surprised the man of God.

Thus the Reverend Winthrop did as he was bid, and more—immediately assembling all the Lincoln Road Methodist Church elders to relate the news and the plan, deal with any objections, and prevailed on his willing and energetic wife to do the same for her church women's groups, as well as her contacting other Methodist congregations and their Women's Christian Temperance Union chapters.

David's father, too, went along solemnly and without murmur, and Siobhan set Wallace Phelan to making the necessary telephone calls from the lengthy list she made up of friends, distant relations, and interested parties from the Windsor community, including the African Church where Lulu Pearl had offered her services and support in the Spanish flu pandemic. David moved his own chair beside Wally and checked off the names as they were called, and could not recognize his father's voice at the end of the long hours.

After his phone calls, Wallace Charles Phelan hugged his son closely and then retreated silently to his carpenter's workshop below. David soon heard the familiar sounds of sawing and hammering that would last for all three nights of Lulu Pearl Phelan's traditional Irish wake.

18 Cuimhneachán
Remembrance

If the two months following his father's moral redemption after Mulvaney's Tavern were the happiest, the three endless days and lonely
nights of Lulu Pearl Phelan's traditional Irish wake were by far the
strangest, the most disturbing.

David had later explained to his beloved Norah McGee that he
found the keening and crying of the succession of female mourners
standing at his mother's side the most unsettling. But only at first.
Siobhan, his cousin Mair, and Mrs. McCrae had tenderly bathed
his beloved Lulu Pearl, washed and carefully arranged her faded red
hair, added just a brush of makeup, and dressed her in a starched and
pristine white nightdress and dainty silk slippers of the same colour.

Mair had surprised David and her mother by insisting she must
help with Lulu Pearl's preparation, now that she was old enough
to assume the family responsibility. When the three women carried
Lulu's body solemnly down from her bedroom to carefully lay her on
the parlour table, it was Mair who spread the white linen cloth and
placed the white satin pillow under his mother's head, and lovingly
arranged her hair. All three were crying softly. Then Mair slipped
away and out to the backyard, and returned a few minutes later
holding a neat bouquet of his mother's wild white lily-of-the-val-
ley, with its deep green, heart-shaped leaves, and placed it in Lulu's
hands after Siobhan had folded them over her breast. The four-point

flowers were certainly past their best season, but his mother had always loved them.

"Yes. A wee bit of the Irish green," his father finally spoke in approval.

Mrs. McCrae carefully placed a silver holder with three tall white candles at Lulu Pearl's head, then walked to the chair at the side of his mother's bier while David and his father watched. "I'll be sitting first." The adults must have silently agreed because Mrs. McCrae took up her position in the hand-carved, polished wood chair and began to knit with a soft clicking of needles.

For those three days and nights, David marvelled at the Irish women's solemn care of his mother. Lulu Pearl Phelan was never alone, never out of someone's loving sight, the flowers were always fresh and carefully arranged, and the tall white candles always burning, softening his mother's now relaxed and distinctive features.

And as was the Irish custom for ages, all clocks in the house were stilled and timeless, and all mirrors draped in black.

"I think we're ready, Wallace." At nine o'clock on Monday morning, Siobhan gathered David and his father, and Garrett and the girls, around Lulu Pearl. All were neatly dressed in their Sunday best, but wearing black cloth armbands sewn by Mrs. McCrae. One by one the sombre Phelan family joined hands around Lulu Pearl's bier. Siobhan watched and waited until the circle of family was complete, then bent her head forward and began a low sound in her chest—so low that David wasn't sure it was a sound at all—and slowly raised her head in time with the pitch of her voice until it was a shrill cry of grief sent Heavenward, and made him afraid with its insistent power and depth of feeling. Mair then took up the keening in her clear adolescent voice, and even her younger sisters looked on Lulu Pearl and slowly added their child's sweetness.

"e-e-e-e-E-E-E! e-e-e-e-E-E-E! e-e-e-e-E-E-E!"

Siobhan's hand vibrated with her effort and squeezed David's own. The apprehension slowly departed his mind and body, and he returned his cousin's pressure in his own support. David had never understood so deeply before: this was family, his family, and he would always have their love and support, and offer them his in return.

He smiled through his tears.

"e-e-e-e-E-E-E! e-e-e-e-E-E-E!" The sweet female voices rose and fell, rose and fell, in a quavering communal rhythm that washed David with love and longing. The keening went on and on, and David felt his own body responding in sympathy, like it was its own natural instrument. He began to sway from side to side in time with the rest.

But on his other side, he felt Wallace Phelan's hand remaining unexpectedly cold and slack, causing David to almost lose his grip. Until his father, too, gave up his private grief, a husband's grief for his darling wife now lost to him forever. Out of the corner of his eye, David saw Wallace Charles Phelan's heavy head sink and his broad chest begin to heave with the emotion he'd fought so hard to repress, when it's release and acknowledgement was his best response to grief. Wallace Charles Phelan at last raised his eyes and voice in turn and gave a deep high groan, like seasoned wood strained beyond its limit to bear: "Oh, Lu! Lu! Lu!" Now the strength of his father's grip made David gasp, but the hand began to warm in his.

In that awful and beautiful moment of realization and release, David could grieve his mother, and could begin to forgive his father.

He slowly grew aware of the tears standing out on the faces of those family around him, but oddly, not his own falling from his cheeks onto the white linen covering Lulu Pearl. On the mantle in front of David, the big parlour clock's usual metallic ticking was silent in sympathy, and the wide-angled parlour mirror, draped in the black cloth of the armbands, was like a bowing head. This was Lulu Pearl Phelan's household and always would be. David had taken Mair and the black cloths around the whole house earlier that morning, and shown her every clock, every mirror, even the ancient ones in his father's workshop. His cousin had taken an appropriate length of the black mourning material and draped each in solemn ceremony.

How satisfying it felt now to David to let the insistent ticking of his bedroom alarm clock run down into silence like a dying animal, the simple power of it, stilling the measure of its metallic beats. Stopping time. Lengthening the moment to take in the great affect of his beloved mother's passing. He nodded, and Mair added the black cloth to cover it.

"e-e-e-e-E-E-E! e-e-e-e-E-E-E!" the women continued.

Now, the hot ball of pain, anger, fear, and resentment, and all the other emotions growing huge in David's gut for the last week rose up, and he was retching it out, so that Siobhan and his father held him up and took the weight of it as family.

"Ah-h-h-h-h-h-uh! It's not fair! Not fair!"

David twisted in their hands in his rage and screamed and screamed his protest to God and the Heavens who had allowed it. It was all accepted, all accommodated by the loving embraces on either side of him, and given back in fullest measure by the familiar voices around him. Then David could cry steadily, take their comfort, and let the women's keening voices begin to draw out the depths of his pain.

David kept staring at the living room mantelpiece and stilled parlour clock above it, at the polished wood bat case with its refurbished glass front. Yes, it was Tyrus Raymond Cobb's hand-carved, chestnut-oak bat. Yet David's mind's eye instead called up Mulvaney's *shebeen* on that fateful night, and the vivid image of his determined mother, wielding its heavy weight in defence of her family, her faith, and her honour.

It was Lulu Pearl Phelan's bat forever after.

The traditional Irish wake's prolonged wailing wound down into silence after a time. When David looked upon his loving mother lying on her white-linen-draped bier before him, he saw her too-short life in every line and shadow of her small, heart-shaped face and pointed chin. When he looked at his cousin Siobhan, she was smiling down on him with watery blue eyes. And David could at last smile back, a little. In that instant of revelation, David knew the unbreakable bond between Siobhan and Lulu, and that he would always be warm and blessed in the love and embrace of his Phelan family, and share that same bond of blood.

"Now the *Cuimhneachán*, 'The Remembrance.'"

Siobhan took up the Phelan family Bible from the mantelpiece with slow ceremony and opened it at a place she'd previously marked. At first David expected his cousin was about to read a special Biblical passage, but he was mistaken. What Siobhan was looking down upon was a careful notation in black India ink on the back of an illustration from the life of Jesus Christ. The Saviour stood on a wide rock with his arms open and looked out over his gathered followers waiting respectfully, his face shining with love. But the followers had shrunk back, their own arms raised in shock and awe at their Lord Jesus's unanticipated return from death and the afterlife on the cross of his crucifixion. "This is what our beloved Lulu Pearl wanted to say to us all, her dearest family, before her sudden passing from this veil of tears."

Siobhan began bravely, struggled to retain her composure, but her voice shook with sorrow and grief near the end, and yet she was smiling through it all despite her tears.

My most beloved Phelan Family:

Do not grieve. Do not blame. Do not regret. But consider I am not gone. I only wait and watch a little beyond your lives and am warmed by what I see. What we have shared, we share still. The precious names I called you in Life: Husband, Son, Aunt, Cousins, all of my loves, I call you now, and it gladdens me. The names you called me, call me still: Wife, Mother, Niece, Cousin, Love. When you talk to me, do it in our old accustomed way, and I will do the same to you. Nothing important has changed. Your hands will always be warm in mine and draw you to my heart, as through the years and the Veil of Death my mother's hands drew me. Remember the secrets we kept together, the fond touches, the times of strain and doubt, the silly laughter, the small offences, all that made us human in each other's eyes. Lay me to my rest with those same fond hands I know so well. Then find out your different lives in the confidence of our unity in love, in blood and in faith, and in the sacrifice of our Lord and Saviour Jesus Christ, anointed of God.

Be cheerful. And visit when you have the need. But most of all, my precious, precious family, until we meet again in Jesus: Be at Peace.

Siobhan reverently closed and returned the Bible quietly to the mantelpiece where it would now remain. At last, even David's father could try a wan smile to overlook them all. When Siobhan turned and spoke softly again, David knew he could love his precious cousin almost as deeply as his mother.

"Lulu Pearl's guests are waiting on us and our hospitality. Garrett, please open the front door, leave it open and welcome them warmly. Wallace, David, please seat yourselves on the receiving chairs here in front of Lulu Pearl and welcome them warmly as they pay their respects to Lu and may offer a few words of condolence. Mair, you and your sisters will prop open our back door, make sure the chairs and tables are ready and waiting in the yard, and help me with the food in the kitchen before taking the trays, plates and dishes out to serve to them."

Now Siobhan looked at each of them one by one to confirm their attention. "All have been strictly warned. All. Warned by me. More than once. But if you see drink or any sign of alcohol or drunkenness at all, do nothing, say nothing. Come to me immediately, and I'll sort the bastards out."

David now became aware of the voices of the large crowd of people waiting respectfully at the front door of their Phelan household, as if he'd come back from a long, long journey. Sorrow, grieving, yes, but also a deep love and hope. He had expected it at first to be quiet and solemn, as it would be in their Lincoln Road Methodist Church. But instead, surprising to him, there was exactly the warm cheer and goodwill in their guests' assorted voices that his mother had so insistently requested, and David found he wasn't offended.

It was only the beginning of his many surprises.

19 Sunlight

Mr. and Mrs. McCrae, with Roddy and Deirdre, were first through the door, but David didn't recognize the slim older man with them. They all stood beside Lulu Pearl Phelan with bowed heads for long silent moments. Finally, Mrs. McCrae reached out a hand and placed it on Lulu's right shoulder for more long moments. Her lips moved in a heartfelt prayer David couldn't quite hear distinctly, but ended with Mrs. McCrae dabbing a lace handkerchief against the corners of her eyes, then finally stepping softly back with a last bow of her head. The rest of the crowd waited patiently in a line some distance away and kept a respectful silence now. Further out the front door voices rose and fell in a manner David now found as soothing as the family's keening, with their neighbourly conversations and laughter now paused in this silent witness.

Roddy's mother came over with the slim man David didn't know at her side.

"Wallace, Davy, I will never in my life be half the neighbour, the care-giver, the woman of faith, the wife, and the mother your Lulu Pearl was. It is our great loss and Heaven and the Angels of the Lord's blessed gain."

"Thank you, Patsy, thank you from our hearts," his father said and embraced her warmly for a moment. "Lulu and David and I owe you a great debt we can never fully repay, for all your neighbourly care and consideration of us in this time of deepest sorrow." David looked suddenly up at his father in some surprise. It was the first time he could remember being called David, not Davy or boyo and such by his father. It felt different, strangely different. But then, so did he, and would continue to feel so into the life ahead of him, whatever it might bring.

"It's as close to grace as I'll be comin' on God's green earth for as long as I may live, Wallace."

"And I also, Patsy, thank you."

She then put a gentle hand on David's right shoulder and squeezed it. "And how are you faring through all this, Davy? I cannot imagine it, but know it is certain hard, especially at your young age."

David fully met her concerned look with tears anxious to flow. He held them back with a concerted effort of will. "It's hard, I guess."

"It is surely that, my boy, and I and my family are the sorrier for it. But you have your mother's stout heart beating in you, and her example shining before you now to guide you always. Know that I've made Lulu Pearl's favourite recipes for roast leg of lamb and her rich sour cream coffee cake, but they'll never be as good as those from her own hands. And remember always, Davy, I'll be having you and Wallace over for proper suppers too, when Siobhan needs some blessed relief." Then Patsy looked fondly down, bent, and kissed David softly on the head.

"Thank you, Mrs. McCrae, really." She nodded solemnly, and now pulled the strange slim man forward. He'd been very patient beside her, standing quietly with head bowed in respect of the occasion and condolences.

"This is Derint Killan. Derint, Wallace and David Phelan, husband and son to Mrs. Lulu Pearl Phelan here beside us." The slight man looked to be in his seventies at least, with his shaggy grey hair hanging, and wouldn't meet their eyes directly, but only nodded politely, holding a worn black case close. "Old Derint doesn't say much with his tongue, but he's for certain sure a dab hand with the bow and fiddle, and lets them do his talking."

The little man looked like what David imagined a spry leprechaun out of Irish legend might—a small red face with round cheeks, a point of a nose and white wisps of hair in trailing sideburns. And with something mischievous playing at the corners of the neat bow of lips, Derint Killan finally gave them a quick look and wee smile of acknowledgement. His suit was old, dark, and badly worn, in both senses of the word, and might once truly have been green. Derint said nothing at all, but did reach out to give each of their hands a firm shake. The leprechaun then deftly climbed onto one of the high stools Siobhan must have brought up from the basement workshop and placed in a near corner. David guessed she'd anticipated or even arranged the fiddler's arrival.

Derint Killan took out his fiddle and bow from their case, both as worn with age and use as he was, but the well-plucked strings still resilient and responsive to his slightest touch. The solemn leprechaun adjusted the tuning and began a slow, soulful Celtic lament that seeped quietly into David's mind and body, and softly touched his heart.

Roddy and Deirdre Bryant looked on, both touched and awkward, as well, in the present situation. The mournful sound of Irish fiddling was exactly the solemn sense and emotion Siobhan intended Derint Killan to inspire for Lulu Pearl's traditional Irish wake. And like David, his two friends were neither quite sure how to act appropriately, nor certain what might need to be said, beyond their quiet looks and "sorrys" to him. But soon the two and their father, Garrett, did finally find their own longer expressions to give heartfelt condolences, and shook hands with both David and his father, who smiled kindly back on them. Heads bowed, the three McCraes continued on to the bustling kitchen and the welcome promise of food, friends and good company.

Now, Mrs. Patsy McCrae stood up straight beside the fiddler with her hands folded and began to sing. Her voice had a rough edge, but it didn't matter, and soon other friends, family, members of the

the Women's Christian Temperance Union and the Lincoln Road Methodist Church congregation in the room joined in, even as they moved gravely by Lulu Pearl and paid their respects.

> *"Do not stand at my grave and weep,*
> *I am not there ... I do not sleep.*
> *I am the thousand winds that blow.*
> *I am the diamond glints on snow.*
> *I am the sunlight on ripened grain.*
> *I am the gentle autumn rain..."*

Next, it was Mrs. Aviva Kirsner, Dr. Gerald Kirsner's wife, who arrived at their door, and then appeared before Wally and David to pay her respects. Mrs. Kirsner was carrying a long, beautifully braided challah loaf, and her husband Gerald behind her, a wide platter of more than two dozen delicious smelling latkes.

"Mr. Phelan, I have baked a loaf of our fresh Jewish challah bread for this solemn occasion. I hope it is to your liking?" Wallace Phelan smiled his pleasure at the sight and inclined his head.

"It is, Mrs. Kirsner, most welcome, thank you. And I, David, my whole Phelan family owe your husband Gerald here a great and lasting debt. Great. And Phelans remember."

"To say I wish I could have done more for Lulu Pearl sounds so common, so pedestrian, Wallace," Dr. Kirsner placed his hand on David's father's arm. "But I surely do. We've offered our most heartfelt prayers for Lulu Pearl and all your family at our synagogue..."

"Thank you, sincerely, Gerald. Your exceptional care of Lu in her suffering greatly eased her pain, and our own. We Irish have a bit of wisdom to offer in these solemn moments: 'God has one mouth and many ears.' David, would you show the Kirsners to Siobhan in the kitchen and see they are well taken care of?"

David was older in that moment, wiser. "Of course. And thank you too for helping my mother all you could, Doctor. This way please."

When David returned, there was some commotion at the door that interrupted the solemnity of the occasion. Wally got up to attend to it, but Patsy McCrae pulled his father back to go herself. "No, Wallace, this is your place, none other."

David soon recognized Windsor Police Constable Carrick, though he was not wearing his uniform. Behind Carrick, just outside the door, stood a tall Negro man and his wife, with two young girls hugging fearfully to their legs at the argument erupting around them. Carrick was lurching and unsteady on his feet, angry at the wall of stern men forming in front of him.

Mrs. Patsy McCrae stood in front of the policeman, hands on her hips and leaning into his face, like God's own Angel of Vengeance, and then gave him a stout shove back for his recalcitrance. "Take yourself off now, Carrick, you sodden fool, and let respectable people enter this house of sorrow." Patsy gave Carrick a second, even greater shove back, and slapped his face, reddening it more. When the drunken police constable protested further and tried to re-enter, the wall of stern-faced men tightened again to block his way. In short order two of the brawniest grabbed Carrick's arms, shouted to clear a path ahead and propelled him out the door to go crashing down the Phelan family's front steps. They waited on the top step, fists doubled and ready, until the policeman cursed them all, promised his certain revenge, but finally took himself off.

Derint Killan had briefly broken into a lively Irish reel to accompany the violent action, then returned to a more subdued lament. His audience nodded its approval and laughed quietly.

Then Mrs. McCrae asked the other visitors to stand aside for a moment, on seeing the Negro family beginning an uncertain retreat from their place on the doorstep. She introduced herself smiling and led the Negro man and his family directly to David's mother. All four bowed their heads in respect while the husband spoke in soft tones David supposed were prayers of condolence. The tall Negro then directed his family to David and Wally. At more hesitation, Wallace

Phelan stood up, reached out his right hand and persuaded the man to shake it, followed by his wife's. "Thank you for coming, sir and madam."

"We've never met, Mr. Phelan. I'm the Reverend Josiah Washington of the African Church, and this is my wife, Abigail, and my daughters, Jenna and Louise. Mrs. Phelan and her cousin Siobhan were of great help and service to our church, comforting our sick and dying when the prejudice of the majority might have kept them away. That this dreadful plague should claim her now.... I can only believe that Our Lord keeps close those souls he loves best. Mrs. Phelan is surely one, and we offer our sincere blessings and condolences to you and your family."

David's father stood stood straighter, bowed his head in acknowledgement and managed a smile. "And my family thanks you, Reverend Washington. So it appears, with Lu. And I suspect it was not easy to bring you and yours forward here this day." The Washington family remained close and Jenna and Louise shy. But Wallace Phelan shook the hand of each of them, even the girls. David smiled and did the same, and the two sisters finally managed a small smile in return.

"I'm sorry for the trouble before you and your African community. Lulu Pearl kept her Methodist faith, a warm and welcoming Christian home, and was a great believer in the brotherhood of all men and women under God."

"A noble sentiment, surely, Mr. Phelan. Thank you, sir."

"And our thanks again to you all for joining us here in our time of mourning. There is ample food and refreshment in the yard behind awaiting you and your family. My son David here will be most pleased to—" But the Reverend and his wife Abigail exchanged a look David couldn't interpret, as he smiled in encouragement and stood waiting to lead the Washingtons through to the yard.

"Thank you, Mr. Phelan. Another time, perhaps?"

"You are my family's valued guests, Reverend. Be assured, all are welcome here." The minister shot a quick glance back out the door as if to contradict David's father.

"With respect, sir, I must decline." A knowing look passed between the two men. Wallace Phelan nodded his understanding, and allowed Reverend Washington to lead his family back out through the door. David also understood.

"There walks a better man than I am, David. How much courage must it have taken to come among us here this day with so much prejudice abroad against his people. Remember Reverend Washington's example, for Lu's sake."

David bowed his head in agreement. "I will, Father."

Hours passed almost unnoticed, with Wally and David receiving sympathetic guests and their heartfelt words. Some of them David recognized from the Lincoln Road Methodist Church, the neighbourhood, the Temperance marches, and Dumfries Fine Ladies Wear. But many more were strangers. It left him in awe. Had he ever really known his mother, and her works and influence in their community and further afield?

Three times, David and his father were practically dragged out to the kitchen by Mair, who insisted they eat and refresh themselves with cups of thick potato soup, crusty loaves of bread and sweet rolls, cold roast lamb, chicken, and ham. Each time Mair stood by to make sure they did. How David loved his older cousin in these moments! Again, David knew the women from Lincoln Road Methodist and the Temperance marches and the surrounding neighbourhood, but others offering up a variety of salads and casseroles and cold beverages, or beginning to scrape and wash the earthenware bowls, the finer china plates and tableware, and cutlery, were strangers to him. Yet they greeted him warmly each time, laughing and chatting together as they filled the plates, and the many people took them out to long trestle tables in the Phelan backyard. All the looks upon David as he sat there eating were tender and kindly.

Siobhan had brought in two geese and three ducks from her husband Garrett's basement larder and had kept them warm on the stove in turn, even making soup from their naked carcasses. David remembered Lulu Pearl doing the same with the freshly shot and hung birds his father brought home into the fall and winter each year. It all helped to reassure him, yet made him sad with the memories at the same time.

"Ah, David, me boyo, I've saved the best of the drumsticks for your dinner with a wee helping of your mother's spiced apple dressing and sweet tea. You must keep up your strength for the duration of this, me lad."

"Thank you, Siobhan. They're my favourites." David was genuinely touched by this gesture.

"And after almost eight long years, now, don't I know it, little man?" A large metal soup-keeper contained steaming black tea while another held strong coffee. Chocolate milk, hot dogs, and corn on the cob with salt and pats of butter, were served to the surprising number of children of all ages who had appeared with their parents, after the end of the working day. It had been mostly elderly people and those not working shifts for those first few long hours at his mother's side. "Mair's out behind waiting for you, David, and has saved your place at the table. So be off with you now."

Their Phelan family backyard, not a small area, was filled to over-flowing with people of all ages and dress, some sitting and eating, others standing in small tight groups, but all laughing, all talking, all seeming to enjoy themselves. More than a few were already turning a shade of brick red from exposure to the afternoon sun.

"I have your place there, Davy." Mair pulled him to the table nearest the back stoop, his father's Gehenna, his Purgatory and former place of exile, and sat him down on the end of the bench. Then Mair surprised him. "Here, boyo, take some of this up your nose, and then have a wee pull on the pipe."

"Uh? But what is it?" David stared at the small dish of brown powder and the long curving white pipe.

"It's a bit of the snuff, powdered tobacco, and a traditional Irish clay pipe of regular tobacco to go with it. It's an offering made to all manly guests like yourself, boyo, in respect of Lulu Pearl and her life. It's like this." Mair mimed taking a bit of the brown powder from the silver dish and inhaling it up her nose. Now David felt the eyes of the people around him watching, waiting, so he did—and immediately sneezed loudly and repeatedly! He reddened with profound embarrassment, while everyone else roared with cheers and laughter around him, patting him on the back, even Mair.

"That's what's supposed to happen, bucko!" She then smiled with mischief, took up her own pinch of the snuff, inhaled it, sneezed, and giggled like a drain. Now David was laughing too, at himself, at Mair's daring, and at those around him who nodded and winked at him in sympathy. "Now this, bucko!" Mair proffered the thin white length of the clay pipe. David took it with some reluctance, was careful on the inhale, but the thick blue pipe smoke filled his throat and stung his eyes, and he doubled over in a fit of coughing, with the same humorous results all around him.

"I think that will be ... uh, enough for now, Mair," David managed to croak out. Mrs. Balleymoney, helping to serve and take away dishes, frowned at David and his cousin, and shook her head in disgust at the two young cousins and the tobacco. Mair ignored her, shot David another mischievous smile and continued her rounds with the snuff and pipe as new people arrived by the minute.

David was finally able to take the first bite of his savoury goose drumstick and discovered he was ravenous. He finished his plate in record time, and Mair must have been watching because she was there at his last bite with a second plate.

"Irish wakes give prodigious appetite, Davy. So, eat up because..."

"...I'll need all my strength?"

"True enough, and none of your cheek, little man." David still didn't like the term any better from Mair.

"I'm not little. And you're not much bigger than me, little woman." Mair shook her head and laughed.

"And do you think I don't know that, boyo?"

David had never been this serious with Mair. "Now you sound just like your mother, Mair."

"And there's a compliment if ever I heard one! And so do you, me bucko, with your own blessed marm's cheek. It's the way of it in Irish families. And we're both blessed by it." Mair bent and kissed David full on the mouth for a long moment, then was gone, laughing, before David could recoil or say more. The unexpected pleasure at the soft touch of Mair's lips on his own was more revelation than surprise.

David surprised even himself by finishing his second plate, as Mair had predicted, and tried to sort through his complex feelings. His cousin Mair was different somehow these last weeks. Noticeably different. David thought about it and finally concluded he must be too.

David wondered again at all the people Lulu Pearl had drawn to her. What struck him then, were the many differences. Dr. Kirsner and his wife Aviva and two sons were at another table, but Mrs. Kirsner got up periodically and cleared dishes from guests' tables, and made rounds with fresh tea and coffee and smiles, working alongside Mair and Siobhan and the other women as if they had never been strangers. Paulie from the Penn Central Railway switching station was still there too, laughing and smoking with a group of men. And no *poteen* in sight, a tribute to the strength of Lulu Pearl's admonitions against spirituous liquors—her phrase, even in death—and to the wicked sharp edge of Siobhan's acid tongue.

Although, as David would later learn from his friend Gar, a tall keg of beer, bottles of Walker's Special Old Whisky, and the inevitable *poteen had* been set up in the McCrae's garage, not far away, to which many of the men and no few women, retired after paying their solemn respects and eating here at the wake.

"And didn't each man and woman there drink a toast to your Ma, and never tired of hearing the story of Mulvaney's and Lulu's bat," Siobhan said later. How had she known? David felt he should mind that, but found that he didn't. And did Mrs. McCrae know, as well? She must have. What else didn't he know, David wondered?

The Irish leprechaun and fiddler came out to the yard with his plate piled high, and when David looked back, the food had disappeared, as if by Celtic magic. While David stared, Gar Langlois' father began to shout: "Derint! Derint! Derint!" Others joined in. A chair was promptly set atop a table, and Derint raised up to sit astride it and send his lively Celtic melodies out over the yard and beyond. No laments this time. The music was energetic and Irish quick, and soon had people clapping in time, singing along, linking arms and dancing jigs, and shouting out more requests.

Wally at last came out and took his own pinch of the snuff and inhale of the Irish clay pipe from Mair nearby. David laughed when his father sneezed mightily as expected, and Wally clapped him on the back and joined him. His mood seemed lighter. "Rest in the sure and certain knowledge Lu will be enjoying this, David, as she smiles down on us from Heaven's verge."

"No *poteen*?"

"That too, to be certain sure, but for certain the respectful and lively celebrations of her family, her friends and her neighbours, in celebration of the life she lived and the example she set."

"I know, Papa. I'm a little happy, but mostly very sad."

His father nodded solemnly in sympathy and understanding

"How are you holding up, then, boyo?"

"It's not what I expected."

"No. I believe that."

"And calling me 'David' and 'little man?' And Mair kissed me. On my mouth."

His father reared back and looked intently. "Did she now? There'll be one for the boys to watch and be wary of."

"Like Siobhan." Wally took a drink of his black coffee, and nodded.

"More like her every day."

"Does that mean I'll be like Mother?" Now his father's cup stopped midway to his lips.

"And where did that come from?"

"Mair thinks I'm like her sometimes."

"I should hope you are."

"But I like baseball and Ty Cobb and learning the duck calls. I want to go hunting with you and Garrett. And make things in the workshop."

"Then I guess a bit of your old Da slipped in somewhere."

"I hope it did, Papa." Wallace Charles Phelan hugged him and David was suddenly serious with him.

"The last time I talked with Mother, before ... before the wake ... she said you blame yourself. Is that true?" Now his father looked away, and the noise around them seemed more distant.

"I'll not deny it, David. A part of me does."

"Mother forgave you."

"Lu did. But can I ever forgive myself?"

"She also said that too. And that I must also—"

"Wallace! I believe you're the one to handle this." Siobhan had inserted herself between them and pointed at a knot of people by the stoop, growing larger by the second. "Garrett is at the front door but he was at a loss as to what to do."

Suddenly, David stared in disbelief.

"Are they...?" Wally saw where David was looking, and a dark shadow passed over his face. His father seemed to shrink back into himself for a moment, then set his face with firm purpose and stood.

"Yes, David. Those are the two saloon women from Mulvaney's. And that's Mulvaney himself with them." Wally shook his head and the laugh this time was bitter. "And I'm guessin' more than a few men here are a little nervous, as am I. I'll see to it, Siobhan."

David had recognized the older, red-haired woman from the saloon, and the younger woman who had come down from upstairs with Constable Carrick and had seemed only half-dressed to his eyes. Mulvaney was short and wide, with a great brown beard and moustache spread across his face and chin. All three looked uncertain, and a small crowd had formed around them, growing quickly. Almost all women. Almost all Temperance. Almost all angry. Derint's fiddling stumbled into expectant silence.

"Stay put here, Davy. Siobhan, you'll need to help me with these other women." Wallace Charles Phelan put down his black coffee with some force, then surprised David by taking the plate of snuff and slim white Irish pipe from Mair, who stood staring in silence beside her mother. But Wally looked back. "No, on second thought, David, you come along with me. Now."

But it was Siobhan who shook her head, extended both arms aggressively, and forcefully cleared the way with her unflinching look and rough shouldering. David's older cousin had heated words with the Windsor Temperance Women that caused them to move reluctantly aside for his father and himself. David felt their heavy eyes on them, and the looks were wary, some judgmental. The two Mulvaney's saloon women in the centre of it all now seemed small and pale outside of their pub and, in the bright sunlight, supremely vulnerable. Maybe they don't get out very much in the daytime, David thought.

After a moment, Mulvaney pushed forward and spoke over the crowd for all to hear.

"I told them it was a daft idea, Phelan. Daft and risky. We know we're not wanted here." This set the two saloon women to flinching back, hesitating, and then murmuring their quiet acquiescence. Now the two women looked down at their simple, ordinary shoes and turned to leave quickly. Up close, David was aware of how plain, how vulnerable they looked, lacking their makeup and stiff hair and bright jewellery. Even the younger blonde one had deep lines of stress and worry around her eyes, and the left side of her mouth seemed to droop.

"No! It is NOT! Not the case, Mulvaney! NOT a daft idea!" His father smiled invitingly and nodded at the two women. "You are welcome here on this solemn day of celebration and remembrance."

Wallace Phelan stepped in front of Mulvaney, forcing him aside, and politely held out the snuff and the long white pipe to the turning women. His father's voice when it came was inviting, steady and certain.

"I'd be most honoured, ladies, most honoured, if each of you would take a bit of the snuff and the Irish tobacco here." Wally smiled, nodded in encouragement, and bowed slightly. "'Tis an old Irish custom in the welcoming of guests." Now the two women exchanged shy looks. "Please."

The older red-haired one finally nodded, took a puff on the slim pipe, and inhaled a pinch of the snuff after his father laid it on the back of her right hand. She sneezed mightily for the curious crowd, yet her laughter that followed was nervous in front of these silent onlookers around her. The younger blonde woman did the same, with the same result, and, after some hesitation, so did Mulvaney himself.

Wallace Charles Phelan stood tall, looked around to those assembled in their yard and raised his eyes and deep voice to the crowd.

"Hear me now! Hear me! All of you! There will be no casting of stones in the precincts of this, Lulu Pearl Phelan's house and home, on this day of all days. None! *All* ... are welcome here! All!"

David couldn't see his father's face, but his jaw was hard-set, and the older Mulvaney's bar woman was looking at him intently. At last Wally nodded to her in acceptance and she did the same back. "Mr. Killan? Something lively, if you please!"

The Irish fiddling started up, and Siobhan intently eyed the other women for a few more moments, until they moved away, talking in undertones. "And would you now excuse us for a moment, Mulvaney?" His father was not asking. Siobhan grabbed the saloon owner's left arm and pulled the big man over to the railroad switchman Paulie's group, who took him in. But his cousin's face was unreadable to David.

Then Wally put a hand on his shoulder. "And this is my only son, David."

David quickly offered his hand, surprising himself, but the older, red-haired woman only nodded, reluctant to take it, and the younger looked down again. Neither would give a name, but the redhead spoke to his father.

"Thank you for that ... that courtesy, sir. I was afraid the worst would happen."

Wally nodded his understanding. "I meant what I said. And we're all of us afraid at times."

The woman smiled, as if embarrassed by this honesty. "Even your wife?"

David surprised himself by answering her. "Yes. I was with my mother. We were both afraid that night. Mama said she understood ... about you being at Mulvaney's, I mean."

This brought a painful look to the woman's eyes, so different from the one David remembered. Her face seemed drained of all life, all hope. She took the younger blonde's hand. "Then maybe there's still hope and some redemption in this weary world yet. We're sorry for your loss, sir."

The woman nodded at David and Wally, and they turned to leave. The younger woman had not spoken once. Siobhan appeared again beside them and led them through the staring onlookers toward the front door, marching like she bore the shield of Holy St. Patrick before her. No woman, no man, no-one, dared utter a single word of censure and risk his cousin's explosive ire.

"But they didn't have any food, Papa?"

"I know, David. I know. You finish up, while I'll be relieving Garrett at the receiving."

David would later learn from Mair that Siobhan had ordered up a generous carry bag of food and refreshments be made for the two of them, and defied any kitchen woman to protest it. Mulvaney himself would get nothing from her. Mair said she was very proud of her mother.

Wallace Charles Phelan walked heavily up the back stoop, his Purgatory. The look on his father's face was identical to the red-haired woman's a moment before.

And more than that.

When an older David thought back over these long-ago events, this was one of the moments that his father's Irishness began to leave him. The lilting rise and fall of his words. The cadence of old-country music at moments of great excitement or solemn pronouncement. The peculiar, sly dictums and hard-won wisdom of Irish generations past, an immigrant's ocean away. The grace notes of melancholy. What his mother had once called "the sparkle of emeralds falling from our Irish lips."

David sat beside the bier with Lulu Pearl from six until nine, the morning of the third and last day of her traditional Irish wake. Siobhan had been the one to convince Wally to let David hold this solitary place, his son's place, alone with his mother. His father went silently back down to the workshop in the basement where he spent much of the nights when he wasn't sitting by Lulu Pearl in his turn. David didn't know if his father slept at all. After each solemn vigil beside his mother, David made his way quietly to his own bed, exhausted, in the evenings, and his sleeps were dreamless and deep. A blessing.

Then some time later, at midnight of the third and final day of her Irish wake, the fine white linen sheet had been wrapped carefully around Lulu Pearl Phelan by Patsy McCrae, Siobhan and Mair, shrouding his beloved mother completely, when the last time of public visitation had passed.

David, his father, Garrett, and his youngest daughters stood humbly by in witness.

David could never know the exact number of people who had arrived at the Phelan household over those three days to pay their final respects to Lulu Pearl, but it was more than he ever could have imagined. He wondered again if he ever really knew his mother.

Phelans would take it in turns to sit by Lulu Pearl's bier from midnight on, through those final hours of her wake.

The long black hearse of A. Morris and Sons Funeral Service would arrive at ten the following morning, and carry Lulu Pearl Phelan the short distance to Lincoln Road Methodist Church for her funeral service and blessing, conducted and delivered by Reverend Winthrop. And then, Lulu Pearl would be transported to the Windsor Grove Cemetery, on the west side of Howard Avenue, for the final blessing and laying to rest.

A private ceremony, Phelan family only.

David Charles Phelan had been waiting for his own final time to be alone with Lulu Pearl. Ty Cobb's hand-carved, chestnut-oak bat hung ceremonially above the mantle in front of him in its case, its broken glass replaced. Yet it was Lulu Pearl Phelan's bat now in a way it had never been Ty Cobb's. David listened to be sure the house was quiet, and that he and his beloved mother were truly alone. Even the sounds from Wally in the basement workshop had stopped, and a pale light was shining through the large parlour window, softening the hard edges of the living room.

It took a minute, now standing up beside Lulu Pearl, to work up his courage. Then David drew in a breath and tenderly unwrapped the white linen sheet from around her face and down to her hands, still holding the last of Mair's lilies, a lonely touch of the Irish green. Lulu Pearl Phelan's face, his loving mother's face, appeared carved from wax, whiter than the linen sheet and her nightdress.

But death and the pale light from the low-hanging moon, had smoothed all the lines, and Lulu looked younger than he remembered her. David had waited those three long days and nights to put his own special gift of remembrance, his *Cuimhneachán*, into her hands with the flowers, but her fingers were too stiff.

In the end David slipped his small, hand-carved basswood boy's boat with his name on it underneath Lulu Pearl's folded hands, hidden, so only the two of them would know it was there. Then David stood beside his beloved mother with his head bowed and quietly wept, after which observance he carefully rearranged the white shroud around her for the last time.

"Be the sunlight, Mama."

20 Black Barrel

It had now been seven long years since his mother, Lulu Pearl Phelan, had tragically passed out of David Charles Phelan's life, when she succumbed to the wide-spread Spanish influenza that gripped most of the world after World War I.

David would never forget that last night of Lulu Pearl's three-day, traditional Irish wake when, during his final vigil beside her bier, he had slipped his small, hand-carved wooden boat, bearing his own name, under her stiff folded white hands. "Be the sunlight, Mama," were his final words and wishes for her.

His father, Wallace Charles Phelan, had never gotten over his beloved Lulu Pearl's death and loss. As his mother had predicted to David on her deathbed, Wally blamed only and ever himself: his breaking of his Temperance Oath of Sobriety to Lulu; his betrayal of his faithfulness and marriage vows by standing next to the 'woman in red,' who was wearing his Detroit Tigers ball cap at Mulvaney's Saloon, on the night that changed their lives forever. Mulvaney's *shebeen* had been filled to the rafters with the carousing, Protestant, Loyal Orange Lodge members that Lulu Pearl despised with a passion, still vowing death to all Catholics, and continuing Ireland's old 'Troubles' in their new Dominion of Canada.

All. All were witness to Lulu Pearl Phelan's shame, visited upon her by her wayward husband and no fault of her own. And their only son, young David Charles Phelan, standing up on the tall black iron base of the lamppost outside, and watching and hearing it all unfold through the wide widows and open doors of Mulvaney's. The huge wavy glass mirror behind the long bar shattered and falling to pieces from the shards of his father's full mug of beer when Lulu Pearl batted it out of his hands with Ty Cobb's hand-carved, chestnut-oak bat. The beautiful White Angel with Lulu Pearl's face that Wally had carved for his mother to entice her to accept his proposal of marriage, first thrust into his father's face, then laid on the bar between them as a symbol of her husband's perfidy. The 'women in red', standing beside Wallace Charles and wearing his precious Detroit Tigers official ball cap. Another kind of insult and betrayal.

David would never in his life forget his mother's words back to his father after Wally loudly ordered her to: "Be off home, woman!"

Then Lulu Pearl's instant reply and response: "Oh, I'll be off home alright, Wallace—but you'll be coming with me!" Followed immediately by the violent sight of his mother wielding Wally's hand-carved, chestnut-oak, Ty Cobb baseball bat, in an almighty roundhouse swing, to connect solidly with the left side of his father's head. The sound was … indescribable. Wally had simply vanished from David's sight.

And that was the fateful night when Wallace Charles Phelan's Irishness had begun to leave him and David cried out in fear, sorrow and growing despair.

But then, some years later, a blessed salvation for David

David Charles Phelan continually thanked God and all angels that he had been spared direct witness of his father's ultimate tragedy and death. That a welcome, much-needed and fateful mercy had been bestowed upon David. It came in the lovely and miraculous-to-his-eyes form and person of Salvation Army Grace Hospital Emergency

Nurse, Norah McGee. Protestant Irish Norah McGee, whom he met, courted and been blessed by, with her consent at last to accept his Phelan family Claddagh ring, and become his beautiful loving wife.

David still considered it a minor miracle seven years later. And Norah McGee Phelan had soon born them both a fine son, Norman George Phelan, to carry on the Phelan and McGee family traditions. And those traditions especially were love of baseball and duck hunting, and Norah's intelligence, generosity, kindness, fairness, and wise counsel to them and all around her. Norman was already following in his mother's footsteps and very proud of her and of himself, compared to other boys his age.

On the second Sunday in September, twenty-six-year-old David, and his wife Norah, with young Norman between them, attended morning services at the newly renamed Lincoln Road United Church congregation. Methodism had been incorporated into the new United Churches Union after the merger of four Protestant denominations in 1925.

After the service, the young Phelan family were moving into their new home in a neighbourhood nearby, on Moy Avenue, one block from the wide-flowing Detroit River shoreline. The original patriarchal home, established by Wallace Charles Phelan and his wife Lulu Pearl Phelan, had been sold following Lulu Pearl's early death from the Spanish flu. And not long after, the disappearance of a troubled Wallace Charles on the often-uncertain winds and waters of Lake Erie while duck hunting. The original Phelan family home on Gladstone Avenue was soaked in those sorrows and losses, and David and Norah made the difficult decision to let it go to new owners.

The move was not far, but much-loved family, friends and neighbours of long standing, took their solemn turns at the leave-taking of David, Norah and Norman. It was as much in memory of Wallace Charles and Lulu Pearl and their long-time home, as for David and his young family leaving it. A tearful Patsy McCrae, with her son Roddy and his new wife Colleen, already carrying their first child, could not seem to let them go. It was the next hardest trial of tears and leave-taking after the loss of Wally and Lulu.

Goodbyes said, the three younger Phelans drove in Wally's ancient Ford pickup truck to the Windsor Grove Cemetery and Lulu Pearl's maple- and chestnut-shaded resting place. The truck box was packed under canvas with only the most cherished furniture and small items—Lulu's sewing bench; Wally's carved duck decoys, calls, and shotguns; his parents' dark-sheened wooden bedstead, with its beautifully turned legs and carved headboard; his mother's fine Irish china; her fateful Ty Cobb baseball bat, now hers after Mulvaney's, and more. The old Phelan family house on Gladstone Avenue had sold quickly, for a good price. But David still found it disturbing, a kind of betrayal of his mother, to leave its sheltering walls. Wally had talked about selling it for a long time after his beloved Lulu Pearl's death, and never could. But when this most recent year had passed, David found his father couldn't bear the new emptiness as David and his new family acquired their own independent residence.

"I think our family's moving in after Lulu's loss helped my father," David said. "Having a woman, a wife, and a mother in the house again, and offering us their bed and rooms. And when Norman was born, having a grandson to spoil and take to Detroit Tigers baseball games."

But then, Wally was gone, and under circumstances troubling and suspicious to David.

Young Norman looked to them both at the mention of his name, and Norah ruffled his hair, drawing a laugh. "Yes, my love, but there was a profound sadness in him too," Norah said. "The way Wally looked at the Claddagh ring on my finger when he thought I didn't notice. And now this new conflict, this horrible great war again so soon after the First World War, the 'War to End All War.'"

"True enough, love. Our family lived in daily fear and consternation throughout the first, a fear as daunting as that war that provoked it."

David pulled the Ford truck into the lee of a broad overhanging maple and turned to Norah beside him. "But here's the worst of it, love—my mother never, not once, thought we'd learn any lesson from it. Now I guess Lulu was right."

David turned off the ignition, and he and Norah took Norman's hands to make the difficult journey down the rough gravel path to the broad row of weathered gravestones, and Lulu Pearl's place of rest.

"I wish so much I'd known her, David, so much." David nodded, but said nothing. Now looking at the grave, what *could* he say?

His beloved mother had been everything to him as a boy, before he met and successfully wooed Norah McGee, now his own beloved wife and mother to their child.

AT PEACE
LULU PEARL PHELAN
1890 – 1919
BELOVED WIFE
OF
WALLACE CHARLES PHELAN
1887 – 1938
GO N-ÉIRÍ AN BÓTHAR LEAT
(GOOD LUCK ON YOUR ROAD.)

"All right, Norm." Norah led their son forward with his Irish green bunch of Lulu Pearl's lily of the valley from the old Gladstone house. She stooped to place the smooth glass vase of water in front of the white cut stone, then guided Norman's hands as he put the lilies into the vase. Norm was seven years old and full of questions about the matter, exactly as David had been when a boy. In an uncanny coincidence, David had been the same age at Lulu Pearl's death. He knew questions about death were normal in a child, but the coincidence still made it eerie.

"Where is Grandpa Wally?"

David looked to Norah, and she nodded and tried to explain it once more to their son, as carefully as she could.

"Grandpa went duck hunting on Lake Erie. In the boat he built together with your father, the *Lulu Pearl*. You remember it?"

"The Evinrude?"

"Yes, that was the outboard motor Wally used. But the weather was bad, Norm, very bad. A heavy storm came up and big waves. And there must have been an accident. The boat sank, and your Grandpa Wally drowned."

"He's dead? Like Grandma Lu?"

"Yes, dear. But Wally's spirit is with Lulu's in Heaven now, and they're together once more as husband and wife forever. So, your father and I put his name on the tombstone too, and we put flowers here to remember them both."

Norm thought about this.

"But where *is* he?"

His son wasn't talking about Heaven. The trouble was, they still didn't know. David took over.

"Wooden pieces of the *Lulu Pearl* were found after the storm, washed up on the beach of Lake Erie. But not your grandfather's body, Norm."

"He's not in the ground with Grandma Lu?"

"No."

"So, Grandpa Wally's not holding the little boat with your name on it?"

On the way back to their empty Gladstone house after the memorial service for his father, David found himself telling Norm about the small boat. How he'd secretly placed his carved toy boat under his mother Lulu Pearl's stiff, clasped hands at the close of her three-day, traditional Irish wake. David still wasn't sure where that impulse came from. Just that it felt right at the time, and now would rest in his beloved mother's hands forever.

The young Phelan family left Lulu Pearl's grave and flowers behind. They walked back in solemn silence to the heavily loaded old Ford truck, and began their drive into a new house and a new life on Moy Avenue.

David couldn't yet call it their home.

"Grandpa Wally can have my toy boat like you gave yours to Grandma," Norm offered, as they pulled onto Howard Avenue. The year before, after hearing the story, his son had immediately asked for a carved wooden boat of his own—an obvious child's request, but David was still surprised by it. So much about Norman George surprised him at first, and later seemed obvious.

"The lot of new fathers." Norah had commented. And his wise, loving wife never seemed surprised.

"What about the lot of new mothers?"

"Well, bucko, when men can get pregnant, I guess you'll find out. Until then, the Creator, the Mother Goddess, in Her infinite wisdom, has made the right choice."

"So did I." David tried a sly smile.

"Oh? So, the choosing was your own, was it?"

"In your infinite wisdom, Nurse Norah McGee, you led me on to believe so." Norah laughed, and they kissed over Norm's head, causing him great embarrassment.

"An insight worthy of Peter the Great," she said.

"Interesting you should bring him up."

"I *like* bringing him up."

"Who's Peter the Great?" Norm immediately wanted to know.

"When you're a wee bit older, my lovely boy, I'll tell you about him," Norah said.

"Ah-h-h! I'm seven!"

"I remember your age, boyo, but not for a few years yet." Norm snorted in frustration.

Later that night, in their new Moy Avenue home, they quietly checked on Norm in his bedroom and exchanged delighted smiles, before retiring to the pleasures of their own.

And bringing up Peter the Great.

David and Norm had worked together at Wally's old workbench on his son's little boat. Sitting up on a high stool, Norm had sanded the white basswood with great energy, then inserted the end of the little mast, coated with carpenter's glue, into the hole David had drilled near the bow. Norm watched with great seriousness as David reached around him and carefully marked his name out in black block capitals on either side: NORMAN P. "And let's make one for Mama! And a new one for you."

Another obvious surprise.

Norah had made a great fuss over her beautiful NORAH P. three days later, when Norm presented her boat at dinner. It took almost a week, but it finally rained heavily, and Norm would not have supper until they had all three put on their slickers and "sailed" their pretty white basswood boats together in the flowing runoff along the curb, the DAVID P. bringing up the rear. "Mine's the fastest! Mine's the fastest!" Norm shouted and laughed, as he splashed along after it.

"Then don't be losing it down the drain, boyo." Norah cautioned.

The memory of sailing his own hand-carved basswood boat with Roddy and Gar, nearly two decades before, overwhelmed David Phelan. Or maybe it was that other duck boat, his father's *Lulu Pearl*, and the ominous suspicion that kept David awake and wondering at night, Norah not quite asleep beside him. And his beloved wife, always attuned and aware, must have sensed something, those nights in their old bedroom back at Gladstone Avenue—sleeping in his parents' own carved wood bed. "What's wrong, love?"

"This house. It has ... too many memories he'd said. Or maybe I've changed." David would close his eyes, and Norah would often hold him to her a long time before he slept. Norah didn't object when David suggested selling the old house and finding one that would be entirely their own, and waiting for *their* memories to be made there.

Yet, handing over the old keys to the new owners had been a deeper, more complicated ending for David than he'd anticipated. The many happy memories were still present, though bleakly overshadowed by the accumulated pains of the bad.

So the new Phelan family house on Moy Avenue, a half-block from the Detroit River, was *their* beginning, his own young family's. But David would never forget his parents and their first house together with him, their only son—or stop missing them dearly. He never, ever wanted Norm to experience a parent dying while he was still a child himself.

It turns the world upside down.

Now his son was excited by the size and expanse of the new basement, long grass-green backyard, and rough grey stucco garage, giving onto a worn cement alley behind, for parking Wally's old Ford truck. Norm constantly wanted to play catch in their long basement after supper, and practice his boy's batting and catching in the wide backyard on the weekends with David's too-large, vintage leather, Detroit Tigers baseball glove. Their new home was a full seven blocks from the Gladstone Avenue house and neighbourhood, and Patsy McCrae and friends, but still only three blocks from Norm's King Edward Public School, and two blocks from their Lincoln Road United Church. Norah had been firm on those geographic conditions, and David knew better than to go against his formidable Irish wife.

Norah loved the textured brown rug-brick, the cream-painted trim, the full-length, grey-painted front porch, and especially the two square rug-brick pillars, with wide grey cement caps that flanked their entrance sidewalk. "Very elegant," David agreed.

"But we will have to watch Norm closely," his wife cautioned him, "against any chance of a climb and fall. Moy Avenue is much busier than Gladstone Avenue."

They had sternly warned their son more than once.

Yet not two weeks later, Norm had managed to climb to the top of of the left-hand pillar with a new neighbourhood friend, and fallen— onto the grass-side verge luckily, and only had the wind knocked out of him. A stern Nurse Norah examined her son and pronounced him a fit boy. But they confined him to his room so he could not listen to the Detroit Tigers game with David on the radio in the basement that Saturday afternoon. Norm thought the punishment was "really crap." Norah warned him again about his language tendencies when angry or trying to provoke her, and he finally hung his head under her prolonged stare.

Still, all three Phelans enjoyed picking out shiny new white appli- ances, Kelvinator, Westinghouse, and General Electric, and slowly adding simple and elegant brown wood furniture to the rooms, bright paints and colourful wallpaper. Norm had always accompanied them and approved of their choices—although Norah had been unhappy about the bright lime-green paint her young son had insisted upon for his bedroom. David had only laughed and helped Norm with the painting. Not the best job, but *their* job, a father and son.

David Charles had turned over the neglected flowerbeds by the garage, and Norah's first official gardening act was to plant the care- fully nurtured lily of the valley and Solomon's seal she had removed from Lulu Pearl's old garden. Norm had helped her, struggling but determined, with the long-handled spade, and the sight of it lifted David's spirits: his wife, his son, his father's spade, his mother's flowers. They were a continuance. And a posterity, as well.

David installed Wallace Charles Phelan's tools and workbench in the basement, built shelving for the duck decoys and a secure storage cabinet for their shotguns, with a sturdy padlock and a stern look at Norm, curious about them. "When you're older, Norman. Not now. Not before."

"But I *am* older, Daddy, almost eight!"

"Not old enough for the guns, boyo. Not for a few years yet. Then we'll see."

"It's not fair! I can be careful."

"And guns can kill. That's enough now." David's severe look was familiar, and Norm knew there would be dire consequences if he went against his father.

"But, my son, there is something that *will* be fair, and necessary."

"Oh yeah? What?"

David smiled and began work on a tall, four-legged stool, with Norm's help. They painted his son's name in big green capitals on it so they could work on projects together at Wally's high old workbench.

But most important for David and Norah, and Norman too, with great ceremony, David mounted the glass-fronted case containing Lulu's bat on the wall of Norm's room, with his young family looking on. And then cheering when Norm realized it was *his* bat now too, in a way. Family.

David had not yet told his son the full story of Lulu Pearl and Wallace Phelan at Mulvaney's that fateful night. He and Norah had agreed on that when Norm was born. They cautioned Siobhan and her family, and their close friends against it as well. Norah's strict warning looks to them had kept the incident to vague rumours. Norm was too young still. David and Norah would sit him down when he was older and reveal the details. They'd also try and provide the best answers they could to Norm's inevitable questions that would follow.

At present, Norman only knew the heavy old chestnut-oak bat had once been hand-carved by the legendary Detroit Tigers player and manager, Tyrus Raymond Cobb—Cobb's bat.' But David's son loved the story of his Grandfather Wally's discovery of it in a trash bin at Detroit's Navin Field ballpark, which he worked on as a carpenter in 1912, and Norm often asked to hear it again.

Alone now, David unpacked the more recent object that was his own treasure and ambivalence, and set it under the light on top of Wally's old workbench. The two-foot piece of African mahogany was varnished but water-worn. David had severed it from a much larger piece of the *Lulu Pearl* that had been recovered from the shores of Lake Erie, just over a month after his father's disappearance during a stormy duck hunt on Erie's troubled waters. A hardy winter beach-comber had discovered a beached section of the *Lulu Pearl's* bow, its front deck, and hull planking that carried part of the name. He'd hauled it up farther on the beach and reported the find to the police in Leamington Ontario nearby. They recognized the name from their original search for its owner. After the police notified him, in the second week in December, David identified and confirmed it as a section of Wally's duck boat.

The jagged piece of bottom planking was not unusual for a boat broken up and rolled and pounded by waves—except for one small area David's master machinist's eye had instantly noted. He put the tip of his right index finger against a perfectly half-round, one-inch-cir-cumference curve, barely discernible in the uneven splintering of one end. Part of a clean hole.

The curve was one half of a round hole—the source of David's ambivalence and upset.

It was the reason he had salvaged this piece, before burning the rest in Wally's old black steel trash barrel, when Norman was not around to ask more of his boy's difficult questions. It was even more painful than David anticipated to see the few identifiable letters of the skiff's name, the *Lulu Pearl*, scorch black and burn to cinders. A kind of cremation.

But David had made his sole decision. He knew he could never bear to keep this deeply affecting fragment of his parent's life and love to haunt him for the rest of his days. Wallace Charles and Lulu Pearl were in his heart forever, where they belonged. His own 'sunlight'.

When David had put one of Wally's old one-inch-bore steel drill bits against the half-round curve in the remnant of the *Lulu Pearl's* hull planking, his worst fears for his father were confirmed: the fit was perfect.

David stood next to the black burn barrel and wept.

David Charles Phelan, recent father and loving husband to Norah McGee Phelan, wanted this first Phelan family Christmas in their new Moy Avenue house and home, to be a happy, a joyful one for his son Norm. He did *not* want it darkly overshadowed by death like their last one. Norah had taken Norman Christmas shopping along the bustling, north-south stretch of Ouellette Avenue that afternoon. It contained some of the city's finest shops with many gift possibilities. And Norm glowed with anticipation and excitement, despite the damp Windsor cold and grey dregs of the last snowfall.

Heat generated by the burning African mahogany of the *Lulu Pearl* was melting a circle of snow around the base of the black steel barrel, but gave David no warmth. The insistent weight of the evidence intruded. David poked at the fire, and the sparks and grey-black smoke whirled into the bleak winter sky like an offering.

That fateful morning that would change their lives forever, Wally had gone duck hunting, alone, on Sunday, the ninth of October, 1938. David suspected later, after thinking about the piece of hull planking, that the choice of the ninth was not random.

The last game of the 1934 World Series had been played on that very same October 9th date, although a Tuesday. His father *only* went hunting on Saturdays, usually with David, but sometimes by himself. Never Sundays. Ever. Sundays and church had been too special to his beloved Lulu Pearl. And special to Wally after Lulu's death. "I feel closer to Lu there, in our church, David. But the feeling is *not* painful, as it is in our home, despite Lu's final wishes for us all."

The Phelan family had always sat together in the Lincoln Road Methodist Church with Siobhan and her family. This had continued after Lulu Pearl's three-day, traditional wake, and David's own marriage and family. Then Garrett Bryant took that sawmill job in Port Alberni, British Columbia, and moved the family away from them. It had been a tearful parting, but the sawmill pay was too good to refuse, with Garrett's growing young family depending on him.

So. The Major League Baseball World Series—game seven, October ninth, 1934. The heavily favoured Detroit Tigers had played St. Louis, going up against the Cardinals' phenomenal Jay Hanna "Dizzy" Dean on the mound, at Navin Field in Detroit. David and Wally were two among 40,902 fans in attendance. They stayed until the end of the sixth inning, when Wally abruptly stood up. "I'll be leaving for the truck now, boyo. I'll wait for you there. How much more pain can a dedicated Tigers gamesman take?" But David left with his father, feeling the same devastation.

In the third inning, St. Louis scored seven runs on seven hits. Before the end of the game, the surly Tigers fans showered the field with garbage, interrupting play again and again. The Commissioner ordered the Cardinals third baseman, Ducky Medwick, to the bench for his own safety. Fearing a riot, Commissioner Kenesaw Mountain Landis had almost stopped the game.

It didn't matter.

Detroit used six different pitchers, but the Cardinals needed only one: the inimitable "Diz." St. Louis got seventeen hits to Detroit's six. The final score was a humiliating 11–0, a shutout. The salt in that deep wound was that Dizzy Dean had bragged from the end of the Pennant Races that he and his brother, Paul, would do *exactly* what they did. Each of the brothers, Dizzy and Daffy, had beaten the Tigers twice from the pitching mound. The media couldn't get enough of Dizzy.

Devastation.

Wally had said nothing at all after they left the stadium, while David drove them through Detroit's Irish Corktown neighbourhood, over the Ambassador Bridge, back to Windsor and the long winter ahead of them....

Four years later to the day, Wallace Charles Phelan quietly rose before dawn, took his duck boat, his shotgun, and his decoys, and went duck hunting alone on the shores of unpredictable Lake Erie and its grey fall storm waves. David woke briefly to the sound of the old Ford truck starting, and smiled at his father's intrepid pursuit of ducks and geese, at all times and in all weathers. A true waterman and Decoyman, and carrying on in Andrew William's proud tradition more than a century later:

> "Here lies the Decoyman who lived like an otter,
> Dividing his time betwixt land and water;"

Then David folded himself against his beloved Norah McGee Phelan's warmth and went back to sleep, almost at peace—

Except, the twelve-gauge shotgun was his father's *third* best, the action loose and past its prime. And the decoys, no more than six, were retired and waiting to be salvaged and refurbished over the winter, or burned in the black steel barrel. And of the polished, hand-carved duck calls David loved, Wallace Charles Phelan took *not* one.

David had discovered only two other objects missing, and neither one had anything to do with duck hunting—the beautiful, hand-carved White Angel with Lulu Pearl's solemn face, and Wally's heavy brace and a wide one-inch bit.

And then that telling piece of the *Lulu Pearl's* varnished African mahogany planking.

But at the bottom of it all was the final thing his father had told David that grey afternoon duck hunt on Lake Erie, a few years before, as the black coffee grew cold in their cups and Lulu Pearl's death was an ongoing ache in their hearts. Siobhan's revelation to Wally.

"Dr. Kirsner was a wise man, David. And compassionate. He told only Siobhan and left it to her to decide. And before she and Garrett went west, Siobhan *did* decide." His father had hung his head. "Lu knew me too well, and never said a thing about it at the time. But I tell it to you now, David: When your mother died, she was pregnant with our second child. *Pregnant.* After seven years of trying again, she was carrying our second child. The curse was my own, David. My own. I am rightly rebuked ... again."

Seven years.

Then the past was in them both, and David still felt its insistent pull on his heart and memories, tears in his eyes. Would Wally never be free of it? Would he?

Now Christmas in their new Moy Avenue house was only two weeks away. David, consciously, with appropriate ceremony, deposited the piece of African mahogany planking from the *Lulu Pearl* into the black steel barrel and leaned into the smoke to watch it slowly turn black.

David Charles Phelan had still not decided whether to tell Norah ... or Norm, when he was older, of Lulu Pearl's second pregnancy and loss.

PART THREE

Cobb's Card

Peterborough, Ontario—1968

21   The Card

David Charles Phelan knew the boy had been right about the rare Major League Baseball card.

It was far too expensive, even as a special Christmas present for his favourite and only grandson. Frank David Phelan wanted it badly, as only a twelve-year-old could, who had made the man his baseball idol and the model for his own playing of the "Great Game." David also knew he must take most of the blame—or credit, for this passion for the game.

The moment Frank had started to walk, David had bought him a small, vinyl fielder's mitt and a matching, sponge rubber baseball, and begun to teach him the rudiments of fielding in the backyard of his son Norm Phelan's Windsor, Ontario, home. Of course, Norm supported him in this baseball training and tossed the ball to young Frank while David crouched down behind the boy and coached his grandson's chubby hands to catch it. Yes, Frank was probably too young, but as David reminded his lovely daughter-in-law, Laura Lindenfield Phelan, he had done the same thing with Norm when he was a toddler. David's wife Norah had to agree, and so she and Laura sat back and let the Phelan men play. "They probably enjoy it as much as we do," David confided to Norm. But neither of the Phelan women made it obvious.

"Fifteen minutes and no more," Laura had said to Norm. She put aside her sunglasses and watched from one of the folding canvas chairs in the shade by the back door, cutting up yellow wax beans without seeming to look at her hands. Pregnancy agreed with his daughter-in-law, David thought. Laura's green and white maternity top looked almost festive. Norah had confided that Laura Linden-field Phelan hoped for a girl this time, maybe one with her own dark red hair and fair skin, German not Irish, but she had never said so to him—or to Norm, as far as David knew. If she had another son though, the four of them might almost have the start of a baseball team. But David knew enough to stay out of it. That had been the point of Norah's disclosure.

"And I do *not* want to hear my grandson end up crying," Norah had warned him next. Norah sat taller than Laura, peeling potatoes with the same careless skill. David didn't have to see his wife's eyes behind her sunglasses to know she was watching every move they made with her first grandchild.

Where Laura was fair and tended to freckle and burn, Norah's skin drew even colour from the sun, so that David could see the fine lines around her mouth. These made her self-conscious, and religious in her application of Pond's Cold Cream each night before they retired. Norah's black hair was cut short and parted in the middle, with shiny bangs just reaching the white frames of her sunglasses. David missed her fall of loose raven hair from their early years. But these days, as women got older, it seemed their hair got shorter, and David stopped mentioning it. In men it was the reverse, with results that were sometimes outlandish, even ridiculous. Did men think they could be shaggy-haired Samsons forever? It was true the menfolk in David's family were blessed with thick hair and no hint of baldness, but he had kept his hair short and neat since adolescence, and Norah had never complained. "Or see Frankie getting over-excited," Norah added later.

"Excitement is healthy for a future young ballplayer. You know the importance of spring training for the boy," David had told her.

"Oh yes, dear, I know the importance of training," Norah replied, "but the kind of training Laura and I did for Frankie was a touch messy and smelly." Her daughter-in-law laughed.

"Smelly!" two-year-old Frank had repeated, holding up his arms in triumph, looking to his grandmother for approval at his mastery of this new word. "Smelly. Smelly."

"Exactly, Frankie. And I don't remember you offering to coach him through *that* skill...?" Even David had had to chuckle.

"I don't either, Norah." Laura went on smiling at their men's discomfort.

"Now that's not fair, honey," Norm said. "I think I did my share of diaper duty. And David helped when he could."

"Yes, such sacrifice! Norah and I are nominating you both for the 'Dr. Spock Father and Grandfather of the Year Awards.' I believe they come with engraved potties attached to giant diaper pins. We'll put them in pride of place on our mantelpieces." David and Norm watched in silent exasperation as Norah had to take off her sunglasses, in turn, because her eyes were filling with tears of laughter at Laura's ready wit. "But while you're polishing your potties and pins, keep the Johnson's Baby Powder handy because in about three months duty will call again."

"Du-ty! Du-ty!" Frank said, and Norm had scooped him up and swung him around and around until the whole yard filled with laughter.

"Enjoy it while you can, my son." said Norm. "Mommy is about to bring a new player into the clubhouse, and it could be a whole new ballgame."

"For all three of you: ten minutes," Laura said.

"Over-excitement," Norah reminded.

"Yes, dear." Both David and Norm had nodded and spoken as one.

By this time in his life, David's son had taken to wearing his rimless glasses for more than just reading, despite what he claimed. David would bet dollars to doughnuts it was the result of squinting at those endless columns of figures all day as an accountant with the Canadian Bank of Commerce, later the Canadian Imperial Bank of Commerce or CIBC, after their merger in 1961. Norm worked at the big CIBC branch at the corner of Ouellette Avenue and Riverside Drive. Folding those long six feet and hunching over a desk all day hadn't done much for Norm's fitness and posture either. Norm had been a tireless runner in high school, after the war, and then a successful pitcher with his Canadian Bank of Commerce baseball team. But in 1956, Norm decided to take a year off when Frank was born. Yet after three seasons, Norm still hadn't rejoined the team. "For God's sake, go out again, get some exercise," David had encouraged, to no avail.

David Phelan still thought of himself as Irish-Canadian, the so-called "Black Irish," also evident in Norah and Norm's hair and dark complexions. Although after Wallace and Lulu Pearl's deaths and the end of their endless Irish stories and legends, David wasn't sure he bought the idea that, four hundred years before, some female Irish ancestor had taken pity on one of King Philip of Spain's swarthy, shipwrecked sailors from the ill-fated Spanish Armada, and invited him into her bed and the Phelan family gene pool. Still, it would be interesting to see how his grandchildren continued to develop in that area. Frank's hair had begun a light brown, thick and curly like his mother's, but had started to darken up, peeking out from under the junior-sized Detroit Tigers ball cap he'd bought him that spring. Later, the family's newest arrival, Fancy Lou Phelan, had hair the palest orange at birth, but at eight years as rich and auburn as her mother Laura Lindenfield Phelan's, revealing its German red roots.

David's new granddaughter, it would later turn out, would have no interest in baseball at all. "Thank you for the Tigers ball cap, Grandpa," she would tell him solemnly on her fourth birthday. Then, wisely checking to see that her mother was not watching, would whisper up to David, "But I really wanted some shiny red shoes."

So much for beginning a Phelan family baseball team.

Despite those early cautions from their womenfolk, serious or not, David and Norm were encouraging little Frank to carry on the Phelan family male tradition of fierce loyalty to the Detroit Tigers into the third generation. Fourth, when you counted great-grandfather Wally, who *began* that family tradition. David had tried to convey the significance of this to Norah, in preparation for her meeting his father for the first time. How as a baseball-crazy kid, before the turn of the century, when the eventual site of Tiger Stadium was just an open ground devoted to baseball, called Bennett Field, and before the Tigers or even the American League were born in 1901, the Tigers of Detroit became Wallace Charles Phelan's one and only team. But even after being married and living with Wally for those eight years, Norah's interest was only a polite concession to her husband's obsession—like Laura's now to Norm.

"Let the Tigers fur fly! Detroit till we die!" had become David's mantra with Norm and Frank.

And since Lulu Pearl Phelan had been dead eleven years before David married Norah, it was just as hard to get his wife to appreciate how Wally's passion for baseball and Ty Cobb was matched by Lulu Pearl's total commitment to Methodism and Temperance. A generation later, it was even harder to make real to his daughter-in-law, Laura Lindenfield Phelan. LIPS THAT TOUCH WINE SHALL NEVER TOUCH MINE, Lulu's signs had warned, and she herself loudly declared on their Temperance marches.

"But literally?" Laura asked.

"It was the times," Norah offered. "And a clever and reliable female strategy, promoting one prohibition by threatening another. I think it began with Lysistrata and other Spartan and Theban women denying their men any sex until the dolts ended their costly Peloponnesian War."

"Then I'll certainly keep Lysistrata's strategy in mind, Norah."

"Ah, but I'm not a heavy drinker, honey." Norm had looked hurt.

"But you like to fool around." She winked at Norah.

"David does too." Now David felt hurt—and embarrassed.

"Still?"

"Still."

"Ladies, please. The children..." David gestured to include his imminent grandchild, as well as Frank, careening around the yard, throwing his baseball, and chasing it down. "The children."

"Exactly, Norah."

"Reliable, Laura." They had laughed loudly, and David made the mistake of trying to explain further.

"Lulu Pearl was a realist too. My mother recognized the necessity of good work and steady income through uncertain times. And even that Wally worked on the Detroit baseball stadium with the reverence of a minister taking a hand in building his own church. That's how our passion for baseball and the Detroit Tigers began. And right in the heart of Detroit's Irish Corktown neighbourhood, as well."

It was no use. The tradition would remain a Phelan family *males'* tradition.

But after three generations, David concluded that the Phelan females had their *own* tradition. Like Lulu Pearl Phelan, they were practical women of strong presence and deep integrity, more ready to laugh, maybe, but with tongues dipped in bitter aspic when crossed. It was as if Phelan men were predestined to keep repeating conjugal history, and were attracted to women whose strong values and firm domestic hands could ensure a good home and respectable family life, and curb their husbands' more wayward impulses.

Yet times did change and the Phelan clan with them.

After the war especially, smoking and drinking in moderation were accepted in both households, although Norah did neither. Laura Lindenfield Phelan had never smoked and quit drinking during each pregnancy on the advice of their doctor, although physician and surgeon Dr. Cyrus Elmore indulged both habits. Now David knew his daughter-in-law liked the occasional rye and coke with friends at card parties, wedding receptions, their anniversaries at Windsor's Top Hat Supper Club, and of course Christmas and New Year's, where she might risk a drag on Norm's cigarette but refused any offer of her own, to his son's great amusement.

And when David encouraged Norm to teach a child who could barely walk how to wear a baseball mitt and catch a ball, he judged their wives were amenable, and more amused than disapproving, unlike some of his mother's generation. "Our own Backyard Boys of Summer," as Laura had begun calling them, after watching their antics.

"Or should it be our own *Backward* Boys of Summer?" Norah had suggested, and she and Laura about doubling over with laughter while the Phelan males stared in bewilderment, even young Frank. However, less than two years later, when the two men wanted to take the women's three-year-old son and grandson across the Detroit River to witness his first battle in the epic war between the Detroit Tigers and the New York Yankees at Briggs Stadium, Laura and Norah had responded with their own single voice: "Over my dead body!"

That was in 1959, the year the Tigers' Al Kaline homered in the All-Star Game and thrilled David, Norm and Tigers fans on both sides of the Detroit River, by winning the batting title with an amazing .530 average. Then it was: "Let the Tigers fur fly! Detroit till we die! Kaline! Kaline! He's our guy!"

Now, almost eight years later, Frank had fulfilled all David's hopes—a Tigers fan, a talented right fielder and power hitter on his Windsor Legion Branch 143 ball team, and a constant companion to him and Norm at all the Tigers home games David could make it down to Windsor for. It took five hours to drive from Norah's big family cottage, on Buckhorn Lake near Peterborough, where he worked as a foreman and master machinist, and she as a private home-care nurse for the Victorian Order of Nurses. David had expanded and winterized the cottage himself, and they planned to retire there.

Of course, Norah, in the truck beside David, was more interested in spending time with her grandson Frank and his three-years-younger sister Fancy Lou than attending Tigers games. Still, both Norah and Laura *did* come to all Frank's Windsor Legion Branch 143 games, sometimes dragging his less enthusiastic sister Fancy Lou along when no arrangements with Fancy's friends could be made, and rooted for him as enthusiastically as David and Norm. "Werewolves! Werewolves! 143! All the way to vic-to-ry! Yeah-h-h-h!"

But Frank was also an avid collector of Topps baseball cards, and spent much of his weekly allowance and gift money to acquire them: first, the Detroit Tigers team for the current baseball season, along with any related, specialty cards like Tigers batting champs or All-Stars or Gold Glove Award winners for their work defending on the field; then all the other American League teams and their specialty cards; and finally, National League teams, especially the pennant winner, and at least the NL's marquee players for that year. The smell of a new Topps card, dusted with powdered sugar from the square of pink bubblegum enclosed in each colourful, waxed paper pack, was heady perfume to Frank and his friends. So, with encouragement and the occasional cash advance from David and Norm, Frank was a very successful young baseball card collector.

But Frank's collection could never be complete. Never.

The boy deeply despaired of ever finding and affording the card Frank coveted most.

A mint condition, 1954 Topps #201—the Al Kaline "rookie card."

22

Who's On First, First?

David knew his grandson Frank did everything right in the quest for a Topps #201 Al Kaline rookie card, a rare baseball card collector's gem. Frank endlessly biked the long Windsor city blocks to multiple different variety stores in Sandwich West to buy the widest range of Topps baseball cards. He shrewdly traded cards with his friends at home and at his J. E. Benson Junior High School. He even solicited opposing players at his Branch 143 baseball games. And everywhere, Frank played card games like "tops" with his doubles and other spare cards, spinning them against a wall until one player's card fell back and covered part of a previous card, to win them all. In no time, the boy was a tops expert, and had become smart enough *not* to show it. "Save it for when a baseball card falls that I really need, that's the best time, right Granddad?"

So David also took Frank to the baseball card shops and trading shows in both Windsor and Detroit. But the few, much-coveted Topps #201 Al Kaline rookie cards they found were either in poor condition or, if mint, far out of Frank's price range, or NFS, simply "Not for Sale." This was especially true since Al Kaline, at only twenty years of age, became the youngest player ever to win the hotly contested American League batting championship. And the cool thing was, Ty Cobb, also as a twenty-year-old, had won the very same title back in 1907. For Kaline, it was in 1955, and Al Kaline was named the Sporting News American League Player of the Year that season, and again in 1963. Kaline's #201 rookie cards were being religiously hoarded by dealers and collectors, and their value only increased with each season that passed and each additional success on the field that Al Kaline and his Detroit Tigers recorded.

"Looks like we struck out again, Grandpa." Frank continued to look down at each subsequent disappointment.

David clapped his shoulder in encouragement. "We'll find one, son. Just need to hang in there, right?" Frank had said nothing.

In the final, ultimate desperation of the quest for a mint Topps #201, David had tracked the vague rumour of an available Kaline rookie card down to a mysterious private collector in New York State. He worked through an exhausting series of phone calls and tips from the Official Detroit Tigers Fan Club, of which he was an early, avid and active Canadian member. This led David Phelan to a contact with the more exclusive Official New York Yankees Fan Club, and the phone number of the rumoured source of that mint condition Al Kaline rookie card. This mysterious private collector looked like David's best and only shot at this special card before the approaching Christmas Day, and he hoped to make a special gift of it to his grandson. And now snow had already fallen deeply at Buckhorn Lake earlier in the week. How much its purchase might cost him left David terrified to imagine. He could likely never afford it—but it remained his last and only very, very long shot....

But when at last a discouraged, exhausted, and hopeless David Phelan finally reached the elusive American at his private home number that late Saturday night, the gruff-spoken man had been endlessly suspicious of the unknown Canadian calling out of the blue, and grilled him for ten minutes—and then became suddenly very cagey, not willing even to admit he might have that specific item.

"Where you say you's callin' from, again?"

"From Ontario. Canada. Buckhorn Lake, not too far from the town of Peterborough," David explained.

"That be anywhere near that big ole city of Toronto I drive through a few times on business…?"

"No, not really, no. Buckhorn Lake is a couple of hours farther east and north. Buckhorn is first and foremost a village. Some farms of course, but lots of woods and lakes and rivers, and quite isolated. Buckhorn Lake is the biggest body of water in the area. What people there are nearby, are spread very thin. So, most of the time I see more deer and fish and ducks than people, but that's why I like it." David knew he was anxious and babbling way too much.

And then David Charles Phelan got lucky—but not in the way he anticipated.

"You think you got you some ducks way up there?" David had to pause a moment at this unexpected detour in the conversation.

"I know I do."

"How you know?" David determined not to take offence and offered the most concrete evidence he could.

"Because I'm looking at my big white freezer in the kitchen right now, where a good dozen mallards, blacks and canvasbacks are just waiting for me to make up my mind when to enjoy them for the second time. We have a saying up here: 'Ducks hate to be hunted, but they love to be eaten.'"

"You a fair hunter then?" David thought a bit and then put aside his natural modesty and told the simple truth.

"Duck hunting is one of the things I live for—besides Detroit Tigers games that is. I believe I get my share." A long silence followed on the other end of the line. Alvin P. Greathwite, "Big Al" to his friends, seemed to be considering the possibilities.

David would later learn that Al was a very successful Chrysler dealer who had worked his way up from selling questionable used cars at cheap, fly-by-night gypsy lots in Brooklyn, to owning no less than three of the premier Chrysler dealerships on the Upper East Side of New York. Big Al Greathwite had no natural modesty to begin with. Or if he did, he'd put it aside as a definite car salesman career-killer so long ago that he'd forgotten. What Big Al did have, what he'd built his sales success on right from the start, was the ability to lie convincingly at the drop of a hat, and good old-fashioned "balls."

Not to mention that Alvin P. Greathwite presently occupied one of the finest reserved viewing suites at Yankee Stadium, "the house that Ruth built," that money, bluster, and persuasive salesmanship could buy. An afternoon spent with Big Al at a New York Yankees home game put his Chrysler staff and potential clients exactly where he wanted them—snugly in his back pocket. Thus, the shrewd Chrysler dealer combined business with pleasure, and left plenty of room in his other pockets for the cash.

Big Al's swagger and charm was also evident in his manner and voice. And although he would never admit it publicly, Al would eventually confide to David that he had come to think of himself as the George Herman Ruth, the "Bambino," of the New York State Chrysler dealership network.

"So, you a bettin' man up there in duck-country-Canada, Dave? Willing to take a big risk for a big reward?" David had to pause once more.

"I guess that would depend on the game, the stakes and the odds." He had no idea where this was going.

"Well, here's what I'm thinkin', Tiger Dave. I'm lookin' at my own freezer down here, so to speak, where no less'n two of the party you're asking after are just sittin' there on ice, all wrapped in plastic and in mint condition just like your ducks. And just waitin' for me to make up my own mind about how I might enjoy them for the second time."

"And?"

"And now, listenin' to you from way up north in Canada there, I just did make up my mind. New Yorkers got a saying of our own down here that I believe might apply: 'Put up or shut up!' So, this is what I'm puttin' up. I'm a fan and a collector, not a baseball card dealer. Even if I was, them parties ain't for sale. Considerin' the stats, their value's goin' nowhere but up. But you want to take the risk and put up, Tiger Dave might just win both them beauties for that grandson of yours. That's the stakes. So, you game, for the game, Tiger Dave?" David still didn't know where this was going, but he desperately wanted that Kaline rookie card for Frank—and for himself, if he would admit it. Two cards would be an added, if unexpected, bonus.

But David Charles Phelan was cautious.

"Well, I might be, Al. Like I said. It depends. What exactly *is* the game?" Alvin P. Greathwite laughed his best car salesman's laugh. He had a prospect kicking the tires. Now to polish the paint job and sell the goods.

"It's kinda like 'Who's on first, first?' The game, if you're game, is game." David had to endure Big Al's long chuckle here at his own wit. "I know I'm one hell of a car salesman—got me three big old car dealerships to prove it. Know I'm a hell of a Yankees fan—got season's tickets, best seats, team citations, fan club sponsorships and Yankees autographs up the wazoo, to prove that. Know I'm a hell of a stud—wore out the best parts of two wives and working on a third to prove that. And the contents of my own freezer, of which you know only two of many, prove I'm one hell of a card collector too."

David could think of nothing to say.

"But here's the thing, Tiger Dave. I like to think I'm a damn fair duck hunter, just like you. Got my own duck camp down the Carolinas near my roots, and I get my share, I surely do. After the Yankees and what a good wife with the right kind of bodywork can supply, it's one of the things I live for too. So, if you're willing, let's see who's on first, first—Tiger Dave from Canada or Yankee Al from these great United States of America, Land of the Free and Home of the Balls. I'm not just talkin' baseball here."

Now it was David's turn to laugh at Big Al's bombast.

"So, what exactly are you proposing?"

"I got me a big international car dealer convention comin' up in Toronto shortly. But first, I stop by your neck of the woods, way up in duck country Canada there, and bring along them items you're interested in. We hook up, and you show me those fine Canadian game birds. We shoot from the same duck blind, use the same shotgun shell loads, alternating but even rounds, and the first one to hit his legal duck limit of wins."

The Canadian was wary.

"It sounds like you've done this before."

"Not exactly, Tiger Dave. Been in a few shootin' competitions though, mostly skeets or retrieving trials with my gun dog."

"What's in it for you?"

"Knowin' who's the best. If it's Tiger Dave, he gets two mint-condition, autographed, Al Kaline #201 Topps rookie cards, knowing he won 'em fair and square and there weren't no other way to do it, and there weren't no money needed to change hands. If it's Yankee Al, he gets some fine shootin', some fine Canuck duck, some fine company, and leaves with the ones that brung him, knowin' he is for sure, one hell of a fine duck hunter on *both* sides of the border. So, you game for the game, Tiger Dave? You got some *cojones* way up in duck country Canada there, to go along with them ducks?"

David didn't have to think it over for a second. But he did have to shake his head at the unabashed bombast and American audacity of the big Chrysler salesman from New York City.

"I'm game, for a game with the game, Yankee Al."

He'd sold the goods! The American chuckled in satisfaction.

"You are one dead duck, Tiger Dave."

Yankee Al from the Big Apple was as good and as big as his words. Even his huge black Chrysler Imperial, with its fat whitewall tires, miles of chrome and his monogram in gold leaf on the driver's door, seemed too small to contain him when he stepped out of it in November, two weeks later, to shake David's hand at the Buckhorn Lake cottage. "Pleased to meet you at last, Al."

In those few seconds, each man took the measure of the other—a study in contrasts, David decided. His tall, quiet Canadian confidence confronted Al's shorter but solid American brashness and the ego that supported it. And neither man found the other wanting. When David looked directly into Al's eyes and smiled his welcome, Big Al did the same. David guessed the man's competitive instincts, like his own, told him this was going to be one hell of a fine contest. "Hoo-ee Tiger Dave, lead me to them ducks!"

"Happy to oblige, Yankee Al. No motels either, you'll bunk right here with us, maybe sample one of those fine Canadian canvasbacks first. Let you know what you might be missing." Big Al laughed at this as David continued. "Another saying we have here is: Don't count your birds before they fall."

"Borrowed that from the chicken farmers, did ya?" David smiled in turn. Al was some quick with the mouth and likely just as quick with his gun—and not just talking shotguns, as his big new New York acquaintance might say.

"Maybe so, Al. Maybe so. So come on in, meet my wife Norah, and smell that roasting bird while we go over the topo maps, and I show you what I have planned.

Norah McGee Phelan walked over from her big aluminum stove and held out her hand in greeting. "Pleased to meet you at last, Al, especially under these rather unique circumstances." Big Al Greathwite took Norah's hand with grace and some ceremony, and just about bowed.

"Always a supreme pleasure meetin' attractive ladies such as yourself, Norah. And yes, our coming together is a bit unusual, but from those savoury smells coming from your kitchen our meeting promises many pleasures." Norah laughed a little self-consciously and turned a bit red.

"Well, I better get back to the stove so the pleasure will be served in good time." Now it was Al's turn to chuckle. David just stood by and shook his head in wonder.

"Now, Al, I pulled a few local strings with my Ducks Unlimited brothers and got your hunting license all squared away last week. After supper, we can pack all our gear on the boat and turn in early. I figure we're up at two a.m., in the blind with decoys out by six, and ready for ducks as dawn breaks.

"Hoo-ee! Sounds good to me, Tiger Dave. Only thing better'n duck huntin' is gettin' ready for duck huntin.'" Big Al scratched at his day's growth of beard. "Well, maybe I was mite hasty there. That first 1923 Yankees World Series win and the charms of my third wife fall into the same pond pretty close. You lucky, maybe I'll tell you a bit about her talents, just between two sportin' men. For now, though, Tiger Dave, I'm so took with your hospitality, I'm going to give you a little peek at them items that brung us together. Then you too can see what you might be missin.'"

"Looking forward to it, Yankee Al." David gave a short, two-note whistle, and the black Labrador retriever that had watched the introductions calmly from his post by the front door, came immediately to his master's side and sat, looking up at David expectantly. "This is my faithful duck dog, Cobb. He'll be doing the retrieving for us." David gave Cobb a small hand signal and the dog visibly relaxed, wagged his tail and allowed Big Al to give him a friendly pat.

"Well, I like the name, Dave. This old boy looks a mite long in the tooth, though." David judged Big Al Greathwite was a skilled hunter, and a skilled hunter knew his dogs. A duck hunter's dog was more important than his gun. Much more. Money could buy a good gun. Money could buy a dog too, but finding a good dog to buy and train up was the hard part. "More exact sayin' might be: 'Don't count your birds till they's back in the blind.'" David put his hand on Cobb's head and nodded.

"True enough, Yankee Al, true enough. Cobb's eleven, but he doesn't miss much. You put a duck down, dead or winged, he'll find it. Al nodded in his turn and gave the big retriever another warm pat on his black head.

"Guess we'll see." David nodded again, gave in to the craving and shook out a Player's Navy Cut from the flat blue and white box in his jeans back pocket and offered it to Al. David was not a youngster anymore himself. He was trying to cut back on the tobacco, save his wind, and not have his grandson Frank pick up the bad habit. Fancy Lou too, he supposed, when she was older.

"Why not try one of these instead, Tiger Dave?" The big American had conjured a textured leather case from somewhere about his person, drew out a thick, six-inch cigar and gave it to David. "Called *Romeo y Julieta*, from Cuba. Still get a few out even though that commie Castro took over, and the place has gone all to shit." David would reserve judgment on that, but accepted the offering. "More my size." Al clipped the ends with a neat gold cutter and lit them both up. Each duck hunter drew in and exhaled a blue-grey stream of pungent cigar smoke. "Smoother'n shit through a goose."

"Expensive shit." David allowed.

"Only shit I got, Tiger Dave."

Satisfied, the two duck hunters and avid baseball fans laughed, already comfortable in each other's company. Cobb sat like a dark shadow made solid between them. Then they stepped out the front door, with Cobb at their sides, to savour these rare *Romeo y Julieta* cigars, and the expansive view out over Buckhorn Lake in the fading light.

A persistent north wind carried the sharp chill to them off the long lake. Foot-high waves carried small shards of ice left over from a sudden cold snap and rolled them onto the shore with a ticking sound. The odd cottage in front of them was still occupied, and lights stippled the dark shores, alternately hidden then revealed by the tall moving pines on either side. The wind swirled and smells of burning hardwood from nearby cottage wood stoves enveloped them in a pleasing rural fragrance. The two duck hunters smoked in silence, adding their scents of rich Cuban tobacco to the natural smells of the night air around an isolated, slate-coloured lake in the Canadian woods, as autumn merged into winter. The stars looked too close and too large and the rising three-quarters moon too bright. Cassiopeia and the Big Dipper were overhead in the near distance, the Little Dipper almost fully risen on the northern horizon. Orion, "The Hunter" out of Greek mythology, was just appearing over Buckhorn Lake to the east.

"A fine evening, Tiger Dave. Thank you. You have yourself a real pretty place here."

"That it is, Al. But the cottage is Norah's. Left Windsor four years ago to take a foreman's job at a big new machine shop in Peterborough. Norah was torn between our grandchildren there and her family here, so we go back to the city a lot, especially during the baseball season. But I lied to myself. The foreman's job was just the means to let me live here in this hunter's paradise. Ducks and geese all around it, and filled with natural wonders and nature's rich bounty."

"Bring'em on, Tiger Dave!"

"Soon enough, Yankee Al. Now let's get inside to Norah and her delicious supper preparations, or we'll both be dead ducks before our time." The hunters laughed and turned toward the lights and warmth of the cottage, and its inviting smells.

"You people religious at all, Dave?"

"Well, Norah and I attend services at a United Church in Peterborough. Why do you ask?"

"Just don't want to give offence to your wife if I happen to take the Lord's name in vain. Forget it, Tiger Dave."

"It's forgotten, Yankee Al." He clapped the big American on the back, looking forward to the hunt, but more than a bit nervous about the outcome of the wager and the fate of those two rare Al Kaline rookie cards.

David Charles Phelan was anticipating a kind of one-on-one, Invitational World Series of Duck Hunting, but a series that had just now come down to the final deciding team match-up. Tiger Dave Phelan and Yankee Al Greathwite were the two opposing Big League hitters waiting in the on-deck circles, in a decisive one-time game that would last from dawn until dusk the coming day. Each hitter was relishing stepping into that batter's box and taking his turn at the home plate. Ahead of them, first base was wide open and beckoning and, as in any great game, the skill of the players would somehow combine with the unpredictable whims of fate and nature, in a venue brimming with possibilities, to decide the outcome—the man who was crossing home plate as the victor when the Invitational World Series of Duck Hunting was called on account of darkness.

Old Cobb must surely have sensed his master David's mood. Over the years, the bond between hunter and faithful retriever had become deep, almost preternatural. The Lab licked David's left hand and put his big black head against David's thigh to be patted. "Thanks, dog. Thank you." He'd had three Labs since Wally's Navin, years before, but Cobb he had bought from a large animal vet and breeder in the local Peterborough area, Dr. Ann Spence. And Cobb was indeed special. Only an avid duck hunter who had trained his dog from a pup to do one thing, and one thing only—spot, point and retrieve ducks—and called on that dog to do it again and again, in the most adverse of weather conditions, and was never disappointed by his performance, might begin to understand his feelings. But David didn't think so. Owning and training his retriever was the biggest responsibility for a successful duck hunter. And in return, Cobb gave David his absolute trust and excelled at his own responsibility in their partnership, retrieving the ducks his master downed with his spotting and pointing.

How the duck hunter loved him in return.

23 Lost Man Lake

Towards dawn, David Phelan and Big Al Greathwite were seated behind their canvas duck blind, as comfortably as two duck hunters can ever get in heavy green rubber chest-waders and black, beige and brown, camouflage-patterned parkas. The blind was located on the marshy edges of a small, well-hidden, nameless lake. From what David could tell from his researches, this little lake was uncharted, accessible only after careful study of the relevant topo map and skilled piloting of his own hand-made, shallow draft duck boat.

He'd called the broad-fronted skiff the *Lulu Pearl II*, after the original *Lulu Pearl* David had built with his father, Wallace Charles Phelan, too many years ago now. That fateful craft was lost with his father on the waters Lake Erie under very suspicious circumstances, which David had finally resolved when a piece of it washed up on shore and was returned to him by an avid beachcomber who had heard of the *Lulu Pearl's* loss some days before.

David still hadn't told Norah or his son Norm of his troubling findings—and maybe never would—that Wallace Charles had used his large woodworker's brace and a one-inch bit to deliberately drill through the bottom, let the duck boat fill up with Lake Erie water, and slowly sink to his death. It was after his mother Lulu Pearl Phelan's own tragic death from the Spanish flu some years before. David suspected that his father simply could no longer take her loss and the deep, unremitting grief that followed, and chose to take his own life and join her in death. The body was never recovered from the brown Lake Erie waters.

Now, seated here in the duck blind beside American Big Al Greathwite, he shook his head and tried to put the painful past behind him once more.

David Phelan had discovered this little gem of a lake years before, in one of those surprising but pleasurable turns of a duck hunter's fate.

David had become completely lost when forced to detour the *Lulu Pearl II* repeatedly, motoring with his left hand on the tiller of the Evinrude outboard. He manoeuvred the duck boat slowly during a fall season of heavy rain and high water, while on his way to hunt another stand he often used. And suddenly, just visible through the pouring rain, there it was, one of nature's treasures: a dozen acres of tea-tinged water, alive with sheltering ducks and pristine in its undiscovered isolation. David had never marked it down on his own topo map, but after careful calculations with his sighting compass, its location became clear in his mind. David christened it "Lost Man Lake," because to his way of thinking, the little lake had found him.

A responsible hunter and dedicated conservationist, David Phelan had kept its secret and hunted it only once in each duck season, no matter his luck in other, less productive stands. It was enough for David just to be there, in the calm and solitude of its promise and beauty. The memory of this secret water sustained David all year, shimmering like a tea-coloured jewel in his imagination. Even after a decade of solitary weekend or holiday visits from their Buckhorn Lake cottage, David had never seen evidence of another duck blind on Lost Man Lake. He valued and respected his rare privilege and the wonderful ducks it might offer up, and hunted it the way others might worship at a sacred shrine.

David was planning to introduce his grandson Frank to its beauty and variety of wildfowl when he was mature enough to be David's duck spotter, and to appreciate and respect the secret—maybe next season. And Frank was curious and already well trained by David on the vintage but pristine Crosman .177 calibre waisted lead pellet air rifle he'd given him for his birthday last year. The pellets were powered by compressed CO_2 cartridges. Next summer, too, Frank might be ready for more advanced training in the care, safe handling and shooting of the vintage Cooey single-shot .22 calibre rifle, and even Norm's old twenty-gauge Winchester, at the local skeet range. David would start Frank with windblown balloons and .22 calibre lead-free birdshot on one of the ponds he knew, then move to the shotgun and skeet. And he would do his conservation best to retrieve and responsibly dispose of the downed balloons.

David had decided to bring the big American hunter to this special place because of his desperation for those mint condition, Topps #201 Al Kaline rookie cards Al had shown him, and because it had always had ducks. He'd shown Big Al only the general map area and was confident the New Yorker could never locate it again, even if he wanted to. Still, he'd had misgivings, and the Canadian hunter had refreshed his memory about two other locations where he'd had success in the recent past. But after three hours sharing duck lore and experiences with Al the evening before, David believed that beneath the brash swagger was a good man, a hunter with integrity, conscience and an unfailing respect for the sport and the gifts of nature that made it possible.

The little Lost Man Lake was presently misted with a near-dawn sprinkling of rain that might continue off and on all day. This experience was so common for David and Al in the fall duck season that they were hardly even aware of it. In the false dawn, he had carefully positioned his twenty-decoy set near an abandoned beaver lodge on the lee side of a small point, beginning the set about thirty feet out from the well camouflaged duck blind. Al was in the stern of the *Lulu Pearl II*, expertly manoeuvring the skiff with the paddle and handing forward the decoys as the Canadian hunter called for them. David had decided on a mix of cans, blacks and mallards, with an inviting opening in their midst where his hoped-for targets could land. And David always included a pair of his father Wallace Charles Phelan's original, hand-carved and painted decoys, rotating them from the diminishing number that remained, for luck and remembrance of the man and duck hunter he loved, and who had passed on that training and love to his son with pride and affection.

"You're still with me, Dad," he said, too softly for Big Al to hear.

Farther out, David placed a set of four Canada geese to mark the forty-yard point of effective shotgun range, and because the sight of geese at rest would give passing ducks more confidence in the safety of the location. David wished he could transport and lay out more decoys, but all the other gear and the size of the large hunter from New York, not to mention the black Lab, Cobb, now waiting patiently in the blind for the familiar ritual to be completed, had left limited space in the flat-bottomed duck boat.

There was only one more Phelan family ritual to complete the setup, but David was self-conscious in front of the American. Would Al think David some kind of crazy Canuck? But David thought of Frank and the rare baseball cards, and decided he could leave nothing to chance. "One more thing, Yankee Al. I'm kind of superstitious about this, but my father, Wally, taught me a poem when we first hunted together in the twenties. I've always recited it after laying out my decoys. For luck."

"A fickle lady. Better get on with it." David stood in the bow and looked over the set. His eye fell on his father's mallard blocks and David slipped into the familiar rhythms of lines on Andrew Williams:

"Here lies the Decoyman who lived like an otter,
Dividing his time betwixt land and water..."

After the poem, Big Al said, "Amen, brother Phelan. That 'crumbling to dust ... like you and I must' is a pisser." David thought of Wallace Phelan's body dissolving slowly into the shallow waters of Lake Erie, and nodded. From that time on he had always inquired as to the source of the yellow perch and pickerel at the Windsor fish markets, and would eat none from that lake. It was irrational, but Norah understood.

"It's from the 18th century, in Britain, when duck decoys were trap ponds where they drove ducks like cattle, during the moult, and slaughtered thousands."

"Never knew that, Tiger Dave. Know Indians used to weave floating decoys out of grass, bulrushes, or cattails. Sometimes stuck feathers or even a whole duck skin on 'em. Clever and effective, I understand. Supposed to have done it here in North America for thousands of years. And Cree Indians still make standing goose decoys from small branches of tamarack. Seen one once at a hunt show." And the two duck hunters and skilled opponents eyed that same slender, reddish-brown tamarack in small clumps around the margins of Lost Man Lake, mixed in with birch, black spruce, and cedar. "Makes a duck hunter think."

"Okay, Yankee Al. Let's get the *Lulu Pear II* under cover, and we'll have a look at the calls," David said.

After Cobb and his shooting prowess, David Phelan believed it was his skill and versatility with his necklace of polished wooden duck calls that had made him the successful duck hunter he was. And for this uncanny skill, David still regularly thanked Wally who had coached and encouraged him in the arcane art of duck call and serenade, at his father's workbench or when hunting from blinds in the marshes around Michigan, Windsor, and Lake St. Clair to the east of the city. David remembered Lulu Pearl Phelan had not approved of "this gun business," but couldn't deny the pleasure it gave her husband, or again, resist the security and matchless taste that wild ducks ripening in the cold-pantry provided. After baseball, the hunting expeditions were some of the best times David had had with his father, and to this day, David could never get enough of either....

The soft grey light unfolding over their heads revealed the humped outline of the beaver lodge, the painted decoys floating invitingly in their patterned array, and the thicket of dark green trees defining a low horizon around the uneven edges of Lost Man Lake. David's beloved black Labrador retriever Cobb sat tall in the blind beside the two hunters, a sleek dark statue with its eyes tracking back and forth above the trees.

The low-seated hunters stopped their quiet conversation, and in a mutual accord, men and dog observed a full half-hour of silence amid the natural sounds and rhythms of the morning's unfolding beauty.

24   Cobb

By the end of the half-hour, their quiet faith and reverence was rewarded with the blessing of a large flight of ducks, moving swiftly in their formations across the far eastern sky, still a long distance out. Cobb immediately stood, silent and observant, as he was trained, until the black Labrador retriever sounded his familiar soft growl, low in the throat. David glanced at the gold dial of his Accutron wristwatch. It was only ten minutes after the permitted shooting time officially began, and the avid Canadian duck hunter smiled in his pleasure at the sight and distant sounds of his favourite game birds, anticipating the challenge he loved.

The hunters had flipped a coin after they first set up their duck blind, and Big Al Greathwite had won the toss. He would be the first shooter, with his two twelve-gauge shotgun shells, premier Imperial factory loads, in the sleek over-and-under barrels of his custom-made, Italian Perazzi twelve-gauge, a shotgun David had never seen before in Canada. David would be the duck spotter and caller, trying to entice the passing ducks to within range of their decoy set beginning thirty yards out, and then mark the fall of any birds the American hunter brought down. Once Al had shot his two loads, and if the ducks were still in range, David might fire himself, at the back-up shooting position. David would still be the first shooter on the next flight whether successful or not, with Big Al as spotter, caller, marker, and back-up shooter. This was how each inning of their private Invitational World Series of Duck Hunting would be played. Each man trusted and understood that his fellow hunter would do his very best to bring ducks into range for his opponent.

After that, all was fair, in baseball and duck hunts.

"Flight of blacks," David said. They were almost too far out, but he recognized the flashing white underwings of the blacks and selected his favourite, newly-polished duck call, a mallard, smoothly dark, oiled and hand-carved by his father years before. David had gotten it on his twelfth birthday, along with his first, small .410-gauge shotgun to begin his duck hunting journey, and they were two of the most satisfying presents he had ever received in his life—the signs of his growing manhood and the respect and love of his father and avid duck hunter. Every time he picked up the now vintage .410, its old, familiar feel still gave David the same confidence, even after he'd moved to his bigger, more standard, twelve-gauge duck hunting guns.

David put Wally's hand-carved and polished mallard call to his lips, and produced the familiar series of highball *burp-burps* designed to get the attention of the passing flock of blacks. Beside him, Big Al had reached under the waterproof rubber military green sheeting, removed his custom handmade Perazzi, and flipped off the safety. Al had had the Italian trap gun modified with a series of full and half-chokes, and the interchangeable double barrels designed specifically for the duck hunting he loved. David knew the American had confidence in the premier duck-man's shell, those fresh Imperial factory loads.

The beautifully turned shotgun looked completely at home in Yankee Al Greathwite's big hands.

At the end of David's second series of duck calls, the curious blacks turned and swung lower over the calm waters for a closer look at their set and found it good. "Range," said David quietly at the long fifty yard point out, and continued with a softer series of *clacks* and *chuckles* that sounded notes of contentment and ease, as of ducks at rest and feeding safely.

Cobb's ears came up, and he strained even further forward in the light rain. His soft growl had first alerted the hunters to the distant shapes, and his keen retriever's eyes followed the birds approaching lower and nearer.

At the word "range" Al stood up immediately, pulled the sleek Perazzi in tight to his shoulder and calculated his targets—their angle of flight, the speed and distance, the necessary lead—and fired two shots that sounded as one.

Blam! Blam!

That single, smooth motion seemed too precise for a large man his size, but Big Al had taken the lead pair of blacks at the most extreme edge of the range, far before the surer shot that a few more seconds of approach time would have given him.

David and Cobb flinched, not from the familiar sound of the shots, but because the two reports had come before they, in their long experience, had expected them.

The following blacks veered out of shotgun range with panicked cries of alarm, but left two of their number spinning brokenly out of the sky into the still grey waters below. David shook his head, and had to admire Yankee Al's skill. Two ducks at over forty-five yards out were a shooting feat few duck hunters could match, and the American hunter had made it look easy. "A great shoot, Yankee Al! Well done."

"Why thanks, Tiger Dave. But I think ol' Lady Luck had a lot to do with it. May have shot me a mite early there. Been a while. Some kinda of duck fever, most likely. Could've blown the whole dang thing." Al smoothly broke the Perazzi's action, pulled the spent Imperial shotgun shells and replaced them with fresh loads, resetting the safety.

"Maybe so," David said.

But the Canadian hunter didn't believe it for a second.

Big Al Greathwite was simply a superb shot with his beautiful Perazzi and had shrewdly decided to take his ducks from as far out as he could, spooking the the rest of the flight, leaving David no chance for his own shots at back-up. This was how a high-stakes gambler played the big Invitational World Series of Duck Hunting, and what *might* have looked like a long shot, literally, to some, David was convinced was a calculated percentage shot for Yankee Al from New York City via South Carolina. The proof was in the making.

Beside them, the black Lab retriever Cobb had not taken his eyes from the falling birds for an instant, and was staring intently in the direction he must go for the retrieve, only waiting for his master's voice. "Cobb! Two! Two!" David held two fingers spread out in front of his beloved retriever, then released him with an extending arm motion to confirm the line of his retrieve. "Break!" And the black Lab bounded right over the lower side of the blind and launched himself smoothly into the rain-stippled waters of Lost Man Lake, his big head moving forward, leaving V-shaped ripples aimed like an arrow at the downed ducks, now invisible to the hunters low in the grey distance.

This was Cobb's purpose, the love of his canine life as a superb retriever.

And David watched in quiet admiration as his good friend, closest hunting companion and pure-bred Lab from a long line of his forebears, pursued his destiny. The two hunters looked on and waited, saying nothing, for almost four minutes.

David was the first to see Cobb's black head, carefully manoeuvring around the abandoned beaver lodge and decoys, and pointed him out to Al, who nodded that he saw him too. The Lab came powerfully out of the water, over the blind again in one jump, and dropped the two trophy blacks at Big Al's feet, with no evidence showing they had ever been in his teeth and mouth.

"That is some fine old retrievin' dog you got there, Tiger Dave." This was the truth, and David reached into his pocket for Cobb's customary large biscuit treat and reward.

"He earns his biscuits." Cobb accepted his master's welcoming pat and warm congratulations, took his favourite biscuit behind the duck blind and, when he was far enough away, also part of his training, shook the dripping water from his coat and settled down to enjoy the reward and pleasure of his own success.

"His name 'Cob', like corn-on-the?" Yankee Al inquired with a twinkle in his eye. David had to laugh despite himself.

"No, Al. His name's 'Cobb' as in Tyrus Raymond."

"I knew that. But you missed your chance to call him 'Peach' or even 'Georgia,'" Big Al suggested, with another twinkle.

"Well, Cobb's male, so that kind of eliminates 'Georgia.' And I just couldn't hold my head up around manly hunters such as yourself, Al, if I called my gun dog 'Peach.' Probably wouldn't work for him with the other Lab retrievers either, so Cobb seemed a good choice."

"You trying to imply some kinda connection between that ol' Southern boy and your dog? Seems a mite presumptuous." Still the twinkle. David considered this for a few moments, knowing Big Al was having his fun. But when he answered, his response was more formal than he intended and surprised even him.

"Well, I never thought about it that deeply before, Al, beyond it being a reflection of my respect for the talent of the man, the player and the Detroit Tigers manager. But now that you ask, I guess I'd have to say that, like his namesake, Cobb loves the game and is a dedicated player and sportsman. He keeps his eye on the duck and retrieves in all weather conditions no matter the time, place or circumstance. But Cobb's still a team player, and when the ducks are down, always does what it takes to earn his biscuit—just like Ty Cobb for the Tigers. Of course, I'd have to say he has a friendlier disposition, so I don't find Cobb hard to live with in the blind, quite the reverse. We're a team and loyal each to the other and no question."

Now the twinkle was in David's eye.

"But maybe that's because you had that poor black Lab fixed so he couldn't be tomcattin' round's my guess. Turn any self-respecting stud into a pansy."

"Yes, I did have Cobb fixed. But not before I let him sire one litter on a fine black Lab bitch in Peterborough that belongs to his breeder, a formidable woman and skilled veterinarian I respect. So, in a few years, when Cobb's ready to retire, I'll have the pick of the litter from his grandchildren, or some such, down the line a bit. Then there'll always be a little of Old Cobb around me in the blind. I take great pleasure from that idea."

"Well, I'll let ya' in on a little secret, Tiger Dave. I got me one hell of a fine retriever too—German wire-haired breed, a champion—probably give old Cobb a run for his biscuit. And he is one-hundred-percent, all-American stud-ready, and hot to trot, just like his master. And I can further assure you, pansy is never goin' be in his future. Like to lose his whole edge. Makes me all squeamy just thinkin' 'bout doing that to another stud male, even a four-legged one. Be a kind of betrayal!" David bristled at this, but didn't want to disagree outright. Big Al had a lot of ego tied up in the issue.

"Could be, I suppose."

"Anyway, I'm betting you can guess my stud-dog's name, just going on his master's prejudices and predilections from our brief acquaintance." And David was really beginning to enjoy the Carolina cornpone Big Al was laying on. Not that he believed it. David appeared to give the matter some consideration.

"Okay, Al. 'Prejudices and predilections.'... Well, based on those, as far as I can understand them from our discussions of the sport last evening, I'd guess you called your dog, 'Bambi,' like the little deer in Walt Disney that starts out cute and cuddly but grows up to be a fine, powerful buck with a big rack to impress the ladies." Yankee Al shook his head and laughed, then turned mock serious.

"That was not very clever and a definite insult, Tiger Dave. Guess again. And try to show some respect for your own male breed."

"Okay. Sorry. Then I guess I'd have to go with 'Sultana', or maybe one of those longer, more impressive sounding titles like 'The Sultana of Swat', since some of those German retrievers are sort of wrinkled looking and a kind of raisin-brown colour. Was that closer?"

"You are really pullin' my pecker, Tiger Dave. So, I'll just confirm what I expect you already know. My stud-dog's handle is 'Babe', as in George Herman."

"That was going to be my next guess."

"Uh-huh. And like his master, he's already workin' on his third bitch and has such a passel of pups I can't hardly recall the exact number. Believe that's what gives him the edge. Like his namesake, Babe's one hell of a hitter and a winner in every retrieving trial I run him in. I tell ya—" Suddenly, Yankee Al broke off his recitation in mid-boast and pointed behind and over David's right shoulder. The Canadian hunter made out a pair of birds skirting the edge of their area at a very oblique angle. David reached under the sheet for his own shotgun, not taking his eyes off the ducks. "Greenhead and a suzy," Al confirmed with the binoculars, keying on the mallard male's iridescent green head and yellow bill against its mate's sand-brown mottling.

"Cobb, heel." David said softly, and sensed the Lab slip smoothly back into the blind and take up his position beside him, his eyes scanning the sky and then locking on and tracking the two ducks. "May be too far out." David observed quietly, not expecting a shot.

But Big Al already had his duck-call to his mouth, a newer, metal-bodied one, and began selling their position to the mallard pair like he was sweet-talking a reluctant used-car buyer into getting out his chequebook and signing on the dotted line. Yankee Al proved to be a master duck-salesman, as well, and his first series of high, quick calls caught the attention of the mallard male which, still out of range, changed course for a fly-by and closer look. Al softened the call series and brought the bird even closer. David was impressed.

"Range," Al confirmed. And David pushed off the safety but held his fire and stayed down. Both hunters and the Lab remained motionless.

The lead mallard must have bought Al's pitch and liked what it saw, for it spun lower and made a run for the set. But David also had his eye on its mate, which was holding back and slower. Al risked one final series of slow calls, and that seemed to do it. The male was into its flare and about to land in the middle water stretch of the set, not yet aware the birds were decoys, when the brown mottled female finally dropped down to follow.

Because of their separation and the alarm that the first shot would bring, David would have to judge it carefully if he hoped to get both birds. He felt a twinge of reluctance at the suzy, as he usually hunted for males only—but desperately wanted those rare Topps rookie cards for Frank. Al Kaline was his grandson's baseball idol.

"Ra—" Al began, reaching for his Perazzi and taking off the safety in case the Canadian left him a shot at the trailing suzy. But his whisper was lost in the punching report of David's twelve-gauge Browning Auto-loader, when he smoothly stood up and seemed to fire without aiming, dropping the far-out female mate.

Before it could hit the water, David swung like well-oiled clock-work and fired at the male. It had picked up speed at the loud report and was now skimming low over the water, headed for the nearest trees, turning away from its original course and almost parallel to the hunters in the blind.

With the report from the second shot, the fleeing mallard tumbled head over tail into the water, already a full ten yards beyond the decoys on their left. Al could tell by the nature of the fall that David had lead the escaping duck perfectly and made a clean head shot at a difficult angle, so that no one later would be picking shotgun pellets out of his teeth when he dined on this fine duck.

"Great shot there, Tiger Dave!" Al said, as he reset his safety, and David picked up his spent casings. "Seem to do pretty good with that Auto-5."

"Thanks, Yankee Al. I manage to keep myself in ducks and Cobb in biscuits. But I couldn't have gotten them both without your calling. That was one hell of a fine duck call, Al. You are a duck-hunting virtuoso on that fine instrument." Al slapped David on the back and both men laughed, enjoying David's parody. It seemed an instant bond between two very skilled and dedicated duck hunters. Two all-stars of the game, and it looked to be a fine series.

"Hoo-ee, ah love this duck huntin' game! Better get ol' Tyrus Raymond out there see if he can round 'em up."

And David did, sending Cobb out twice to retrieve the widely separated birds. And for that, he thought his loyal Lab deserved a double ration of biscuits as a fellow all-star and his partner in the great game.

Cobb happily agreed.

25   Gamesmen

But Big Al Greathwite was not finished his recitation that the ducks' appearance had so pleasantly and fortuitously interrupted. He resumed as a harder rain began to fall, and David unpacked and shared out a measure of Norah's delicious, warm duck broth for them both, as well as thick ham sandwiches and a can-full of Cobb's favourite dog food for the slavering Lab. All three players relished the break. And if fortune and the gods of duck hunting continued to smile upon the hunters, they would need all the energy and stamina they could get in the worsening weather on Lost Man Lake.

Big Al waved his soup spoon in David's face like an orchestra conductor. "Now, gettin' back to our earlier discussion of the merits of the Bambino, I know any straight-shootin' duckman like yourself can't just help but agree that ol' George Herman Ruth was simply the best damn Major League Baseball player, ever to put spikes on his feet, a pitch on the plate, and wood on a baseball." Yankee Al paused the spoon, looking David straight in the eye, and giving the fellow sportsman his chance to agree. David nodded in consideration, swallowed a mouthful of duck broth, savoured the full flavour of Norah's culinary arts, and marshalled his points of argument in response to the big American's expectation of agreement.

Now the Canadian hunter's spoon conducted his own symphony. "Well, Yankee Al, I would certainly have to agree that no player in history could put wood on a baseball as *hard* as the Babe, especially considering the time and situation of the earlier 'dead ball' era he was playing in, with those baseballs inferior to today's more lively and responsive ones. And don't forget all those cagey pitchers on the mound who didn't hesitate to load them up with tobacco juice, chewing gum, and all that other illegal crap."

"Damn straight, Tiger Dave! Damn straight! The Babe battin' southpaw, hitting seven hundred and fourteen dingers lifetime, with a .690 slugging percentage, and a sixty-run romp in that shorter season, and one hundred and fifty-four game playing schedule. Record still stands! Ol' Commissioner of Baseball Ford C. Frick made the right ruling there when he officialized them stats. Now, I do admire our Yankee slugger Roger Maris, but boy had him another eight whole games in a season to get them sixty-one dingers, and that livelier ball to boot. The Bambino led that whole league in dingers for ten whole seasons—ten whole seasons, Tiger Dave. Ball never knew what hit it, that ol' pin-striper from Baltimore come up to the plate. Never knew! But Major League Baseball and the whole damn world soon did. 'S God's truth." Big Al nodded his certainty and paused his soup spoon and symphony of baseball statistics.

David Phelan nodded thoughtfully in response, paying quiet attention to Big Al's arguments as he continued.

"Can't forget them two thousand an' fifty-six walks, neither. Boy was some kinda stud batsman! Pitchers just about wet themselves, he come to that plate swinging his lumber. George Herman was hell on spikes on them sacks and hell on wheels *inna* sack. Stud after muh own heart. Had him some bat, Tiger Dave! Some kinda bat!" The Canadian laughed and shook his head in wonder at Big Al's command of baseball lore, and the sheer force of his Southern expression, bombast, and continued cornpone.

But David Charles Phelan was no slouch himself when it came to Major League Baseball matters, and stats and history either.

"And I would also agree, Yankee Al, that the Babe was an outstanding pitcher when he began with the old Red Sox organization. I believe Ruth played five seasons there and won almost ninety games for the Soxers, before being sold to the New York Yankees. So yes, the Bambino also knew how to put a baseball on home plate, too."

"Hoo-ee! Tiger Dave, you do know your stats! I'm impressed. Yep, 1914 to 1919, that ol' boy won eighty-seven games and lost only forty-four. But that poor ol' Red Sox owner Bernie Frazee needed money so bad, man was forced to sell *the* greatest player a baseball diamond ever seen to the Yanks. Bet you didn't know, however, the Babe retired as the only studsman to have thrown over one thousand innings and still a lifetime batting average over .300! Was .304 to be precise." Yankee Al Greathwite caught his breath and took a big bite of Norah's thick ham sandwich, well satisfied with the case he had made.

"Very true, Al, all very true. And I do seem to recall that he pitched the longest complete game win in World Series history at Ebbets Field, when he beat the old Brooklyn Dodgers in the early twenties."

"You continue to impress, Tiger Dave. Yep, was in 1923. Went fourteen innings and ended 2–1. The 'Sultan of Swat' made the Yankees all they are today. Got them pin-stripers into that new house called Yankee Stadium, and kept them there with seven pennants and four Series wins." Al finished his sandwich in record time and reached for another, hunching over to shield it from the falling rain. "Can't be any doubt about it. George Herman Ruth is 'The Man' and always will be!"

David seemed to consider it some more while automatically scanning the skyline around Lost Man Lake for any further duck action. It had been more than an hour since he took down the mallard pair. The Invitational World Series of Duck Hunting was tied for the moment.

David, too, reached for his second sandwich, choosing another Canadian bacon. He stared at it thoughtfully and said just one thing: "Five thousand, three hundred and twenty-five."

"What was that, Tiger Dave?"

"Five thousand, three hundred and twenty-five," he repeated.

"And what might that be?"

"That would be the total number of the 4,189 hits, 724 doubles, 295 triples and 117 dingers of Tigers Tyrus Raymond Cobb, lifetime. Not to mention .366, which would be the highest lifetime batting average ever recorded. These, against .342 and 4,229—the first of which you would be familiar with, and the second whose relevance I'm sure you can guess."

Now it was Yankee Al's turn to pause and consider.

"Yep, I believe I can." Al was a successful salesman in a business where running numbers quickly in his head was crucial, and by now second nature. He soon verified the accuracy of David's adding up of the Babe's batting stats, and his lifetime average. "So, you got some point here, Tiger Dave?"

"I believe I do, Al, and it's this: though I would have to agree no player put wood on a baseball as *hard* as the Babe, the 'Georgia Peach' sure put wood on the baseball more *often*. And I might point out, besides the highest lifetime average, the Peach still holds the record with his twelve years leading the Major League in batting. So, I allow Ruth was well endowed in the big bat area, but it's also clear that having the biggest bat isn't everything. The number of times you can swing it successfully is just as important." David stopped and consulted his bacon sandwich, giving Yankee Al some time to digest this point and his own sandwich. Then the Canadian tore off a generous piece of the Canadian pork and fed it to the reclining Cobb, who seemed to be alertly following the hunters' dialogue with a level of interest that David and Al, dog-lovers both, found very engaging. But Cobb also scanned the darkening grey sky like clockwork. The big American spoiled the black Lab retriever with a piece of his own sandwich. Still, David knew this dedicated Yankees fan would stick to his shotguns in these matters.

Big Al didn't disappoint.

"That may be, Tiger Dave, but you can't deny the Babe was *the* most exciting and dramatic! Why, that time he pointed to the sky and swatted that leather-covered pill into the upper deck for that ailing little boy ... hoo-ee, Tiger Dave!"

"Well, that *was* exciting—in legend at least, Al. It's sort of in the realm of myth though, a bit like the 'Black Sox' 1919 Series scandal and Shoeless Joe Jackson's 'say it ain't so' situation, with another kid. I'm not saying 'it ain't so.' But I *do* know one of the most exciting moments in baseball history *was* so, and it produced what many fans and sportswriters agree is *the* most dramatic photograph in the long history of major league baseball. You know the one I mean, Yankee Al?"

Al thought a moment. "Would it be that 1910 shot by sports pho-tographer Charles Conlon, of ol' Tyrus Raymond going down low and dirty, and stealing third base in a cloud of dirt?" David had to shake his head again.

"You continue to impress, Yankee Al. And I believe that memor-able, historical moment was caught on film forever in none other than your own, beloved New York City, at Hilltop Park." Al took his biggest bite of bacon yet and chewed vigorously, unable to let his mouth admit it. But David and Cobb were both looking at him so steadily, with the laughter playing at the corners of David's mouth, that after a few seconds of stalling, Big Al was laughing a little himself and had to shrug his reluctant admission that it was so.

"Course, George Herman Ruth was the more valuable and versa-tile player than Cobb, being both a fine pitcher and a fine slugger."

"Well, Al, I'd argue Tyrus Raymond was both valuable and versatile himself too, being a record-setting hitter, an aggressive base-runner and then a player-manager with the Detroit Tigers for five years at an unheard-of salary of $35,000 a year. I seem to recall a big controversy about Babe Ruth wanting to manage the Yankees, but I don't think he ever did." David waited and watched Al turn more than a bit red as Cobb's stats unfolded.

"That's so, Tiger Dave. Was 1934. Such a damn shame too. That Jacob Rupert was one large hoss's ass, only offering a player of the

Babe's stature a farm club to manage. Just a hoss's ass. Lost him to those Atlanta Braves. Then the boy retired in 1935 after hitting that boomer over the roof of ol' Forbes Field in Pittsburgh.... Never see his like again, Tiger Dave. Never!"

David and Cobb chose to remain still and silent, and respectfully allow Yankee Al Greathwite his moment of reflection and tribute to the Babe. With only a few reservations, they had to agree.

26   Rain Keeps Fallin'

Rain was falling more heavily as the long afternoon stretched and wore on.

Time was passing like slow cement and both duck hunters knew it, but chose to remain stoic and say nothing. This was all to be expected, all part of the Invitational World Series of Duck Hunting, and neither wanted to show disappointment or impatience before the other. The elderly black Lab resolutely continued his scanning of the skies, a true champion retriever in all weathers and conditions. Duck hunting, like baseball, could be a slow game. And they were all three, men and dog, dedicated Major League professionals at it.

Now, American Big Al Greathwite looked at Canadian David Phelan with some curiosity. "Since we're throwin' round numbers, how bout explainin' how you seem to have these facts and figures so handy like. I can see you being familiar with ol' Ty Cobb, being a Detroit Tigers fan an' all, but why the Bambino?"

"Well Yankee Al, I guess you could say I've been a part of many heated arguments about who is the greatest player to ever play the game, for most of my life. It all began with my own father and avid baseball fan, Wallace Charles Phelan, in the early 1900s, who took me over from Windsor, across the Ambassador Bridge and through the old Irish Corktown neighbourhood to Detroit's Tiger Stadium, after the First World War, when it was still called Navin Field. Of course, I was very young, but I got a chance to see some of the greats play on that wonderful old turf—Babe Ruth and Lou Gehrig and Tris Speaker, of course. Hans Wagner's last season at shortstop with the Pirates in 1917. Lots of others. But the Sandwich West Windsor Phelans, my whole family, were diehard Detroit Tigers fans, first, last and always, and my greatest baseball pleasures came in the twenties when Tyrus Raymond Cobb was the Tigers player-manager and the whole outfield lineup, Manush, Heilmann and Fats Fothergill, were all hitting over .400. Those were the red-letter days for diehard Tigers fans like me and Wally."

David poured out more of Norah's rich duck broth for them, now barely tepid, and tried to block the sudden inrush of a familiar unease.

David decided he would *not* tell Big Al anything about both his parents' tragic deaths, especially that of his mother, Lulu Pearl Phelan. How it shattered him and his father Wally, and how both of them clung to baseball and duck hunting like desperate life rafts. How Wally had stopped shooting female ducks entirely without explaining why. Some complex, deep connection to Lulu Pearl's memory, and Wally's burden of guilt in the matter of her death. And how David began to do the same for reasons he too, could not fully express. The suzy he'd downed beside Big Al earlier had been the first in decades, and sat heavy on his conscience. David had still not told his beloved Norah the truth about Wally and his intentional suicide on Lake Erie, nor his son Norm either.

David forced himself to go on with Al and the Phelan males love of baseball.

"The tradition continued with my own son, Norm, and now my grandson Frank, who's ten. Their family still lives in Windsor, and young Frank's just as crazy about Al Kaline as I was about Ty Cobb. We never miss a Tigers home game when Norah and I go down to visit, as we often do. And with my son and grandson sitting cheering beside me and scoring the games on their cards, arguing about who's the 'greatest' now, or then, or ever ... well, it's very, very special. I cherish every minute with Norm and Frank like it was my last—I guess because I know some day it will be."

"Yep. Not many of us get them extra innings, Tiger Dave." This was cutting too close.

"But I'm sure now there'll be another Phelan living and dying with the Tigers, who'll remember the Georgia Peach and what he added to the lore of the game—that hands-apart batting grip, the double-bat warm-up, wearing weighted spiked shoes to train for speed on the bases, and his dirty trick of wetting down the batter's box to screw up the sacrifice bunts for opposing hitters. The man died in 1961, but I want the pleasure Tyrus Raymond Cobb gave me to live on in Frank, like his legend lives on in baseball stories and the record books. Might be a bit selfish too, wanting that little bit of me to live on in my grandson." Big Al sat silent in quiet tribute to a great Tigers player, now gone, and a great baseball lineup.

"Course, speakin' of great lineups, Tiger Dave, you may recall that 1927 was a pretty good year for history, specially the way them poor ol' Pirates was gunned down in four straight Series games by eight batters in the greatest hitting lineup the world has ever seen. I'm speaking of course of the infamous 'Murderers' Row,' wearing their proud Yankees pinstripes and led to glory by the pitching of Pennock, and the bats of Gehrig and Ruth as the big guns at the heart of the Row. Fourth game was amazing, tie in the ninth and the Buck's reliever, Miljus, threw him a wild pitch with two out and let that Yankee Coombs just dance his way across that plate from third. Ruth and them '27 Yankees was the first American League team ever to sweep a World Series. First ever!" Yankee Al Greathwite finished his sandwich, wiped his hands carefully on the chamois David had thoughtfully provided them, and made his final pronouncement:

"The prosecution for the proposition that George Herman Ruth is just *the* greatest baseball player in the history of the game now rests its case."

David finished his own sandwich, took the chamois from Al, wiped his own hands and declared:

"The defence for the proposition that Tyrus Raymond Cobb was just naturally the greatest baseball player to play the game, ever, now *also* rests."

Both duck hunters and baseball fans, American and Canadian, dissolved into hearty laughter and slapped each others' backs in pleasure, sympathy, and friendship.

"Fair enough, Tiger Dave. I believe the jury's still out on this one. So, I suggest we still got us a game here and first base is still open and beckoning. Now, let's us get back to them fine ducks and see just who wins this little Invitational World Series of Duck Hunting here, and goes home with two young Al Kalines in his kit bag. I believe we's all tied up at two and two ducks apiece, and we've had our seventh inning stretch—

"Bring on them birds! Hoo-ee!"

But Lady Luck seemed to have turned her fickle face away.

The two duck hunters waited anxiously in their blind, neither able to relax, and the slow afternoon began to slide by in a cold mizzle of rain and angry storm-fronts pushed by a bitter, fitful wind. The once lively repartee slowly petered out to an occasional desultory comment, and eventually died altogether, when the hours slipped by with no prospect of ducks, much less a possible shot to bring one down. The anxious duck men carefully put away their shotguns under the green tarp and hunkered down in rain-slicked military green ponchos, squeezing and kneading cold gloved hands to retain some hint of flexibility and feeling. The streaks of green and black camo grease each man wore under the brown, Jones-style, short-peaked duck hunting caps, with the earflaps down, gave David and Al the appearance of two sad clown faces. Their chest waders squeaked each time they stood or shifted position to fight the stiffness and find what little comfort they could.

The elderly Cobb too, retreated, crawling under a sheltered corner of the blind David had rigged for him, lying down with his big black head on his paws, looking over at David from time to time and making low, whimpering sounds in his throat. "Easy now, Cobb, old boy, we've both been here before."

In front of their now-sagging duck blind, the wide set of carved duck decoys bobbed and blew around erratically beside the abandoned beaver lodge, a few even drifting out of position, dragging their anchors in the stronger storm gusts. Some ducks, mostly mallards and canvasbacks, did pass them by, far out of range and at long intervals, and were not even worth a duck call.

But mostly, it was long Vs of wild Canada geese, naturally wary and at a distance, returning after a long day of foraging and heading to their roosting grounds somewhere beyond Lost Man Lake to settle down for the night. It was their constant honks, the wind in the trees and the cold rain pattering the water, that competed with the silence of the two men and dog at the near end of small Lost Man Lake.

David gave Cobb a biscuit and a pat to keep up his spirits, but the Lab only toyed with it a while and left it sitting between his paws in front of his nose.

It didn't inspire optimism.

The men wordlessly shared out an ounce of Norah's now cold duck broth from the thermos for a brief relief. And as the wan fall light began to fade, David poured out the final swallows of the now tepid coffee, heavily laced with sugar and a tot of dark rum, to give them a bit of warmth and energy against the chill.

"Well Yankee Al, the light's fading fast, and it looks like we may have to call it a game and a day." The Canadian hunter finally voiced what each had been thinking. And David had really, *really* wanted those rare, Topps #201 Al Kaline rookie cards for grandson Frank. It had now come to nothing. Maybe he should risk a direct cash offer for *one* of them when they got back to Buckhorn Lake and his waiting Norah—what David could afford anyway. He didn't hold out much hope though.

"Yeah. Looks like you may be right-on there, Tiger Dave. Big damn shame though. Big one! Day starting so well an' all. Looked like we might limit out before noon and be home to dinner early, with five fine birds each in our pockets. Surely did. Most of them birds seemed headed for other parts of these swamps, flying so high and not even cruising our set. Feels like bein' all het up and ready to rumble, and then forced to sit on the bench too long on account of some damn rain delay. Now our big Invitational Major League Duck Hunt's been rained out and called on account of dark both."

Big Al was all out of hoo-ees.

Part Four

Cobb's Crisis

27

Shot in the Dark

The two avid gamesmen and duck hunters had stayed long as they possibly could behind their sagging duck blind. Cobb came a little alert as they began to shift under the still heavy rain, pulling their soaking gear together.

The last vestiges of grey light were just about gone on the shores of Lost Man Lake to the northwest, when they rose stiffly and began to pack their gear into the large, waterproof canvas kit bags. Both David and Al were slow and shivering despite the ponchos, sugar and rum. Now Cobb climbed slowly to his feet with a long whine and stretched repeatedly to work out the tightness in his retriever muscles and the joints of his flanks and shoulders, almost painful from the chill and inactivity of the last few hours.

Then the big black Labrador retriever walked deliberately out behind the blind to give his soaking fur coat a good shake and urinate noisily—and so Cobb was the first to hear the next skein of Canadas, coming up behind them from the southeast. Cobb listened for a few moments, shook himself a last time and then walked back and sat next to David while his master and the American sportsman finished packing the last of their duck gear.

Out of long habit and instinct, the retriever kept his eyes and ears on the geese that were now tracing a course to pass right overhead of the blind. Cobb made a small growling noise in his throat as the flock approached, and David stopped long enough to shush his Lab when he too heard, but ignored, the familiar honks. "Quiet, Cobb. It's just more Canadas."

But David was mistaken—very mistaken....

And although he would never after know how Cobb had sensed it in these adverse conditions and at that distance, and under the persistent honks of the Canada Geese, his beloved big black Lab went abruptly rigid with tension and continued to look, listen and growl low in his throat.

Then Cobb stood up straight and went stiffly into his familiar retriever duck point.

Birds! Ducks! Must be!

Now David and Al froze as well, and looked up and out through the cold streaming rain at the honking Canadas, while they passed almost directly overhead in a high, ragged V. But it wasn't the Canada Geese that suddenly drew David's complete attention—it was the very much smaller covey of peppercorn dots trailing behind and below them, seeming to show indistinct flashes of what might be narrow white belly as they flew northwest, to where the last rays of watery light had almost vanished behind the heavy rain.

Both duck hunters remained motionless and intent, no longer from the cold, but from complete and utter disbelief—

It might have been only vivid imagination and desperate wishful thinking, yet underneath the receding voices of the geese, David began to think he heard short whistles, peeps, and the occasional sharp quack. Cobb must've shared the same hallucination and brushed his big black head deliberately against David's left leg, too disciplined to bark, but wanting to snap his master out of his lethargy.

"My God! It's teal! Teal! Take them, Al!"

But was it already too late for these smallest and most unexpected of ducks?

Yankee Al Greathwite reached quickly under the green rubber sheet for his custom Perazzi twelve-gauge, stood straight up and pulled it to his shoulder, nimbly fingered off the safety and tracked the little flight of green-winged teal for the barest fraction of a second.

The small flock was rapidly disappearing into the heavy rain and overcast, already forty-five yards out.

Bam! Bam!

Alerted first by Al's sudden movement, and then by the two loud shots that followed, the green-winged teal revved up to their maximum speed and approached a panicked thirty miles an hour within a few short yards.

But in his haste not to lose them, and on the thick muddy ground, Big Al went slightly off balance and out of his rhythm, yet had fired twice in desperation and disgust—with no effect....

The little covey of teal merged with the sooty grey of the horizon and flew on, almost disappearing into the opaque darkness that all but closed them in.

David too, had his Browning twelve-gauge up and ready, safety off, but still careful to track safely ahead of Al. Before the echo of the big New Yorker's second shot began to fade, and Al could expel the first of his curses of frustration, David fired once into the rain and grey gloom—

It was over sixty yards out, far ahead of, and above, where the last of the small flock of green-winged teal vanished a moment before. And as soon as he fired, David knew he shouldn't have.

"Damn my stupidity! Damn it to hell!"

David loudly berated himself for his *utter* lack of shooting discipline. He was a better duck hunter than that! The wasted shot meant the persistent shotgun pellets would fall into Lost Man Lake to no purpose, and very possibly pose some risk to other wildlife that might take it up, although the pellets were not the older, more poisonous lead of previous times. But worse, it might leave a shot bird down and wounded to die a slow lingering death from shock and exposure.

"So bloody stupid! Just stupid!"

The hollow reverberations of the three twelve-gauge shotgun reports faded slowly over the dark lake, swallowed up in the cold, heavy air and dampness. Everything was suddenly eerily quiet, save for Al's continuing imprecations beside him. David would have joined him in voicing the same angry sentiments, but it was not really his habit, and the big Chrysler salesman from New York, by way of South Carolina, was doing it loudly and well enough for them both.

"Goddamn! Didn't see 'im in time. Goddamn it! Too old. Too cold. Too slow, Tiger Dave. Who would've thought them sneaky little teal bastards would come over behind them big honkers. Dumbest shots and cleanest misses I had in a long time. Waste of good shells. Now, who's the ass end of a hoss?"

"Yeah. Me too, Yankee Al. Lost my usual discipline and don't like it one little bit. Don't know why the hell I fired even that one shot. Not just old and cold and slow, but stone stupid too. Might have risked some poor teal cripples dropping into that frigid water to suffer a lingering death. Just not sporting." David worked the big Browning's well-oiled action and recovered the spent casing and second shell. "Well, dumb is done. So, let's get the gear in the boat and start collecting the de—"

Both men heard the sudden splash in the grey gloom in front of them.

"What in hell? Cobb? Cobb, that you? Where are you, boy?" David left the blind with sinking muddy steps and moved to the edge of the rain-dark water. He cupped both hands around his mouth, "Come back here, boy. Cobb! Heel, dog! Heel now!"

But David Phelan was too late.

His loyal Labrador retriever had jumped the duck blind completely and disappeared into Lost Man Lake, a black Lab in a black water wilderness and thick grey gloom of rain. In thirty seconds, even the sound of his Lab's swimming efforts died away. David was left shouting hoarsely over the now invisible lake, and then cursing himself and his retriever as he rummaged clumsily for his flashlight and tried to cover his increasing worry, now verging on panic.

The minutes dragged by.

Rain fell like Judgment.

There was no sign of Cobb returning at David's repeated commands.

The hunter's voice went hoarse, his nerves vibrated with his worry and worst fear: that he might lose his most beloved canine companion forever. Forever! The heavy word jarred and echoed in his head. "Stupid!"

David didn't know if he meant Cobb or himself, but suspected the latter.

"Okay, Tiger Dave. Okay! I'll work the damn light. You keep calling out," Big Al ordered. The big Chrysler dealer's Carolina cornpone and hush-puppy accent were now totally absent, and David did as he was told.

"Co-o-o-b! Here fella! Co-o-b! Come on, boy! Come to me, dog! Heel, Cobb! Heel!"

Not a sound.

Eight minutes had crawled by like slow caterpillars, according to the glowing dial on Big Al's gold Rolex, while David paced the muddy shoreline calling, gesticulating, cursing himself. The big New Yorker was becoming alarmed at the growing desperation, anger, and self-reproach in David's voice, growing more strident and hoarse by the moment. The Canadian hunter had seemed so quiet and controlled that this change was completely unnerving. And Al really didn't know David all that well. He wasn't quite sure what to expect.

The man obviously worshipped that elderly black Lab of his.

Three more minutes crawled by on caterpillar feet, and David was shouting less, a deep pit of cold panic and growing dread opening up in his gut. David knew the lake water was mercilessly frigid, that even good, experienced dogs could become disoriented, lose their way in the dark and rain. Swimming Labs, in strange dead-wood waters, could gut themselves on the sharp spikes of submerged snags, could become fatally tangled in old fishing line or anchor rope, or just succumb to hypothermia and pure exhaustion, and sink to their dark, solitary deaths—even smart, strong dogs like Cobb. And truth be told, at eleven years of age, Cobb was no longer young, his prime duck retriever years behind him.

More minutes passed. More Judgment fell.

David paced and called, cursed, and begged. The Canadian could already begin to trace the empty black hollow inside himself, in his days and his life, that would be left if the dog he'd loved and trained from a pup were suddenly taken from him in this tragic way. Simply lost at night on a small, dark lake in wilderness, his exact fate unknown. No chance to stroke that big black head a last time, to say don't be afraid, I'm right here, to say thank you for the years of love, loyalty and companionship, years of service in the quest for ducks. No chance to take his intimate, proper leave, and let Cobb lovingly go at last. First Lulu Pearl, then Wallace Charles, now this.

It wasn't fair. Wasn't!

"The boat! Shoulda thought ... get to him, pull him in, be all right..." David scrambled for the overturned *Lulu Pearl II* under the camouflage netting, and began to try and heave it over in the dark—

Big Al Greathwite encircled David's waist strongly from behind and held on, dropping the flashlight in the process when David struggled.

"Easy, Dave! Easy! I'm so goddamned sorry, so sorry, but Cobb's gone. He's gone. Been almost twenty minutes. Way too cold. It's over! Cobb was a mighty fine retriever, Dave. Did what he was trained to do. But it's too dark, too cold, too late now to risk your life too. I understand. I truly do. Doing something heroic ... but too risky, getting your own self in trouble. Putting your own life in danger. Think of Norah."

But the Canadian duck hunter continued to struggle against Al's restraint.

"Come on now! I'm with you here, Dave. Take it easy now. I understand. I'm with you..." And Al held him in his large embrace until David slowly went limp and slid down in the marsh grass and mud at the edge of the black water. He sat with his back against the duck boat, put his head in his hands, and softly wept.

Big Al retrieved the fallen flashlight, but kept it pointed at the ground while he slid heavily down too, to sit beside David. There was no real sound, but Al could feel the deep sobs shaking the Canadian's body through the hull of the *Lulu Pearl II*.

"Big damned dog. Foolish action. No command. Never said a word. Why'd he do it, Al? Why?"

Big Al shifted toward David in the rain and dark, and draped his arm over the Canadian's shoulder in sympathy. The two hunters remained that way for some minutes, each in his own silent thoughts.

Until—

David Phelan felt Big Al Greathwite's hand press against his left thigh in sympathy, and he could take a deep, shuddering breath and begin to resign himself to the reality of Cobb's death and loss. Get ready for the bitter journey home in the cold, wet dark without his beloved friend and companion. David murmured his quiet "Goodbye" to the lost Lab and began to shift to his feet. "Right, Al, right. Have to face it."

Al's hand never moved.

And when David reached down in the dark to squeeze it, the hand was a head—wide and wet and panting. Something soft as a baby's breath dropped into David's lap. A familiar, slobbering tongue found and licked his exploring hand. And before his duck hunter's brain could register it, David Charles Phelan's mouth was open wide and laughing hysterically one second, babbling incoherent nonsense the next. His excited hands lovingly stroked the thick black fur and his stiff arms hugged and rocked his great wet dog, a dog that was too exhausted, too weak to do more than pant and shiver and collapse heavily against his master, now mumbling constant nonsense.

David bent down, ground his face again and again into the dripping scruff of Cobb's neck, inhaling his rich, familiar Lab smell. Big Al turned the flashlight on David and the exhausted black Lab retriever, and was only slightly more articulate, his Carolina cornpone flooding back—

"Well, I'll be screwed, blued and double-tattooed, if it ain't ol' Tyrus Raymond hisself, back from the dead, bigger than sin and twice as ugly! Don't know whether to shit or spit stones. Hoo-ee, Tiger Dave! That is one hell of a fine retrieving dog you got there. Just lookit this here! Jus' lookit it!"

David at last lifted his cheek from Cobb's thick ruff and looked down on his lap—where Cobb's head rested and Al's flashlight invited him—at the small, soft-feathered body of a green-winged teal.

Then David couldn't help himself again. Couldn't. He began to sob and shake and hold his big black dog close, rocking back and forth, completely overwhelmed by yet more and stronger emotion.

28   Dr. Ann Decides

David was so deliriously relieved at having Cobb back from the dead that it took him another minute to fully realize something was very, very wrong with his loyal black Labrador retriever.

Cobb's entire wet body was shaken by spasms of shivering and periodic muscle contractions that verged on convulsion. Cobb couldn't seem to hold up his heavy head. And when David used the flashlight, he saw Cobb's eyes partially rolled-back, showing white and unfocused, and his tongue lolling.

David called his name and tried to get the Lab to stand, but the retriever only collapsed back against him, and Cobb's movements were feeble and lethargic.

From immense relief and joy, David's emotions ratcheted down into the depths of near uncontrolled panic: Cobb was seriously hypothermic. Seriously at risk of his life—the life he'd risked for this lovely small green-winged teal and the master he adored. Now, if David didn't take exactly the right remedial actions instantly and at speed, his loyal aging Lab retriever and best friend in the world, would die right here in his own arms....

"No! You can't die, Cobb! You can't!"

David took a deep, steadying breath, got his duck hunter's iron control and purpose back, and jumped into action.

"Al, Cobb's in very bad shape. Very bad! Got critical hypothermia. He was in that frigid water way too long and completely exhausted himself retrieving my goddamned teal. My stupid shot in the dark! Now he's shaking himself to pieces, eyes rolling up and losing consciousness. We've got to get him out now. Right goddamned now!" David was already vigorously rubbing down Cobb's wet fur with the chamois and then wrapping him tightly in the spare wool sweater from his dry pack, tying it on with the arms. Yankee Al Greathwite was extremely relieved to see his duck hunting companion decisive and rational again, even if the circumstances were dire, even hopeless, he feared.

Yankee Al was ready as well, and jumped into his own decisive action. "Right, Tiger Dave! I'll round up them decoys and then we can get going pronto."

David thought of his father Wally, all those years after blaming himself for his beloved Lulu Pearl's death and finally seeking his own death in self-retribution. Whether irrational or God's just punishment, the result was the same pain, the same guilt, and the ongoing agony of self-reproach. David had done his best to follow his mother's last deathbed request, to not blame his father for her death, to live his life to the fullest and not look back.

Did he succeed? Had Wally suspected? What was he thinking about his only son David when he drilled those one-inch holes through the heartwood bottom of the *Lulu Pearl* on the similarly frigid waters of Lake Erie? The emotions surrounding those fraught events were too tangled to say with certainty. But David *did* know he would blame his own self forever after, if Cobb died because of his own careless risk and stupidity, his loss of duck hunter discipline in taking that impossible shot.

"I said I'll get the decoys, Tiger Dave, so—"

"Forget the decoys! No time to waste, Al. Pack the guns, throw the soft gear in the front of the boat, get both flashlights out and launch it. Right now! I'll sit up in the bow holding Cobb and direct you back downstream to the truck through this rain and darkness." David stood straight up with Cobb in his arms, amazing the big American with his sudden Herculean strength and will. "I know these little channels well now, Al, but it's pitch black, so we'll use just the electric trolling motor and make the best time going with the current that we can. Okay? Don't want to risk an upset with the outboard's speed and collide with something."

"Got ya, Dave! Jus' take care of ol' Tyrus Raymond there and leave the rest to me. That son's gotta lotta heart. He's gonna make it. You'll see." Yankee Al still had grave doubts about that, but this was exactly the wrong time to voice them.

While the big American duck hunter packed and manoeuvred the *Lulu Pearl II* into position in record time, David dug out the first aid kit and ripped open the packaging of his newest addition to the emergency supplies, the wide silver foil of a thermal blanket. He cut a length of anchor line with his old folding hunter knife, and tied the foil thermal blanket around Cobb and the sweater to preserve what body heat remained, so that only his Lab's greying muzzle showed. David kept shaking Cobb's head gently and calling to him to hang on, repeating his name continuously. He was very afraid of ever letting him lose consciousness.

That would likely be the end of them both.

The big Lab heart seemed to be beating much too slowly now, and Cobb's breathing was fast and dangerously shallow. David had the sudden premonition they just weren't going to make it. Weren't. The thought that he would feel Cobb's heart sputter and stall right beneath his hands was unthinkable. That goddamned Topps #201 Kaline rookie card bet seemed so juvenile, so pointless now, for a man of his years. Yes, David had wanted it for his grandson Frank. Yet David would never forgive himself, never, if his rash actions killed his beloved dog because of a stupid baseball card and a shot he should never have taken.

Out of the darkness, more rain fell like more judgment. David continued to berate himself under his breath. It had been too late in the day, too dark, too great a range, so goddamned, Christly stupid and unlike him, and this was the result.

David unscrewed the top of his thermos, tilted Cobb's head back a little so his mouth hung open, and began to slowly pour the last last few dregs of cold duck broth into the side of his Lab's mouth, stroking his throat and speaking constant encouragement. It was too little. Cobb seemed on the verge of choking, so David adjusted his ministrations and at last managed to get him to swallow only a last ounce or two. The rest dribbled away.

It would have to do.

Big Al Greathwite was soon ready with the wide, flat-bottomed duck boat, and David waded determinedly out with Cobb in his arms and placed him on their flattened packs in the bow for a moment. He covered the Lab with his poncho and stepped in swiftly, retrieving the two flashlights from Al in the stern and again amazing the American.

"Go! Go! Go!"

David gave the word, and Yankee Al launched them and started the *Lulu Pearl II* downstream as safely, but as fast as he could. The small Minn Kota trolling motor's thirty-two pounds of thrust, combining with the fall current, pushed them along at a surprisingly good clip. David now held Cobb on his lap, kept the rain off him as best he could, wished in vain for a clear night and a bright fall moon, but using the flashlights and his best recollections, gave directions to Al that kept them mostly in the main channel.

Twice, David, and Cobb with him, were almost swept overboard in the blackness, when his directions brought the determined hunters into the branches of overhanging deadfall, David losing his lucky hunting cap the second time. Once, the *Lulu Pearl II did* ground on a gravel bar when taking a bend too sharply—

"Damn! Goddamn!" David exclaimed, despairing.

But Big Al jumped nimbly out to push them off the grating stones and hopped in again at the stern. Amazing, really, for a man his size. Yet both duck hunters retained a firm composure, though leavened throughout with an unending stream of course salty comments from Al.

Still. Still. The hazardous journey in the dense rain and dark, which an impatient David judged must be close to seven miles, was taking far too long....

David Charles Phelan sensed Cobb's heartbeat was still slow now, but the periodic spasms were less frequent. He didn't know if this last was a good sign, but suspected it was the exact opposite. David kept calling regularly to Cobb and shaking the Lab's great head, willing him to hang on. The diminishing light of the second flashlight showed the rain like silver metal, with the feel of shrapnel against his face. The channel turned grey-green, became surreal and went to matte black as the flashlight blinked out.

The hunters covered the last half-mile in the total dark: the rain-filled duck boat sloshing and scraping from shore to shore; David shouting directions; Cobb a dead weight; Al cursing the motor and the uncertain world from the darkness behind them.

The low iron bridge and the parked, half-ton Ford F-150 truck and trailer were angular black masses that David sensed rather than saw against the wet streaming sky. The two fraught duck hunters were almost under them when he shouted to Al to kill the Minn Kota and felt for the cement bridge abutment to stop the duck boat. Almost an hour had passed like a struggling year, each man knowing what that meant, what had to be done.

"Bring the guns. Leave the boat, Al! Unhook the trailer. I'll see to Cobb and start up the damn truck." David slipped to his knees twice, cursing and scrambling up the sodden mud riverbank, but finally released the Ford's door handle, heaved the limp mass of Cobb onto the front passenger seat, scrambled over him, fumbled with the keys, but at last started the engine and turned up the F-150's heater and fan to their fullest.

Big Al Greathwite said not a word.

But, panting heavily, the American duck hunter quickly secured the *Lulu Pearl II* to a low-lying scrub cedar and let the current swing it out of sight under the bridge, where he hoped it would be safe from potential theft. He splashed loudly up the slippery bank with the duck guns and more choice comments. Big Al then whipped off the trailer's chains and released the hitch in record time, jumped into the driver's seat and stowed the shotguns behind them with a dangerous rattle.

"You drive, I'll navigate, Al." David urged.

"No problemo, Tiger Dave! Carolina boys got moonshine an' road grit in our blood. Don't just sell that big Chrysler iron, not know how to ride it." Yankee Al hit the brights, put the half-ton Ford in drive and crushed the accelerator, peeling away on the white-lit gravel with the Ford as much off the road as on—pounding the wheel, straightening the curves, and showing complete disrespect for soft shoulders, overgrown bushes, and the occasional warning sign. Al rode those back country roads at breakneck speed and with a dangerous, insane disregard for any limits.

David hugged Cobb close in his silver-foil blanket and wool sweater, and prayed to whatever gods, Christian or pagan, were listening. He directed them quickly onto the black, two-lane highway, where Big Al continued to ignore the speed limit, passing the few other vehicles dangerously close and drawing lingering blasts of horn. They sped on into the night until at last, the two keyed-up duck hunters pulled up to the neat residence of David's friend, and skilled veterinarian, Dr. Ann Spence. He had purchased Cobb from Dr. Ann as a superbly bred black Lab pup, the best of the litter in his opinion, and Ann's too. Cobb had not disappointed. Now it was David's turn to do everything he could to repay the bounty of those many years of love, loyalty and retrieving service with which his beloved gun dog had blessed him.

David *must* not, *could* not fail....

Dr. Ann Spence was an experienced, well-respected, large-animal vet, who kept this smaller, in-town house and treatment facility for lesser domestic pets and animals, in the thriving village of Stoney-brook. David just hoped like hell and prayed to those same pagan or Christian gods that she would be in town this evening when he could not have a chance to call ahead and alert her. Dr. Ann's much bigger large-animal veterinary surgery and cattle-breeding operation were on the other side of Stoneybrook, much farther away. David was taking a huge gamble, but was certain his dying Lab would never make it as far as the Spences' cattle ranch.

Big Al was skeptical. "You sure you trust this here lady vet with ol' Cobb's life, Tiger Dave?"

"No one else, Al. More than my own doctor. Ann bred Cobb true."

29 Care and Cattle Sleeves

It was eight thirty p.m. and near pitch dark when David Charles Phelan kicked loudly and repeatedly on Dr. Ann's steel-clad, front security door.

By this time, Cobb was totally unresponsive, unconscious and fading fast. Was it already too little, too late? Had he failed his beloved gun dog when the faithful retriever needed him most? David didn't know.

But by all the gods in all the firmaments, he had to try—

Luckily for David, Dr. Ann Spence *was* indeed in her clinic, but very upset at having her big steel front door kicked loudly and repeatedly, this late in the fall evening. She yanked it open to confront the intruder.

"What in the goddamned heights of hell you think you're doin', kicking at my front door like that this time a' night?" Ann was a large formidable woman and had her big right fist cocked back and ready to do serious damage. "Why, I oughta..." It took Dr. Ann a few dangerous seconds of shocked, angry disbelief before she recognized the strained face staring white-eyed at her under its thick smears of green and black camouflage grease. "David Charles Phelan! It's you!

What d'ya mean puttin' your muddy damn boots to my door like that at this hour? Like to scare the livin' shit right outta me!"

Dr. Ann Spence was in her early forties and filled her own doorway like a female Hulk Hogan, and looking like she could wrestle even Big Al Greathwite to the ground and not lose a breath doing it. And Ann was in an aroused and explosive mood to do exactly that, David had no doubt. Big Al was pushing David, holding Cobb in his arms, hard through her front door from behind and right into Dr. Ann, forcing the "lady" vet to give unaccustomed way in her very own home and clinic.

Then the big brash American duck hunter made matters much, much worse.

"Sorry, ma'am! Sorry! Not a damn second to waste! Got us a sick Lab pup here, half-dead from freezing water and hypothermia, and plumb exhausted. Needs help very damn quick or ... well, the big ol' boy, he ain't gonna make it, no way, no how. Money no object whatsoever. None! Whatever it takes, spare no expense, none. Got muh big fat chequebook open and ready for the finest care and treatment money can buy 'round here."

David winced heavily back and felt himself cringe, despite his own exhaustion and agitation, knowing exactly the force five hurricane that was coming and dreading it.

The Canadian duck hunter knew only too well that Dr. Ann Spence, the "lady vet," had been given this exact species of loud, crass, arrogant marching orders from some of the wealthiest, most entitled and domineering male breeders around, whether of cats, dogs, sheep, horses, cattle or titmice. And Dr. Ann invariably went absolutely livid with outrage at the bald-faced insult and lack of respect for her expertise and long years of specific care—and most especially at the least suggestion that she would ever, ever put money before the health and well-being of the distressed animals she had dedicated her life to serving.

Dr. Ann Spence didn't mince words. She fired them, like exploding, Imperial load, twelve-gauge shotgun shells from an automatic cannon. But first, Ann lunged abruptly forward with both hands out and shoved Big Al Greathwite back so hard he cried out in surprised alarm, fell awkwardly back, arms windmilling, and only saved himself from landing on his fat ass by grabbing at Ann's door frame as he went by—

"A-a-a-a-h! What in hell!?"

Dr. Ann Spence bent forward with both fists on her hips and morsels of her white spit stippling Big Al's camo-greased face for emphasis as she shouted at him.

"I don't know who your lard-assed, goddamned friend here is, Phelan, but he better believe I got my big right fist cocked, ready and willing here, and if he doesn't knock the fuck off with that chequebook bullshit, I'm gonna put on my plastic cattle sleeve and give him a rectal he'll remember for the rest of his sorry-ass life!"

Big Al spluttered his own saliva nonsense, bugged his eyes in surprise, but straightened abruptly to step hurriedly back from the unexpected vehemence of the vet's threat.

Dr. Ann Spence immediately took the heavy, wet black bulk of the unconscious Cobb from his master's sagging arms. David Phelan fell back against her door frame in relief, panted deeply, but managed to get his words out.

"I'm ... sorry, Ann. Really. I'm so sorry. We're both very upset ... in bit of a panic to reach you here, and ... thank the gods you're in. An emergency. Cobb on a far-out retrieve. Swimming in the dark, in near-freezing water. Trying to find a downed duck I didn't ... didn't realize I'd shot. Was too long ... way too long. Maybe wasn't sure either, but Cobb went into the water before ... before I could stop him. Thought I'd lost my dog in the dark forever. Stupid damned shot. So goddamned stupid! Seemed like hours. Drove me crazy. Still don't know how in hell Cobb made it back to the duck blind.... And with my green-winged teal in his mouth. Unbelievable. My own damn fault. Too risky shot from too far out in the dark. Did what we could, Ann, but ... but he needs the best, so..."

"Okay. Okay, Phelan. I got the picture."

Big Al Greathwite stepped cautiously through the steel door, and pulled it closed behind him, still hesitant to enter. But Ann Spence was already turning away, speaking over her right shoulder.

"Now cut the shit, Phelan, deal with the guilt later. Follow me out back. See what we can do for the poor old boy. But have to say up front, old Cobb doesn't look good. Not at all. So don't go getting your hopes too high. And get ready for the worst. The worst. Understand?"

David hung his head in resignation and nodded at the likely possibility of Cobb's loss, as he followed Ann into her examination room with its long, padded veterinarian's table.

"Both George and Billy are down in Peterborough for that big Peterborough Petes hockey game tonight, so get the hell outta that goddamned wet rubber right now. You'll have to assist. And you give your loud-mouthed buddy here your number too and show him the phone. He needs to call Norah right away and fill her in on what's happened. She'll be worried half to death about you already, and waiting for some word."

In his continued anxiety and deep emotional distress, David had completely forgotten about his beloved wife Norah. He pounded his forehead with a fist. "I am so, so stupid!"

"Yeah, so are we all at times, Phelan! Now get a goddamned grip and let's get this started. If there's still time; it's about to run out for your old Lab retriever."

Al bristled again, but kept his mouth shut and did as he was told at the telephone. He tried his best to reassure the anxious Norah, and promised her repeatedly that David would call with news of Cobb as soon as he could. Then the American duck hunter joined his new Canadian friend and the formidable female veterinarian in her small-animal clinic at the rear of the house.

The term "lady" had been seared from Big Al's tongue, never to be uttered again in her presence.

David explained what he'd already tried to do for Cobb, while Dr. Ann unwrapped him on her examination table. She immediately covered the big Lab again with an electric thermal blanket, setting the controls for a slow increase in temperature. She inserted a rectal thermometer, and then checked Cobb's heart rate, lungs, eyes, mouth, and paw-pads. All the time, David hovered and fidgeted and said small, silent prayers to any god or goddess, pagan or Christian, who might listen and take pity on his elderly Lab. Ann checked Cobb's heart again and then pulled the thermometer and consulted it. She shook her head.

"I'm sorry, Dave. I truly am. But it doesn't look good for the old boy at his age and in this condition. Cobb's body temperature is so low from the exposure, the freezing water, and his heart has suffered a great deal of strain. The beat is weak and uneven. He must've been swimming in that frigid water the whole time, and I'm beyond amazed he made it back to you at all. Cobb's heart and liver, especially, are chilled and his metabolism is slowed. That's why he finally lost consciousness. In my long experience, the old boy should be dead already. But you did all the right things with that bit of fluid, Dave, the thermal blanket and sweater, and trying to keep him conscious."

"Please try, Ann. Anything you can do, even it if it seems hopeless ... please." David begged. Dr. Ann looked at David with a sly smile.

"Said, it *looks* real bad. Didn't say hopeless." She squeezed David's arm. "Of course, I'm going to do all I can. Just want you to be prepared for the very worst if it doesn't work out. So, you got hold of yourself? You ready to go to work?"

"Anything, Ann. Just tell me what to do."

"Okay. We need to get some warm glucose and nutrient fluids into Cobb. That will help reverse the internal heat loss and give him some energy, get his metabolism primed to get his heart rate and circulation up. Got to keep Cobb's heart from passing the critical temperature point and stopping altogether. Get the heart and the liver warm enough for return to normal function. So, Dave, you hold his head firm and steady, with his mouth open, while I insert this feeding tube into Cobb's stomach."

David did as he was instructed. His beloved Lab was still unresponsive.

The hunter watched with great trepidation as Dr. Ann skilfully inserted the flexible tube, filled a large syringe with a viscous mixture of glucose and other nutrients, attached it, and steadily fed the fluid into Cobb's stomach. Then the vet carefully withdrew the tube. "Now, Dave, we've got to get him conscious and active, so you start working his legs slowly, getting them going, making them walk, while I massage him. And it wouldn't hurt to call Cobb's name and encourage him to come around and respond." Ann held David's eye.

"Yeah. Been doin' that for a while now, Ann."

David tried his level best and resumed the pattern of calling and encouragement he'd begun hours before, while working Cobb's front and hind legs, and smoothly rubbing his wide black face. Ann massaged the prone Lab's body with some vigour, and periodically monitored temperature and heart rate.

And David was hardly aware of Big Al Greathwite watching it all silently, slightly behind and off to the side. No sign of the American Chrysler dealer's usual banter or brashness or even words of encouragement, as if he were slightly amazed, now that he had a chance to reflect on it all. That he, a duck hunter from the United States of America, a stranger and newcomer, found himself amidst an energetic, critical fight for an old dog's life, in the small Canadian village of Stoneybrook that he'd never heard of.

Big Al Greathwite shook his own wide head in quiet amazement.

David would not realize until much later, the depth, power, and impact these events were having on his fellow duck hunter. That Big Al, a bombastic, cornpone-spouting Chrysler dealer from New York, was impressed as all get-out by this old Lab's loyalty and will to retrieve for his beloved master in the direst of circumstances; by David's stolid and complete determination to pull Cobb back from the brink of death; by Ann's candour about Cobb's near-fatal condition and risk; and by the formidable vet's total commitment to doing the utmost she could to give the big black Lab his last fighting chance, when it looked to Big Al like no chance at all....

For Big Al Greathwite, it was a moment of unsought, unwanted, and uncomfortable witness and self-reflection, the like of which he had rarely allowed himself. The sudden process was decidedly uncomfortable and deeply disturbing. Big Al's wealth, his trophy wives, his slick salesmanship, his chronic bombast, his affected cornpone expression didn't matter here. Not a goddamned whit.

In this unlooked-for place and moment, he had no standing. None.

Al had been a professed Roman Catholic for all his long years, and three marriages along the way. What had happened to that Catholic faith and belief he so easily, so thoughtlessly professed? He was no longer sure. Had he been lying to himself like some gormless fool? For decades? Yes.

But not now. Not in this sudden moment of uncomfortable self-reflection.

Now, Big Al Greathwite wanted very *much* to matter—to himself, to David, to Dr. Ann, to the Catholic Church, to his God and to the wider world. He wanted very much for old Cobb to live. For that impossible retrieve from the brink to mean something. For his fellow hunter and now unexpected Canadian friend David's sake, but very much for his own sake, as well. Without apparent volition, the lapsed

Roman Catholic Chrysler dealer from New York found himself quietly reciting words his conscious mind had forgotten—the *Our Fathers* and the *Hail Marys* of his boyhood, on Cobb's behalf.

David Charles Phelan tirelessly laboured, in full commitment and concentration, on his task, but he finally noticed and processed the murmurs of Big Al's subvocal prayers and appeals. "You say something, Al?" The American duck hunter was shy, reticent.

"Just something from my childhood, Tiger Dave. Thought it might help."

"I'm very, very grateful to you, Al, in your debt forever. No matter what happens. You'll always have my gratitude for what you did for Cobb." Yankee Al nodded gravely in acknowledgement; the murmurs resumed; and David continued his grim, heroic struggle for his beloved Lab's life....

And maybe it did help—Al and Cobb both—because Big Al was the first one to notice, and leaned in to make the momentous announcement.

"Son's awake! I think Cobb's awake! Hallelujah!"

And sure enough, old Cobb's tired eyes were open and trying to find their focus. It took a long while. And as David steadily repeated his dog's name with increasingly joyful relief, the elderly black Lab wagged his tail feebly and tried to lick his master's hand. Dr. Ann bent closer and quickly confirmed Cobb's return to consciousness, the stronger heartbeat her stethoscope revealed, and a body temperature that was steadily rising.

"Right, Dave! Old Cobb is officially back from the brink and in the land of the living. Now we need to hold him here. It's crucial. So next thing, Dave, is to keep Cobb conscious, eyes open, heart pumping and get him active. But slowly, steadily, a little at a time, by getting the old boy on his feet and supporting him while you begin to encourage him to walk a bit. Being active will continue to warm his heart and liver to a level of more normal function, and allow them to reheat the body and then, slowly, his extremities. So, you get at it, David Charles Phelan! Life or death. Get at it!"

This treatment of forcing the elderly Cobb to walk, appeared counter-intuitive to David, when the Lab seemed mostly, and sensibly, to just want to sleep and recover his lost strength. But David's faith in Dr. Ann Spence was absolute. He did exactly as he was bidden by the talented vet and breeder that had brought his beloved Cobb into this world, and his own life, in the first place.

The exhausted but relieved Canadian duck hunter soon had a groggy, lethargic Cobb upright and on his feet on the floor, and was bending to support his faithful companion of many years, slowly encouraging the black Labrador by voice, name, and gentle pressure to begin a slow, unsteady walk around the examination table. David supported him at his side and led Cobb to do a half-dozen shaky circuits under Ann's direction. And then Big Al found himself volunteering for the next half-dozen, taking a genuine warmth and pleasure in Cobb's increasing steadiness and willingness to keep doggedly putting one paw in front of the other, even in his much-depleted state. David then took over again from Al....

Dr. Ann Spence stood proudly back, nodding and smiling with increasing confidence at the success of all their faiths and tireless efforts. Now David held only Cobb's wide leather collar this time and led him around without any support, and marvelling at his resilience after coming as near to death as any living creature could. And at his elderly age and condition ... what a dog!

David could only shake his head in wonder, unaware of the tears now streaming down his camo-greased cheeks.

Ten minutes later, with the humans at his side, Cobb was walking on his own and following, albeit slowly, shakily, where David called and led. Dr. Ann Spence smiled hugely and shook her own head in wonder. Big Al clapped and grinned and likewise too shook his own big head in unabashed awe, and with Tiger Dave Phelan, new

Canadian friend, duck hunter and dog lover, laughing continuously in nervous relief beside him.

Cobb looked blearily up at all three humans, wagged his heavy black tail slowly and managed to give out a weak bark, now aware that he was the centre of these three approving humans' attentions, and just recovered enough to begin to enjoy it.

A shadow had passed.

30   Mort Le
                            Merde

"Right, disaster averted, Dave. Now Cobb needs his rest and so do I."

Dr. Ann Spence began to push the men out of the examination room and toward her front door. "The two of you the same. This big old Lab retriever will be spending the night here at the veterinary clinic, so I can check on his condition later tonight and in the morning. I need to monitor his intake of fluids and his urinary output just to make sure his metabolic function is returning to normal. If all this checks out, I'll start your dog on some simple nourishment and work out a diet and recovery regime for him. I'll give you a call at home some time after nine tomorrow. Now, I'm kicking you sorry-ass hunters out, bedding down my patient and hitting the sack myself. So, scoot. Norah will be worried to a frazzle and anxious as all hell to hear the good news. I'll call now and let her know you're on your way."

The two bedraggled duck hunters had begun to sag themselves.

David Phelan couldn't stop the tears of relief and gratitude. He reached into his back pocket for his wallet and an initial payment that would never be enough.

Dr. Ann slapped his face. "Cut that shit."

The two duck hunters took their leave, each thanking Ann sincerely and repeatedly for the wonder of Cobb's recovery, and each being firmly and repeatedly reminded by Ann that it was "just my job. Could have gone either way. Now git!"

But neither David nor Big Al believed it.

And David was glad Big Al Greathwite had learned his lesson and wisely decided to avoid the threatened cattle-sleeve rectal by not mentioning his own payment again. In the fullness of friendship and time, his debt to Ann Spence would be paid, one way or another. Al knew, as well, that when David recounted her efforts on Cobb's behalf to his wife and friends, this would add to Dr. Ann's formidable reputation and respect in the surrounding Stoneybrook and Peterborough communities.

Lady vet, indeed!

David was shaken and asked Al to continue the driving, taking them back to his Buckhorn Lake cottage. He was exhausted but weirdly exhilarated at the same time. After a few minutes, Big Al summed it up for them both: "That is one hell of a damn fine vet, Tiger Dave! One hell. And a lady to boot." David had to laugh quietly at the American's continued use of the term.

"You don't know the half of it, Al. I saw Dr. Ann Spence for the first time at the annual livestock fair in Peterborough, must be fourteen, fifteen years ago..."

David Phelan had known without doubt that veterinarian Dr. Ann Spence was Cobb's best chance at life, because he had been present among a group of friends and farmers to witness firsthand the memorable event that had forever and always established the "lady" vet's formidable reputation in the Peterborough community, and far and wide. Afterwards, Dr. Ann was in immediate, constant and loud demand, with more requests for her skilled services than she could ever hope to fulfill, and was being offered increasing fee bids unheard of in Peterborough and the surrounding farms, ranches, towns, and villages.

David had been standing on the fringes of a group of cattlemen, rough and hard-spoken, who were actively and loudly admiring

"Mean Mort" Lardashe's fine looking, prized Hereford bull, in its holding pen at the annual Peterborough Livestock Fair, with its much anticipated, hotly contested livestock breeding competition. And there was the unsubtle implication by its owner, Mean Mort, that he himself and the well endowed "Mr. Magnificent" were *both* potent and formidable specimens in that most definitive of masculine domains.

Mean Mort Lardashe was the first one to catch sight of, and recognize, the new "lady vet" offering her services to the community, who had just set up a large animal clinic on her Stoneybrook farm that spring—the first female veterinarian any of the cattlemen had ever seen. For that reason, and their unfounded suspicions of her skills and quality of services, she had had few calls on her time from any of them.

It hadn't looked good for Dr. Ann.

So the whole skeptical male assembly was intensely curious, as they watched Dr. Ann Spence working her way slowly down the prize cattle pens toward Mean Mort Lardashe and his tobacco-smoking and -spitting cronies, examining the different breeds and classes of the cattle, with occasionally a friendly word or question for the proud showmen and women. All were hopeful, energetically grooming their impressive animals to get ready for the expert judges' appraisals, and the honour and satisfaction of the multiple awards, ribbons, trophies and enhanced reputations on offer. True to his nickname and wide notoriety, Mean Mort Lardashe just couldn't resist this golden opportunity to further confirm that "Mean" reputation. David Phelan had seen this all before; knew it would be its own sideshow; knew Mean Mort loved to perform before an audience of his male fellows, and welcomed any opportunity to take the stage.

As soon as Dr. Ann Spence was fully within earshot, Mean Mort Lardashe began speaking over-loudly about women and cattle, especially bulls, not mixing. "No way. No how. Not ever!" And this being most particularly true of "lady" vets, who might be too fussy and reluctant to undertake some of the coarser and more grossly intimate demands of the cattle and bull breeding business, which all the old, experienced *male* vets of his acquaintance handled, literally, as routine.

"You hear what I'm sayin', boys?"

Mean Mort's coterie of fellow breeders coughed, smoked, spit, took quick drinks from illegal concealed bottles, and nodded and affirmed their complete agreement, all with ill-concealed amusement and sly derision directed Ann's way.

At first, David had thought Dr. Ann Spence had chosen not to hear or acknowledge these crude and insulting remarks, because the *lady* just continued her calm appraisals of the cattle and her inquiries of their breeders, not glancing Mean Mort Lardashe's way even once. When at last the lady vet reached the smirking, self-admiring Mean Mort, now fully relishing his own malicious performance and his attentive group of cronies enjoying the show, Dr. Ann approached him with a friendly, open grin. She nodded at the big bull, himself seeming to enjoy the audience admiration, then asked politely if Mean Mort would permit her to have a closer look at his prize Hereford stud, Mr. Magnificent?

At this, Mean Mort exploded with laughter and surprise, almost bent double, and then looked directly at Dr. Ann with genuine disbelief on his fat, bearded red face.

Then the stout Peterborough cattle breeder and showman looked around, inviting his sympathetic, grinning audience to share this most unusual, unanticipated pleasure. It was just too much. Mean Mort Lardashe bowed as deeply as his belly would allow in comic insult, and invited the "Little Lady" to "be my guest." His term of address was more overly respectful and thinly sarcastic than accurate.

Dr. Ann Spence was a large, strong, formidable young woman, descended from two generations of a big cattle-ranching family on the Alberta prairies. But Ann did her veterinary studies at the University of Guelph's Ontario Veterinary College, acknowledged to be the best in Canada. And she had recently married a young cattleman from a family of Peterborough cattle breeders of good reputation, and they'd started their own breeding and veterinary operation on their extensive farm outside Stoneybrook.

With some apprehension, David Phelan had watched Dr. Ann's large, work-hardened hands as she thoroughly patted down, soothed and examined every significant physical feature of Mr. Magnificent, from nose and curve-horned head to tail—not neglecting to weigh and assess the potency of the big red bull's impressive testicles in both hands and judge the general quality of his breeding equipment and potential.

All this to the increasingly loud, thigh-slapping amusement and low derisive commentary of Mean Mort and his smoking, spitting, drinking band of cattlemen.

Then, still grinning and sincerely thanking Mean Mort Lardashe profusely and loudly for his kind patience and the generous opportunity to examine Mr. Magnificent, Dr. Ann Spence grinned even more widely and offered Mort her big right hand for a grateful shake. With a look around him of supreme relish, a dramatic pause, and an unconcealed air of great public condescension, Mort Lardashe deigned to extend his own right hand and shake it.

And that was Mean Mort's mistake—

Ann's own expression shifted immediately to one of intense personal satisfaction, as she clamped down on Mean Mort Lardashe's fat right hand with a grip so intense, so powerful, so crushing, all around them heard the hand and finger bones crunch dramatically. Mort squealed like a prized fat Duroc hog facing imminent slaughter, then screamed out his unbearable agony and surprise. And then, after too-long seconds of the bone-grinding pressure, began to sink begging and whimpering to his knees, with runnels of tears streaming into his bushy black beard.

But Mean Mort Lardashe never made it that far—

Before his knees could reach the muddy ground, veterinarian Dr. Ann Spence jerked him powerfully forward like a fat Raggedy Andy doll in faded plaid shirt and overalls, and grabbed the sagging seat of Mort's jeans with her other big hand as it flew by.

Of course, Mean Mort Lardashe was by no means a small specimen of masculine cattle breeder, and the collective jaws of the onlooking male audience dropped in stunned amazement, cigarettes and liquor dribbles falling from their tobacco-stained lips to the straw-strewn muck below.

Yet, with a prodigious show of strength akin to that of Mr. Magnificent's own, the like of which no cattleman present claimed ever to have witnessed in his life, before or since, the "Little Lady" propelled Mean Mort Lardashe a full seven feet through the air—headfirst into the sizable pile of fresh manure steaming and ripe at the rear of Mr. Magnificent's pen!

And that was the ultimate demise of the reputation for sarcasm, cruelty, and abuse of Mean Mort Lardashe.

Now, an exhausted and increasingly relieved David Charles Phelan shook his head in amazed wonder at the memory of it, finally becoming aware of the discomfort of camo grease and old sweat on his tired face. "And so, Al, Mort's been known ever since that fateful and surprising day as 'Mort Le Merde,' or more commonly, 'Mort the Shit,'" David said with a lingering smirk and hint of laughter.

Yankee Al Greathwite hooted gleefully, also relieved, and pounded his big right fist repeatedly on the steering wheel of the Ford F-150 in his own American awe, as David continued. "Colourful accounts of Mort Le Merde's public humiliation, and Dr. Ann Spence's clever and forceful instigation of of it before that disbelieving male audience, spread lightning-quick around Peterborough and even as far west as Toronto. It grew with the telling. And there was even mention of 'Mort Le Merde's' humiliation as a 'local rumour' in the *Peterborough*

Examiner. Almost instantly, Dr. Ann Spence had more business than any professional vet could ever hope to handle. Offering substantial service fee increases and endorsements for her wide expertise, some of the wealthiest cattle breeders and showmen pounded on Ann's door, chafing at the bit to get a face-to-face look and fuller sense of the "lady vet"—although no man after dared use the term, conscious of the odoriferous fate that might follow."

David expanded on the story.

"So absolutely everyone, Al, far and wide, wanted to meet the formidable woman who had put Mean Mort Lardashe headfirst into his own bull's bullshit. After that, it was Ann's extensive knowledge of first-class, pure-bred cattle breeding and her utter competence in handling their stud service and breeding lines, and any weaknesses or ailments. Now *she* takes the biggest trophies and ribbons at the fairs, and ambitious cattlemen pay a hefty premium to bring their stock from all over to stud at her Stoneybrook cattle farm. And not a few of us have Ann's fine black Labrador retrievers too, Al—premium-priced, but the best damn retrievers any duck hunter could dream of owning, training, and loving like family, which is what they become, as you know yourself."

David paused to hold Big Al Greathwite's eye and make his next point clear.

"And no one, Yankee Al, absolutely no one, even the most insufferably arrogant and entitled cattleman, ever risks insulting or demeaning Dr. Ann Spence to her face. Ever.

"Hoo-ee, Tiger Dave! One hell of re-e-doubtable woman! Lucky to have escaped with my big ass and thick skin intact. I surely am!"

"Agreed, Yankee Al. Maybe only three other women I've ever met can match her. My father, Wallace Charles Phelan, married the first one, Lulu Pearl Connor; I was smart and lucky enough to marry the second, Norah McGee Phelan; and my son, Norman George Phelan, did himself a lifetime's favour when he was fortunate enough to attract the third, my daughter-in-law and Frank's mother, Laura Lindenfield Phelan."

David smiled and looked over at Al for some agreement.

But Big Al Greathwite didn't share David's tired smile of amused contentment and marital pride. Abruptly, all the larger-than-life bravado and car salesman's energy and drive went out of the man, and Al's large hands tightened on the Ford's steering wheel.

The silence between the two new friends and ardent duck hunters deepened, lengthened, and grew unexpectedly heavy

"You all right, Yankee Al?" The formidable American Chrysler car dealer stared straight ahead, and appeared mesmerized by the highway's broken white dividing lines disappearing under the truck in the headlights' glow, as they drove through the dark forested landscape toward Buckhorn Lake and Norah Phelan. The constant, heavy rain had finally stopped, and the windshield was misted only by the damp, humid air, but not enough to use the wipers.

David was about to speak again.

"All right? All right? I thought I was, Tiger Dave. Now, I'm not so sure. Not so sure at all." Al's words were simple and direct, all bluster and Carolina cornpone absent, and made David uncomfortable—and even apprehensive.

"Anything I can do, Al? Anything at all? I owe you so goddamn much for my gun dog's life back there, when I dreaded the absolute worst. And all because of me. The stupidity of that impossible shot that sent him off. A shot no experienced duck hunter should ever have taken. My heart was breaking."

"Yeah. I hear ya'. But that's just it, Dave. That's the pisser. Sometimes, especially in the worst of life's unexpected circumstances, you can't do any damn thing at all. Nothing." David stared at the sad set of Big Al's camo-greased face, waited a few tense moments, fearing to go further ... but then took a long nervous breath and went further anyway.

"I'm not completely sure I understand, Yankee Al. And I'm very sorry to have to say so." Then it was the big American who took his *own* few, tense moments.

When he began to speak, Big Al Greathwite was somewhere else.

"My first wife, Dave, was Jenna Wills Greathwite. We took a big risk and decided we'd try coming up east together from the Carolinas, after that awful Second World War and its devastation finally ended. We were both of us tired, exhausted really, and hoping desperately for a better life, like the millions of others around the world coming out from under that long shadow of war. Best I could find was workin' long hours hustling used cars from those unlicensed gypsy lots day or night, all around Brooklyn and New York, while Jenna Wills worked consecutive shifts in a steaming hot hospital laundry room. Took us more'n four years, but we saved every dime we could, till I caught a break at last and bought into a small Chrysler dealership in Brooklyn that was going under.

"Jenna Wills and I worked twice as hard and brought that failing damn dealership back to profitability. Wanted to forget all that war, the sufferin' and deaths, the constant rationing. A big old shiny white 1950 Chrysler New Yorker, carrying our trunk fulla dreams, was our ride into a new, better life. Least we hoped so. Jenna Wills and I moved further uptown, to a small Brooklyn apartment and a growin' neighbourhood. Jenna could quit that sweaty laundry job at last, so we could begin the family we'd been planning on havin', but weren't sure we could afford."

David nodded his understanding and sympathy, now completely drawn in by Big Al's narrative about Jenna and their hopes and dreams.

"Jenna's poor hands had been red an' cracked, and pained her for years from that hot water and strong bleach. All them laundry chemicals used in that big old hospital laundry room. Now, they slowly came back to pink and soft again with some loving care. Made me so damn happy. Still not the same as before. But beautiful hands, Tiger Dave, and I could never stop holdin'em. Then, had my sharp eye out for another Chrysler dealership, larger, more prosperous, somethin' a bit prestigious."

Big Al Greathwite paused his account and glanced a long moment into the F-150's wide rear-view mirror, seeing in its reflections those times of struggle and hope now put behind him, by his and Jenna's own effort and determination.

The Canadian duck hunter reached out and squeezed Big Al's right shoulder in his own admiration of that determination. "Sounds exactly like what it takes to be successful in those difficult times, Al." Yet David Charles Phelan, sitting beside his new friend and fellow duck hunter, tried to forestall the arrival of the revelations that the stiffening hairs on the back of his neck and hands foretold were coming, with the only defence he he could muster in that moment: words.

"Sure sounds like you and Jenna Wills paid some heavy dues, Al. Things were certainly difficult for Norah McGee and I, living up here in Canada after that awful war too. Although we Canadians never had to directly experience the years of Nazi invasions and occupations, and the massive bombing raids on both sides that levelled London and Berlin and so many other cities and towns across Europe, though not your United States, thank God. And Norah and I were beyond fortunate that Canada's huge war effort in support of Britain and the Allies was crucial and ultimately successful. And then, after the conflict finally ended and some measure of peace was restored, that Canada needed dedicated Registered Nurses and skilled, experienced machinists like me to care for the "Baby Boomer" babies and tool up the factories in Windsor for your new Chryslers and Fords and everything else. My son Norm was born into the depression in 1932, and then came that long war, but through it all, Norah McGee and I still had our work and our home. Then this job in Peterborough..."

"Yeah. Jenna and me were happy, despite it all, Dave."

Then David felt Big Al Greathwite's mood becoming his own, carrying them both back to those complicated, uncertain times. He guessed the American Chrysler dealer's revelation would be bad when it came, and he was exactly right.

Big Al shook his big head and began.

"Started with headaches, blurred vision, trouble keepin' her balance, an' only got worse and worse. The seizures began. And Jenna Wills' personality slowly but completely changed. Completely. Until I hardly knew her, that pretty woman I loved more than my own life, Dave." Big Al took a few moments to look into the rear-view mirror, then continued, with an effort to maintain his composure. Tumour was all through Jenna's brain—*glioblastoma multiforme*, they call it now. Couldn't cut it out. Radiation and chemo pointless. Took her three months to die after the diagnosis. Three long painful months, for both of us. Was the worst time in my life, those damn months. Still fight 'gainst it every day to stop those awful images of Jenna Wills flashin' in my imagination. Change was night an' day, Dave. At the end, that pretty, lovin' woman didn't even recognize me. All those lost years we shoulda had. Lost forever."

As if the very weather itself shared Big Al's grief, rain started beating against the windshield once more, a pathetic fallacy, as though God Himself was listening and acknowledging Big Al Greathwite's burden of pain. After waiting a few moments, David Phelan reached over and quietly turned on the F-150's wipers again, their persistent rhythm a counterpoint to Yankee Al's words.

"It changed me, too, Tiger Dave. Changed me. Don't know why I'm tellin' ya this..."

David reached across and rested his left hand on Al's shoulder. "I'm truly sorry, Al. Truly. I can't, for the life of me, think of anything to say."

That was a lie. Well meant, but a lie nonetheless. David Charles Phelan knew what he *might* say. *Might* reveal. Would the sharing help them both?

"Back there with Cobb, Al, with Dr. Ann's help, we *could* do something. We *did* do something. And it made all the difference in the world, Al. Not just to Cobb, to me too: a man and his dog. No matter what the outcome, for both of us, even the worst, you'll always know you tried. It's the helplessness that kills you."

Big Al nodded his agreement, glancing once more into the mirror. "Yeah. It surely can, Tiger Dave. When you asked me what I was sayin' behind your back there at Dr. Ann's? It was a buncha Hail Marys and Our Fathers I haven't spoke for years. Lotta years. Jen and I had been devout Roman Catholics, true believers. But after seein' her pain, her long sufferin', an' then not even able to recognize me, nothin'. Well, I was damn sure through with that Roman Catholic Church and all the preachin' about faith and succour, through with the Lord God Hisself. I blamed Him, Dave. Blamed Him alone."

Big Al Greathwite paused, set his face, then continued in a mocking, dismissive tone of sarcasm.

> *"Praise be to the LORD,*
> *for he has heard my cry for mercy.*
> *The LORD is my strength and my shield;*
> *my heart trusts in him, and he helps me.*
> *My heart leaps for joy,*
> *and with my song I praise him."*

Big Al huffed in derision.

"It's Psalm 28, Dave. But the *Good* Lord. The Lord of *Mercy*. He didn't hear *my* cry for mercy. Where was His justice and mercy for Jenna Wills Greathwite? I was filled to the brim with my anger at Him, Dave. Been that way ever since. Why my Jenna Wills? Why His faithful servant all her life? What had Jenna done to deserve such a long, painful death and suffering? And so young? So damn young?

That big trunk fulla dreams we shared was empty, bare, Tiger Dave. *I* was empty."

Big Al's hands were white and rigid on the Ford F-150's steering wheel.

So, maybe it *was* time. Time for David to tell the story of his own childhood trauma and loss.

In the heavy silence that hung between them, and with his beloved Cobb's near death still vivid, David took a deep breath and slowly began to unfold his *own* deepest pain and suffering. His own harrowing loss of the person dearer to him than any other at the time—another sudden loss. "I know, Al. I know. I was just seven years old, back in 1919. After World War I, The Great War. The so-called 'War to End All War'—as if that was ever going to happen. It was when the 'Spanish lady', the Spanish flu epidemic, was really taking hold across the world, spreading widely with the returning troops. My mother was named Lulu Pearl Phelan. A devout and outspoken believer in the Christian Methodist Movement. She was a very formidable woman, a staunch leader of the very active women's temperance movement in Windsor, Ontario—speaking out, marching, carrying signs, campaigning against the widespread consumption of beer, alcohol and 'spirituous liquors,' as she liked to call them...."

A half-hour later, the two bedraggled, exhausted duck hunters were pulling the Ford F-150 into the Buckhorn Lake cottage's long gravel driveway, the shared memories of deep grief rendering both men fully silent and sombre. Norah McGee Phelan was waiting for them outside, huddled in the heavy rain, wet, white-faced and anxious in the Ford's yellow headlights.

In seconds Norah was wrenching open his door and pulling David into her arms. The rain hid her tears.

How he loved her.

31   Cobb's Teal

David Charles Phelan's nervous relief and energy had evaporated.

The Canadian duck hunter felt completely hollowed out by the harrowing ordeal with Cobb and Dr. Ann Spence, the emotional stress of Big Al's account of his first wife Jenna Wills Greathwite's drawn-out suffering and death—and his own sharing of his mother Lulu Pearl Phelan's premature demise and agonizing, irremediable loss. Now David was more than ready to follow Dr. Ann Spence's strict prescription and get some much-needed rest in the comfort and care of his loving wife Norah McGee Phelan's welcoming arms. In this rare and unforeseen moment, he'd never appreciated this beautiful woman more and thanked whatever god, if any, that had brought her into his life, love, and welcoming embrace.

But later, over the sweet honeyed tea and salmon sandwiches Norah had waiting for him and Al, slowly recounting the day's troubling events to Norah and answering her many questions, David wasn't fully aware of the profound change slowly overtaking Big Al Greathwite across their kitchen table. The big American duck hunter had let David do almost all the talking among them. And where, at the end of the long conversation, David was even more exhausted and anxious to fall into bed with the wife he so adored, Big Al was fully charged and acutely focused in a way that he was hardly aware of. So, David and Norah both were beyond surprised by Big Al Greathwite's announcement—

"Very sorry, Tiger Dave! Very sorry. And you bein' so damned hospitable Norah, so damned kind and supportive. But I've just gotta be on my way. Gotta! Can't wait another damned second. And you are one damned lucky duck hunter and husband, Tiger Dave, special wife like Norah here beside you in your life. Waited too damned long already. Can't stop saying 'damned' neither." Al laughed a hearty laugh at himself and the situation. "Too many people I gotta see and thank and apologize to. Gotta help. Things I gotta do shoulda done years ago. Years! Damned selfish and ornery, thinkin' only of muhself and muh troubles. Been one damned big hoss's ass, I surely have. But time's up! Been up too damned long already...."

At first David, and then Norah, had tried to insist that Al must at least stay the night as planned. That the big American had to be completely worn out after the exhausting ordeal of the drenching duck hunt and dangerous boat ride out of the marshes in the dark. Only to be followed by the stresses and near-death crisis with a hypothermic Cobb and Dr. Ann. That Big Al driving this late at night in the continuing rain, in rural areas he didn't know well, on roads he wasn't familiar with, would be needlessly risking his own safety and life. But Yankee Al Greathwite adamantly refused, shaking both Phelans' hands and energetically thanking the protesting Canadians for their hospitality and hoping "ol' Cobb" would fully recover his health and retrieving prowess soon.

Norah just managed to hug him once before Big Al was out the cottage door.

So at the last, Big Al Greathwite was leaving the Phelan household with an abbreviated but very sincere invitation to David, Norah and Cobb to visit him next fall season at his duck hunting camp in the Carolinas. "Get you two Canucks some old-fashioned South Carolinas' hospitality and cornpone, and especially, I promise you, some mighty damn fine ducks."

Norah was still more than a bit offended at his declining her ready hospitality, when the man must be almost out of energy and about to take a risky drive to who knows where. He wouldn't say.

David finally said he would indeed consider it "an honour and a rare pleasure" being offered them by Yankee Al.

Then, with Big Al Greathwite sitting behind the wheel of the huge black Chrysler Imperial in their driveway, his fancy gold monogram on the driver's side door, the brash duck hunter sincerely promised to be in touch to arrange it all when the occasion, the timing and the mighty fine ducks were perfect. And then Yankee Al Greathwite and his black Chrysler Imperial slid smoothly into the wet Canadian night, his left arm waving out the window, were … gone! Yes, just gone. But too large, too impactful, too impressive ever to be forgotten.

"What in great God's heavenly creation came over that man?" Norah asked for them both, shaking her head in bewilderment.

"I'm not quite sure, my love." David admitted, shaking his own head in amused wonder.

Norah McGee Phelan finally took her worn-out husband's left arm and pulled him back into their Buckhorn Lake cottage, David sagging heavily against her side. "Right! Now to bed, David, both of us. But first, we each need a healthy dose of that expensive, Premium Canadian Club Rye Whisky Norm and Laura gave us so thoughtfully for our anniversary. But no funny stuff after!"

Norah laughed, but David Phelan could only nod like a bob-ble-head doll and let his lovely wife take him to their dining table and pour the libations, knowing this day and night, its extremes of action and churning emotion, inspiring and terrifying both, would never be forgotten.

Not forgotten, no, because two weeks later, Dr. Ann Spence called David in surprised wonder to inform him that their Peterborough Humane Society she sometimes assisted, had just received a generous check in the amount of ten thousand US dollars, in the name of Dr. Ann Spence, from an anonymous New York donor. And because yet another morning a month after that, a boxy Canada Post delivery van pulled into David and Norah's drive, to hand deliver a very special parcel covered in red and white warning stickers, too fragile and too large for even their capacious old steel mailbox.

Old Cobb, not quite the black Labrador retriever he once was, but still instantly alert, was the first to hear its arrival, and his familiar bark from inside the front door alerted David and Norah. Winter had come on in a full white fury of cold, wind and heavy snow, and Buckhorn Lake had begun to fully freeze up. It had already begun to bloom with ice-fishing huts erected by those who craved the best spots for bass, perch and pickerel, and were foolish enough to risk it. David's much-loved Lab, unhappily, spent most of his time inside the cottage now, lying in front of the big, central McClary cast iron wood stove, its original black faded to grey by heat and time.

Dr. Ann Spence had informed David with a strict teacher's stare that Cobb's swimming, hunting, and retrieving days were over, finished—as if he didn't realize it himself. But the hunter dutifully nodded, still beyond grateful to his vet and dear friend, for her vital role in his retriever's miraculous survival. The black Lab's great heart had been permanently weakened by the stress and exertion of that last unbelievable, over-long retrieve in the freezing dark waters of Lost Man Lake. But Dr. Ann's veterinary opinion was that, with further care from her and the support of a heart medication David must administer daily, Cobb might have a couple more years of quiet life. David held up his right hand to swear he would do his best to make it so.

David was deeply thankful for this prognosis every day, and with Norah's support had soon moved old Cobb's sleeping basket and extra blankets into a corner of their master bedroom, so they could all be close day and night, a family. It just seemed the right and sensible thing to do. And dog and master, husband and wife, enjoyed the cozy arrangements.

No invoice for Dr. Ann Spence's heroic intervention had arrived, and when David brought it up with Norah, she gave him a pointed look. "Don't you dare insult Ann by asking, David, or I'll give you another slap in the face myself!" Huh? David could only raise both hands in surrender, and wonder how she'd known. Norah continued, "We'll make our own contribution to the Peterborough Humane Society in Ann's name. She'll hear about it, and the money for a good cause will please her, and show our gratitude for Cobb's remaining years she made possible."

Women, even his own wife, were still a mystery to David at times.

David signed for the big Canada Post box, carried it inside and placed it on the kitchen table, shaking his head at its mysterious arrival. "It's from Big Al, Norah, all the way from New York!" And with Norah and Cobb closely looking on, he took out his old Buck 110 Folding Hunter Knife and carefully cut away and peeled back the clear, heavy sealing tape. The parcel was much bigger than a breadbox and the assorted stickers cautioned FRAGILE and THIS END UP, and it carried a sizable US postage sticker and a black Canada Customs stamp dated a few days before. Big Al Greathwite had addressed the parcel to all three members of the Phelan household, and now all three were staring at it, curious to discover its mysterious contents. David and Norah sat on the old, high-backed, polished oak chairs, Cobb attentively on the floor between them, his head cocked to one side, apparently as interested as they.

David opened the wide cardboard flaps with some reverence. Digging carefully into the mass of Zest white foam packing, he found and removed four individually wrapped objects, setting each on the table and then putting the box on the floor behind him. David looked at Norah and Cobb, who both seemed to nod minutely, and decided to start with the large brown manila envelope that turned out to be a handwritten letter from Big Al Greathwite himself.

"Well, don't just sit there staring like the Rock of Ages, David, read what the man has to say," Norah hectored. So, David began, and found that the brash New York Chrysler dealer's written communication was disappointingly ordinary, getting the job done, but lacking the size, colour and distinctiveness of Big Al's spoken idiom, which David had come to enjoy fully during their heated baseball dialogues and arguments some weeks before.

Tiger Dave, Norah, and Cobb,

Thanks for that phone call a while back to let me know that old Cobb pulled through, though his retrieving days are over. I'm sure that new young descendant of his you'll be picking up at Dr. Ann's and begin training next month will be a chip off the old dog biscuit, just as you planned. Still, that boy will have to go some to beat his great granddaddy, and my guess is, he probably never will. I believe special retrievers like Cobb come around only once in the lives of a handful of sportsmen, and what I witnessed out on Lost Man Lake that dark stormy evening makes me certain you are one of those lucky few, Tiger Dave. Which brings me to my first gift in the way of a lasting tribute to old Cobb's accomplishment. It gave me a great deal of pleasure to commission it, and I trust that you and Cobb, likewise, will enjoy it and find it fitting. Your lovely wife Norah too, although she didn't directly witness those events with us.

As I'm sure you knew, but were maybe too polite to point out, Tiger Dave, Tyrus Raymond was one of the original five players inducted into the baseball Hall of Fame, in 1936, getting 222 out of a possible 226 votes, or ninety-eight percent—still the highest vote percentage in Major League Baseball history, American or National. And I know you know how much it pains me to admit that this was seven more votes than those for the "Bambino" himself. Like his namesake, I now consider old Cobb to be of a similar stature and uniqueness in the annals of duck hunting and retrieving, and this is my vote for his induction into the

Retriever Hall of Fame. I think Cobb retired when all true champions should—at the peak of his talents and the pinnacle of his career.

Norah used David's Buck Hunter to slit the tape and open the largest of the objects, an oblong box with Cobb's name on it, also covered with white and red warning stickers. What she removed from its own bits of foam cushioning was a large glass dome on a solid walnut and brass base. And mounted on that base was one of the most ethereally beautiful and elegant pieces of feathered taxidermy David had ever seen: a green-winged teal, in full flight—wings upswept, feet tucked back, head straining forward, eyes glittering—held invisibly by some alchemy of the master craftsman, and seeming to ride so naturally, in art, the same air that had supported it in life. "Oh, David!" Norah turned the display case so David too, could read the inscription on the small brass plate affixed to the walnut base.

COBB'S TEAL
THE RETRIEVE OF A TRUE CHAMPION
LOST MAN LAKE
CANADA
1967

David was deeply touched by Al's vision and unlooked-for generosity, so evident in the form this perfect tribute took, and by the tacit admission from one of the Babe's most knowledgeable and ardent fans that Ty Cobb, the arch-rival of his greatest hero, had bested Ruth in the most sacred of Major League Baseball's shrines. It seemed that a gentler, less self-centred, more genuine Yankee Al Greathwite had emerged fully, like a spreading of wings, in this supremely kind gesture. David turned the globe slowly and completely around so he, Norah and Cobb could admire it from all angles. Cobb barked once, immediately stiffened into his traditional black Lab retriever point and vigorously wagged his tale. David and Norah both looked at each other and broke into laughter. It was Norah who knelt and gave their old Lab a long, loving hug. Family.

David patted Cobb's big black head and carefully set the elegant display gently down on the floor in front of his dog, who sniffed at it cautiously, then circled and examined the glass globe closely from all angles. He finally looked back up at his master and barked twice more in complete approval.

Mad dogs and duck hunters! Who really knew? David settled himself, nodded at his wife, and continued with the letter.

Now, this talented taxidermist confirmed something that seems almost impossible to me, Tiger Dave: that a single pellet, only that one, which he discovered, removed, and carefully kept from the mounting process, brought down this duck. I do remember firing my own two shots at that surprising flock of green-winged teal that came out of nowhere. And I know my Perazzi's shot pattern was too late and too low. You got off just that one shot, Tiger Dave, after they disappeared into the rain and dark. And I'm as certain as an experienced duck hunter can be, that this single pellet was yours, Dave, and so was the duck it brought down. Yes, it seems near-on impossible, that shot, Tiger Dave—but it's so. I'm saying it. The teal belongs to you too. Without any warning or command, ol' Cobb risked his own life to prove it and make it official. So just accept it and honor his effort.

If you look closely at the wooden base, above the brass plaque and behind the glass, you'll see that very pellet where I had the taxidermist mount it, as well. If it was a Major League Baseball, I'd ask you to autograph it. That hit was out of the ballpark, Tiger Dave! It was that good. Pat old Cobb for me!

And so, this brings me to my next package, the one for your grandson, Frank.

David paused as Norah returned with two hot mugs of coffee for both of them, and a handful of biscuit treats for Cobb. David cut away the tape and brown paper wrapping on the small, rectangular package with Frank's name on it. Again, it had its own set of warning labels. He continued reading, now warming to the experience and its mysterious surprises.

And you seem to have forgotten the original reason we came together that memorable day on Lost Man Lake, Tiger Dave. And with your fear and concern for Cobb's near-fatal condition, which was crucial and much more important, this is completely understandable.

But we had us a wager, Tiger Dave! Who's on first, first? Remember? That pellet and this beautiful little green-winged teal it brought down, with Cobb's impossible retrieve, prove you won that wager: Tiger Dave Phelan. How ol' Cobb knew? Why he jumped into that dark, frigid water and went after that teal without any command from you—well, I guess we'll neither of us ever really know. Maybe it's that kind of rare instinct and total dedication to his calling that makes a champion unique. I believe Cobb has them in spades.

Now David was shaking his head and staring in wide-eyed wonder at a mint condition, Topps #201 baseball card, 1954, tightly sealed and carefully displayed between two ten-inch pieces of glass, in a pewter frame with its own support stand. He then realized it was *two* cards. The top one showed the American League Detroit Tigers Al Kaline, a smiling young rookie outfielder in his spanking new number six Tigers uniform, looking right back at David. The card below it was the *back* of that second card, showing his stats and career history in Major League Baseball. It was the same arrangement on both sides of the square glass display. Or so he thought. But not exactly!

When David peered more closely at the second Topps #201 face card, he saw there were *two* Kaline signatures—one the standard and expected Topps print version, but the other was Al Kaline's very *own,* hand-written signature, in fine black ink pen mark—an original, early autograph! "Holy shit, Norah! Take a look at this!"

Norah gave her husband a sharp, disapproving emergency-room-nurse look, but examined the card and the ink signature David was pointing at. "Okay, so what am I looking at specifically? I see Kaline's signature on his Topps baseball card? So? Al showed them to us. That was the bet and the prize."

"No! No! Don't you get it, Norah? This is a *genuine*, mint condition, Topps #201 rookie card! Do you you have any idea how rare this is? How much it's worth?"

"I guess not, but I'm sure you can't wait to tell me, David."

"Okay, okay, yes, the cards have Kaline's standard printed Topps signature. But this isn't his signature, Norah, it's his damn autograph! Al Kaline's personal autograph!" The implication finally dawned on Norah. Big Al Greathwite had never shown them *this* side of that Topps #201 rookie card!

"Holy shit! Sorry, I mean, wow!" Norah took the square display glass from David for a closer look. "Wow!" Shaking her own head in wonder. Phelan men were baseball fans, Detroit Tigers fans, forever, and Phelan wives and mothers by extension knew something about baseball cards and their history for fans and collectors.

To tell the absolute truth, after his quieter reflections over the weeks that followed their harrowing duck hunting adventure, David had an idea what this package *might* contain before he opened it. After all, as Norah said, the cards were the wager. Yet the solid physical reality, the sensation of actually holding these rare, sought-after cards his grandson so intensely coveted, was more magic still with this totally unexpected and much rarer autographed version. Now David, and Norah too, he suspected, were both already anticipating the immense pleasure of Frank's surprise and enjoyment, when the boy opened this special Christmas present from his grandpa in a month's time. David could hardly wait. Now he handed the Kaline cards over to Norah with conscious ceremony, and she nodded her approval and carefully set the silver pewter frame aside.

"One to go." Norah handed her husband Big Al Greathwite's final surprise, but with no less interest to her and Cobb too, already with his sharp retriever's eye on it.

So, one other large, flat rectangular package remained to be discovered. This one had "Tiger Dave" written on it in large black block capitals. David and Norah and Cobb now had his beautifully mounted green-winged teal and the Topps #201 Al Kaline mint condition rookie cards, but David could not for the life of him think of a single thing that might remain from that experience so fraught with risk and extreme emotion.

Now it just so happens, Tiger Dave, that I also had in my collection of baseball cards, memorabilia and souvenirs, another couple items beyond the immediate, that I believe you would enjoy more and better appreciate than an old, dyed-in-pinstripes Yankees fan like me. Especially for the reasons I will explain in a moment. Anyway, open your package now, if you haven't done so already. And believe me Tiger Dave, I would give a big old, mint condition, black Chrysler Imperial to see the amazed expression on that reserved Canadian face of yours when you realize the truly remarkable nature of these items. My deepest gratitude to your lovely Norah and to you, Sir, for the warmth of your hospitality, that truly unbelievable duck hunt, the energy we exerted pulling ol' Cobb back from the brink, and the best damned baseball discussions and arguments Yankee Al Greathwite ever had. The best!

The items David then carefully unwrapped, without the merest hint of expectation, as Norah and Cobb looked on, were part instant recognition, part total enigma. Both the larger and the smaller items were framed neatly together in the same attractive and professional manner as Frank's Al Kaline rookie cards. But David did rightly guess that the smaller item was also, itself, a baseball card, and one David never expected to see, much less be holding it in his own two hands. The card *did* show a stern-looking but fully recognizable Tyrus Raymond Cobb, yes. But this was no ordinary, standard looking Topps card from the recent years. No. David was now looking at another mint condition baseball card, but it was one from a much earlier era, one of the first cards of its kind, in fact. This remarkable and unexpected card was a *vintage* Major League Baseball card, from the era when the game's greatest hitter and most aggressive base-stealer was still actively playing baseball, and establishing his most memorable Baseball Hall of Fame records and firsts.

When David looked more closely, the old baseball card did begin to seem a bit familiar, but the Canadian baseball fan still couldn't quite place it. Something from his early boyhood? Something classic? Maybe only glimpsed?

The larger item that accompanied the vintage Ty Cobb card *also* looked like something from a bygone era. It appeared at first to be a kind of diploma or legal document or fancy certificate, or something of the sort, with plenty of impressive black and gold engraving and scrollwork on the borders and in the body. The name 𝕿𝖍𝖊 𝕮𝖔𝖈𝖆 𝕮𝖔𝖑𝖆 𝕮𝖔𝖒𝖕𝖆𝖓𝖞 appeared scrolled across the top. A round, gold, medallion-style logo containing the stylized image of a stately, romanticized female figure and the year "1919" occupied the bottom centre of the document. David's stomach immediately tightened and he drew in a breath when he read that fateful date. Both Norah and Cobb stared closely at David, heads cocked to one side in question. Oddly, the word "COMMON" appeared in larger, lighter-coloured grey letters, stencilled diagonally across the middle of the document from top left to bottom right.

But David shook his head and shrugged his ignorance at Norah and Cobb. He knew he'd need to consult Big Al's letter for an explanation. Norah held the document down to Cobb for a thorough look and sniff, and examined the two items more closely herself, but was equally puzzled. Again, he read aloud:

I know you will recognize Tyrus Raymond, Tiger Dave, but maybe not this specific baseball card series. While Cobb was still playing in 1901 and there were only the eight original teams in the American League, the makers of "Cracker Jack," established in 1871, brought out a collection of baseball cards showing 122 players. It probably had something to do with the popular song, "Take Me Out to The Ball Game," written about that time, and including the line, "Buy me some peanuts and Cracker Jack." Anyway, Dave, I never had a complete set, but I did have this very special one and thought you are the Tigers fan that would appreciate it most, and should have it. What's that you say, Tiger Dave? Thank you so very, very much, Yankee Al? I am forever in your debt, again? You're most welcome, my new Canadian friend and fellow duck hunter. But the best is yet to come!

The second item you're looking at is my latest untiring effort on your own behalf. It took me over a month of searching and inquiring, but finally, one of my accountants, himself a longstanding fan of the Great Game, told me about this little gem and tracked it down for me. It earned him a generous bonus and cost me a pretty penny, but I think you'll agree it was worth it, Tiger Dave. This is the skinny.

As you may or may not know, Coca Cola was first introduced by its inventor, Dr. John Stith Pemberton, in 1886, in Atlanta, Georgia. A banker named Earnest W. Woodruff and a group of investors eventually bought the manufacturer out. They took the company public in 1919 and started selling Coca Cola shares at forty dollars apiece. Quite a steep price back in those days. And what you're now looking at and holding in your lucky hands, Tiger Dave, is one of those first, original share papers. Those ol' boys sure made themselves rich, millionaires all. My perceptive accountant calculated that if just this one, original share was held until now and hadn't been cashed in, what with all the dividends re-invested, it would itself be worth almost a million dollars! Did I hear a big hoo-ee!, Tiger Dave?

So now, what do you have to say? Can you possibly guess why this particular surrendered share paper might be of very special interest to a dyed-in-the-stripes Tigers fan like you? Know any shrewd investors, Dave? Know any millionaires you might be acquainted with? If not, Tiger Dave, just open your eyes wide and examine the signature on the back of the certificate carefully. I'm sure you'll find it downright fascinating. Downright!

And suddenly, before Tiger Dave Phelan could gingerly turn the framed vintage Coca Cola stock certificate over, it all came together, and David suspected what he'd find. But, like Big Al Greathwite, he never in his life imagined that such a unique piece of Major League Baseball memorabilia, in this most unusual of forms, ever existed or would be available to a collector like Al, even with his deep pockets. David had absolutely no idea what something this rare and remarkable might be worth, but it all fit: Atlanta, Georgia; Coca Cola shares; 1919; smart investor; millionaire—

There, on the back of the share certificate, above the line marked "Owner," was the printed name and distinctive signature of Tyrus Raymond Cobb!

David was speechless.

Norah's mouth hung open in wonder beside him. And it was left to the black Lab, again, as he looked from one of his stunned humans to the other, to express the inexpressible—with a robust bark and drawn-out Lab retriever howl, a kind of canine "hoo-ee!" that finally broke the spell of enchantment cast over the humans. "And you can say that again, Cobb." David reached down and gave Cobb a satisfying, drawn-out scratch behind the ears.

All Phelans present were content.

After a long minute to let it all sink in, Norah motioned at the letter, "Let's hear the rest, David." And the avid Canadian duck hunter and Detroit Tigers super-fan began again, now on its fourth page.

Amazing but true, Tiger Dave. Of course, I knew Ty Cobb was very financially successful over his long Major League Baseball career. But I damn sure didn't realize Tyrus Raymond also did it by investing early in companies like Coca Cola, and so became one of early baseball's first millionaires. But it's so! And as of this moment, Sir, you now own a solid bit of that proof and history. So, enjoy!

And now, sadly, Dave and Norah, this last is some news that is a bit less welcome and no call for celebration. I'm still not even sure why I decided to tell you both about it, but I seem to be less sure of a lot of things these last few weeks since Cobb's Big Adventure we shared. Anyway, you do remember the rectal the formidable Dr. Ann threatened me with, wearing her plastic cow sleeve, that night? Well, I did finally get that rectal, though I chose to have it done by my own personal G. P. and not my local vet with a cattle sleeve. Unfortunately, his initial findings were not so good, and the Doc sent me to a specialist in the area for further tests. I am now awaiting the results.

At any rate, Tiger Dave, I still fully expect you and Norah and ol' Cobb, if he's up to it, to be my guests at my duck hunting camp next season, where we can pick up where we left off with new friendship, ducks, and baseball. However, Dave, I feel it's only sporting and just to warn you that I'm continuing to study up on all the Bambino's stats and history with the New York Yankees I can find! And I strongly advise you to do the same for ol' Tyrus Raymond and the Detroit Tigers. Because by the time we get together again, I suspect I may well be the foremost authority on those particular subjects in these whole United States, if not the whole of the civilized world. Ha! Until then, you're now near the top of my special, exclusive Christmas card list.

Fair warning, Tiger Dave.

Warmest regards to all,
Al

"Maybe you should open this one first?"

Frank David Phelan looked at the relatively small square package his Grandfather David held out to him, wrapped in its simple white tissue paper and Christmas red ribbon. Frank had been reaching out to take the much longer and bigger present, also in white and red, that he was certain would contain the much-coveted, Major League, aluminium baseball bat he'd begged for over the last three years. But his parents and grandparents kept telling him: "When you're a bit older and bigger, Frank, and can handle it."

Now, at almost thirteen years, apparently Frank *was* older and bigger, and couldn't wait to hold its smooth aluminum length in his own two hands, and take his first mighty swing. So, Frank hesitated, eyes on the bat, and his whole Phelan family watching: Grandfather David, Grandmother Norah, dad Norm, mother Laura and three-years-younger sister, Fancy Lou Phelan. But it was the serious look in those black Irish eyes and the firm nod from his Grandmother Norah McGee Phelan that left him no choice. Grandma Norah rarely brooked any argument from anybody. Especially her grandchildren in her own home.

David forced himself to take the proffered Christmas package from his grandfather.

It was 9 a.m. on a snowy, but otherwise clear and sunny, Christmas morning, a virtual Yuletide fairyland. The whole Phelan family had spent the previous two days at his grandparents' spacious Buckhorn Lake cottage, outside of Peterborough Ontario. Laughing, hugging, singing, hiking, tobogganing and festive feasting. But his mother and grandmother would absolutely *not* allow Frank or Fancy Lou anywhere near the brightly lit and lavishly decorated scotch pine Christmas tree, with its trove of colourful presents under its wide, dense green branches, until a full Christmas breakfast was consumed by all: rich yellow and white mounds of scrambled eggs and bacon, with butter rye toast and his mother's delicious homemade strawberry jam. Fresh strong black coffee for the adults; a rare taste of coffee and cream for Frank and Fancy Lou. And lastly, his mother Laura's delicious, freshly baked chocolate muffins, topped with generous, snow-white icing, and decorated with out-of-season summer strawberries she had defrosted from her freezer's larder especially for this Christmas holiday occasion.

Now, Frank held the big Christmas breakfast in his full stomach, and held his Grandfather David's square-boxed present in his hands, and just wanted to get the unwrapping and discovery over with, and get to that aluminum baseball bat. Pronto!

He felt the curious weights of his Phelan family's eyes on him, even Fancy Lou's, equally anxious to get at her own Christmas gifts, especially the possibility of those shiny red leather shoes she'd been begging to have, also for the last three years. It would be her *second* pair of bright red footwear after her initial pair years earlier. His more mature sister now imagined she would be Dorothy, from her favourite *Wizard of Oz* movie, and wearing the magic red shoes, able to click the heels together three times and "not be in Kansas anymore," but some magical world of wonders. Of course, in Fancy Lou's case, it would "not be in Windsor Ontario anymore."

Frank's Grandpa David and Grandma Norah suddenly laughed in anticipation of the impending revelation, and the rest of his Phelan family increased the intensity of their curious looks and expectations, obviously unaware themselves of the mysterious present's contents.

"Well go on, get to it, Frank!"

He looked to his mother Laura, then slowly, and with some ceremony, Frank unwrapped the the square-boxed Christmas present. With equal ceremony, Frank slowly opened the small white box revealed and examined the contents. And that was it! All thoughts of aluminum baseball bats vanished in an eyeblink.

His thirteen-year-old boy's entire universe stopped. Abruptly. Completely.

Were these what Frank thought they were? Was it even possible? And how? Impossible! A deep mystery waited to be unfolded...

Avid Detroit Tigers Major League baseball fan and disciple, Frank David Phelan, appeared...appeared to be holding two, *two* mint condition, Topps #201, Albert William Kaline rookie cards, from 1954.

His Grandfather David laughed, hugged wife Norah, and then reached out to hug his grandson and nod vigorously in confirmation to Frank's unspoken question. "Yes, they're genuine, Frank. Authentic. The real McCoy. I won them for you, Frank. In the most bizarre, most unlikely of circumstances. Here's the skinny."

And his grandfather David Phelan unfolded the amazing tale and circumstances to his now extremely attentive Phelan family. All were now seated before their brightly-lit Christmas tree in the Buckhorn Lake cottage's wide living-room and its comfortable couches and chairs. And David's loyal, much-loved and heroic black Labrador retriever, the elderly Cobb, who had made it all happen—right there with them.

A bet with a big American duck hunter and dedicated New York Yankees fan, called Big Al Greathwite, who owned *both* these rare, mint condition, 1954 Al Kaline rookie cards. But the big American hunter would *not* sell them to David for any amount of money the Canadian could afford to offer him. He was a wealthy Chrysler Car Dealer, from Brooklyn New York, so didn't need the money. Instead, Big Al challenged David to a *duck hunting contest*!? A duck hunting shoot. Whoever shot the most ducks within the day's legal hunting hours, would win both those fabulous and much sought-after Topps rookie cards.

Frank David Phelan could only shake his head in confusion, trying to grasp what his Grandfather David was telling him. Even Fancy Lou was fascinated. But his Grandmother Norah nodded in definite confirmation of this seemingly impossible story. A bet? A duck hunting contest? With a New York Chrysler Car Dealer named...Big Al!?

"But Grandpa..."

"I know Frank. I know. But it gets even more serious and unlikely. At the end of the day, we were exactly *tied* for ducks brought down, packing up our gear to leave for home. I had lost the bet. Lost the cards...when I took a stupid, stupid shot I never should have taken. Never. Too cold. Too dark. Too far. At a small, surprise covey of Green-wing teal in the distance over Lost Man Lake. And then, before I said any word of command, old Cobb was throwing himself into that frigid water and swimming out of sight.

Al and I waited. Shaken with fear and anxiety—

I called and called for him. But too much time had passed. Way too much! I was frantic with worry and shouting at Cobb through that dark pouring rain, until finally...finally, I just collapsed. In tears. Angry at myself. Angry at my reckless, utter stupidity and lack of professional hunter's discipline."

"Geez! What happened, Grandpa?" Now Frank was rapt. As were his whole Phelan family.

"A miracle, Frank! I swear to you all, it was God's miracle!" Norah reached out and hugged David close, again.

"I felt something drop. Right into my lap. Reached down and felt the soft body of what I knew must be a small Green-wing teal! A teal!"

Now Frank's Grandfather David unexpectedly laughed, shook his head, and hugged his wife. Norah kissed him.

"Old Cobb too, just collapsed against me. I felt him more than saw him in that rain-dark night. Exhausted and hypothermic. Near death. How Big Al and I got him all the way back to Stoneybrook, to Dr. Ann Spence's small animal veterinary clinic, I can hardly recall? But Big Al was one hell of a driver of my Ford half-ton. And we did. We made it. Hid the *Lulu Pearl II*, the decoys, duck blind and gear under the bridge. Took only the shotguns and the now unconscious Cobb, wrapped in my wool sweater and the thermal blanket. Grabbed the truck and made it to Stoneybrook in record time. Broke every law in the book. And Dr. Ann performed her *own* miracle and saved the life of this sweet old boy here. My hero. Forever!"

David reached down and patted his beloved and loyal retriever with deepest affection and gratitude. Norah joined him in a loving hug for their friend, and Cobb barked his response to their attentions, tail wagging furiously. The other Phelans watched with their own broad smiles as Cobb thumped his tail more and leaned into his humans' emotion.

"But Cobb's retrieving days are over, Frank. I can never repay Dr. Ann. Never. Not in this lifetime."

There were more tears in his grandfather's eyes at the memory. His wife Norah McGee Phelan stayed by his side and embraced him with soft words Frank would never make out. Would he himself ever find a wife as loving and loyal as his Grandma Norah and his mother Laura? In that moment, he hoped so.

His grandfather got a measure of control back.

"Now, Frank, have a closer look at your new Al Kaline rookie cards. Notice anything unusual about Kaline's printed written signature on the bottom card in the display frame?"

Frank *did* look more closely. Examined the signature minutely. When the lightbulb suddenly lit, David and Norah laughed in unison. Now his whole family crowded around him, even Fancy Lou, for a closer look themselves.

"It's...it's not a signature?"

David smiled at him and nodded for Frank to continue.

"Is it a...a real autograph!? Al Kaline's autograph? You mean he signed this card personally...himself? Really, Grandpa?"

David laughed. "Really, Frank. Very really! You are now the proud new owner of a genuine, mint condition, 1954 Al Kaline rookie card, signed by the man's own hand in black Sharpie."

Suddenly, unexpectedly, his sister Fancy Lou Phelan grabbed the card frame out of Frank's very hands and examined it closely. "Are you sure, Grandpa?"

"Very, really sure, Fancy Lou. Now give your brother back his rookie cards."

Frank's Grandmother Norah looked pointedly at his sister. "And, Fancy Lou Phelan, don't you ever, ever do that again! Or your mother won't be the only one to give you a hard spank where it hurts." His sister looked to their mother for support. But Laura Lindenfield Phelan shook her head at her daughter and gave her an equally stern look.

It was almost as satisfying to Frank as now owning these rarest of rare baseball souvenirs. Almost.

32   Safe At Home

David and Norah Phelan, and black Lab Cobb, did indeed receive a cheery Christmas card from American Big Al Greathwite, and sent one of their own in return—but the Canadians and their old retriever never made it down to the New York Chrysler dealer's hunting camp in the Carolinas for his hospitality, fine ducks and Major League Baseball discussions and debates.

Instead, David got an unexpected long-distance phone call from the Big Al's son, Duane Greathwite, early one morning in the last week of April, 1968. It was very difficult to process its news, and later, to share the uncomfortable details with his beloved wife, increasingly anxious at his side. The call went on for some minutes, until Norah finally put a hand David's shoulder in sympathy and support. Even old Cobb sensed the increasing tension in his humans and trotted over from his accustomed place on the carpet in front of the big cast iron McClary wood stove, and sat beside them solemnly, looking up from one to the other and whining nervously.

And then, after discussing the sad news at length with Norah, and getting her ready agreement and Cobb's air of resignation for what-ever was coming after his loving pats, David Charles Phelan booked his Air Canada flight to New York via Peterborough the next day with a heavy heart.

Big Al Greathwite had indeed passed away, in some pain and much lingering discomfort, of an undiagnosed, metastasized colon cancer, caught late, which a series of extreme radiation treatments and medical interventions could not defeat, long before the opening of the 1968 duck hunting season. David Phelan's elegant, personal invitation to Yankee Al's funeral service and reception after, arrived within four days of Duane Greathwite's phone call. Norah agreed the gold-embossed invitation was a bit of a surprise, the Phelans knowing Big Al for such a remarkably short time. Although the Canadian couple *did* agree that short time was more than intense, with its full gambit of emotions from fear and despair to desperate hope and vast relief.

David Charles Phelan arrived in New York City, "The Big Apple," on schedule, rented a car, and got directions to the impressive Roman Catholic Cathedral from the Hertz car rental agent. The Canadian was decidedly apprehensive and unsure of what to expect.

The funeral service David was witness to was as large and lavish as Big Al Greathwite himself, held in the foremost church in Big Al Greathwite's home diocese and community, a prosperous, spacious, and ornate Roman Catholic cathedral, St. Michael and All Angels, in upstate New York. David was not at all surprised. He judged rightly that Big Al's wealth, reputation and standing in his New York business community and surrounding areas qualified the successful car dealer for a final funeral and interment service conducted by no less than the head of his Roman Catholic diocese, one Bishop Blythe.

Canadian and Protestant United Church member David Phelan was but one of hundreds in reverent attendance, seated in St. Michael and All Angels' elegant, polished oak pews. The recently arrived acquaintance considered himself lucky to locate the church as easily as he did, and then to find an empty parking space for his rented Ford Galaxie only six blocks away, and finally, an ideal viewing position in the second row of the upper church balcony. From that high precipice David could overlook the solemn Roman majesty of St. Michael and All Angels and its smartly dressed congregation.

Even as a young boy, David had been an observant member of the Wesleyan Methodist Church, raised to its strict Methodism by his formidable mother, Lulu Pearl Phelan. He eventually became a United Church member as Protestant worship grew and evolved a few years after her death from Spanish flu in the early twenties. David's father, Wallace Charles Phelan, had told young David more than a few old stories of the lavish popish services conducted by the Roman Catholic Church in Ireland, before members of their Phelan "clann" or *fine* emigrated to Canada during the famine years of the 1850s and 1860s, known as "the Great Hunger." "Idolatrous, they were, Davy! Full of gaudily painted graven images of saints and angels, of the Lord Jesus, Mary of Magdala, Mother Mary and Joseph of Nazareth, and all its popish bishops and priests in their own gaudy ceremonial robes to match, all present and speaking loud Latin sermons no congregation could decipher to understand!"

And now, sitting in his tightly packed, polished oak pew and looking about him, David Phelan *did* find the formal Roman Catholic rituals, amidst the radiant images of saints, sculpted statues of Jesus and Mary, and rosy cherubic angels, far more ornate and ritually impressive than the Peterborough United Church spiritual observances he and Norah were used to.

Yet David still had to shake his head and smile quietly to himself.

The opulent service, with Big Al Greathwite lying in royal state on a raised dais at the centre, hands crossed solemnly on his chest, seemed a good fit in his gold and silver coffin. Like the three huge black Chrysler Imperials, one with his gold monogram on the driver's side door, parked ceremoniously in front of St. Michael and All Angels and draped in black crepe, it suited the man's size. The shiny Imperials had carried Al's son Duane, and all the principal members of the Greathwite clan and their families, to the elaborate Roman service.

So Canadian duck hunter David Phelan gave himself over to the moment as a sombre, early-middle-age Duane Greathwite left the family pew at the front of the wide nave and, with head slightly bowed, approached his father's coffin and nearby podium. Duane unfolded a stiff sheet of pure white paper with nervous fingers and smoothed it on the podium. He adjusted the microphone with a crackle of static and looked out over the wide Roman Catholic assembly in front of him, then up to the pews above him where David sat. Big Al's son paused a moment, nodded once in silent acknowledgement, and addressed the hundreds of mourners who had taken the time and made the effort to attend Big Al Greathwite's funeral service—

"Yogi Berra once said, 'Always go to other people's funerals, otherwise they won't go to yours.'" Duane smiled slightly and visibly relaxed at the congregation's subdued laughter. "I want to sincerely welcome you all here today, on this sad and solemn occasion, on behalf of myself and my Greathwite family. And of course, for my dad, Big Al Greathwite, lying in rest before us. I see so many familiar faces, so many, and it warms my heart, as I know it would Al's. You are active, involved, and busy people, and dad would take your presence here this afternoon as a great kindness and compliment. I would like to speak to you now of my beloved father for a few minutes." Tears had begun to brighten the son's eyes and a slight shudder shook him. David judged it was not easy for the man.

Duane paused to gather himself in his worsted black mourning suit, a white rose in its lapel, and began his tale of Big Al Greathwite and his varied life.

In his eulogy, Duane spoke fine, sincere words concerning his father's life experience, colourful character and larger-than-life influence. He paused occasionally to ask his audience's indulgence as he was overcome by emotion and tears, and in need of his white linen handkerchief. In contrast, the assembly laughed and nodded quietly at the narrations of Big Al's brash acts and acerbic humour, so often leavened with sharp wit and his signature Carolina cornpone.

David had met Big Al Greathwite only the once, and so missed many of Duane's references to family members, family history, and Big Al's consequential and defining life-moments. Yet the quiet Canadian from Buckhorn Lake readily agreed the expressed sentiments were accurate, and typical of the New York car salesman, devoted Yankees fan and skilled duck hunter he had known so briefly, and in such trying circumstances. His son Duane was also openly candid about the less than flattering elements of his father's life and character, and David much admired the man for the honesty and measure of courage it took.

Duane allowed that his dad was "one helluva of a slick-talkin' salesman," sprung from deep, southern Carolina rootstock. A profuse and tireless self-promoter, too often decidedly autocratic and stern when it came to his Chrysler dealerships, family decisions and positions on matters. That at times, Big Al's family relations were strained to breaking, sometimes *did* break, and were too overly painful to be borne.

Duane looked up and took in the whole sober assembly for long seconds.

"And who of us here in this audience this afternoon, in Big Al's presence and Our Lord's, me most especially, his loving son, is without a measure of life's flaws that render us human and fallible?"

The audience nodded their silent assent.

"I ask you to remember dad as *I* choose to remember him: the loving man and caring father, the household head; the tragic husband, almost broken by life, angry at Our Good Lord over beloved wife Jenna Wills Greathwite's too early, too painful death; the man who so recently struggled to recover his Roman Catholic faith; the man who became once more, in these last troubling months of his life, a believer."

Duane Greathwite paused with a slight smile and wiped the tears from his eyes. David's own eyes were glistening, as were the eyes of many of the assembled mourners.

"And I must admit to you all, confess in our Lord's presence, that this recent recovered faith and generosity was so abrupt, so unlooked-for, that Big Al both surprised and inspired us all."

Here Duane had to take a shaky breath, look away a few moments to recover composure.

Then Big Al Greathwite's son was proud to say that what failings as a Roman Catholic, a father, grandfather, and husband, were indeed redeemed by the new and sudden respect of his friends, his Chrysler dealer peers. But were most redeemed by the recovered loyalties and affections of his Greathwite family. Even to his second wife, Duane's own mother, because Big Al had been at such pains to make amends.

Still, David was a bit surprised to identify the two attractive women, who must *both* be wives, sitting there below, easily recognizable now in the front row of the nave. Both dressed in black, both blonde, both quietly composed and shedding silent tears down cheeks reddened by emotion. The younger wife, on the left, sat with a boy and a girl, no doubt hers. The older wife on the right with her older children and their families.

Duane Greathwite made only one more solemn reference to Al's first wife, Jenna Wills Greathwite, and her tragic early death that affected his father so profoundly. "As the years passed and my father became more and more successful, acquiring his three big Chrysler dealerships, dad also became embarrassed by his lack of a formal education. As some of you will no doubt know, Big Al made a continuing, conscious effort to instruct himself in the knowledge, wisdom and experience he lacked, and filled his large study with the many notable books and authors he came to admire, to love, and to quote on occasion. And dad also took a keener interest in current events in New York city and state, and more widely around the world as well, endeavouring to keep up with the news and ready to argue and express his personal views on matters."

Now Duane was most proud to formally announce to all present the establishment of the Jenna Wills Greathwite Trusts, to be administered through New York University and the City College, providing substantial scholarships for inner-city high school students without the financial means to pursue their educations further. And Duane was at pains to emphasize, "Not the best or the brightest, but those students whose hard work and records of service and support to their peers and communities are still very deserving. Our guiding principle in selecting the worthiest recipients will be taken from the small brass plaque above the wide oak desk in Big Al's study: *Labor omnia vincit*—Work conquers all things. I think my father lifted it from Virgil. Of course, I was only a boy at the time, so whenever I begged him for something I thought I absolutely must have, Al translated it more freely as: 'Show me the sweat, son.'"

David saw most of the audience smile and nod in familiar recognition.

"My wife Carol and I, along with my mother, stepmother, and an admissions staff member from each of two of New York's largest post-secondary institutions, are most pleased to take an active role in this qualification process by helping to review these worthy applicants."

Now David appreciated even more how complicated Big Al Greathwite's family life must have been, and the profound effects it must have had on his son Duane. But of course, the elements of the big American's life with which David could most identify and sympathize were his passion for duck hunting and his fondness for retrievers—and, most definitely, Al's complete dedication to the New York Yankees. Early on in the funeral service, Duane had drawn the gathered mourners' attentions to the representatives of the current New York Yankees baseball team and management, in respectful attendance in a place of prominence near the front of the cathedral: "And a special thanks to Ralph Houk, Mickey Mantle, Mel Stottlemyre and those others in attendance with us here today, whom I know you'll recognize. Big Al would most certainly have enjoyed this." Each of the named players nodded in quiet acknowledgement.

It also turned out that many of the impressive, multi-hued displays of flowers, ribbons and tributes that filled St. Michael and All Angels Cathedral were donated by the entire 1968 New York Yankees lineup, and sported the ribbons in the traditional Yankees pinstriped black and white pattern. "And of course," Duane continued, "it is more than a little ironic that an ol' Southern boy from deep in the heart of the Carolinas would come to support a Major League Baseball team called the 'Yankees.'"

David nodded in smiling agreement and joined in with the audience's quiet laughter.

"And now, my friends, family, and valued guests, I would like to end this eulogy with an almost certain prediction: That if I know my father, Big Al Greathwite, and I do, it won't take an eternity before all the saints and angels in Heaven are driving shiny white Chrysler Imperials. Thank you."

The audience tension and solemnity eased completely at this "almost certainty," and their laughter was comfortable and unrestrained.

As was that of the Canadian duck hunter from Peterborough.

33   Laid to Rest

David Phelan thought the applause had begun somewhere in among the prominent New York Yankees team members and representatives, softly at first, then spreading and growing in volume and enthusiasm. But it *was* Yankees fielder and first baseman Mickey Mantle, "The Mick" or "The Commerce Comet," who first rose to his feet and smiled, followed one by one by his Yankee teammates. David rose himself, with surprising energy, solidly clapping with the rest of the assembly. Bishop Blythe, in his rich Roman Catholic regalia at the altar, seemed more than a bit taken aback at this unexpected spontaneous action, but soon smiled and rose with the rest and added his own applause to Big Al Greathwite's tribute.

Son Duane Greathwite allowed himself a long pause to overlook the appreciative assembly, then smiled through the steady flow of tears he made no effort to staunch, and finally bowed his head in gratitude before rejoining his fellow Greathwite family members, weeping and clapping, in their front pew.

David was acquainted with no one in this congregation but the deceased, and him only briefly. And so he felt humbled, somewhat lost and out of place, as well as a bit shabby, in this assembled cohort of well-dressed natives, business associates, players, friends, and family members gathered in memory of Big Al.

Later the lone Canadian looked on again from the fringes of the crowd, while Big Al's mortal remains were laid to their final rest with lavish ceremony—not in the holy ground of the cathedral, but in a beautiful marble vault in the stone mausoleum on the cemetery grounds that surrounded the church on three sides.

Al's vault was a large, Romanesque structure, in an area of similar but older mausolea, with **GREATHWITE** carved above the wide-open black iron doors. Below the name were two other entries. On the left: "**Alvin Peter Greathwite, Loving Husband, January 17, 1922 – April 19, 1968**." And on the right: "**Jenna Wills Greathwite, Beloved Wife, June 14, 1925 – December 17, 1949**." The loving couple were reunited again at last, after Jenna Wills' remains were disinterred and transferred, and David suspected that Big Al Greathwite was finally and truly, indeed, at rest. Although this sculptured structure was most impressive, the pure elegant whiteness of it reminded David of another, lesser stone, and the memory of Wally and Lulu, his own loving parents, also finally at rest, although most disturbingly *not* together.

It was so unfair to his father, and now to David, but it was so. Nothing could change it. The flood of his own grief shook the Canadian once more, and he felt his own eyes water.

Then Bishop Blythe did a final incantation and sprinkling of holy water amid the general weeping and dignified observance of the hundreds of mourners. The black iron doors of the mausoleum were closed and sealed, and Big Al Greathwite was at rest in a sumptuous setting befitting the wealthy Chrysler dealer and New York Yankees fan's size and reputation.

It was a sobering moment for all in attendance, and David Phelan knew he would dearly miss the American who shared his passion for ducks, retrievers, and baseball, and whose unstinting efforts in their time of harrowing crisis had been so critical to saving his beloved Cobb's life.

David waited quietly as the crowd of mourners slowly thinned and dispersed in front of him, before moving forward to stand in front of Big Al's final place of rest. When he was alone, David reached into the inside pocket of his suit jacket and pulled out the very last of the *Romeo y Julietas* Al had left for him on the kitchen table, just before his abrupt departure the year before. He had planned to save it for their anticipated visit to Big Al's duck camp in the Carolinas, that would now never happen. David carefully unwrapped it, put the cellophane in his jacket pocket, trimmed the end cleanly with his Buck pocketknife, and carefully applied the flame from his nickel-plated Zippo lighter to its end. When the expensive Cuban cigar's tip was an even, glowing red, he placed it between his lips and slowly drew in the rich, fragrant smoke, and held it in his mouth a long time before exhaling. "Smoother 'n shit through a goose."

"Expensive shit, Tiger Dave."

"Only shit you got, Yankee Al." David smoked in silence for a few minutes and wondered how it was even possible to miss a stranger so much after meeting him only once. The thought of that Carolinas duck hunt they would never share was a bleak void in his mind.

A short while later, near the end of the *Romeo y Julietas*, something about the polished, black iron doors of Big Al Greathwite's crypt drew his interest. He approached for a closer inspection and stared in some puzzlement, until ultimately resolving the slowly emerging motifs portrayed there. David took a step back in wonder and surprise to take it all in—then nodded his head in sympathy and agreement as the full recognition finally sank in.

There was the familiar New York Yankees team logo of baseball, bat and Uncle Sam top hat, with its American stars and stripes, decorating the left-side black door. But the right-side door was the one that had caused David to step back in wonder. It displayed a black Labrador retriever's image, in full point at a flock of mallards lifting off from a cattail pond, wings outspread and reaching for the sky. A strong mallard male followed his flock of suzies like its herding master ... but it was the leading duck that David concentrated on. This bird was done differently. It took David a few seconds to fully realize that it was "caught" and moulded in mid-transformation, becoming an angel, and the duck behind it just beginning a similar change. In the upper right corner of the door was an impressive figure, obviously an angel, waiting with a long trumpet to its lips. After a few moments' deliberation, David thought it might be the Archangel Michael.

But the amazing thing was something only Canadian duck hunter and Lab retriever owner David Phelan would ever recognize—that *this* black Labrador retriever, in full point on the left, was his very own Cobb! And the smaller duck it was pointing at was surely a green-winged teal! How did Big Al manage it? It was nothing specific but, the closer he looked, the more certain David was. It was somehow most appropriate.

The full realization and deep irony staggered the Canadian duck hunter.

Head bowed, reaching out to place his right hand on the unexpected artistry of the black iron doors, his cheeks trickling with tears, David Phelan said a small, heartfelt prayer for all of them.

"It seems we both had the same idea."

David turned in surprise at the interruption. A Catholic priest in neat white collar and well-cut black suit under an open black topcoat, was standing a few feet away. He looked to be in his early forties, with brush-cut dark hair and a noticeable gap between his front teeth that made his smile disarming and engaging. His eyes were a light grey and his look steady and perceptive. But most amazingly, he was smoking a cigar, and not just any cigar—a Cuban *Romeo y Julieta*. David was certain of it from the size, the cigar band, and the distinctive scent of the smoke. It was the scent of quality, of "expensive shit," of Big Al Greathwite.

"I'm Father Alonzo, head of the local parish." The priest's handshake was warm, dry, and strong. "St. Michael and All Angels is my church."

"Phelan. David Phelan."

"From Canada?" David was at a sudden loss.

"Is my citizenship so obvious, Father?"

"I *do* know my congregation, sir. And by now, most of Al's family and friends, as well. But yes, maybe something in your quiet manner. Your obvious recognition and appreciation of Al's choice of decorative artwork. But mostly the scent of your cigar smoke. Big Al didn't give away his precious *Romeo y Julietas* to just anybody. And I *do* know you were one of his favoured recipients." The grey eyes twinkled in mystery.

"More likely my old suit here, not quite up to the style and expense of the congregation's refined dress. But, Father, how would you know such a thing?" Father Alonzo smiled and nodded.

"Well, I do also know Al wasn't interested in you for the quality of your suits." David felt increasingly uncomfortable.

"You still have me at a disadvantage, Father Alonzo." The man laughed a comfortable laugh, obviously enjoying their exchange to this point. He bowed his head in acknowledgement.

"I do, sir. And I apologize. But I do also think we need to talk. I was planning to take you aside at Big Al's reception, which I trust you will attend, but this may be a better occasion for the matter we should discuss. More private." David's continued nervousness and discomfort must have shown. "Please. Al spoke of you to me at some length recently. Now I believe there are some things you should know."

David considered a few moments before answering. Where was all this going? "Alright."

"Good. Are you parked?"

"Yes. I have a rented car five or six blocks away."

"Fine, David. Big Al's reception will be as lavish as you'd expect for a man of his wealth and stature, and will no doubt go on for some time. Why don't I drive you to your car after we talk, and you can follow me there later?"

"Yes, that would be very helpful, Father, especially as I'm sure parking will be easier."

"No doubt. But first let's walk together up to the church rectory, have some refreshment, and we can speak more comfortably and privately. My housekeeper gets testy if I don't let her spoil my guests and me regularly. As you might imagine, after just a few visits there, Big Al Greathwite had her completely charmed. And if I do say so myself, it is a pleasant walk through the grounds here—that is, if you're not averse to cemeteries." David thought of Wally and Lulu Pearl's white stone amid the spreading elms and maples at Windsor Grove Cemetery, but said nothing, just nodding his agreement.

"Yes," the priest continued, "I, myself, had somewhat the same experience with Al's wit and charm almost from the moment I got to know him." Father Alonzo filled the ten minutes it took them to reach the rectory with some of the history of St. Michael and All Angels church and grounds. How the original building and graves dated back to just after the conclusion of the American Revolutionary War, also known as the War of Independence in 1775, almost two hundred years before. "And of course, we *did* do a little better in that one against the British Empire than we did in the War of 1812." David had to shake his head and chuckle a bit.

"Yes, Father, I guess we British Canadian colonists and our native allies in North America like our independence too."

"Indeed."

Father Alonzo's housekeeper must have seen them coming, for she was waiting in front of the rectory door as the two men approached, laughing quietly together. She had her hands on her hips and an admonishing look on her handsome, swarthy face.

"Don't either of you two men even think of bringing those stinking cigars into my clean kitchen. I've just now taken the hot *cassata* out of the oven. It's cooling and it smells wonderful."

"Of course not, Teresa! The kitchen is your territory. I wouldn't dream of it, and the cigars are almost finished anyway. But I would like you to meet Mr. David Phelan. From Canada. A friend of Mr.

Greathwite's. David, this is Mrs. Teresa Pugliese, my very capable housekeeper.

"Sure. How are you, Mr. Phelan?"

"I'm fine, thank you, Mrs. Pugliese." David smiled, nodding a little warily. "And good to meet you." At the mention of Big Al's name, Teresa's face had turned sad and she shook her head in memory of him.

"That man, that Mr. Greathwite—what he do for my son Theo, we never forget. Never!"

"Yes. It was generous, Teresa. May we have some of your fine coffee in the kitchen?"

"Yes, yes. I make some fresh, Father. A piece of *cassata* too."

"Do you know how many games of squash I have to play to work off the calories in even one piece of your *cassata*?" Teresa looked hurt. "But one heavenly piece is worth a dozen squash games." Teresa nodded and smiled widely, in complete agreement, then headed through the doors to *her* kitchen.

The April spring breezes had almost died, and bright lemon sunlight showed through the lines of slow-moving cirrus clouds overhead. The Austrian pines surrounding the rectory were a darker hue than the grass, and the oaks and maples nearby were showing hints of green buds. Here and there, bright bunches of flowers "in remembrance," in a wide scattering of vases, stood out against the greens at many of the graves. David guessed that Big Al Greathwite's funeral service had inspired some congregants to mark their own remembrances of lost family and friends.

David Phelan and Father Alonzo stood in an unexpectedly comfortable silence on the sculpted stone porch overlooking the peaceful scene, finishing Big Al's *Romeo y Julietas*. David concluded that he was averse, just a little, to so much death marked out before him now. But *not* to an enveloping serenity, as well. The Canadian husband, father and grandfather decided in that moment that he would take his whole family, all three generations, to the Windsor Grove

Cemetery for an afternoon of family reminiscences, stories, and contemplation, the next weekend he and Norah were down to the city. Together, the living Phelans would remember Wallace Charles' and Lulu Pearl's carved white stone and what it meant. The many family gifts they conferred on David and later generations, intangible, but the more precious for that reason, and the pain and sorrow, as well. That needed to be fully acknowledged, explained, and not forgotten. It had been too long. Too long.

David felt his tears returning.

"Makes a person consider his own mortality, his past history and coming prospects for the time remaining, even if he's *not* religious," Father Alonzo suggested.

"It does," David said. More discomfort. "And I see what you mean about Teresa spoiling you."

"Yes. Teresa is one of God's blessings in my life. I thank Heaven for her. Her son Theo, as well."

"And she did seem very fond of Al."

"Oh, yes. But a sad story, David. Teresa's husband was killed in a construction accident, and the insurance and compensation were not enough to let them keep their house and live decently. This happened six years ago, and about the time the previous St. Michael's parish priest was transferred, and I took over the parish. I was a bit awed by the responsibility for such a large cathedral, its cemetery grounds and congregation, with those many demands. The priest's old housekeeper decided to retire at the same time, and before I knew it, Teresa showed up one afternoon with her young son. She had a handful of admirable references from her friends and neighbours in the congregation, and applied for the position before I'd even had a chance to think about it."

Father Alonzo laughed to himself at the memory.

"Then I felt more like *I* was the one being being interviewed. Evidently I passed muster, and she and Theo have lived here ever since. And I wasn't exaggerating about the quality of Teresa's cooking. It's impossible to resist, as my increasing waistline will attest." The two men were careful to extinguish their *Romeo y Julietas* underfoot and deposit the stubs in an old juice can, put there for the purpose. It already contained more than a dozen cigarette butts. "I'm trying to quit," Father Alonzo admitted.

"Me too," David admitted, sheepishly.

"Confusion to the Marlborough Man."

"And the horse he rode in on."

Now the priest's laughter was throaty and long. "I second that! Shall we go inside, Mr. Phelan?"

"Coffee and, uh, *cassata* sound good, Father. And call me David, please."

"And I'm Joseph. Joe." David's couldn't hide his embarrassment at being invited to be so familiar with a Roman Catholic priest he didn't know and had met only a half-hour before.

"You're not Catholic?"

"Protestant. United Church."

"Ah. Well, since the advent of Pope John XXIII and Vatican II, ecumenism is encouraged and priests are allowed to be a bit more informal, and, I hope, more obviously human and fallible. Still, to Teresa, even after four years, I'm always and only 'Father Joseph.'"

"Father Joseph" led the way into a spacious front hall, panelled in dark, polished woodwork, where they hung their coats. He then indicated a long central corridor, panelled in more dark wood, with a broad stairway on the right. The foyer held a large, painted-wood statue of the Virgin and Child on a low pedestal, her hand extended in invitation. Someone, probably Teresa, had put out-of-season white lilies in a cylindrical recess at the feet of the Virgin. A vintage silver crucifix was mounted on the opposite wall, and the passage was lined with colourful oil paintings depicting scenes from the Old and New Testaments, and the cruel deaths of saints or martyrs David could not name.

The Canadian looked discreetly, as he preceded the priest, but could see no illustrations of Christ and his followers after the Resurrection, or, thankfully, of Sodom and Gomorrah. That image still took David back to the troubling scene on his own Phelan family back stoop, his father condemned to a three-day-long exile by his mother, the lurid, full-page colour illustration in the family Bible of the departing Lot, his wife turned to a pillar of salt, still vivid in David's memory after almost five decades.

The kitchen of the rectory was large and old-fashioned but, like the Conception, immaculate. Teresa Pugliese stood proudly beside the gleaming refectory table set with fine gilded china, silverware, and cloth napkins for two, aware of the effect it had on David. "Your kitchen smells wonderful, Mrs. Pugliese." David bowed his head in sincere acknowledgement of her efforts. He was enveloped by scents of sweet rum syrup, citron, cinnamon, and vanilla rising from the cooling *cassata* sponge cake in its place of honour at the centre of the table. David was now very self-conscious, and the smells reminded him of weekends long past in Lulu Pearl's kitchen, when his mother was doing her delicious baking for the week to come, and she allowed her son small tastes as he stood eagerly by, as had become their custom. Different smells, certainly, but equally inviting nonetheless.

How David missed them!

Teresa must have been aware of him struggling over her last name. "You must call me Teresa, please, Mr. Phelan. Mrs. Pugliese, too much like an old woman." David judged the Italian housekeeper was in her late thirties, fine-boned with glossy black hair in waves, parted on the side.

"Very well. Teresa."

Next to David, Father Alonzo laughed in surprise. "Old woman, Teresa? Mr. da Lentino doesn't think so," Father Joseph suggested, with a sly grin that made the gap in his teeth most obvious. Teresa interrupted her pouring of the coffee and setting out two pieces of *cassata* to scold her priest and employer.

"You should not say such things, Father Joseph. A decent widow with a son to raise up." But David could tell Teresa was pleased again as she finished serving and made to leave them alone.

"You and Theo are a treasure, Teresa. And Mr. da Lentino is a lonely man who knows it." She snorted at that.

"I must get Theo." But her son was already on his way, his footsteps sounding on the stairs and then running toward them down the hallway. He erupted into the brightly lighted kitchen and veered straight to Father Joseph.

"See, I'm getting faster, Father. Aren't I?" His mother smiled a smile only a loving mother could smile, and silently nodded her approval. Father Joseph kneeled to feel the boy's left foot and hold the ankle, gently working it back and forth.

"Maybe too fast, too soon, Theo. Give the foot time to heal completely and get stronger. Don't put too much strain on it yet, please." He messed the boy's black hair, drawing a laugh and nod of consent.

"Then can I try out for the Little Yankees this summer? I need to be fast to play centre field. Will you let me, Father?" But for the darker hair and eyes and his outfit, Theo could have been David's grandson Frank. Theo was dressed from cap to stockings in a boy's version of the New York Yankees team uniform. Even his high-top running shoes were black and white.

"And you be careful with that glove."

"Only for this afternoon. When we visit Mr. Greathwite." David noticed Theo's beautiful, brown leather fielder's mitt, still a little big for a boy's hand, was covered in a maze of inked signatures. David guessed they might be from the whole of the New York Yankees Major League Baseball team. Al's doing, he was sure. Theo's mother opened the commercial-sized refrigerator next to her and brought out more of the white lilies in preparation for their visit to Big Al's final resting place.

Father Alonzo turned to David.

"This is Mr. Phelan, Theo. From Canada, across the Detroit River. He was a friend of Mr. Greathwite's, too." Teresa gave her son a look, and Theo came around and shyly shook David's hand.

"I admire your baseball glove, Theo. Although, I'm a big Detroit Tigers fan myself."

"I got 'em all! Here's Mickey Mantle. I met him. And he was in church today, too."

"They look beautiful. My grandson Frank is a big fan of Al Kaline, and he enjoys playing in right field on his own Little League baseball team in Windsor Ontario, across the Detroit River."

"Yeah. The Tigers look good this year," Theo allowed.

"Hey! 'It ain't over, till it's over.'"

"Yogi Berra! He's cool too."

"Enough now, Theo," Teresa said. "We get our coats and leave Father Joseph and his guest to have their coffee and *cassata*." The priest reached out and made a fist.

"Yankees pride!" The boy went over and punched the end of it with a fist of his own.

"Every day! All the way!" Theo finished and departed, grinning, with his mother.

"Kids and baseball," David said, and shook his head fondly after them.

"Big kids, too, David. Like Al. We have him to thank for that." He nodded after the boy, then indicated David should sample the sponge cake. He let a piece of Teresa's *cassata* melt on his tongue.

"Manna from Heaven, Father." David looked to the decorative ceiling above, followed it with a second bite of sponge cake, a sip of strong black coffee and sat back, more at ease than he imagined he could be.

He waited for Father Joseph Alonzo to begin.

34 The Little Tigers

"'That boy hits baseballs over buildings. He runs as fast as Ty Cobb,'" Father Joe apprised David Phelan, offering the challenge. He wasn't speaking of Teresa's boy, Theo.

"Well, let's see. That would be Casey Stengel, manager of the championship New York Yankees in the early 1950s, talking about the 'Commerce Comet,' sometime in those early years. When Mickey Mantle was starting to attract attention. No doubt about 'The Mick's' hitting power, either. He was a slugger from day one."

"Impressive! I see Big Al was right, David. You certainly know your baseball stats. And Cobb's speed on the bases?"

"There I'd have to disagree, Father. Ty Cobb was obsessive. Hunted wearing leaded shoes in the off-season. Practiced his slides till his pants had holes. Maybe it was being a kid, not much older than Theo, but seeing that fleet-footed Tigers base runner steal a base at the old Navin Field in Detroit's original, Irish Corktown neighbourhood was like watching infielders trying to tag smoke. However, I would also have to agree that Mantle *is* the greatest switch hitter Major League Baseball has ever seen. A fitting successor to 'Joltin' Joe' DiMaggio, the Yankee Clipper was."

"Yes. I guess growing up, DiMaggio gave me the same thrills and a love of the game that Cobb did for you. And marrying Marilyn

Monroe! Divorced in less than a year. Unbelievable. Those must have been great years after the war."

"The best. Until my ... until I grew up," David recovered. "Part of me anyway, like everybody. But my son Norm and grandson Frank are just as thrilled today."

"It's a wonderful tradition."

"So, you're a true fan of the Great Game too, Father?"

"Joe, please. Well, I liked to *think* I was—then I met Big Al Greathwite, and the experience was humbling. If you'll pardon the limp cliché, for Al, baseball was a religious experience akin to the Resurrection and the Light. How we first connected. But I know he *did* consider you his equal in that respect, David. And not just in baseball." David laughed.

"One hell of a fine duck hunter. No offence."

"None taken." David waited again. "Al told me about your dog, your elderly Labrador retriever, Cobb. That unbelievable retrieve of the green-winged teal in the pitch dark, in heavy rain and chill. How Cobb won you those rare Al Kaline rookie cards, and how it nearly killed him from exhaustion and hypothermia." David had to look away, overcome for a few moments. "As I'm sure you've guessed, if you looked closely, that's Cobb depicted on the black iron door of Big Al's mausoleum, with his teal." The Canadian could only nod, a mix of emotions overwhelming him, but finally spoke.

"Then I'm surprised, I guess. I thought I might be the only one that figured it out."

"One of a few. Myself. His present wife, Linda, of course. Duane and his wife. I think that's it."

"I owed Al more than I could ever repay, Father. It still troubles me. He saved Cobb's life, as much as anybody."

"Yes, I know. And I would surely like to meet the 'formidable' Dr. Ann Spence some day—'one helluva fine vet,' as Al put it. But to the contrary, David, Big Al believed that whole experience *was* a kind of repayment. And him being a part of it, that you and Ann and Cobb saved *his* life—or maybe, helped him to regain it would be more accurate." David covered his confusion by taking more of Teresa's heavenly *cassata* and a sip of her strong black coffee. "He told you about Jenna Wills, did he?"

David looked down, at the memory of Al's sad account. "The tumour? Yes."

"But maybe not that it destroyed Big Al Greathwite's Roman Catholic faith, his belief in a loving and caring God, and Al turned his back on his Lord and his church. For many years."

This was cutting much too close again. David was Protestant, United Church, but he could suddenly better appreciate the attraction of Roman Catholics to the confessional. Deep emotions of this nature could indeed become insupportable burdens. Sharing them privately, with a person with knowledge of, and sympathy for, these powerfully affecting experiences, receiving words of comfort and support, would help relieve some of that burden. To be able to at last confess it, shift its load even a little to someone like Father Joseph, would be a measure of much needed relief. Big Al had chosen his confessor well. David went to church regularly, but as to his personal relationship with an almighty God...?

"I and my wife Norah attend the Protestant United Church in Peterborough, Ontario, Joe. But I don't think you could say that I'm particularly religious." Was David now making his *own* confession to the Roman Catholic priest he hardly knew? Would he be advised to repeat a few Hail Marys and Our Fathers?

He paused in thought, then looked Father Joe in the eye. "But you exaggerate my importance, Father." Even after the invitation, using the priest's first name didn't seem right. David was becoming Teresa, and was that such a bad thing?

"I think not, David. Standing there beside you in Dr. Ann's veterinary clinic at that crucial time, your own presence along with Cobb's, the dog you loved so deeply, dying in front of you, Al began to say his own prayers for the first time in many, many years. Wholeheartedly, sincerely, invoking God's and the saviour Jesus's mercy, the power of faith and prayer granted to us all—and Cobb recovered! He lived. Was it indeed a miracle? Big Al sincerely believed so."

David nodded slightly, smiled, but shook his head. "Please. I don't mean to be ... too skeptical, Father. But it was Dr. Ann Spence who—" But Father Alonzo held up his hand before David could finish.

"That's where faith must serve, David. And you? Did you pray yourself?"

"Are you asking for my confession?" Father Joe chuckled.

"Well, I *am* duly authorized. But no, let's just call it professional curiosity."

"Then I believe I did, Father."

"And in that perilous moment, did you, *believe*?" David looked down at his plate and stalled with his coffee and *cassata* again, but he was fast running out of both.

"That time, Father. That time I believe I believed."

"Father Alonzo chuckled to himself and nodded, but then gave the Canadian a shrewd look. "Ah, David. I believe I sense some previous disappointment in this sensitive area in your own life." He leaned forward and waited until David would meet his eyes. David felt exposed and wished for the traditional screen of the confessional between him and this perceptive Catholic priest, to render him invisible and anonymous before that too-knowing stare. "It's true we don't always receive the answer we're looking for. But Cobb survived. And Big Al felt the hand of God in it. That's when he looked me up for the first time, and he sat right in the chair you're sitting in now." David made the effort to keep still in the seat, but worried at the crumbs of *cassata* on his plate with the fork. "I apologize, David. Your discomfort was not my intention."

"What *was* your intention, Father?" The priest took his own bite of *cassata* and sip of coffee that had become lukewarm.

"I guess, to tell you what Al would have told you himself: the whole experience of Cobb's crisis, his recovery from near death, and Al's role in it, made facing his own death easier. And that even before Big Al knew he was dying, that he … how did he put it? Yes, that he was no longer 'standing by.' I won't go into detail, but in the months following those events, he dispensed many gifts. Many. Big Al Greathwite changed people's lives for the better. Made this community a kinder, more welcoming place. Al left a thoughtful legacy of good works that lightened his own spirit in turn, and he will always be remembered with fondness. Theo was one."

"His foot?"

"Exactly. When he was still quite young, before they emigrated from their village in Sicily, Theo fractured his foot very badly in a fall. It was not well set, and he arrived here with a severe limp. He couldn't speak the language or keep up with the other boys. They were cruel, as boys can often be, and he was lonely, isolated. His parents had accepted it as the price for a new life. And, after a time, so did Theo."

"But not Big Al?"

"Not Big Al. Our first meeting together here was hardly over before he used his persuasive sales skills to talk Teresa into taking Theo to see the same orthopaedic specialist that consults with the New York Yankees on any serious breaks. She was hesitant. But a week later, Al asked for another meeting with me and showed up with the man himself. Quite a feat, I'm guessing. But to cut to the chase, this skilled surgeon operated on Theo less than a month later, supervised his recovery therapy, and you see the result. With new confidence and a little help from his mother's *ginettis*, Italian sweet cookies, he has good friends who love to come over now and be spoiled. Then Mickey Mantle himself visited Theo in the hospital after his surgery and presented him with his own branded and autographed glove, and a Yankees uniform. Theo has since become a different boy. The boy he should have been, now able to realize his potential, in baseball and in life. Teresa believes Big Al is a saint. Someone right out of Charles Dickens and *A Christmas Carol* after Scrooge's own enlightenment. Really believes. She's worn out her knees on the floor of the front hall asking Holy Mother Mary to intercede with God on his behalf. Prays that God takes Big Al straight into Heaven, selling Chryslers to the saints and angels, as Duane said. No time in Purgatory for past sins."

"It does sound like Al became a new man, too. And the man he *should* have been, achieving his own potential on God's green Earth."

"Yes, David, Al believed so. At least the man he was before Jenna Will's tragic death. The breakup with his second wife, Duane's mother, was very bad. She remarried and has two children with her second husband. Maybe you saw them in church?" David remembered two young girls and probably their father, sitting with the youngest of the blonde wives and other Greathwite family members. "With Linda's encouragement, Al humbled himself and worked for two weeks to persuade Donna to bring her husband and Duane's half-sisters to their home for a dinner before Christmas. He asked me to be there for support, but in the end, all it took was his own sincerity. In this, as in other things, Al Greathwite was truly contrite, and his family, his church and his community opened their arms and received him back. A Prodigal Son come home. Now the two families visit regularly and have become close as families should, especially in times of need."

Father Joseph got up and refilled their coffee cups from the carafe on the stove.

"All this *is* a bit overwhelming, Father. Especially given that I knew Big Al for only the briefest of times. But I'm very glad he had his family with him at the end, all of them, sad as it was."

David himself would never forget the tireless support and kindness of his mother's cousin, Siobhan Bryant, as Lulu Pearl's demise was imminent. The sheer power of Siobhan's whole Bryant family, *his* family, gathered around him and his father for three days and nights at his mother's traditional Irish wake. David himself should have been with his father Wally at the end. But who was the selfish one? His father, for leaving him, for taking his own life too soon and choosing to do it suddenly and alone, and blaming no one but himself for Lulu Pearl's death? Or David, for resenting his father's choice?

"I performed Al's Last Rites, David, and can tell you Al was at peace with himself, his family and his God." David nodded but could think of nothing further to say. Father Alonzo went to his briefcase on a side table and returned with two framed pictures. "I'm going to bring these to the reception as part of the display of remembrances, *memento mori*, but you might like an explanation."

David looked at the first, the classic photo of a Little League baseball club.

"These are the 'Little Yankees' Theo was talking about," he guessed.

"They are. We've had a few baseball practices since the snow left, but the real spring training begins in May."

"I do recognize Big Al." The man was smiling, but David thought he was noticeably thinner. "And is that...?"

"Yes, it is. Little League baseball coach Alonzo—in a different uniform."

"And ... are those girls?" The Roman Catholic priest chuckled.

"Some of my best infielders, David, to be sure. Great hands. And Blacks, Whites, Italians, Hispanics, you name it. Big Al formed and funded an umbrella organization among all the Chrysler dealerships on the northeast coast of the US. Got the dealers to agree to donate one-quarter of one percent of profits to what he called the 'Teams of America.' Doesn't sound like much, but it's tens of thousands of dollars in Manhattan alone. Amazing really. And even more amazing, Al was adamant: No Chrysler dealer public media promotion, no dealer logo or advertising on the uniforms either. None. Little League local team name only. Strictly for the kids, their families, and their local communities.

"There was definite resistance at first. But Big Al persuaded several dealers to commit to a trial period first, then judge by the results, and not just their sales statistics."

David laughed and nodded. "Big Al at his best!"

"Better than best, David. The initial dealers' group were blown away after four months of team organization and game play. Not

336

by sales statistics, but by the local communities' positive response, appreciation, and new respect. The Chrysler dealers were lauded for their generosity, charity, and support of young people. Community members began to shun the Fords and General Motors and Jeeps, looking at Chrysler offerings first. Supporting the dealers supporting their kids."

"*Et voilà!*" David shrewdly guessed.

"Exactly. Sales statistics began to steadily increase and, just as important, the Chrysler dealers were proud of their new standing in their communities. The other dealers fell in line. Then Al worked through the Roman Catholic Church networks to find those kids who couldn't afford the uniforms and equipment, or afford to pay for the field time any other way. Now each Little League team rents practice time on its own playing field, and donated Chrysler vans with parent volunteers drive them to their away games. The plan, eventually, is that each community area will build or buy its own field, maybe even a small neighbourhood park for all sorts of kids' activities. In just ten months we had twelve teams here in New York."

"That's more than amazing, Father." David smiled. "Its own kind of miracle, in a way."

"And Big Al had his own lawyers handle the new education scholarship setups, something he wanted to do himself. Lots of boys' teams, even a few a girls' teams, but Al was the first to suggest mixed male and female teams like these. Now those Chrysler dealerships, even the hesitant ones, are basking themselves to sunburns in the widespread positive publicity their charitable donations have generated. Al swore it increased their sales."

"That makes sense. Back in Windsor, Ontario my grandson plays for teams sponsored by the Canadian Legions and War Veterans. My son does the accounting and taxes, some coaching and plenty of driving. Boys only, though. So far."

"Well, maybe that can change." David nodded. Not a bad idea. Not a bad idea at all. Although he doubted his granddaughter, Fancy Lou Phelan, would be interested in any baseball team.

"And you must know of the race riots and fires that shut down Detroit for five harrowing days last year, David?"

"Too well, Father. Too well." Father Alonzo hung his head, as if in shame before the Canadian duck hunter. "My son Norm's family lives just two blocks from the Detroit River in Sandwich West, right across from the tall Penobscot Building. Tanks, armoured personnel carriers, Huey helicopter gunships, the Michigan National Guard, regular troops sent in too. They saw the towering black smoke hanging over the Motor City for almost a week. Norm and his family, and most of Windsor, lined the riverbanks for hours and could see and smell the burning cars and buildings when the wind was right. Saw it all day, every day on the American and Canadian news networks. My grandson, Frank, swears he even heard the bursts of gunfire while he played baseball on a field near the riverfront. We were all shocked, saddened and upset, and didn't go to any more games at Tiger Stadium that year."

"Then you'll be interested in this." Father Joseph showed David the second picture. It was a team photo too, but most of the faces were Black. Recognize the uniforms?" David took in the familiar black, orange and white logos on the chests of the players.

"Don't tell me—the Little Tigers?"

"If I had another of Al's cigars, you'd win it the first time. Al went to Detroit himself and persuaded the owners of the Chrysler dealerships there into sponsoring three Little League teams made up of kids from the worst hit areas of Detroit, mostly Black neighbourhoods like Virginia Park. Al paid for their uniforms, equipment, and local field rentals for the first year. The dealers supplied the Chrysler vans and basked in the positive public opinion. The local Black churches co-operated in spreading the word to the kids in the community and organizing volunteer coaches and drivers. Of course, three teams are a small league, but he hoped it would grow." David looked more closely.

"I don't see any girls."

"There's one." Father Joseph pointed to a smiling face in the front row. The slim young Black girl had tucked her hair up under her ball cap. "Ellie Fitzgerald. Like the jazz singer. Only girl starting as a pitcher in either league. I guess the boys on the teams can't believe it, but Ellie's the best, reads batters and pitches smart. Passion and heart, Big Al said."

"That might do it."

"Al showed me a letter from Ellie's father, a Baptist minister, thanking him for giving his daughter and other girls the chance to play on a team that promoted racial and gender equality. I gather he and his Ellie are huge Tigers fans."

"Something I can certainly appreciate, Father."

David heard the front door of the rectory open, and the voices of Teresa and her son returning from the funeral. Theo waved at them solemnly from the front hall and went upstairs. His mother came into the kitchen, her eyes looking shadowed and bruised by her grief for Big Al.

"How is Theo?" Father Alonzo finally inquired, as his housekeeper remained quiet and morose. Teresa Pugliese finally looked at them both.

"Bad, Father. Bad. First his father and now Mr. Al." The priest nodded in silent sympathy. "But you will be late for Mr. Greathwite's reception. You should leave, Father."

"Are you sure you won't come, Teresa? You and Theo have your invitations from Duane."

"No, Father, no. Enough death for one day. And you make sure you eat something there." The men stood as Teresa began to clear her kitchen table.

"Your *cassata* was delicious, Teresa, and your coffee," David said. "I hope everything goes well with your son's recovery from the surgery, too. That Theo makes a fine Little League player."

"Thank you, Mr. Phelan. Good to meet you." Teresa made a shooing motion. "Go, Father, go."

35   The Reception

Father Alonzo dropped him at his rented Ford Galaxie, and waited until David pulled out behind him so he could follow the priest to Big Al Greathwite's after-service reception. By the end, their conversations had stirred up old memories for the Canadian, drawn him again into his past and some of its most troubling, indeed tragic, memories.

Too much death. Teresa Pugliese had it right. Yet Big Al had done all the generous and philanthropic things he'd done, knowing his stage four colon cancer was literally eating away his life from the inside. And in a matter of months. Where had the big Chrysler dealer found the energy and will? Found his renewed Catholic faith? David still had a hard time seeing himself as an "instrument of God." But hadn't he prayed for Cobb? For all of them, at Al's tomb?

David still felt uncomfortable and out of place here in New York, and by the time they'd reached the Galaxie was on the verge of ending his visit with the service, the cemetery visit, and his private farewell to Al. But after meeting Father Alonzo, and Teresa and Theo, he didn't want to appear ... cowardly in front of the priest. Or Al either, if he was looking down on the whole thing. And Duane, in that phone call, had asked him specifically to attend the reception, after David had agreed to attend Big Al's funeral. The son said it was important, but hadn't said exactly why. Now David resolutely followed his religious guide's car through a fashionable residential area to Al's home. His guide in more than this, maybe.

Big Al Greathwite's residence was impressive, he had to admit. A fancy black iron gated entrance, with a long drive curving back on itself through professionally maintained grounds. The drive ended at a handsome, brownstone two-storey home with a pool, tennis courts, and a parking area almost big enough to accommodate the mass of invited guests. As it was, he and Father Joseph had to tuck their humble Ford and Chevy behind the line of mostly luxury Chryslers along the head of the drive with the overflow of late arrivals.

"We are a bit tardy, David. My fault."

"Not at all, Father. But I guess it's *not* fashionable to arrive late at funeral receptions, even in this exclusive neighbourhood." The Canadian undid his topcoat and attempted to straighten the travel creases from his good blue suit one more time—with the same lack of success. The priest led him through the sea of better dressed visitors up to the double doorway, their invitations in his hand. David judged the discreetly liveried functionary at the entrance would have given him more than cursory scrutiny if Father Joseph, in pristine black suit and white collar, had not "parted the waters," so to speak.

After a solemn nod from the doorman, they moved through the long formal atrium past more domestic personnel, who relieved David of his topcoat and gloves, indicating the way to the central staircase with discreet nods. He let the priest thank them, and then almost panicked when a prosperous looking older man suddenly appropriated Father Alonzo and led him off to the side for some hurried conversation.

David took a calming breath and continued upward, as directed, with some sense of intimidation at the continuing opulence of his surroundings. Across a wide landing, through polished wood double doors, into a stately dining room on the second floor. Where, amidst the solemn, well-dressed crowd, the Canadian couldn't say he blended well.

Still, the family reception line of wives, children and in-laws received him politely with slight smiles and nods of acknowledgement.

David remembered by name only the son, Duane, at its head. "Ah, dad's new Canadian friend. Very pleased and grateful you came all that way to join us. I wasn't sure how you would respond to my invitation." Further introductions were exchanged, and almost immediately forgotten on David's part, but it was all very gracious and civil.

The Canadian continued into the crowded room, accepted a glass of wine from a passing waiter, ignored the impressive buffet, and quickly discovered a far corner where he could hide out. David planned to stay for a seemly amount of time and then slip quietly away to his hotel to spend the night and catch his morning flight back to Toronto. At least, that had been his original plan, before meeting and speaking with Father Alonzo. Those conversations had been both revealing and somewhat upsetting, causing David to reflect on his mother Lulu Pearl Phelan's life, love for him, and her tragic demise, followed not long after by his father's suicide. And now David found himself reflecting upon and questioning his own values and religious beliefs.

He scanned the brightly lit, crowded room, but could not pick the Roman Catholic priest from among the milling dark suits and fashionable but subdued dresses.

A few guests *did* approach David in the next half hour, while he nursed his expensive red wine and hoped to avoid having to ask for bathroom directions. But for these prosperous New Yorkers, he sensed, one look at his respectable but dated suit was enough cue for just a quick nod and a hasty flyby toward more significant and familiar guests. Now David was at the point of complete discomfort and poised to escape, when someone took his right elbow and then faced him squarely to offer his hand—again.

It was Duane Greathwite, Big Al's son who had delivered the eulogy.

"Ah, here you are, Mr. Phelan. Took me some time to find you in the crowd. Thank you sincerely again for coming all the way from

Canada to attend Big Al's funeral service and this reception. I know dad would have been most pleased."

Duane's handshake was longer and warmer than expected.

"You're most welcome, Mr. Greathwite. I suspect you must know that Al and I only met for a couple of days last fall, duck hunting up in my Peterborough, Ontario, neighbourhood. But I enjoyed your father's company very much in that short time. His heroic efforts helped saved Cobb, my beloved black Lab retriever's life. I could never repay him, but wanted to honour him with my attendance here at this sad time. Now, after hearing your eulogy, I respect Al even more. Anyway, Big Al was most generous to me and my wife Norah with some gifts he sent us a short while after those harrowing events. Most were unexpected surprises. Norah and I were quite moved—overwhelmed, really. And Cobb absolutely loves the mounted, green-winged teal he retrieved, and those special Al Kaline #201 Topps rookie cards. Neither my grandson Frank nor I thought we'd ever see, much less own them."

"Yes, we were more than a bit surprised ourselves, Mr. Phelan. That sudden and mysterious duck hunting trip in Canada? Then those gifts? And especially that black Lab on the door of Big Al's mausoleum. Cobb?" David nodded. "But we may know less than you might think. We understood dad was just attending another one of his usual automobile dealer conventions in Toronto, but I'm not surprised he found some time for ducks. He did sometimes take his Perazzi twelve-gauge with him, depending on the circumstances. The duck hunter in him was dedicated, and even a bit vain, as I guess you found out. Never talked much about that Peterborough hunt though. Said he met some friendly Canadians and witnessed some fine shooting by you, Mr. Phelan. And he *was* most impressed by your Lab retriever."

Now David wasn't sure, himself, how much he should say.

"Please, call me David."

"Only if you'll return the courtesy and call me Duane?" Al's son paused and took a fresh glass of wine from a passing waiter, then hesitated again before holding David's eye with a serious, decidedly inquiring look. "Dad was different after that duck hunting trip in Canada, David, very different—a changed man even, although none of us could quite put our finger on it. Big Al stepped back from his prized network of Chrysler dealerships and began to give more control to the local managers and staff. Never happened before. Like ducks, his dealerships were his life and love. Also, and the most surprising and notable really, dad immediately sought out Bishop Blythe and then Father Alonzo, and said he was committed to becoming a practising Roman Catholic again, a man of faith, and requested their support and counsel."

Duane's curiosity had increased as he observed the changes in Big Al upon his return from that mysteriously fateful and life-changing Canadian duck hunt.

David nodded his understanding. It had changed his life too.

"Yes, Duane, I think I understand. I spent some time with Father Alonzo today, after the service. It was ... revealing, to say the least. Caused me to reflect deeply on my own life and values and beliefs."

"Did you, now? Anyway, this whole sudden transformation of Al's was something of a shock to my Greathwite family, and Al's fellow Chrysler dealers and friends. All but my father's first marriage were civil ceremonies, and, of course, the Catholic Church doesn't recognize divorce. Must have done a hell of a sales job on Bishop Blythe, if you'll pardon the expression. Not surprising, I guess, Big Al being Big Al. And I would like to add that 'all hell broke loose,' but no. It was quite the reverse, as you have no doubt heard from the good Father Joseph?"

It was a question, and David felt uncomfortable again.

"Some of it, Duane, yes. Your father was a most persuasive man. Besides the shooting ducks, we had some fine and detailed arguments over baseball and baseball statistics. Ty Cobb and Babe Ruth especially—who was the best, and in what areas. I'm a longtime Detroit Tigers fan, as Big Al worshipped the New York Yankees."

"Yes, I think I understand, David. And no real surprise there." Duane was thoughtful for a moment. "Well, after the discovery of Al's colon cancer and his inevitable decline, dad attended mass religiously, took communion and made regular confession." David's mouth felt dry, and he took a sip of wine before speaking.

"I hope it gave Al some comfort."

"Thank you. I believe it surely did. And so, it all progressed from there, as I recounted in my eulogy, culminating in Bishop Blythe conducting the funeral service personally and, most surprising, granting an exception and consenting to dad's entombment on the hallowed grounds of St. Michael and All Angels. A dedicated self-promoter to the end." David raised his glass in a toast to Al's persuasive sales talents.

"One of those Biblical 'lost sheep' who repented. A Prodigal Son who returned to the fold. Maybe God had a change of heart?" David said."

"Well, by whatever term, Al was a devout Roman Catholic by the end of it all. Although somewhat surprising to us, dad never pressured any of our family to follow his example, I will say that for him. Claimed it was just his personal choice."

Duane Greathwite waited expectantly, looking intently at David, but the now self-conscious Canadian said nothing more.

"As you may expect, I'm one of the executors of Big Al's will, David, and there *was* a large endowment, in the form of a perpetual trust, to the diocese children's home and its attached school for Catholic orphans and children in need." Duane smiled with mischief. "And that *might* have had something to do with the good Bishop Blythe's allowing a wayward and divorced Roman Catholic like my dad back into the Lord's sacred fold." The Canadian considered this.

"Well, as you probably know, Duane, Babe Ruth was *forced* to attend a school for wayward boys, in Baltimore, when he was quite young. I guess his family and home life weren't the best, and the Babe was picked up for repeated thefts or something before he became famous. So, Ruth was a little wayward too."

"You're right. And I did know; my father was fond of that story. A priest named Father Gilbert ran the boys' school, and it was him that encouraged Ruth's baseball talent. Even got him a pitching tryout with Jack Dunn's Orioles. Dunn was so impressed he became Ruth's legal guardian, and the other players called him Dunn's 'babe,' right? I just never put the two together," Duane admitted, impressed.

"I didn't know your dad well, but it seems like the kind of two-birds-with-one-bequest deal Big Al might have worked out with the bishop."

"Mr. Phelan ... David, I think you knew my father better than most. I can see why he liked you." Self-conscious, the Canadian duck hunter could only politely demur.

Then Duane Greathwite launched a mystery of his own with his next revelation.

"David, the reason I asked you to make a point of coming to this reception is that you were named in my father's will—a recent codicil actually, but perfectly legal and binding."

"Named in Al's will? Why me, of all people?" David drained his wineglass to have something to do with his hands, then shook his head in bewilderment.

"Yes, we too were a bit surprised, since, well, we don't really know you at all, apart from some brief accounts from dad. Anyway, it was a bequest—not money, but something very specific. After the reading, it did make some sense. So please, come with me while we have a few minutes."

David Charles Phelan followed Duane Greathwite, moving as quickly as was politely possible through the knots of milling people, many wanting to shake hands and say a few words to Big Al's son. But eventually, with lingering apologies, the two reached a far door of vintage carved oak at the back that Duane unlocked.

He flipped a light switch and ushered David in. "My dad's study."

36 A Study in Contrasts

The wide square room was a subdued off-white, wood-panelled in light browns and centrally occupied by two desks—one, an old-fashioned wooden monstrosity still covered with business papers and correspondence and positioned with the sitter's back to the oversized fireplace that dominated one wall; the other, a more modern, elegant metal and black-painted wood version, holding three phones, an IBM Selectric typewriter, a large electric calculator, and what looked like a dictation machine of some kind with a foot pedal.

But there was so much more.

David was entirely caught up, feeling for elements of Big Al in the room, and was discovering the big Chrysler dealer and duckman was a very complex man. Very. Duane watched the Canadian's expression for a few long moments, nodded to himself, then didn't hesitate. "Why don't you look around for a few minutes, David? This was my dad's *sanctum sanctorum*, his holy of holies. I think you'll find some of this interesting and even surprising."

"Thank you, Duane. I'd like that."

"Be back in fifteen minutes." Duane headed out the door, and David heard it close firmly behind him. The disturbed air smelled faintly of cigar. The Canadian walked to the middle of the room and began a slow turn around.

Four low tables and most of the wall area were covered with pictures, souvenirs, awards, and trophies from the different worlds of car dealing, baseball, and duck hunting, as well as family mementos of various kinds. But tall bookshelves stood on either side of the fireplace, and the books and magazines they held were carefully organized and well thumbed. Current affairs magazines like *Time, Life, The Economist* and *New Statesman* dominated the periodicals, with shorter series like *National Geographic* and even *Scientific American*.

But David was surprised to see a shelf of poetry, mainly American, with Whitman, Frost and Wallace Stevens well represented, but also some Yeats and Auden! Below these, Hemingway seemed to be all there, even a novel, *Islands in the Stream*, which David had never heard of. He did recognize Fitzgerald's *Gatsby* and assorted books by Salinger, Steinbeck, and Faulkner. But who was Ring Lardner or Hart Crane?

Now Arthur Miller's *Death of a Salesman* made eerie sense. Yet he never expected a set of Shakespeare's plays and sonnets, in some antique edition, bound in leather and gold leaf, that was prominently displayed and permanently finger-stained from Al's handling over a period of years. It even included works like *The Life and Death of King John, King Henry VI* in three different parts, and *The Famous History of the Life of King Henry VIII,* none of which David could remember. Duane had not exaggerated in the eulogy when he said his father was mainly self-educated. Apparently, Al was more eclectic and refined in his tastes than he'd let on. And the big man never did anything by halves, of that David was certain. It explained why Al's letters were so different from his conversations with David at Lost Man Lake. As if Al could fill his mouth with Southern pone or the Bard of Avon, at will. "*Did* only meet the man once," he murmured.

"Quite a collection." David looked back at the study door to see Duane Greathwite nod at the books. Al's son was smiling fondly, but a smile touched by pain.

"Not what I expected."

"Yes. I believe this may be more in line with your acquaintance." He invited the Canadian over to a low bookshelf opposite the desks, which had been converted into a glass-fronted liquor cabinet and contained a fine selection of spirits—Scotches, ryes, and bourbons— that seemed more typical of the small experience of Al that David possessed. How his mother, Lulu Pearl Phelan, a staunch Methodist and Temperance crusader, would have protested this dissolute supply of alcohol so close to Al's hand! Methodism. He found he could smile at the changed times.

"Something amuses you?"

"My mother. She was a determined Windsor Women's Temperance leader and marcher in Windsor in the early 1900s. I marched and carried signs with her as a child."

"I'm sorry. If you'd rather not, I can come back with a soda or juice."

"Times change. I'll try some of that Southern Comfort Janis Joplin prefers. Seems only appropriate." Duane laughed.

"Dad did have a taste for it, long before Janis." There was no evidence of an ice container so David accepted two fingers of the bourbon neat. "And Canadian Club for me, also appropriate in the circumstances. The son smiled again, enjoying the irony, and making David feel a bit sheepish.

"Thank you. Canadian Club *was* his rye whisky of choice, on the occasions when he took a drink." David raised his glass in salute and took a sip of the bourbon. He nodded his approval at the smoky taste.

"You seem surprised at Big Al's book collection," Duane observed. David looked away and said nothing, reluctant to offend a dead man's son by any suggestion that his father may have lacked civilized refinement. "It's okay. I can understand how my father's rough edges gave most people the impression he was uneducated. And as I said, that was the case, in the formal sense. But as dad became more successful, I know he felt the need for more polish, and discovered that he came to genuinely enjoy the books he began to buy and read. Many more than once."

"I guess he had me fooled, Duane."

"You and many others. Al enjoyed it."

"Well, he was entertaining company."

"And American to the core. Dad was a Yankees fan in more ways than one, even though he originally hailed from the South and had a wide rebel streak. Probably contributed to his success in a competitive profession like car dealing." Duane finished his Canadian Club rye and put down the glass. "And speaking of surprises, excuse me while I retrieve the item in question." He shook out his keys and headed for another door in a far corner of the room. "You might also find those display cases of interest."

Under the large mullioned windows were four low display cases housing some of Big Al's baseball collection. David recognized period pictures of the Babe on a dozen cards from different issuers like Old Cardboard and a vintage one of P. M. Clarkson from Old Judge Cigarettes packages of the 1870s, considered the first true baseball cards. But the pristine 1908 Cy Young card from Victor Publishing he'd never known about. There were also three vintage New York Yankees ball caps and a wonderful old New York uniform, complete down to stockings and spikes, from the 1920s David was sure. They shared the long case with a half-dozen old leather mitts, well-worn and webless of course, and most of them surprisingly small to his eyes, as if heroes could have little hands and still be giants in the "Grand Old Game."

A second, smaller case, held a number of programs, ticket stubs and pennants from Yankees World Series home games, but the centrepiece was a 1923 program and two vintage tickets from the first game ever played in the newly built, triple-tiered Yankee Stadium. His father Wally would certainly have appreciated those. Now David had son Norm and grandson Frank, but still missed that older time of sharing the lore and experience of early Major League Baseball with the man he loved and deeply missed—especially so in the tragic circumstance of Wally's death by suicide, overcome with grief at the early passing of his beloved Lulu Pearl.

All items were in their own clear, protective sleeves and cases, and looked to be in beautiful condition. The other cases displayed a beat-up but intact vintage home plate and old-fashioned base-pad from the early period of "Ruth's House," together with one of his autographed Babe's bats, dark with a wide band of pine-tar and surrounded by a dozen dead-ball era baseballs, each loaded with hieroglyphic signatures that appeared, as well, to be mostly Yankees. Some were faded or smudged, but most were barely legible under the glass. Was Ruth's among them? Or even Cobb's? In Al's private place, he would bet on it.

David couldn't help thinking of another vintage, hand-carved Ty Cobb bat in rare chestnut-oak from Georgia—the one that carried so much of his personal Phelan family history. "Past doesn't mean gone, that's for sure," he reminded himself. And how much death is too much? Of that David was not so sure. "Not like God gave you a choice," he murmured. Death will come to us all.

All these ball players are dead David told himself, but wished he had the temerity to ask his host to unlock the cases so he might touch their remains. Sinful? Sacrilegious? For him, emotional and fighting his memories, maybe just risky. Instead, he told himself it was just good manners and maybe natural Canadian reticence that forbade it, especially in this personal place and under the sad circumstances of Big Al Greathwite's passing.

As well, David sensed Duane was anxious to get down to the business at hand when he returned, five minutes later.

"Okay. Here we are, David."

David took one of the two comfortable leather armchairs Duane indicated, positioned to either side of the dead fireplace, and set his empty whisky glass on the marble coffee table that sat between them.

David thought he could recognize two of the three pewter-framed pictures at one end of the marble coffee table. The first was a picture of a handsome German short-haired Pointer, sitting obediently behind a trophy, that David took to be Al's prize-winning retriever, Babe. The second was a recent Yankees team picture from their last 1962 World Series win over the San Francisco Giants. Yet it felt a little surprising now, when he gave in to temptation, leaned forward, picked the framed picture up and took a look through the back glass. Not surprising, it was covered with player signatures. Duane smiled his encouragement to the Canadian.

The difference was that now David too could appreciate that Al was more than his image of bombast, duck hunts and baseball.

Duane nodded for David to look also at the last picture, which was really two pictures, as the son remained standing and held the two long flat leather cases that he had brought back with him at his sides. With some effort, Duane sat down in his own armchair and positioned the largest in the centre of the marble table, and the smaller case on the floor beside him.

"Those last two pictures in a single frame are really the most remarkable, David. The first is dad and Jenna Wills on their wedding day; the second is dad with my mother, Janice, and my stepmother, Linda, taken earlier this year. I never in my life thought I'd see them together like that. A kind of Greathwite family reunion miracle, really. At the end it became Al's favourite, in the room with him upstairs when he died. I don't know why, but my family decided *not* to display it publicly with the others. Something too private maybe. Somehow, I don't think dad would mind you seeing it."

David bowed his head in recognition. "I'm pleased, and honoured. Thank you, Duane."

"You're welcome." Duane smiled and leaned forward. "And now, here are your keys." David accepted the small bunch of them from Duane, who motioned for him to unlock and open the larger of the hard-leather cases. David quickly found the right key and opened the sleek flat case. He removed the legal-sized brown envelope sitting on top. Then, after a moment of confusion, David recognized Big Al's beautiful, hand-tooled, twelve-gauge Italian Perazzi shotgun, lying in its custom-made case with its Perazzi Company manual, spare barrels, cleaning and tool kit. The kit carried the Italian manufacturer's distinctive brass identity plate. Each piece in the assembly was perfectly cushioned in its own green-velvet recess and secured under neat leather straps. David shook his head and whistled softly. It must have cost Big Al a fortune. But well worth it.

David stared in duck-hunter wonder and said nothing for a full minute, not daring to touch any part of the Perazzi twelve-gauge set. It would be too much like touching Big Al himself. He felt the water behind his eyes, fought to contain it, but in the end couldn't and openly wept.

Duane remained quiet and looked away respectfully for a few minutes, until the Canadian regained a measure of control.

"The envelope contains all the documentation needed to verify your ownership of the Perazzi, and the necessary information to allow you to transport and declare the weapon, and carry it legally through both American and Canadian customs—at least, according to our lawyer. His name and number are also included, should you need his services at any point during the crossing."

The son waited a beat. "I think there's also a letter."

David sensed this was both information and a request to share. He opened the envelope and took out two stiff beige pages rendered in Big Al's now familiar hand, and couched in the same, more standard idiom as that longer letter the previous year that came with Al's gifts to him and Cobb. On closer inspection though, the script was spidery and uneven in places. Duane looked his request at David, who nodded and began to read aloud. The note was dated from the second week of February, in the New Year, and began without preamble.

"I am dead," Tiger Dave.

Hamlet's three words to his friend, Horatio, before the flights of angels sang him to his rest. They pretty much sum it up for both of us. In my case the "potent poison" is colon cancer. I now have faith that the flights of angels in my case will be Catholic too—and that we will be heading north! Ha! I have recently recovered my Roman Catholic religion and Christian faith, and my return to mass, prayer, and confession has given me some of the strength I need to face my own death. For the rest, I have called on my family and friends, all my family.

But the "melancholy Dane" was right when he said that old sergeant Death is strict in his arrest. He sure took me by the scruff and shook me. It's left me little time to put my affairs in order. I am trying to deal with the spiritual, but this is a smaller, material affair that concerns us here.

I know now Dave that we'll never have that return visit and shoot together at my Carolina duck hunting camp. And I found that I miss this small thing, this shared experience and love, too late and much more deeply than I thought. I really wanted you to meet my own retriever, Babe, and see him in action with some accommodating ducks. I was also looking forward to showing a fellow enthusiast and student of the game my Yankees collection, and to more fine baseball arguments. But I'm pleased to know you enjoyed my gift box last fall. It gave me great satisfaction to send you those items because I know they will be kept well and cherished by one who understands and values all they represent.

That box was a tribute to the passion for the game we share, Tiger Dave. But I wanted to do something about our love of duck hunting and that second round I'll be missing this fall. I decided that if we couldn't get together at my camp, I might join you in spirit, so to speak, although the metaphysics get a bit tricky here. So, I would be most pleased if you would accept my favorite gun, the Perazzi, as a gift from a fellow shooter. And if you would use it this coming season to bring down a few fine ducks and remember big old Al Greathwite, all the way up there in Peterborough Canada, well, it'd be a bit of compensation for the hunt we missed. We'd be together in that way, and it would give me pleasure. I want to look down from that big hunt-camp in the sky, God willing, and see you holding my fine Italian Perazzi. Banquo said, "There's husbandry in Heaven," and maybe a few fine ducks, if the Lord allows.

Now, getting to the second case. When I ordered my Perazzi some years back, Duane had been married for less than a year, but I already had visions of being a grandfather and introducing my new grandson to the pleasures of baseball and duck hunting, much like yourself. But Duane and his wife decided to postpone starting a family, it being the sixties and what with the Pill and all that. Now I pass the contents on to you and your grandson, Frank. Like a good hunter and his loyal gun dog, it would be a shame to break up a fine team and a well-matched set. I know once more you'll understand and value it.

So, this is thank-you and farewell, Tiger Dave. Give my warmest regards to your lovely Norah and old Cobb, and even Dr. Ann. What a woman! She sure put me in my place that night. And speaking of Cobb, it still amazes me that two strangers like us not only loved baseball and duck hunting, but both chose to name our gun dogs after our baseball heroes. I got to thinking about old Cobb being retired and how you plan to train one of the pups he had a paw in siring as your new retriever. Can I offer a suggestion? Why not carry on that fine, Phelan fan tradition you're so proud of, with your grandson? Not just giving him that rookie card set last Christmas, but also calling your new Lab Albert William Kaline, or just Kaline for short? Be like combining Cobb's championship tradition and a Tigers rookie-champion-in-training. Only a suggestion, Tiger Dave. May all your ducks line up for you. Remember me.

Best regards my Canadian friend,
Yankee Al Greathwite

Both David and Duane were silent for a few moments, unashamed of the tears in their eyes. Then Duane nodded his appreciation of this sharing of his father's thoughts and motioned for David to open the second, smaller case, which he set on the table to replace the first.

The leather cases were identical.

David used another key. And what he saw on opening the case looked, at first glance, in every respect like a smaller version of Big Al's twelve-gauge Perazzi. Duane explained.

"As he said in the letter, dad was really looking forward to a grandson, and we planned to oblige, but not right away. Time passed, the years slipped by, and suddenly it's too late for dad. I now regret waiting, but who can know what the future will hold. Anyway, dad also put in a special second order with the Perazzi factory representative, and this is what those Italian gunsmiths came up with."

The Canadian hunter took the shorter, slimmer, lighter rifle out of the smaller case. This Perazzi was an elegant, polished wood sibling to the bigger, heavier twelve-gauge.

"Bore's too small for a shotgun." David examined the barrel.

"Right. Perazzi gunsmiths took one of their famous .22-calibre match rifles with interchangeable barrels, and converted it to a .177-gauge pellet rifle, powered by high-pressure, compressed CO_2 gas cartridges that fit into the stock. But being a custom match gun, Perazzi didn't do things by halves. They made provision for adding a *second* gas cartridge to the first, for even more range and power. I fired it a few times with the double cartridges, and it really packs a wallop. If it wasn't for the lack of a bang, you'd think you'd hit the target with a real .22 calibre bullet. The pellet will go right through quarter-inch plywood at even medium range."

David examined the pellet gun more closely and shook his head in wonder. It was another Italian Perazzi masterpiece, beautiful but deadly in its own way. "My grandson has your standard Daisy air-rifle, but nothing like this, Duane."

The son laughed.

"No one does, David. It's strictly a one-off, according to the company. The rifle loads twenty waisted lead pellets from the butt and, like a modern .22 calibre, it uses some of the gas from each shot to re-cock and reload, making it semi-automatic. As you can see, being a precision rifle with some range, it also comes with a custom-made telescopic sight. It's necessary for complete accuracy. So, I think dad was right. They'll make a fine set for you and your grandson, and I'm sure too that both Al's Perazzis will continue to be in exactly the right hands. Try it."

David took only a minute to screw and snap the pellet gun's components together, so experienced in gun-handling he needed no instruction. He checked the safety from habit, and decided not to load or dry fire it. The converted Perazzi's elegance and spare economy of purpose, its balance and surprising lightness, amazed him. This was no boy's air gun, no toy—this was a serious rifle. Frank would love it! But not without David's supervised instruction to appreciate its dangerous potential, and learn to use it with safety and confidence. Well, that's what grandfathers and responsible duck hunters did, wasn't it? David would do right by Al and this unique gift.

The occasion felt very formal. Very right.

"Be assured, Duane, Frank and I will handle them both with deserving pleasure and respect."

And David found himself looking forward to it. Frank was twelve and ready to graduate from his Daisy. This would be the perfect rifle for his grandson to own and practice safe shooting habits with, before stepping up to David's old Cooey .22 calibre and the lighter .410-gauge shotgun. And then, when Frank was bigger and well trained, the Winchester twelve-gauge duck gun.

Too many young and inexperienced shooters still ended up dead or maimed each year; his father Wally had impressed him with that. Funny that both Big Al's son and his own son, Norm, showed no inclination or desire to take up shooting. David thought of Norm's formidable wife, and his own daughter-in-law Laura, both in a long line of loving but strict Phelan wives keeping their husbands and children in careful check. He would have to do his level best to persuade Laura about all of Big Al Greathwite's reasons and generosity in choosing to bequeath his treasured Italian Perazzis to David, a virtual stranger, and Frank. David swore to himself he would do a thorough training job with Frank, too, under her watchful eye. Even his own wife Norah, accustomed to her gun-toting husband, would need to be very sure when it came to her dear grandson Frank and his safety. Very sure.

"It's been a pleasure, David. A sincere pleasure and honour to meet you in person, and understand why Big Al enjoyed and respected you so deeply."

They stood, and Duane Greathwite shook the Canadian's hand with both of his. David Phelan did the same, and expressed his admiration and fondness for Big Al one last time. Then the Tigers fan and dedicated duck hunter left with the two cases—unexpected and impressive legacies, feeling humbled by Big Al Greathwite's thoughtfulness and generosity.

He would remember.

Part Five

Cobb's Legacy

37 More Alike Than Ever

David Charles Phelan had delayed it for as long as he reasonably could, and knew it wasn't fair to his valued canine companion and gun dog. To wait longer would strain both duck hunter's and retriever's loyalty and affection, and only postpone the inevitable, making it even more difficult for them both.

Cobb, the retriever David trained and had loved for so many happy, productive years, had to be retired and replaced.

His faithful black Lab had earned the best retirement David and Norah could provide him. David shook his head, still barely believing Cobb's impossible retrieve of the green-winged teal on the wettest, darkest, late-night hunt of their lives. The retrieve that won a grandfather two rare, mint condition, Topps #201 Al Kaline rookie cards for grandson Frank, but almost killed Cobb, and left the aged Lab forever weakened.

But finally, it was time.

And so it was with deepest reluctance, but also a sense of duty, one overcast Sunday afternoon in mid-May, that David made the confirming phone call and drove off in the Ford half-ton pickup truck by himself. The Canadian duck hunter was halfway to his breeder's farm, located outside the small village of Havelock, Ontario, when he pretended not to know why he'd taken his foot off the gas and coasted to a stop in the middle of the deserted highway.

"Oh hell! Hell!"

The angry duck hunter turned the steering wheel sharply to the right, swung the Ford pickup around and back, and with a spray of grey gravel, accelerated to retrace his route home. He parked in another slide of gravel, stomped back into the big cottage on Buckhorn Lake to face a strangely smiling Norah Phelan, in the middle of sour-apple pie preparations at their kitchen sink. His loving wife simply waited, with the paring knife and a half-peeled apple in her hands, trailing a red serpentine strip. David stood abashed, met her sharp black eyes, and twisted about beside her like a chastened schoolboy.

"I couldn't go without him."

Nurse Norah nodded solemnly, as if this had been obvious to her the whole time, and she had only to wait patiently for her dim-witted spouse to realize it. His wife pointed her chin down at the elderly Cobb, lying forlornly at her feet. The black Lab retriever had looked up at David as soon as he re-entered the kitchen— but made no move toward his master.

"I've got his lead on," Norah said. "We've been waiting for you."

David hung his head, briefly nodded his guilt, and motioned Cobb to heel with a single finger. The Lab barked sharply once in his pleasure and came immediately to his place at his master's side, his lead neatly coiled, hanging from his collar. Man and dog turned to leave, and his wife went back to lengthening her peel. Then, David stopped in the kitchen doorway, looked an appeal to Heaven, and turned around once more. Norah interrupted her preparations a second time and looked up.

"You know I couldn't live without you."

"I know," she said, smiling her love. "Give my best to Ann."

David drove off in the Ford truck with no spray of gravel, and Cobb sitting tall in his usual place on the seat beside him. The hunter kept his foot steady on the gas.

"Idiot!"

Dog and master arrived at Dr. Ann Spence's impressive ranch and cattle-breeding operation fifty minutes later. This was where Ann and her son and husband had built their big house, some distance from Peterborough in the green, rolling countryside. Cattle country. And here, in two large cattle barns in classic hip-roof style, sided in shining aluminum, was Ann's large-animal veterinary station. It held a half-dozen quarantine stalls, large rehabilitation pens, and a spacious examination room and operating theatre. The thick reinforced stainless steel table and oversized medical equipment on surrounding steel storage supports were large enough to handle a prize Hereford bull or a Clydesdale. Stainless chain hoists and trusses dangled overhead.

David knew that Dr. Ann Spence kept the original, smaller house and clinic in Stoneybrook, where she had heroically treated the hypothermic and dying Cobb some months before. That extended life-and-death ordeal seemed a long time past, but was vividly lodged in David Charles Phelan's imagination and memory forever. There Dr. Ann continued more her occasional small animal work for needy locals, often children, often without charge, and kept a regular schedule twice a week. The Stoneybrook community worshipped her like the Archangel of Veterinary Medicine, and woe betide any person foolish enough to say a word against her, especially doubting her expertise because she was a woman. "Mort Le Merde" had become legend.

In all the excitement of that trying, near-death time with Cobb, David had not told Big Al Greathwite that Ann was also the breeder he had taken Cobb to, back in his black Lab prime, to be bred with the vet's own line of fine Lab retriever bitches. Cobb was more than willing. But much time had passed since that successful coupling.

Now, it was a pack of Cobb's great-grandchildren David was about to look at.

Ann's reputation as a conscientious and expert breeder of healthy black Labs meant her pups were always in high demand. Nevertheless, the skilled veterinarian *was* very careful about screening her prospective buyers, demanding excellent references, and had been known to outright refuse a sale when her instincts made her suspicious of the party.

Dr. Ann had quickly sold Cobb's offspring to deserving owners, and had saved only one handsome male, with strong Lab conformation and quick instincts, to continue that line. In time, Cobb's son had been bred in his turn, and a grandson with desirable retriever qualities after that. By now, Ann Spence had been fending off other anxious inquiries for the pups from this third breeding for quite a while, in deference to David and Cobb and their original agreement, having promised him the pick of the five-pup litter. The two were old friends from Ann's earliest days in their Peterborough community, when David witnessed Dr. Ann's hilarious chastening of Mort Le Merde, pitching the loud-mouthed, sexist cattle breeder literally into his own Mr. Magnificent's shit. That had instantly made her reputation among the smoking, spitting, cynical male cattle breeders around them. David had done a lot to promote her black Lab retrievers to well-respected groups like his Ducks Unlimited chapter.

But these pups were almost five months old now, and Dr. Ann Spence was justifiably testy as he drove up, feeling avid Lab owners and duck hunters' breaths hotly down her neck.

"Well, well, well. The Duckman cometh! At last." Ann's big arms were crossed in front of her broad chest, and she was smiling widely as if in welcome. But the vet didn't offer her usual hand in greeting. Not a good sign. David reddened deeply and nodded, but said nothing. This was the second respected woman, along with his own dog, that he'd disappointed in less than an hour.

"Okay, Phelan. The men are off to the trots at the Peterborough track, and I'd be joining them, if it hadn't been for the arrival of this momentous occasion at long last. So, get a move on and let's have some strong Cuban coffee, while you tell me the latest on Big Al. And then we'll get this thing done. Every pup has been spoken for.

For months." Ann gave David her sternest look. Allowances for close friendship went only so far.

The duck hunter had to hang his head in acknowledgement of this unforgivable lapse in response.

"But I told 'em of our standing agreement. That one of 'em would just have to be disappointed. That they could put in another order for a pup from the batch on its way. Cobb's Lab breeding bitch was retired after that one litter he sired, and I made damn sure she got a good home that will appreciate her quality and cherish her accordingly. Fixed this current dam too, after breeding her with the Lab stud I judged to be the best of Cobb's grandsons. So, we got us some pretty fine pups here, four males and a female. I think the bitch came last. Now, let's get that *café Cubano* and you fill me in on Al."

David and Ann, with Cobb lying on the floor between them, sat at her kitchen table with large mugs of her terminally strong coffee, while David recounted the details of his subsequent experiences with Big Al Greathwite: the terminal colon cancer, his letters and wonderful gifts, the funeral after Al's return to his Roman Catholic faith, speaking with Father Alonzo, meeting son Duane in that surprising library study, and then the handing on of Big Al's fine Italian Perazzis—the biggest, most unexpected, most personal surprise of all. Dr. Ann Spence shook her head in genuine wonder at it all and kept refilling their mugs with her thick black *café Cubano*. David had to excuse himself to use the bathroom twice, and Ann once.

"Well Dave, I have to say this passing of Al's in those lamentable circumstances is certainly most sad and almost tragic. Being your new duck hunting partner and friend, an avid baseball fan like you, I thought I might see that American again up here, especially considering all we went through together that dark and rainy night. I'll miss the loud-talking reprobate. But that story was certainly more engrossing than the Peterborough harness races, almost Shakespearean.

Religion, wives, Whitman, charities, and Big Al's own Roman Catholic mausoleum, with old Cobb here featured on those decorative memorial doors at the entrance. And that green-winged teal! Who could have guessed?"

Ann stared into her *café Cubano*.

"Feel a bit guilty about it all, somehow."

"You and me both, Ann. If Yankee Al hadn't been right there beside me in those life-and-death circumstances, to help bring Cobb in for your support and treatment for his exhaustion and hypothermia, well, the worst would have happened. Just wish like holy hell I'd had the chance to know that big New York Chrysler dealer longer."

"Yeah, Dave. Would have been some trip, no doubt," Ann agreed, standing now, and washing out their coffee cups. "Got to take another hell of a pee, so you and great-grandpa there go out to the dog pens at the back and start looking over those pups. I'll join you directly."

"I need to relieve myself, too."

"Then you can just go on off to the old outhouse behind the barn like the rest of the local males. Dr. Ann laughed. "Consider it part of the penance for your tardiness in picking out a new Lab pup." David could hear the vet cackling even after she closed the bathroom door.

"*Mea culpa. Mea culpa*"—a prayer from the Roman Catholic confessional that David guessed Father Joseph Alonzo would think appropriate for his transgressions in the matter.

With Cobb trotting obediently at his side, David Phelan visited the outhouse, then made his way around to the side of the big aluminum-sheathed grey barn and entered the large lean-to shed where Ann kept her black Labs. She had six adult dogs lodged in the front half, two males and four females, each in its separate aluminum-barred pen. All sleek, fine-looking animals, hyper-alert and immediately focused on the two visitors, especially Cobb. They began a loud barking and whining, and the elderly Cobb was ready to join in—until a touch from David invoked obedient, duck-blind silence and discipline.

David didn't have the heart to deny his loyal gun dog some sniffing at the curious females, but finally grabbed Cobb's lead and ordered him to heel. "Easy old boy, you've had your fun. Your mind may be willing, but your heart is weak and your manhood's fixed. Time to rest on your laurels." Cobb didn't agree, so David quickly walked him, stiff-legged, to the other door behind which he could hear the high-pitched yips and whines of the excited pups. Cobb took a last long look at the four handsome bitches and, refusing to believe his era had passed, whined in consternation. David hated to admit it, but Big Al might have had a point, back there in the duck blind, about fixing him. But done is done.

"That's enough, now, Cobb. Deal with it. We have other business."

The duck hunting partners entered the second room, where all five black Lab pups strained against the hurricane fencing of their communal pen, now louder and more excited than the adult dogs, full of high-pitched yips and impatient whines. Their tails were wagging so frantically, David thought they could fly right off. Old Cobb was abruptly quiet and a bit bewildered, hanging back and not quite sure what to make of this gaggle of young'uns. David noted the hesitation. "What's the matter great-grandpa? Don't you recognize the fruit of your own loins? Don't seem at all bad, either. Let's have a closer look." But, perhaps sensing what was coming, his beloved Lab retriever hung back by the door and sulked. Yet another era that was passing. David carefully approached the young Labs alone, and Cobb whined with the pain of his master's betrayal. "I know, fella. I know."

David slowly kneeled at the fence and let the excited youngsters sniff and lick his hands. The pups smelled clean and healthy and all Lab.

"A pretty damn handsome bunch, aren't they, Dave?" Ann had slipped in and was instinctively fussing over Cobb, so he wouldn't feel so neglected. But the dog only had eyes for David. "Maybe you shouldn't have brought the old boy along. Must be pretty damn uncomfortable for him. Knows what's coming, sure as manure and taxes." David Phelan gave his breeder a look.

"Yeah, I considered it, Ann. I did. Turned the Ford half-ton right around halfway and went back though. Cobb deserves to be here from the start. See it all up front. And wouldn't you know, Norah had him all leashed and waiting till I smartened the fuck up. I'm a most fortunate husband. Damn fortunate."

Ann nodded her agreement and could sense David's turmoil—dog and master more alike than ever.

"Norah says hi. And maybe Cobb will have an opinion here, if he ever gets used to the idea. You know how long it takes to train a good retriever. I'm hoping Cobb will eventually accept the pup and help me out. Pass on his long experience as well as his genes. But we'll have to see."

"Yeah. Right now, though, I think great-granddad just wants to pass, period."

"Seems so, but let's get on with it, Ann. Like to take the pups out one at a time, if you don't mind?"

"Be my guest. It's your dime, and about time, too."

David did. Over the next hour, the avid duck hunter evaluated each pup thoroughly. Gently examining their strength and con-formation. Wrestling with them a bit. Getting them to jump up for small treats he held. Then showing them the treat and throwing it to the other end of the room, with the command "Fetch!" Watching carefully for the alertness, the willingness and speed of their chasing it down. Next, David bounced a white, sponge rubber baseball and observed how each pup reacted, tracked it down or caught it, and returned to play again, or not, when called. Did they quickly give it up when told to "drop," or bite down harder and tug away, when David held the ball while still clamped in their teeth? Was the mouth likely to be "hard" or "soft" in future, when retrieving birds?

Dr. Ann Spence watched it all from the comfort of a lounge chair she brought in from her yard and unfolded, and sipping yet a third *café Cubano*!

How did she do it? Breed such excellence, so damn consistently. A mystery to David and many others. One, he told himself, he need not solve. Just let it continue and reap the retriever benefits on every damn duck hunt.

The experienced duck hunter was amazed when he could find virtually no significant differences among the five. The pups were young, of course, and each had its strengths and weaknesses, but nothing David couldn't work with. Their temperaments were balanced and equal as far as he could tell. All seemed to be fine dogs with the right instinct, even the smaller female.

Cobb watched this whole long process with an uncertain detachment.

David could tell his old Lab was excited by the white baseball, in spite of himself, and had the ingrained instinct and experience to retrieve. The dog resented his master's involvement with the pups and seemed to disdain the lack of skill and wasted energy of the immature dogs, when they played and performed. It made David wonder if, like human adults, a dog could forget his own youthful misdemeanours and condemn the pups out of hand for the mere fact of being young.

Dr. Ann Spence looked on with a fine breeder's pride.

"Well, duck hunter Dave? What d'you think of this excited passel of pups?"

"They're champions, Ann, no doubt," he nodded. "Retrievers, security, seeing-eye, pets and companions—it won't matter a whit. The right care and training, these handsome little dogs will do whatever's asked of them, first time, every time. Make their owners proud." Ann beamed. This was just about the only man whose opinion she trusted as much as her own when it came to black Lab retrievers.

David had then dutifully brought each pup over for Cobb's consideration, after putting them through their paces and calming them down, wanting his dog's involvement in the trials. The pups sniffed at Cobb with interest, wanted his attention, but he turned away after his own cursory sniff, and in one case, made to nip the smaller female when she tried to jump up at him in an attempt at play.

Ann had held Cobb in check, and David warned him—mildly. Just because the reaction was predictable, didn't make it any easier. He thought of the green-winged teal an exhausted, hypothermic Cobb dropped in his lap not so long ago. "Shit." This selection process in his own dog's presence was even more difficult, more painful than what he'd anticipated.

Not nearly as difficult as Cobb is finding it though, he thought, so quit your whining, accept the guilt and get on with it.

"Well, which one do you like?" Ann tried to move him along.

"That's just the problem, Ann. I like them all. Very much. And Cobb likes *none* of them."

"That's his prerogative and not surprising, David. But you have to make the choice. So?" So, David considered.

"You still have that big exercise yard out there?" He watched Dr. Ann Spence sigh and roll her eyes briefly, but she finally motioned him to follow.

"Yep. Even bigger than before. And I had George dig out a fair-sized pond with the backhoe since you were here last. Gives the Labs a taste of water. Got it sown in ryegrass too, but it's too wet and mucky right now. All that rain last week." David said nothing and waited. "What do you have in mind, Dave Phelan—as if I couldn't guess?"

"Okay if I take the whole pack out and see them together? How they behave in the open? In the water?" Ann hesitated, and he knew she was imagining a messy canine five-ring circus. But she bowed her head in resignation.

"Right. But when they get as wet and muddy as you know they will, you're the lucky amigo's gonna stick around and get them washed and brushed before I bring them back in. They *are* pups you know."

"And you're a good friend, and a champion breeder." David laughed and gave Dr. Ann Spence a sudden hug. "Fair enough."

Ann pushed her good friend away, but laughed despite it all.

38 One for the Angels

David Charles Phelan slid aside the big rear door of the aluminum-clad cattle barn with a sound of steel wheels on steel tracks.

The open door revealed a long rectangular acre of rough-packed earth yard, criss-crossed with tire tracks. David considered the possibilities, then turned back and, with hands on knees, called the clamouring black Lab pups out in a high-pitched voice.

"Okay, pups, c'mon now! C'mon! Show me what you can do! Let's see who's on first, first!" It felt right to use Big Al's own expression from that too memorable, too stressful duck shooting contest. Dr. Ann Spence, still holding a straining Cobb by the collar, opened the wire pen.

David didn't have to call twice.

The pups exploded out the wide doorway into the yard, tumbling over one another in their youthful eagerness to explore and experience. As David watched, with Ann and Cobb beside him, the young black Labs roared around the big fenced enclosure—sniffing, barking, chasing, nipping, and finally, testing the water of a large pond at the far end.

Ann was right about the wetness and dirt. The little dogs were soon happily covered in both, to their great joy. Old Cobb surveyed it all with a jaundiced retriever's eye and remained aloof, not responding to David's pats or words of encouragement. The Canadian hunter's feelings of guilt and betrayal continued, and Cobb seemed completely unwilling to let his master off the hook.

Nor did the elderly Lab show any inclination to join this raucous canine circus.

David watched the antics of the roiling mass for ten minutes, trying to see if any one pup stood out and caught his eye. But none did. So when the young Labs had burnt off their initial burst of energy, David knelt to call them over, enticing them with a handful of fragrant canine treats, careful to distribute them equitably among the squirming siblings.

Ann retrieved her lounge chair from the barn and settled down for the show, shaking her head in both wonder and anticipation. "I don't suppose there's any popcorn and cokes? Maybe some licorice whips?" She threw her her big head back and laughed like a barn's gurgling waste-water drain. David ignored her and concentrated.

Now he had the pups' avid attentions. Ann's too.

He showed them the white sponge rubber baseball again. Genes fired. Adrenaline rushed. Their eyes locked on like the retrievers they were.

The duck hunter stood up fast. Drew his right arm back. Hurled it toward the far fence, some hundred and fifty feet distant.

All the Labs had watched intently when David's arm shot forward and the rubber spheroid flew, a high, fly-ball trajectory. And there was great joy in Mudville as the noisy pack took off after it as soon as it left his hand.

All but one.

One pup had begun racing forward as soon as David cocked his arm back to begin his throw, staring straight in front of it and then picking up and tracking the white ball's course as it flew by overhead. The ball landed. Bounced once, twice, three times. And the pup was there to jump up and catch it, before it could hit the fence. But the rest of the dogs strained close behind, tongues loose, yipping with excitement and ready to wrestle it away.

"Here dogs! To me! To me, now!" David loudly called them back with a quick series of repeated commands, bending over and slapping his knees, encouraging speed and building even more excitement. And the pup with the ball was about to come—but not directly.

Sensing its pack was imminent and would certainly block the return and steal the prize, the young Lab suddenly raced to its right, around the far perimeter of the nearby pond. The sudden strategy confounded the pack, which piled into one another in a confused jumble of heads and tails. It was truly a one-ring circus.

"Hoo-ee, Ann! That is some kinda mess."

The big female vet looked at him strangely, and it took him a moment to realize what he'd said. David shrugged, and Ann nodded and smiled. Then both roared with amusement at the bewilderment of the young Lab pack.

Cobb sat as still as stone.

A few moments later, the victorious pup had dropped the white sponge rubber ball at David's feet, panting and barking and ready to go again. The two humans shook their heads at its youthful energy, its enthusiasm for the chase. Under the muddy make-up, David thought he recognized the young Lab, but wasn't sure. The elderly Cobb deigned to give the pup a single, appraising glance, then turned away again.

The rest of the dogs arrived back and clamouring and, after giving them time to recover and another round of fragrant treats, David drew back his arm. Again, the rubber spheroid flew, just as hard, just as high, but aimed more carefully.

It landed exactly where David intended—in the deep water, near the far end of the long, shimmering grey pond.

The young pack was off once more, and this time, having quickly learned its lesson, was running as soon as he moved his arm, anticipating the throw to come. "No fleas on these doggies, Ann," David said, impressed.

"And did you expect anything different?"

"Ah, no ma'am. Reprimand recognized, accepted, and deserved."

"Good." But said with a smile.

From what David could tell, the previous winner was merely one of this small pack, its earlier advantage lost. Now the pursuing Lab pups, yipping and panting furiously, approached the edge of the water, paused, jostled, sorted, and lined up like Olympic swimmers taking their marks. Then breeding and instinct kicked in. With barely a second's hesitation, the pups plunged in en masse and were soon swimming energetically for the white ball that floated so enticingly at the far end of the pond.

All but one.

It seemed seemed hesitant and even afraid, left alone on the verge.

"What's wrong there?" David looked to Dr. Ann, who shook her head. Then Cobb barked once, very loudly.

When the humans looked back, the lone pup was racing along the edge of the pond at top speed, mud and ears flying. Upon reaching the point of the far perimeter closest to the ball, it sprang smoothly into the water in a canine racing dive, swam straight for the bobbing white ball, grabbed it, and swam swiftly back to the same point of departure.

Dr. Ann stood up to overlook the unfolding scene. The surprised mass of Lab siblings, newly arrived where the ball *used* to be, yipped and paddled in confused circles.

This time, the two human and one canine observer were riveted by these tactics, watching speechless until the victorious pup returned with its trophy, mud and ears flying, and dropped it at David's feet. And though clearly on the verge of exhaustion, the young black Lab barked up at him, game to go once more. Its brothers and sisters were still swimming in confusion behind it.

It was irresistible.

David dropped down on one knee for a closer look. It was so. This was the same pup again—the smaller female.

Cobb walked over to sniff her and barked twice. The tactics and raw talent of the rookie retriever had impressed even him.

"Is that one paw in favour I hear?" Ann asked.

David knelt on both knees now, with his own instinct for training taking over, and gave her the customary reward. By reflex the duck hunter ruffled her neck fur, scratched her behind the ears and told her what a good dog she was. The Lab pup squirmed with pleasure and ate it all up—the treat, the petting, and the praise. In those few seconds an ineffable bond was permanently forged between dog and man. Master and Retriever. They were together now, in the best possible sense. It swelled David Phelan's heart with a unique satisfaction, the burgeoning of a new partnership with years of potential and mutual discovery ahead of it.

"Make that one paw and two muddy hands, Ann," he said.

As a veterinarian and superb breeder of black Lab retrievers, Dr. Ann Spence had been right to be impatient with him. David had waited far too long. Old Cobb barked once more and seemed to agree, despite sensing he was being retired.

The bright little female had earned her biscuit.

The rest of the Lab pack had arrived, treating Cobb and the humans to a shower of muddy water from shaking, furry black bodies. David took it in stride and laughed and wiped the brown spatters from his face as he distributed their well-earned treats. Still kneeling, the avid Canadian duck hunter reached in his jacket pocket, took out a small, well-worn leather collar and fastened it around the pup's neck. She sat patiently for the process and didn't appear bothered by the new addition, as if she knew she was no longer one of a pack.

David looked over, but Cobb made no objection to the banding of their young protege. The faded red circlet had been his own collar when he was a pup. "Seems unanimous," Ann said, when David stood up.

"Yeah. Got off track there for a while. Took an old dog, a Yankees fan, two good women and a smart little girl to get me straight.

True to his promise, David Phelan took a full half an hour to wash down the pups, one at a time, using the hosepipe and the old stock-watering butt Ann kept outside the door of the kennel for just that purpose. He then squeezed out the excess water, rubbed them down with a chamois and returned them to their heated pen, where Ann let the young Labs calm down and rest before their evening feeding.

David kept his own new pup until the last, washing gently and then drying her carefully with the chamois, while Cobb looked on—benignly, even grand-paternally, David wanted to imagine. He took more time with the process and fussed over the little Lab, massaging and smoothing until her coat shone with a healthy, blue-black gloss in the watery sunlight.

The duck hunter loved the rich, young-Lab smell of her and rubbed his cheek against her warmth. Then, while the pup stood patiently by, he took the chamois to Cobb, first letting him smell the pup on it, and rubbed him down until his coat, too, was burnished in the old familiar way. Cobb snuffled in enjoyment and pushed his head under David's hand for a pat and a scratch.

"Right, champ. Been too long, hasn't it?"

Finished with the older Lab, he snapped a second lead onto the new pup's collar. It had also been Cobb's, from the days of his earliest training. Then David walked her around and around the front yard, with Cobb trotting along freely on the other side, until Dr. Ann Spence came out with the pup's breeding papers in an envelope and attached the veterinary shot tags to the young dog's collar.

Ann then took a few moments to pet and say goodbye to her Lab pup. "So, Dave, have you decided on a name for the latest generation?" She inquired. The longtime Detroit Tigers fan smiled and nodded.

"Albert William Kaline. Kaline, for short." Ann shook her head.

"Impressive sounding. But isn't that a guy's name, another ball-player? How did you come up with it? David looked down at his pup—which looked right back up at him, as if asking the same questions.

"It was the suggestion of a friend. And the fit is perfect. In more ways than I can explain."

"Big Al?"

"No fleas on this breeder. Right, Kaline?" The pup barked its agreement. David shook Ann Spence's hand in firm gratitude and walked the Labs to his half-ton Ford truck. He reached through the passenger-side window to open the glove compartment, turned, and handed his breeder the cheque for Kaline. "That the price?"

"To the penny." Ann stared at it for a moment, and David suddenly knew what she was going to do.

"Wait!" Ann stopped with the check half-torn in two.

"Why?"

"Big Al, I guess. The story you told me. Cobb that night. This pup today. Even the way you stood apart from the rest of those fool cattle-breeders way back with Mort Le Merde, before I even knew your name. Didn't think I noticed?" The vet smiled slyly at David.

"Okay. Your pup, your choice, Ann. But maybe instead of tearing up seven hundred dollars, why not donate it to one of your worthy veterinary causes?" Dr. Ann laughed once more and shook her head.

"Okay, will do, Dave. Lightning really has struck twice!"

"I don't understand. What lightning?"

"Exactly. And what I didn't tell you. The chairman of the Peterborough Humane Society dropped by to thank me in person for the generous contribution I never made, about three weeks after Al left. Five figures. US money order. Would've bought twenty Kalines." Ann was fully enjoying this turning of tables. "The look on your face right now, Phelan! So, any money owing's been paid and more besides, especially with this seven-hundred-dollar donation on top."

"Full of Yankee tricks, even now. Al never mentioned it."

"But you're right about tearing this up. With your permission, I'll match it and give the chairman another call," Ann Spence said.

"Yeah, Al would like that. And with gestures like this, Ann, you really should meet Al's priest, Father Alonzo." She laughed and slapped him on the back.

"I'll allow that's a compliment, David. Unlikely to happen. But I guess it never hurts to know a good Catholic priest and man of God if the time comes."

"Al thought so. *This* Roman Catholic priest anyway."

"One for the angels," Ann concluded. David nodded, hugged Ann, and got himself and his dogs into the Ford truck and started it up. Another bond between duck hunters, between students of the Great Game.

Tricky metaphysics again, but good for the spirit, his spirit.

David raised his hand in farewell, then drove out of Dr. Ann Spence's wide barnyard and hit the highway for home and the loving wife he couldn't live without. The elderly Cobb sat up on the passenger side and the pup Kaline perched alertly on the well-worn grey seat cover between them—all eyes, ears, lolling pink tongue and panting excitement. The other cars and farm vehicles passing by, the wide fields on either side of the highway with their sturdy cattle and almost fully ripened grain. The occasional tall aspen, white oak, and pine bush, with streams and small lakes just about visible in the far distance on their right.

It was a lot of world for a young Lab to take in.

More than once, Kaline strained eagerly forward with her paws just reaching the truck's dashboard for a better view. David laughed, shared her pleasure and excitement, her puppy curiosity, and didn't try to discourage her discoveries. Kaline was young but sweet-tempered, and her retriever training and discipline would begin soon enough.

Old Cobb too, seemed content, accepting, sitting straight up, maybe recalling his own early puppy years. And very important, David was sure Norah would approve of their choice. His grandson, Frank, as well—especially the name.

It was Kaline's time to revel in her retriever youth and exuberance, strive to discover and achieve her black Lab potential, and David's time to take the fullest pleasure in her enjoyment. Big Al Greathwite's unexpected death, the fine Carolina duck hunts and heated arguments over baseball statistics and interpretation they would never share, showed the thoughtful Canadian that stark truth again. David Charles Phelan had a choice, maybe the only choice available that made the pain bearable across families of men or beasts.

Embrace life.

He and Cobb had a new pup. A bambina. To initiate into the mysteries of duck hunting and retrieving. David laughed at the prospect, slapped the dashboard himself and embraced the ironies.

"Thanks, Yankee Al! Thanks, buddy."

Low rays of lemon sunlight broke through a gap in the trees. Kaline closed her eyes but stayed in its warmth. The world was transparent. David saw what he was thinking and why. For this moment, life was good.

All his ducks were in line.

End

acknowledgements

Writing a novel is setting off to climb a mountain. It's daunting, arduous, harrowing and long. But when you look down from the top and hold your latest novel in your hands, the sense of achievement is breath-taking. I could not have reached the top of my *Better Angels* mountain without the active support and confidence of my many guides who lent me their hands.

My wife of fifty-three years, Eileen Floody, is razor-sharp, widely read and knowledgeable. Eileen's nickname as a public librarian was, "Ms. Know-it-all". I second that emotion. I love you deeply, honey. I'm a very fortunate husband and writer.

What can I say about my friend, fellow writer and superb editor Greg Blanchette? Never enough. Greg, your honest criticism and suggestions for improvement made *Better Angels* the novel I hoped it would be and more. Sincere thanks, Bro.

No writer can succeed without the support of other dedicated writers who share his passion for writing. Thanks to all my friends in the long-running Clayoquot Writers Group. Your critical feedback blended with humor is energizing. Shirley Langer, a founding member, fellow novelist and dear friend, we've shared so much I'm grateful for. Thank you, Shirley. Love and hugs. To Joanna, Janice, Chris, Shirley M., Helen, Erin, Clodagh, Britt, Adrienne and others at a distance, you guys rock!

To my wonderful and beloved Toronto Floody family, your feedback and family friendship at a distance always give me a lift. Brian, Lorraine, Dylan and Claire, I hope you will all visit us again before too long. Love to you all.

To freelance graphic designer and artist, Felicity Perryman, your cover designs and layout have made my novels attractive and readable, and helped me realize my author dreams. My sincere thanks to you, Felicity, and hope we can work together again soon. Hugs.

And finally, I can't forget my two left-pawed kitties, Tommy Douglas and Libby Davies. I overlook your dragging me away from my writing for treats in return for your furry love and affection.

David Floody,
July 2023, Tofino BC, Canada.

author biography

DAVID FLOODY, B.A., B.ED., M.ED. is a retired Secondary School Academic English teacher, writer and the author of the Young Adult novels: *The Colour of Pride*, *Insect Youth*, and his newest, *Better Angels*, in 2023.

David's thirty years of teaching experience have given him a lifelong interest in the coming-of-age years and experiences that challenge us all. *Better Angels* is the sequel to *Insect Youth*, based on his experience of the 'unlikely heroes' in his own life who made a difference.

In this sequel: a formidable mother and Windsor Ontario Temperance Campaigner confronting her wayward husband; a lovely Emergency Room nurse whose Irish black eyes and laughter are completely bewitching; and an elderly black Lab retriever, near death from a heroic duck retrieve, after a shot that should never have been taken.

David is a member of the Clayoquot Writers Group, the Federation of BC Writers and the Canadian Authors Association. He lives and writes on the west coast of Vancouver Island, in breath-taking Clayoquot Sound, with his wife Eileen and two left-pawed cats, Tommy Douglas and Libby Davies.

He invites you to visit him at www.davidfloody.com.